Breakdown at Clear River

BREAKDOWN at
Clear River

Eliot Parker

Mid -Atlantic Highlands

Mid-Atlantic Highlands

Huntington, West Virginia

Cover Photo: Allison Lake
Cover and interior design: JoAnne Thompson

10 9 8 7 6 5 4 3 2 1

First edition, first printing
Printed in the United states of America

ISBN 978-0-9833947-8-5

Mid-Atlantic Highlands
An imprint of Publishers Place, Inc
821 Fourth Avenue - Suite 201
Huntington West Virgina 25701

www.publishersplace.org

For my dad, Brent, who loved football and good stories.

one

CULLEN WORKED THE FOOTBALL in a circular motion around his head, under his arms, around his waist and each knee, finally playing catch with it between his legs.

"Reverse!" Cullen shouted, although nobody was close by to hear him. He changed the direction of the rotating football.

He rose up, spun the football in his hands. Cullen locked his hands around the ball, squeezed it and pulled it close against his chest. He loved the smell of a slightly worn football. He loved the feel of a rumpled pigskin between his fingers.

Cullen dropped the ball, then grabbed it. He faced forward in an under-center position. Cullen looked left, then right, and barked out the cadence.

"Red 89. Red 89, hut, hike!"

Cullen dropped back and executed the bootleg, faking a handoff to his left, and then bootlegging to his right and throwing the football towards the sideline.

"Damn!" Jordan exclaimed.

Cullen turned, a smile covering his face.

Jordan shook his head. "The boot sprint-out-and-throw is one of my favorite pass routes and you ran it without me."

Cullen removed his helmet. Wiping the sweat from his brow, he walked closer to the sideline to face Jordan, slapped him on the back and said, "I told you to hang out with me after practice."

"Doesn't matter. We ran that play last year against everyone and scored, with the exception of the Shepherd game."

Cullen chuckled. He remembered that game a year ago. The Shepherd Rams had always been a defensive-minded team, with a history of WVIAC All-Americans like James Rooths and Dan Peters roaming the secondary. It took a Clear River punt return and a defensive interception return, both for touchdowns, for the Cougars to beat the Rams last year 14-0.

"Just because that pass route worked last year doesn't mean it will work this year against everybody," Cullen reminded Jordan. "Shepherd taught us that last time we played 'em."

Jordan tugged at his shoulder pads. "It's easy for me to stand here and say that when we've crushed other teams running that play."

Cullen nodded. "Practice does make perfect."

Jordan crossed his arms. He cut Cullen a sharp look. "You worry too much about practice. Just let the game flow. You're good enough." He snorted. "Well, just average without *me* as your go-to receiver. Anyway, Coach has given us the weekend off. Why don't we go into Beaumont and get some beers and flirt with some hot women."

Cullen had played football with Jordan since they were seven. They had met playing pee-wee football for the Lindside Lions. Jordan had always been relaxed, energetic, sarcastic, and a bit selfish. But he truly loved spending time with Cullen. Their friendship grew stronger as they grew older, including becoming offensive teammates together at James Monroe Middle School, where the coaching staff believed Cullen's burgeoning arm strength and Jordan's speed would make an unstoppable quarterback-wide receiver tandem. The staff was right. Cullen and Jordan went on to play for James Monroe High School, helping the school win two state championships in football and shattering school records for passing yards, passing touchdowns, and receiving touchdowns.

"I can't," Cullen replied flatly. "I need to go home and see Dad. I haven't talked to him since April."

Jordan counted on his fingers. "That's four months."

Cullen shrugged. "With Mom gone, we don't have much to talk about anymore."

"Yeah," Jordan added. "Your dad likes to talk a lot with his hands and fists, not with his mouth."

Cullen took off his helmet and looked past Jordan. The late morning blue sky, well-veiled in clouds and occasionally darkened by mists, turned nearly turquoise as it met the mountains behind the end zone. It was a typical late-summer West Virginia morning.

"Look, Brewer, I'm sorry about what I said. I didn't mean it to come out the way it did," Jordan apologized.

Cullen waved off the comment. Bitterness twisted his mouth. "Boxing in those stupid amateur leagues in Huntington was more important to Dad than our family. Even when Mom was sick, Dad didn't care much about how she was feeling...just boxing and beer was all that mattered to him." Tears welled up in his eyes.

Cullen thought about the small locket in his locker. The long, tarnished gold necklace, regal and solid, held the last two pristine pictures of Kathy Brewer before breast cancer took her health and her life. Cullen liked to roll the locket around in his hand.

Cullen sniffed. "Just like Dad used boxing to stay away from Mom when she was sick, I use football—in high school and now—to get away from Dad. What does that say about me?"

A silence fell. Jordan stared at his cleats, then cleared his throat. "I know things haven't always been easy between you and your dad, but I know your mom would be pumped to see you playing football."

Cullen massaged the folds of skin under his eyes as a tear slid between his fingers.

"Besides, football helped us get to college—well, helped me. Your grades were always better than mine. I really *tried* to make good grades."

Cullen flashed a sheepish grin at Jordan. "You always hated homework and studying."

Jordan grinned. "So I lied about that part. But hey, let's go hang out." He nodded toward the locker room. "I need to change. So do you."

"Nah. I need to get some reps in before I go." As Cullen searched the far sidelines for the football, a muscular young man hidden beneath a helmet jogged towards them. Cullen looked over at him. "Dane, you made it."

"I lost track of time." Dane bent over and fumbled with his shoelaces.

"Mike was going to give me a ride back to the dorms, but I remembered I told you we'd run some plays." He swallowed large gulps of air as he spoke, then retied the shoelaces. "How many drills have you done?"

"Three," Cullen replied.

Dane pulled off the helmet and teased his dark bushy hair with two hands, trying to get the thick bands of hair that had been tossed around under the helmet to straighten. The hair matched his small, round, dark eyes and mocha-colored skin. Finally satisfied, Dane put the helmet back on.

Jordan shoved Dane. "Outta my way, man."

Dane stumbled, but caught himself.

Jordan glanced at Cullen. "I can run these routes with Brewer in my sleep." He smirked at Dane. "You underclassmen need to watch and learn."

"Can't you say excuse me?" Cullen asked Jordan, pointing at Dane as he spoke.

"Excuse me," Jordan said, still looking at Cullen.

"Smartass." Cullen shook his head. "Say *excuse me* to Dane."

"Jordan rubbed his chin, collecting small droplets of sweat on his fingertips. He wiped them off his pants. He glanced quickly at Dane and then leveled a look at Cullen. "What's he doing here?"

Cullen swallowed. "I invited him. After practice today I told him that we would go over some passing drills."

Jordan scoffed. "I talk to sophomores only on Saturdays."

A look of confusion washed over Dane as he crossed his arms. "Look, if I have come uninvited, I can leave."

Jordan cast a sideways glance at Dane. He flashed a toothy smile. "Nah, I'm just joking, Marcelli. I'm glad you're here."

"It's Antonelli," Dane replied.

"Whatever. I'm tired anyway. When you give it everything you've got each day in practice for a month, you have nothing left to prove."

Dane chuckled and sidestepped Jordan. "I gotta loosen up the muscles in my legs."

Jordan craned his neck. "Doesn't matter how loose he gets, if he doesn't even know the playbook."

"Just drop it," Cullen replied.

Cullen motioned to Dane and dropped to one knee on the ground. Cullen picked up the football with his right hand, put the ball to his ear with his left hand also on the ball, and threw it to Dane. Dane caught the ball, placed it on the ground and threw it back to Cullen.

Jordan walked onto the field and stood between them. "So, when are we going for beers?" He flipped through a stack of cash held together by a silver money clip, rolling through several large denominations, including a stack of one-hundred-dollar bills.

"That's a lot of cash to be carrying around," Cullen said.

Jordan shrugged. "Just some walking-around money Dad gave me. Said he liked the way I played in our scrimmage last week against Wesleyan."

Cullen searched his mind, trying to remember what Jordan had done during that game that would warrant that kind of money. In the first half, Jordan made two great catches on passes that were thrown behind him. Cullen's shoulders tightened. He'd been responsible for throwing those passes. Coach Miles took the starters out in the third quarter, but not before.

"Yeah, you got flagged twice for unnecessary roughness," Dane chided.

"There's nothing wrong with playing with intensity." Aggravation edged Jordan's voice.

Cullen studied Jordan. "I think Coach Miles thought you were a little too, uh, *intense*. I thought you'd never get done running laps during Monday's practice."

Jordan sneered. "Dad likes my intensity. He says it's something that can't be taught."

"That's true," Dane added. "You either have it or you don't."

"Yeah, yeah," Jordan mocked. "Why don't you losers keep practicing and I'll go drink some beer."

Jordan picked up the football laying in front of Cullen. Jordan threw the ball hard at Dane and it whizzed past his right ear. "Underclassman," Jordan snickered.

Dane stared after him.

"It's okay," Cullen said. "That's just Jordan being Jordan. He doesn't mean anything by it."

"I'm going to have some beer, are you two losers coming or not?"

With downcast eyes, Dane covered his mouth, hiding a smile. He looked up solemnly at Cullen. "I'm underage. Are you sure you want to drink with me?"

"Please. We're friends and teammates," Jordan said. "We look out for each other. Nobody's gonna tell anybody nothing."

Cullen raised an eyebrow. "I need to head home, but you two take it easy."

"If you can get me in, I wouldn't mind having a beer," Dane said to Jordan as they watched Cullen saunter away.

two

CULLEN PEERED INSIDE the trunk lid. The collection of works by John Steinbeck and the notebooks full of notes and freewriting exercises for his summer class lay in a disheveled pile near the back of the trunk. Cullen slammed the lid shut. He stepped away from the car, a Honda Accord he'd borrowed from his friend and teammate Mike Ochoa, and looked at the trailer. A few plastic chairs lay scattered in the yard, surrounded by small tables underneath a sagging blue tarp.

The land, enclosed on two sides by steep ravines, had grassy pasturelands planted with alfalfa, trefoil, and timothy. The morning fog was thick, so the treetops merged with the gray sky. Cullen hated the weather in mid-August. The topography of the Monroe County hardscrabble farmland trapped the trailer in a cocoon of humid heat.

Cullen took a deep breath, his emotions oscillating like they always did at home. He felt an aching in his bones he couldn't explain. Was it worthlessness? Vulnerability? All he knew for sure was that after a two-day visit, he was ready to leave.

He needed to go back into the house one more time to make sure he had all of his belongings. Cullen stepped onto the frontward-leaning wooden deck. The deck absorbed his weight and bowed slightly in the middle. He looked up and noticed that the siding was smudged with mildew. He opened the front door and entered the living room, dimly lit and wallpaper yellowing with age.

From the back room came sounds of his father stirring. Cullen frantically dug into his pockets to make sure he hadn't locked the car keys inside the Honda Accord. It had happened before.

He grinned when he heard the keys jingle in his pocket. He quickly ran through his mind the list of everything he needed: clean clothes, clean football uniform, shoulder pads, money, backpack, and Kroger's groceries. Cullen gave one quick look around the room. The odor, which he hadn't noticed earlier in the weekend, now left Cullen a bit nauseated. The room smelled like someone had holed up in it with dirty clothes and rotting food. Cigarette butts filled every ashtray. Flecks of ash were sprinkled here and there on the stained carpet.

Cullen turned to leave. A droplet of blood slid onto his arm. He looked down and dabbed it with a finger. He caressed his swollen lip with the back of the same hand, and felt a slight sticking pain course through his mouth. He curled his lips and placed a hand on the screen door.

"Where you going, son?"

Cullen froze. He straightened his back and spoke into the screen. "Back to school, Dad. I told you on Friday, I could only stay for a couple days. Coach Miles needs me back to show the new freshmen around a little more."

"I was hoping you'd stay longer."

Cullen let out a long breath. "I'm just lucky Coach gave us a couple of days off." Cullen turned around to face his father. Wendell Brewer, fairly thickset, had creases running across his round face. A mop of brown hair, tinged with gray, jutted from his head in various directions, a wisp hanging low on his forehead. His small eyes and fleshy lips were open. Cullen waited for his father to say something.

"I'm sorry we didn't get to spend enough time together this weekend, you know, as father and son."

"Save it, Dad. I came home to check on you. Where were you on Friday? At Maggie's Bar in Union? The only thing you did was leave me the past-due bill notices on the kitchen table." Cullen felt his lip pulsing in pain, although the bleeding had stopped.

Wendell stepped back, his mouth trembling. "I didn't want you to worry about those."

Cullen set his shoulders. "You really don't remember what happened when you came home, do you?"

Wendell raised an open palm at Cullen. "Son, I had been drinking a little...and..."

"You staggered through the front door around 4:00 a.m. and went straight for the fridge looking for another beer. You saw the bills lying on the table and began screaming at me. You wanted to know why the bills hadn't been paid. I told you I didn't have any money to pay them right now. You went off! You picked up dirty plates from the sink and threw them at me. One of the plates broke against the wall and a piece cut my lip!" Cullen pointed at his mouth for emphasis. "Then it happened again on Saturday night; sleep all day, drink all night, with a little bit of fist-fighting-your-son thrown in."

Wendell looked down at the floor. "...I don't remember."

"Because you blacked out! When I tried to calm you down, you took a swing at me and told me that I was a disgrace and an embarrassment. You said you wished I had been the one to die from cancer and not Mom. Do you know how that makes me feel? Do you know how it makes me feel to see you like this every time I come 'home' for a visit?"

"Don't you talk to me like that!" Wendell demanded. "You never come back here anymore to visit...not at Thanksgiving, Christmas, nothing. When you do, it's usually because you want something or need something. It's okay for you to ignore your old man most of the time, but it's funny how you come back when something's wrong."

Cullen folded his arms and shook his head. "You can't be serious. I never come home, Dad, because it kills me to see what you've become. The dad from Friday and Saturday night is all I remember anymore. I want the dad that watched me play football since I was eight, the dad who raised all of that money for our high school team at James Monroe so we could get new uniforms. That dad is gone. Now, I'm stuck with a drunk. I swear I don't know how Mom put up with it as long as she did."

Wendell's eyes blazed. He knocked off a small lamp resting on a table near the wall with one swipe. The lamp cracked into two pieces as it hit the wall. He kicked it over the table. Cullen felt every muscle in his body tighten. He stepped back, bracing himself against the door.

"You watch your mouth boy! You know nothing about your mother and me. I loved her and she loved me. Do you have any idea what it's like to lose your job and your wife in the same year? No, no you don't."

Cullen lowered his voice. "That was five years ago. Mom died and you got fired from the state park because of your drinking. And yes, I know what it's like...I loved Mom. She meant everything to me. Instead of us helping each other, you became even more of a lush than ever before."

He reached back and pressed the latch on the screen door. "Look at you. No job, no family that wants to be with you, and soon you are going to lose the farm. Well, I'm done. I'm not going to be your punching bag anymore, just like Mom got tired of it."

Wendell charged at Cullen, but Cullen slipped out the door, leaped down the deck steps and tossed himself into the car. He managed to get the key inserted in the ignition and throw the car in reverse as Wendell tried to pounce on the hood.

Cullen flushed the pedal to the floor of the car, kicking up pieces of gravel and rock as he climbed the driveway. He refused to look back at the trailer, but he did cast a look back at the farm, which grew smaller until it disappeared into the fog. He climbed the ravine and guided the car onto West Virginia Route 12.

Cullen settled back into the seat and began to sob. He gripped the steering wheel, unsure whether to be angry or sad about his dad and their relationship. Cullen sped through a stop sign just outside of Peterstown. A beige van slammed on brakes as a horn sounded. Cullen nearly leaped out of his seat and waved apologetically at the female driver, then buckled himself in.

He knew the route from Lindside to Beaumont quite well. In fact, he had the trip memorized. West Virginia Route 12 would become U.S. Route 219. The route then headed north through Peterstown and entered rural southwest Monroe County. Passing through Cashmere, Ballard, and Red Sulphur Springs, Route 12 met West Virginia Route 122. The highway paralleled the Greenbrier River and passed Big Bend Mountain before it joined West Virginia Route 3. The route then wound northeast along the river to Barnettown before heading north through another mountainous area, eventually leading onto Interstate 64.

Thinking about his father troubled Cullen, but it made the drive seem short. As the car pulled up to the main arch entryway into the Clear River

College campus, Cullen noticed several cars parked in a small lot just inside the arch.

Cullen swung into the parking lot and saw three men surrounded by their families. As Cullen got out of the car, their hushed whispers grew silent.

The emotional weight of the morning lightened. "Ya'll must be here for a tour of the campus. I'm Cullen Brewer. Welcome to Clear River and welcome to the Cougars football family.

"Cullen shook several hands and spoke to each player and parent. As he began to circle the group around him, a pert and trim woman with a lemony expression approached him with her son, whose hair was windblown and whose chest stuck out. His self-confidence seemed impenetrable. He acted like someone who's convinced he is liked.

"I just wanted to thank you for all the times you met with Blake here last year. We came up for several recruiting visits and trips and you always made us feel comfortable and made Blake feel wanted." She leaned in to Cullen. Waves of floral perfume wafted between them.

"Blake's never been away from home before," she whispered. "Hedgesville is several hours away, but I know that you'll look out for him."

Cullen smiled and looked back at Blake, who grinned widely. "Thanks, Cullen, for always answering my questions and my emails about school and everything."

"You're welcome," Cullen replied. "I will do my best to make sure you have a good freshman year. If either of you needs anything, you know how to reach me. Just don't tell Coach Miles that I gave you both my cell phone number and email address."

As the rest of the group huddled around him, Cullen felt a vibration in his pocket. He retrieved his cell phone. "Just a moment folks."

Cullen looked down at the screen. The displayed number and description indicated the call was coming from Lindside. It was his father. He squeezed the phone's "end" key a second and then stuck the phone back into his pocket.

"Let's head to the football stadium," he told the group.

three

NOT YET NOON, the Monday overcast sky promised rain—a promise Cullen hoped it delivered soon. The late August heat made practice tiring. Jordan and Dane each ran their assigned routes. Cullen dropped back and threw the ball to Jordan. It spiraled left and landed in Jordan's outstretched arms. Cullen grinned. The trainer tossed him another ball, and he threw it to Dane. A bit high, Dane jumped and snagged the ball from the air. Cullen couldn't help but laugh. With two quality receivers, there would be no stopping them this year. What a sweet way to end his college career.

Tiny raindrops turned into steam as they sprinkled on the field.

Coach Miles blew his whistle and motioned for the team to join him on the sidelines.

Dane ran up to Cullen. "Thanks again for the invite to go bowling last night. I had fun."

Cullen looked at Dane, his big bright eyes and impish grin expecting a reply. "I'm glad you came."

Dane tucked the football helmet under one arm, curling a wrist around the facemask to hold it still. "It seems like you and Jordan have done that bowling thing for a while and I hope me being there didn't cause problems."

"Not at all," Cullen said.

Jordan, still out on the field, finished a few squat thrusts, then scooped up his helmet and headed to the sidelines. He caught up with Cullen.

"I'm going back to the dorm tonight after practice and studying the playbook a bit more," Dane said. "With Coach wanting me to play more this year, I need to have those passing plays memorized."

Jordan raised his eyebrow. "You've got to have them memorized if you want to start."

Cullen looked at Dane from the corner of one eye. Dane's eyes widened as Jordan approached, letting the awe shine through.

Jordan smirked. "I've had the plays memorized since my freshman year. You need to be able to recite them to yourself in your sleep."

"I'm almost there, thanks to Cullen," Dane replied, turning to face the quarterback. "I used the notecard trick you told me about. White cards for plays where I will be blocking, blue cards for short routes, yellow cards for intermediate routes, and red cards for deep routes. I put the play on one side, the responsibility on the other, and I quiz myself. It's really worked. I'm going to do whatever it takes to play well and help us win." Dane slapped Cullen on the leg, peered at Jordan, and then called back, "See you in a bit."

Dane ran across the field to meet with some other teammates.

"I'm going to do whatever it takes to help us win," Jordan mimicked with an eager voice and exaggerated mannerisms. "I hope he can back up his homework and play."

Cullen chuckled. "He's going to be fine." He paused and looked at Jordan, raising an eyebrow. "Jealous, much?"

Jordan scoffed. "Me? Shit no. I've got nothing to prove. We're seniors. He can work into things slowly, like most good sophomores should."

"Get after them, Jordan!" Tom Hancel, Jordan's father, barked.

The words, coming from a hoarse voice, startled Cullen but made Jordan grin. "I'm going to all-out today."

Cullen looked behind him to see the oblong-shaped silhouette of Tom Hancel become more defined as he neared the field. Cullen waved faintly. Tom returned the wave, following it by jabbing an index finger into the air at Jordan.

Before Cullen spoke, Jordan cut him off. "Dad has a meeting later this morning, so I told him to come over and watch us practice."

Standing at mid-field, Coach Miles blew the whistle three times, the signal that the offense would gather for a quick meeting and then begin running simulated plays.

Dane and the rest of the offensive line made it to mid-field before Cullen and Jordan. Once together, Coach Miles surveyed the huddle, nodding as he counted each player.

"We are working on short and deep routes today. First play: the wheel route. It's when a receiver or running back runs five yards forward, five yards towards the sidelines, and then turns back up-field for about ten to twenty yards."

The coach stopped in front of the group. He slid an arm around Dane and Jordan.

Looking at Jordan, Coach Miles continued. "Hancel runs this route to perfection. We call this play a lot because teams often bite on the out route that Brewer throws to either Hancel or Ochoa."

Mike Ochoa, standing just on the periphery of the huddle, ran steadily in place. He listened while his head bobbed and weaved.

"So the corner comes up to the line of scrimmage thinking he's running a simple five-yard route." As Coach stopped to flick raindrops from his shirt, his voice sounded unexpectedly small, but tense, carrying a threat of excitability, as if something were coiled and ready to spring. "All of a sudden, Hancel runs back up field. We should have a big completion as a result."

Coach Miles dug his fingers into both of Jordan's shoulders, squeezing tightly. He bent down and placed his lips near the helmet earhole.

"Hancel, Antonelli watched you run this route most of last year. Now I want him to get some reps in running this route. Mentor him. Got it?"

Jordan nodded, though Cullen could almost hear him seething under his breath.

"I've got the second team defense playing man-to-man. That means Hancel and Antonelli will be covered by a defender who's going to follow them around the field and try to defend the pass." Coach Miles scanned the huddle. Dane and Jordan nodded at Coach Miles in agreement.

Coach Miles stood upright. "All right, Brewer, call it in the huddle and run it."

The players ran back onto the field. Cullen stepped into the middle of the huddle and dropped to one knee. The rest of the offense encircled him.

"We'll run the eighty-six left cut on three," he commanded. Locking eyes periodically with his teammates and smiling briefly, Cullen ducked and turned his gaze. "First pass, the ball goes to Jordan. Second pass, it goes to Dane." Cullen clapped. "Break!"

The offensive line, anchored by Andre Gibson, sauntered to the line of scrimmage. The light drizzle turned into a more steady rain, slicing through the languid sky and increasing the sticky feeling in the air.

Barking out the formation and play calls, Cullen slid both hands under Andre. He looked left and noticed Dane had lined up at the widest point on the left side of the line of scrimmage. Looking right, Jordan occupied the slot position on the right side of the line of scrimmage. From the corner of one eye, Cullen noticed Coach Miles, arms crossed, chewing on the tip of a pen and staring at the quarterback intently.

Cullen hedged his remaining calls, then bellowed "Hike!" He dropped back and held the football tightly near his collarbone. He scanned the field, first looking left, then right.

Jordan ran five yards down the sideline, digging his cleat into the turf. The motion allowed him to make a sharp change of direction into the middle of the field. The defensive back slipped, and Jordan ran behind the stumbling player. Once Jordan achieved separation, he thrust his hand into the air, signaling Cullen.

Responding to the signal, Cullen scanned across the middle of the field. The defensive safety sprinted toward Jordan. Cullen leaned back and threw the football.

The ball rose in the air in a slow arc, then accelerated as it fell. Cullen timed the pass perfectly; Jordan was open and made the catch.

Jordan's frame faded into the distance, the milky sky and rain acting like a cloak of disguise.

A whistle blew.

Jordan trotted back to the huddle, shaking his head. Coach Miles marched to him, mumbled a few words hidden behind a cupped hand, and slapped Jordan on the helmet.

The team returned to the huddle.

Cullen looked around Jordan at Coach Miles. Coach made several awkward gestures with his hands, raking them up and down his legs and dragging fingers across his shirt and face. The discombobulating movements Cullen interpreted precisely. He prepared the next play call.

"Guys, we are running a slant route. It's the fourteen-flood-right play on the play sheet."

A couple of linemen looked at each other with bewilderment.

"It's the play we ran last year against West Liberty that tore them up."

Slight murmurs of understanding, coupled with light taps between the huddle, refreshed their memories.

"Dane, this one's going to you."

"Got it. I'm ready. This is my favorite pass play we run."

Jordan bumped Dane. "Just remember, Brewer and I have made this play ours. Don't forget how to run it right."

Dane dropped his chin and leered at Jordan. "I need to learn how to run it *better* so I can do it when you can't. Oh, and don't worry, I won't screw it up."

Cullen caught Dane's eyes, then Jordan's. "Fourteen flood right, break."

The rain grew steadier and the droplets of water pelted their helmets. Cullen walked to the line of scrimmage. Coach Miles had instructed the defense to blitz, and the linebackers crept closer to the line of scrimmage.

With Dane lined up parallel to the line of scrimmage on the right and Jordan lined up to the left, Cullen snapped the ball. He took in a deep breath. The internal clock inside his head began ticking. Dane needed to run into the space between the linebackers and the safeties.

Dane took a couple of steps then ran to the center of the field. Suddenly, Jordan cut a sharp angle on his pass route and headed for Dane. Cullen slowed his drop back from the line of scrimmage. Two defenders chased him. Cullen jogged to the left, escaping the blitz, and waited for either Dane or Jordan to clear the middle of the field.

Jordan avoided a collision, but clipped Dane with one leg. Dane slowed his run and lunged toward the ground. Jordan stuck his arm into the air once again, waiting for the pass.

Coach Miles barged onto the field and blew the whistle several times. Unsure of what to do with the football, Cullen held onto it, just long enough to be tackled by the two blitzing linemen.

"Stop, stop!" Coach Miles yelled. He set his hands on his hips. "Take a break, all of you!" Veins bulged from his neck and forehead.

"Hancel and Antonelli, get your asses over here. Now!"

Cullen picked himself up from the ground. With a fresh smattering of trampled grass and mud splattered on his jersey, he jogged to the sideline, where Coach Miles had already begun lecturing Jordan and Dane.

"What the hell were you two doing out there? Hancel, I told you the play was going to Antonelli the second time. He ran the slant; you were supposed to keep running down the field."

Jordan looked away as Dane leaned closer to him. "Why did you clip me? I have a right to run the pass routes without having you trying to come after me. I'm just executing the play that's called. If you don't like it, take it up with Coach."

Jordan whipped his head around. "We started running that slant play when Brewer and I came here. That's *our* play."

Coach Miles cocked his head to the side. "Boo-hoo, Hancel. I plan on running that pattern with Antonelli in the formation more and more this year. Both of you are as fast as hell and I want to put pressure on defenses to defend you both." He raised an eyebrow. "You clip him again, Hancel, and you'll sit on the bench and run laps until you puke. You got it?"

Cullen sneezed, drawing a glare from Coach Miles. "You need something, Brewer?"

"No, sir."

"You three had better figure this out. I've said all I'm going to say about it. We have an offense that is going to be the best in the conference this year. For it to work, all of you are going to have to play together. Hancel, you're the veteran. Antonelli, you're the new guy. You both have talent and *both* of you are going to have a chance to make plays. Neither of you will do as well without the other this year. I can't have my two fastest and most talented wide-outs wetting the bed over catches. Now go out and run that play again—correctly this time."

"Sure thing, Coach," Dane said enthusiastically.

Jordan rolled his head from side to side and he and Coach Miles exchanged a long, silent glance. Jordan backpedaled and went back onto the field.

As Cullen turned, Coach Miles called out to him. "You're the leader of this offense, Brewer. Make sure it works right."

four

CLEAR RIVER COLLEGE President Dr. Neal Burcham slouched in his chair, spun it around, and looked out the large bay window onto the Clear River College campus.

The rain had stopped by mid-afternoon and the sun had broken through clouds, to explode the horizon with color as it began dropping behind the mountains that cradled the campus and the town of Beaumont.

Someone rapped lightly on the office door and Dr. Burcham turned to see his Chief of Staff, Jack Dillon, arch his neck into the entry space.

"Coach Miles is here to see you, sir."

Dr. Burcham smoothed his gray blazer and plaid shirt and pushed his horn-rimmed glasses to the bridge of his nose.

"Should I have him wait, sir?"

"No, Jack. Send him in."

Coach Miles burst through the entryway into the office, approaching the wide, narrow oak desk separating him from the president.

Dr. Burcham settled a look onto the coach. Tall and trim, Coach Miles had a face full of symmetrical creases and folds that often gathered in worry.

"Coach, it's good to see you. Thank you for coming by. Please have a seat." Dr. Burcham motioned to the couch in the middle of the office.

Coach Miles shook his head. "I'd rather stand, if that's okay with you. I just came from practice and I'm too wired to sit."

Dr. Burcham nodded. Coach Miles's clothes were slightly wet and he smelled sweaty, like a combination of salt and soured milk.

"Gary, the board and I met this morning, and, as you know, we discussed athletics and facilities. The board is looking at funding options to improve the facilities, especially football."

The coach's shoulders bounced and he shifted his weight from leg to leg. A sly, sideways grin washed across his face. "We have so many needs. The field needs re-sodded. The locker rooms and the weight rooms are crumbling. With some improvements, our school will have a tremendous recruiting advantage over other schools in the WVIAC."

"I know that. The improvements have been needed for some time. But with our inability to issue any more bonds during the last few years for upgrades, the board didn't have many options."

The coach rubbed his chin. "So, what's changed?"

"Well, the student center bonds will be retired next year. With those bonds retired, the legislature is giving us approval to go ahead and re-issue a new bond for facilities upgrades. The board has been meeting, and with some input from me, a master list has been created of campus upgrades. Sports facilities and a new residence hall are at the top of the list."

Coach Miles smiled and relaxed, almost serene.

"There are some strings attached."

Coach Miles straightened.

Dr. Burcham took a deep breath. "Gary, the board wants the football team to be a winning program—"

"We have been," Coach Miles said. "Three conference championships in the ten years I've been here. We are poised to win another this year, if we can play well and stay healthy."

Dr. Burcham steepled his hands. "I know that. But the board would like to see a championship every two-to-three years. They think the program is at a point to really excel, and if these improvements are made...well, then there will be no reason not to expect a championship each season."

Coach jutted his jaw outwards. "What did you tell them when this was said?"

"I defended you and your record. This office has nothing against your performance. You are an excellent ambassador for our program and our school. The summer high school football camps you put on are quite popular; you always agree to speaking engagements throughout the state;

your players graduate; there are not disruptions inside the classroom for our faculty; and the program has been without incident, except for—"

"That was ten years ago! Ten years! I was a new coach then, running a football program for the first time. I made a few mistakes and I learned from them. Not a day goes by that I do not think of that first season and what happened to that kid."

Dr. Burcham stood up. He traced a ring of dust on the desk with an index finger. "I have a short memory. Some people on the board do not."

"Like the board president, Tom Hancel? Is that who you mean?" Coach Miles folded his arms. His face crinkled harshly. "This wouldn't be coming up if my contract wasn't up."

"Gary—"

"No, I got it. I understand. If we don't win conference this year, then we get no upgrades and I may be gone."

"Coach, that's not what I meant."

"But that's what is on the line, no?"

Dr. Burcham paused. "The board president is putting pressure on me to make sure we have the type of season that will make selling bonds more attractive to the rest of the board. It's my duty to keep you informed as to what is going on."

"Political games, that's all this is. Well, if you want a championship season, you'll get one. Pass that message on to Tom Hancel for me." Coach Miles stalked off.

*   *   *   *   *

Jordan grimaced as a taut wind blew across the parking lot of Darby's Bar. The air, soft and hazy, melted into the rich, mellow sunlight sweeping across the mountains. The bar, crammed against a narrow embankment near the edge of Highway 33, signaled the beginning of downtown Beaumont, now growing quiet as dusk set in.

Jordan took two short breaths, then lifted both arms. The sweet aroma of cologne wafted around him as he strode to the entrance.

Darby's, with its sloped roof and wood-paneled façade, had been open only an hour before Jordan's phone rang, followed by an invitation for drinks. Now Jordan reached the flat concrete pad near the front door. The building pulsed with the blare of music and televisions, along with loud conversation.

Flecks of chipped paint littered the stoop. The chips were a variety of dull, dark colors.

He opened the door and stepped inside. An early Friday evening crowd filled the room. The bar, veiled in a thick haze of cigarette smoke, was darkened by jagged shadows. The tiny bar—an inverted horseshoe—dominated the center space as patrons huddled around it. The smallish bar always made Jordan uncomfortable. At the far end, he saw a group of guys drinking and laughing, slapping one another on the backs and arms.

As he scanned the room, a hand swayed back and forth at the bar. Jordan smiled and approached the waving hand.

"Hey, Dad!"

His father's face brightened as Jordan neared. "Hey, buddy. I'm glad you could make it. I thought you might be busy bowling tonight with Cullen and some of the guys."

"That was a couple of nights ago," Jordan replied, finding it necessary to raise his voice amid all the noise. He pulled up a stool, sat down, and s traightened his shoulders.

"You guys looked good in practice today," Tom said as the bartender approached. "Two Coors."

The bartender nodded.

"Except for that dropped pass," Jordan said. "Shit, I have run that route for four years now and I've got the timing down perfect. I know when Cullen is going to throw the ball, either at four seconds or when I get at least three yards of separation from the defender."

The bartender set two draft beers in front of them. Tom Hancel reached for one and took a generous swig. "It's early in the year, son. You'll get back into rhythm once the games start counting."

Across the bar, a shot glass smashed into several pieces. The guys laughed and shushed each other as the bartender raced over, pointing a finger at the group. Jordan rose partially from the bar. Through the haze, he saw Dane throw back two shots of a reddish liquid and wipe the excess from his chin with his arm.

"You know those guys?" Tom asked.

"One of them. Unfortunately. I mean, fortunately. Hell, I don't know. The one guy is Dane Antonelli. He is a sophomore receiver this year and Coach really wants him to be a big part of the offense. I mean, he played good at the end of last year and all, but Coach is all hung up on him." Jordan took a swig of his beer. He lowered his voice. "Cullen is too."

Tom put the beer back on the counter and swirled the liquid inside the bottle. "That boy came in last year and played mop-up duty. It'll be interesting to see how he does when a defense plays him tight from the first quarter."

Jordan slammed his fist down on the bar, causing his father's glass to vibrate.

"Ah, I take it you don't like him."

Jordan looked at Tom, his doughy face scrunched up against thoughtful, hooded eyes. "He's a good guy. I just want him to know that I am still the captain and a senior on this team. This is my year to shine."

Tom drew his arms to the edge of the bar. "And that's why you clipped him on that pass route?"

Jordan looked away, heat warming his face.

"Hey, I'm glad you sent that kid a message. Sometimes talking to a guy doesn't work. Sometimes, you have to use other means to get the message across."

"Coach didn't see it that way." Jordan took another swallow from the bottle. The raucous noise and laughter continued on the other side of the room as the bartender dropped a fresh round of beers in front of the group. Jordan didn't recognize any of the others with Dane, although a couple of them appeared to be older.

"Well, Coach Miles needs to win and win big this year," Tom said.

The statement made Jordan freeze on the stool. He slowly turned and locked eyes again with his dad. "What's that supposed to mean?

"Nothing," Tom replied, somewhat dismissively. "We had a board meeting this afternoon and the subject of Miles and the football program came up. Let's just say the board has high expectations for the team this year." A sinister grin crept across his face as he took another drink.

"That's no different than any other year," Jordan said.

Tom scrunched his brow. "Coach Miles is in the final year of his contract. I made it a point to hold an extension and some facilities upgrades as leverage. I told Burcham to pass it along."

The group of drunks down the bar, becoming more obnoxious, received a final warning from the bartender.

"Want another round?" Tom asked. Jordan nodded, and Tom motioned for the bartender.

The party on the other side finally pushed themselves away from the bar. Dane stood in the middle of them as they all stumbled to the front door.

I think your friend has had a little too much," Tom said.

Jordan watched them fade into the darkness outside. "Yeah. Interesting. Especially since he's underage."

five

DANE COULD NOT MOVE. That realization ricocheted through his mind like a stray bullet; piercing stomach cramps and nausea overwhelmed his senses.

Earlier, a slight headache had irritated the fleshy folds of skin below Dane's eyes and progressed upwards towards the bridge of his nose. As the minutes passed, the headache evolved from a dull ache to a searing, blinding pain that dropped him to his knees. Now, lying on his side, arms cradling his midsection, Dane's stomach quivered violently.

He had almost made it upstairs to his dorm room, back to where he could relax comfortably in the soothing emotional warmth of familiar surroundings. Dane wasn't exactly sure how long he had been lying on the cold, sooty tile floor; time seemed irrelevant. Turning his head slightly upward, he caught a glimpse of the tiered underside of the metallic staircase above, dotted with rust but illuminated with speckles of color. He was familiar with those bright splotches—he had added his own chartreuse sphere to the collection last year in the form of a sticky mass of used chewing gum.

Dane's head snapped backwards against the floor as his stomach muscles retracted. Saliva trickled from the corner of his mouth. He reached a quivering hand forward, his fingers slightly grazing the frosted egress window less than two feet away. The cavernous, hollow stairwell was dark and eerily silent, but a ray of moonlight dimly lit the window face. With two fingers tracing an invisible pattern down the smoky glass towards the base of the window, Dane tried to speak, but his parched throat could not make a sound. Hope was dwindling. Nobody could see his outstretched hand or hear his gasps.

Dane's headache returned slowly. He remembered drinking beer with friends at Darby's in downtown Beaumont and sharing plenty of stories, some of which were laced with ridiculous exaggerations and hyperbole. The experience left him charged and drained.

Tired, Dane had left the bar and anticipated getting some sleep. The walk back to his apartment was routine and uneventful, and he enjoyed the warm, humid night air. He loved summer, especially late summer, with its hazy, lazy days and nights filled with drinking and chasing women. This would be his last weekend of summer, as the school semester began in three days. Then a sudden, sharp pain erupted from his rib cage.

From that point forward, Dane's foggy memory provided no additional clues or details. Yet he clearly understood how precarious his situation was. He'd never felt this type of pain before in his life.

Another sharp pain jolted Dane's attention. His mouth, still as dry as a charred forest, became inundated with a warm liquid that burned the lining of his throat. He swallowed, attempting to suppress the fluid, but nothing changed. The liquid charged up his throat again, this time more insistently than before.

His body trembled violently and heaved upward; his chest wheezed from lack of oxygen. Then paralysis began. He tried to force his leg to move, but it wouldn't. He ordered his arm to rise, but it lay lifeless. Even his finger refused to obey him.

A slow, piercing squeal disturbed the silent night. A gust of warm air cascaded across Dane's shivering body. The squeal subsided, followed by a robust boom. Dane's spirits lifted.

Why would someone be here? Do they know I'm here? Is someone coming to help me?

The pattering of footsteps echoed around Dane, growing louder and closer.

More violent spasms shook his body. The pain and shaking rolled his body sideways, like a fish desperately seeking water.

A rush of coagulated blood settled inside of Dane's chest and seeped thickly out of his mouth. He coughed, but that did nothing more than coat the floor with a smattering of blood.

The pain reached an unbearable pitch. Ahead, the silhouette of something or someone stood near him.

With one last violent shudder, his body grew rigid. A hand reached for him, but his vision was so blurry he wasn't sure if it was real or not. His eyes tumbled backwards.

six

STILL SORE AND FATIGUED from football practice, Cullen rubbed his eyes. They felt like hot stones being stoked by a poker. He glared at the clock on the computer screen. Friday, August 17. 4:08 a.m.

The library was silent, with only a few students still roaming the shelves. Plump moisture droplets rolled off his Mountain Dew bottle and splashed onto the computer keyboard.

Moonlight streamed through a small window, decorating the manila carpet with gashes of light.

Cullen wiped a drop of water from the delete key, plopped his pencil between his lips and resumed typing.

Steinbeck's characters exist, compete, and sometimes cooperate with one another in instinctive environments. For some reason, his characters have instinctual needs.

Satisfied, although unsure of the coherence of the last sentence, Cullen smacked the *Enter* key on the keyboard with his right ring finger.

"Damn conclusion paragraphs," he mumbled.

Conclusion paragraphs always troubled him. Familiarity with the rules did not make the process any less arduous. Instead, the challenge for him was to stop writing, stop typing, and stop thinking. Yet after six hours of drafting, revising, and finally typing an essay on John Steinbeck's use of characterization in *East of Eden*, Cullen's brain was frazzled.

His essay was due at 8:00 a.m., followed by football practice at noon and then film sessions all afternoon. Cullen fixated on the numbers 4, 1, and 5 on the computer screen. His chances of catching some sleep this morning would be nearly nil.

He stood up, leaned back and extended his arms, stretching and exhibiting a generous yawn before sitting down and saving the essay onto a USB flashdrive. As the computer muddled through the task and the blue flashdrive light faded, Cullen forwarded the essay to a printer.

Luckily, his Smith Library computer station was positioned closest to the printer terminal. Thus, Cullen did not have to circumnavigate other computer workstations or collide with the handful of students still working.

Smith Library had so many computers and printers that nearly every student at Clear River College could find one available at any moment. The library study center, open twenty-four hours a day, had saved Cullen's academic career on multiple occasions, and he knew it. Amidst all his responsibilities, he capitalized on every second out of every hour. He spent many precious hours on schoolwork, albeit in the early morning in the study center, feverishly reading, studying, and typing essays.

Cullen wandered from the computer station towards the printer terminal, which featured a printer secured by silver metallic cords bolted into a small, wobbly metal stand. Reaching below the small printer, Cullen jerked his essay from the paper tray.

He examined the first page, and noticed that he'd forgotten the appropriate heading. He grunted and smacked his right hand against the printer terminal, almost causing the metal stand to collapse. Shaking his head in disgust, Cullen retreated and flopped down dejectedly in the chair in front of the computer station. He held the nameless essay in front of his still-burning eyes, and glared at the monitor.

I would like to show John Steinbeck my instinctual "needs."

*   *   *   *   *

Twirling a generous lock of curly strawberry-blonde hair, Serena Johnson fixated on the blinking cursor on the computer screen. A small box inside the screen, trimmed in purple with the words *Instant Messenger* highlighted, framed the image of a generic face and head.

Adjacent to the Instant Messenger box was a photograph of a large field, void of grass or vegetation. Instead, golden pockets of dirt sat haphazardly around the field.

The phrase "reporter1001" was highlighted in red and bookmarked with a colon, the cursor ready for a word to be typed.

Serena continued twirling a strand of hair as she tucked one leg under the other.

Her thoughts were disturbed by a quiet whisper. "What 'cha doing?"

Serena angled her head backwards. The broad shoulders and wide stance of her roommate Crystal filled her vision. Crystal flashed a wide smile.

Serena lowered her head, wiggled her shoulders, and focused again on the blinking cursor.

Crystal leaned forward. When she did, her backpack slid off her shoulder and collapsed onto the floor. Her perfume, a fresh and sweet fragrance reminiscent of springtime potpourri, filled the computer lab.

"Looks like you're still not giving up," Crystal whispered again, this time just inches from Serena's ear.

"Too bad I'm paralyzed by my own thoughts," Serena replied.

Crystal stood upright once again. "I remember when you cut that picture from the campus newspaper and hid it from me for three months."

Serena stopped twirling her hair. "I did it because I knew you would make a bigger issue of it than it actually was."

Crystal pressed her lips together tightly and folded her arms. "A bigger issue than it was? It looks like this issue still *is*."

Serena sighed. She typed into the box next to the screen name, but deleted the words as quickly as she typed them.

Crystal laughed. "I'm not there. I'm right here."

Serena yawned. "Sorry, it has been a long night."

Crystal took a chair from a vacant computer terminal and aligned it next to Serena's seat. The moonlight, which had illuminated Smith Library's computer lab with geometric patterns, now faded. The computer lab, an elongated cylinder-shaped room fragmented by computers, chairs, and tables, seemed cavernous. The faint sounds of pressed computer keys could be heard along with the slight rustling of papers.

Serena wiggled uncomfortably in her seat while Crystal leaned forward again. Crystal's thick, jet-black hair was pulled tightly into a ponytail. Her chubby cheeks and high cheekbones were fixated harshly against her otherwise round face and cast a reflection in Serena's inactive computer screen. Crystal's lips were small and her mouth narrow. Her bright blue tee-shirt and tan shorts accented her round hips and somewhat flabby stomach.

Crystal took a deep breath and sighed. "I cannot wait until you get over this writer's block, or whatever you journalists call it. I mean, you have been staring at that photograph for two weeks and you have done nothing with it. I thought journalists were writers and storytellers." Crystal's right hand moved in a semi-circular motion, inviting Serena to agree with her point.

Instead, Serena tapped her fingernails nervously against her leg. "I keep thinking there is something more here than just a green field covered in sand." She knew the field well. It was used by students during the fall and spring semesters for physical education classes and by students looking for a place to read, talk, or nap between classes. When she'd been a freshman, she'd lounged around that field frequently, watching the cute guys.

Serena exhaled deeply. "It doesn't make sense. The field can't be used by students this fall, and whenever I ask anyone for an explanation, I can't even get a comment."

"Have you asked yourself why this field?"

Serena nodded. "There is nothing special about this field. I have spent hours in the college archives researching it. Maybe the reason nobody in the administration will comment on it is because nobody cares. If it were going to be used for a building project, there would be activity at the site." Serena locked eyes with Crystal. "The place would be buzzing with construction workers and equipment. Yet there is nothing going on there."

Crystal leaned closer towards the computer screen, pushing aside

Serena's arm. "Why not do a column or an editorial on that point? You can argue that the field being covered in sand takes away valuable space for students."

"It's already been done," Serena replied. "Ben Caster, our executive editor, wrote a column raising those points. Then he passed the story on to me."

A dull noise caught Serena's attention. A short, portly student with greasy, thick brown hair seated at the first table had knocked over a chair. The student winced and squatted near the overturned chair. The noise brought a welcome moment of distraction for the few students remaining in the library.

Serena blinked and re-focused on the photograph.

Crystal sighed loudly. "Serena, you cannot create a story if there isn't one to tell."

Serena scratched her chin. "I was hoping that Ben's screen name would appear on Yahoo Messenger and he could tell me what story I need to write."

"Why aren't you in the newsroom? Wouldn't that be a better place for thinking and writing?"

"I spend so much time in that newsroom that sometimes I need to be someplace else to gain perspective," Serena said. "However, it looks like I am not getting anything from being here."

Serena pushed the seat backwards, nearly crushing the chair into Crystal's knees. Serena flung her arms in the air. The few occupants of the library looked up from their books and computer stations and then dropped their gazes back into their work.

Serena bent down quickly, pressing several keys on the computer keyboard. Within seconds, the once-colorful screen featuring the daunting picture of the field faded to black.

Serena turned and stared at Crystal momentarily. A feigned smile spread across her lips.

Crystal's eyes narrowed. "Can we go now?"

"Sure," Serena replied, smiling.

seven

CULLEN JAMMED PAPERS and his paperback copy of *East of Eden* into his blue nylon backpack and tossed the backpack over his shoulder. Snapping his left wrist towards his chest, Cullen saw the hands on his watch inch closer to 5:00 a.m. He wanted a chance to shower and shave before football practice.

Cullen shoved the chair he'd been using under the desk and hurried towards the exit. The chipped pewter tile floor generated friction under his sneakers, which squeaked as he walked.

Once Cullen burst through the metal doors of the library, he surveyed the campus. The limited space outside of the Smith Library Study Center placed exiting students almost in the middle of the street. The library, located on the southwest corner of the Clear River campus, sat adjacent to the college's Administration Building and Fine Arts Building.

Two streets bisected one another in front of the library. Second Street, a small narrow road that was an exit route for the southwest corner of campus, cut right in front of the library. High Street ran alongside the west end of the library and circled behind the southwest corner of campus, eventually leading all the way around the campus perimeter.

The moon, now quite dim, revealed a raven black sky speckled with a few stars. A thick, humid breeze washed across Cullen's face. Clear River's Administration Building and Fine Arts Building held patches of late-summer honeysuckle granules across blocks of white stone, while the naked spots of exposed stone shimmered in the weakening moonlight. Soon, night would fade into dawn.

Looking down Second Street and glancing backwards onto High Street, Cullen walked away from the library towards the back quadrant of campus—the area specifically reserved for student athletes. The campus, compact yet picturesque, showcased lush green fields with large trees, complete with sagging branches and freshly mulched flowerbeds sporting geraniums, daffodils, and phlox.

Cullen sprinted through one of the small, grassy pathways between the President's House and the Science Building. On the other side of the pathway was North Brent Street, part of West Virginia Corridor 33 and 119. That intersection, normally overwhelmed with pedestrian and vehicular traffic during the day, was quiet at night.

Looking at his watch, Cullen saw that seven minutes had elapsed since he'd left Smith Library, although it felt like he had been walking longer. His heart raced as the seconds on his watch ticked by.

Gyrating lights flashed and moved across the President's House and Science Building. The hum of engines grew louder and closer. Cullen took several steps across the green field and found himself standing inches away from the North Brent Street curb. The hum grew into a voracious roar which approached from the west. Flashing red lights danced with dull blue lights.

Three vehicles sped past him with such power that Cullen was nearly knocked backwards.

As the cars disappeared into the darkness, Cullen spied an apricot inscription emblazoned on the back doors of the last vehicle as it listed slightly: Upshur County Ambulance.

eight

THE SILENT, sultry night at Clear River College dispersed as streaks of pink and copper light smeared across the sky. The appearance of sirens and emergency vehicles caught Serena and Crystal's attention. Serena's head ached from fatigue, but her mind raced. "I have to go." She dug through her small brown purse, refusing eye contact with Crystal.

"Go where? I thought we were going back to the dorm to get some sleep," Crystal complained.

Serena cast a long stare towards the flashing lights on the opposite end of campus. "Something is going on, Crystal. I have been a student at Clear River for four years and I have never seen that many emergency vehicles on this campus at one time. Not to mention at this time in the morning...." Serena's voice trailed off as she located a notepad and blue ball-point pen in her purse.

"Always chasing a story." Crystal shrugged. "I'll see you later then."

Serena nodded and began running. Jackknifing her way through campus, she passed the theater on the southwest corner, ran through several parking lots reserved for faculty and staff, and finally through and behind several open green spaces dotted with walking trails and benches. The uneven juxtaposition of concrete pavement and grass hurt Serena's feet. But the more they ached and the more her body became drenched in sweat, the more determined she was to get to the scene.

The last main building before the campus entrance was Stokley Hall, a co-ed dormitory for freshman and sophomore students. Stokley Hall was Serena's destination.

Serena slowed her sprint to a gallop and finally stopped in front of Stokley Hall. The sandstone building rose high into the sky; early morning sunlight, which now had transitioned into a dark phosphorescent orange, encased the building.

The hushed conversations of emergency personnel caught Serena's attention. Men and women clad in a variety of uniforms etched with symbols, shields, and responder designations scurried back and forth. The glass doors in front of Stokley Hall were opened with such force that the glass panels flexed inside their metal frames.

With pen and notepad in hand, Serena weaved around and through the people. She counted at least fifteen police and ambulance officials and three West Virginia state troopers along with several campus police officers.

Serena climbed three steps in front of the metal frame door outside Stokley Hall and swung it open. Everyone else turned right. She followed their lead.

Once down a narrow and dimly lit hallway, Serena stepped inside another doorway and found a knot of responders hunched over the athletic body of a male student. The boy's face, chest, and neck were covered in dried blood and his arms rested in pools of blood. His eyes had rolled backwards, his lips were slightly parted and his face spoke of a torturous passing. The stairwell smelled of death. Serena gasped and took several steps back.

A few responders stood together whispering, while others sidestepped the body. Their movements resembled a ballet dance. The discussions created a muffled echo in the stairwell, but the words were indiscernible. Behind them, the staircase wove upwards like a curling vine.

Clenching her notepad and pen tightly against her chest, Serena approached the body. A tall, wiry man with a thin face and beady hazel eyes snapped pictures. The stitched yellow patch on his navy jacket read UPSHUR COUNTY EMS. The man ran around the body, leaning forward and backward, snapping photographs at such a frantic pace that the hot white flashes of light forced Serena's eyes to close. Dropping her weight on one knee, she looked closely at the body. His neck and shoulders were muscular and bulges of lower shoulder muscles on each arm crept through his blood-stained shirt. A disheveled, wet mop of stringy jet-black hair covered the forehead and ears. Serena looked closer; the student's eyes were closed. His square face and hooded eyes stood in stark contrast to his small, button-like nose and thin mouth. Serena unclenched her fists and started writing.

She was interrupted by five fingers slithering down her shoulder. "Miss, you are not allowed to be here. This is a crime scene and only authorized personnel are allowed."

The raspy words and warm breath startled her. Almost feeling like a captured escaped convict, she momentarily froze. Shifting her weight, Serena stood up, careful not to release her grip on the notepad and pen. She turned and locked eyes with a West Virginia state trooper.

The trooper exhaled a disgruntled breath as his nostrils flared. His green irises were hard.

"This is a crime scene, not open to the public!" The trooper reached down and grabbed Serena by the wrist. "Leave now, miss, or you are under arrest for obstructing an investigation."

Serena swallowed. "I am a reporter with *The Record*, the campus newspaper here at Clear River. I have a right to investigate too." She was impressed with her vocal inflection that made the words seem resolute and truthful.

Unfortunately, Serena did not have her press credentials. She fumbled within her purse, trying to find them.

The trooper's tone turned gruff. "Miss, I do not care who you are or who you represent, but this is a restricted area—a crime scene. A statement by the college will be issued soon and then you can do all the snooping you want."

Serena closed her mouth quickly. *A statement by the college.* The phrase stuck in her mind. She immediately wanted to know more but was reluctant to ask.

The trooper placed a large hand around her elbow. He led her towards the doorway and into the main hallway.

"Hey, I am not finished taking notes here," she said.

"Yes, you are. Move on."

A fleeting moment of righteous indignation for being treated in such a manner as a member of the press swept through her, but her mind was now focused on the statement from the college. Who would be issuing it? And when?

nine

CULLEN MANAGED A SHOWER AND A SHAVE, although he could not shake all the early morning images of emergency vehicles racing through campus. He rested an arm against the powder-blue tile wall in the dormitory bathroom, his curiosity at what he had witnessed causing his chest to brim with anxiety. His racing thoughts, coupled with the speed of the shave, left Cullen's face with splotches of irritated bumps that glowed fiery red under the halogen bulb's yellow light.

After sprinting from Cougar Village across campus again, he climbed the narrow stairwell on the east side of Franklin Hall, his essay for Contemporary American Literature in hand. All he had to do now was turn it in.

Franklin Hall buzzed with activity. As an upperclassman, Cullen was familiar with the pre-semester routine. The last session of summer school at Clear River College always featured a mixture of oddities. Some students were frantically trying to finish up the term while professors balanced their current teaching responsibilities with preparing for the upcoming fall semester.

The fourth floor of Franklin Hall housed the Department of English. The faculty offices were near the middle of the hallway. Cullen cut into the right side of the blue-tile hallway and opened the cream-colored metal door.

Four chocolate brown office doors appeared, two on each side. Straight ahead was an empty conference room encased in glass. The first left door was slightly ajar, and Cullen pushed it gingerly.

Inside, Dr. John Petry, pudgy and grandfatherly in appearance, was reading quietly. His desk was littered with file folders in a plethora of colors from dark blue to light pink. Behind the desk stood four bookcases filled with literary works and books on English composition. The office had a musty smell mixed with the fading aroma of Old Spice cologne.

Keeping his gaze on the book in front of him, Dr. Petry almost dismissed Cullen before looking up.

"Lay your essay on the desk. It will be graded by Monday. Grades are due on Tuesday and will be posted Wednesday. The first day of fall semester is next Monday. Enjoy the rest of your summer." The sentences flowed in a rehearsed cadence. Dr. Petry turned a page.

"Dr. Petry, here is my essay. I just wanted to say I enjoyed your class, especially our discussion on Steinbeck's use of characterization." Cullen placed the essay delicately on the corner of the desk, trying not to disturb the professor.

The last statement was not totally accurate. Cullen truly had enjoyed the discussion on Steinbeck's use of characterization—until Dr. Petry made that the requirement for the last essay in the course. What followed was a long, mentally agonizing evening of writing and revision.

Turning another page, Dr. Petry finally looked at Cullen over his wire-rimmed glasses and scratched the white stubble on his chin. "Thank you, Mr. Brewer, for your kind words. Anything else I can do for you?"

"No, sir, that should be all."

Dr. Petry inched his face closer to the book. "Mr. Brewer, if there is nothing else, then I bid you a good day."

Cullen, however, could not bring himself to leave. Despite all the negative comments and rumors that swirled throughout campus about Dr. Petry, Cullen loved him. He'd been warned that the professor's expectations were too high and that he graded harshly, but Cullen believed that he'd matured as a reader, writer, and student of literature thanks to Dr. Petry's standards. The professor could and would challenge students to take a position on characters, plots, syntax, and other issues in the works of contemporary American writers, often at the expense of polarizing the class. Cullen had learned from those experiences.

The room's silence made Cullen edgy. Although he had never been a student who took advantage of a professor's office hours, mainly because of his coursework and the practice and game schedule created by the Clear River College Athletic Department, coming to Dr. Petry's office seemed okay.

Dr. Petry reared back in his seat, startling Cullen. The professor folded his hands behind his head and shot a disparaging glare at the student. "Mr. Brewer, since you seem content to stand there and not leave, the least you could do is sit down."

Cullen noticed an empty green chair tucked under an overhang at the end of the desk, pulled it out and sat down.

Dr. Petry crossed his right leg over his left, leaving portions of the right knee squished against the desk. He pursed his lips, almost cueing Cullen to start talking.

Cullen did not move or speak.

"Why don't you talk to me a bit about this essay you wrote? Judging by your weary looks, I'd say you spent half the night writing this paper."

Cullen nodded. He wanted to elaborate on the great lengths he took to write, rewrite, and revise the essay. Instead, he bit his lip.

The professor ran his hands through his coarse, white hair. Cullen finally responded, although his voice sounded reedy. "Well, sir, I dealt with the issue of instinctual needs present in *East of Eden* and how that impacts the themes of the novel."

Dr. Petry's nose twitched. He dropped his gaze and fixated on Cullen's essay, lying still at the end of the desk. The gaze immediately returned to Cullen. "That's quite a bit to accomplish in a short paper."

"I just felt these characters have instinctual needs and these needs force the characters to compete and cooperate with each other to get those needs fulfilled."

The professor waved his hand. At first, Cullen started at the flailing fingers, but then he realized that Dr. Petry wanted to examine the essay. Cullen pushed the stapled essay across the desk, where Dr. Petry grabbed it and began flipping through the pages anxiously.

"Now, Mr. Brewer, you know that although some of Steinbeck's characters are mentally deficient and morally corrupt, the difference between them and lower animals—including most characters in naturalist fiction—is that his characters have free will."

Cullen struggled to understand.

"Furthermore, their ability to choose may ultimately prove insufficient for them to alter their material circumstances, but their consciousness of choice creates the possibility for moral distinctions, delusions, unhappiness, personal improvement, and social reform."

Dr. Petry looked up at Cullen, then back at the essay. He placed the essay inches from his nose and began reading some sentences while breathing heavily. "I am sure all of those salient points are discussed in your essay, correct?"

"Well, not to the level of analysis you just demonstrated, no, but I think it has some good information about the novel."

The professor furrowed his brow for a moment and then tossed the essay aside. It flopped on the desk, covering his book.

Cullen's razor-burned skin grew heated. All he wanted was to leave quickly, although he could not figure out a polite way to do so.

Dr. Petry smirked. "Well, we will see, won't we?"

"Yes, sir, I suppose we will."

The professor stood. "Have a good day, Mr. Brewer." His voice was once again low and grumbling.

Cullen jumped up and grasped Dr. Petry's extended hand and shook it firmly. As Cullen cleared the doorway, Dr. Petry called his name.

Cullen stuck his head inside the partially-open door space once again.

"Mr. Brewer, I have high expectations for you... this year—and beyond."

Cullen flashed a relieved smile and disappeared.

*   *   *   *   *

"Good lord, how did this happen?"

Jack Dillon fumbled through a small stack of papers. "We're not sure, sir. The state police are assisting the Beaumont Police Department in the investigation."

Dr. Burcham dropped his chin into a cupped hand resting on the cherry-finished writing desk. He gazed at the intricacies of the desk, including beautiful moldings and antique brass-finished hardware. Featuring burl wood inlays on the desk top and sides, the back of the desk was adorned with elegant molding emblematic of the regal elegance the president appreciated.

Dr. Burcham pushed his horn-rimmed glasses towards the bridge of his nose. Peering around the room, he honed in on the contrasting cross pattern of quarter-sawn oak and walnut flooring in his office. The school seal, etched carefully into the floor molding, made the italic writing of *Office of the President* seem vibrant and alive.

Jack cleared his throat. "We do know a couple of details about the student. His name is Dane Antonelli. He is twenty years old and a sophomore from Clarksburg." Jack held the papers upright, allowing the blazing early morning sunlight shining through the large bay window behind the desk to illuminate the report turned in by the Upshur County Paramedics.

Dr. Burcham sat upright and rested against the plush embedded grooves of the leather chair. The president smoothed over his fresh-pressed navy suit with both hands and bent down, adjusting both argyle socks. "Go on."

"Another student, Elizabeth Hastings, discovered the body in the southwest stairwell of Stokley Hall at about 4:30 this morning. The boy had been lying there for quite some time. It appears he died of a massive heart attack, although we will not know conclusively until the State Medical Examiner in Charleston completes the autopsy."

Dr. Burcham exhaled. "My God." The words hung in the air. "I'll need to speak to Ms. Hastings at some point."

The president removed his glasses and rubbed his chin. Jack rocked forward slightly and then returned to an upright stance once Dr. Burcham had picked up the glasses on the desk.

"I have spent over thirty years in higher education, and I am greatly distressed when students die." Dr. Burcham's eyes darted towards Jack.

Jack's experience as a reporter for The Associated Press in Charleston, along with the contacts he had inside the West Virginia Legislature, would benefit everyone at Clear River College. This morning, for the first time, Dr. Burcham was thankful Jack was his Chief of Staff.

Jack attempted a response, but Dr. Burcham cut him off. "I never imagined a student would die on my campus while I was president." He turned sharply in his chair. "Where was Dane before he was found?"

Clearing his throat, Jack spoke softly. "A receipt from Darby's Bar in Buckhannon was obtained by the police. They phoned the bar, and the bartender confirmed that Dane Antonelli had been there earlier in the evening with some other guys, possibly students. The police are trying to contact the others in his group."

"Have we apprised Dane's family of the situation and the investigation?"

"We have, sir. I had the Student Affairs office handle that first thing this morning."

"Good."

Through the open window, faint conversations hummed, muffled by the hypnotic drone of cars negotiating their way through campus and around pedestrians.

"What about the media? Do they know anything?"

"Not yet, sir, but it will only be a matter of time. They'll catch it on the police report."

Dr. Burcham stared intently at Jack. The president curled his lips. "Please prepare a statement on the situation and send that statement to every faculty and staff member through campus email. Even though most of the faculty hasn't returned from summer vacation, I do not want any assumptions, presumptions, or more importantly, *accusations* flowing around campus once they return. We are going to handle this situation through good communication."

Jack nodded.

The president held up his hand. "Yes, and something else. I want you to call Robinson and McElwee in Charleston and advise legal counsel of the situation. Tell them we should expect a lawsuit from the Antonelli family."

"Good idea, sir," Jack said.

"What is the socioeconomic status of the Antonellis?"

Jack bent the manila file folder backwards and rustled through the pages inside of it. "Dane Antonelli's father owns a large computer company in Clarksburg." Drawing the folder's contents closer, Jack's eyes widened. "They have the state government contract for computer networking."

Dr. Burcham sighed heavily and stood up. His eyes, glistening with earnestness, focused on the folder. "Tell the legal team to prepare for a lawsuit from the Antonelli family."

A crimson light flashed on the president's phone. Edging backwards, Dr. Burcham pushed the desk chair against the window.

Jack leaned in and grabbed the receiver. "Dr. Neal Burcham's office, Jack Dillon speaking." He scratched his face as he lowered his head. "Yes, yes, sir. Yes, sir, I totally understand, and I want you to know this office is being proactive in our response."

Dr. Burcham turned and lifted his head, as if that would help him hear the other side of the conversation better.

"Goodbye to you, sir." Jack hung up the phone. "That was Tom Hancel, chairman of the Board of Governors. He wants to see you as soon as possible."

The president's stomach sank. "Tom's going to have questions. Right now, I have few answers for him."

ten

CULLEN SPRINTED TOWARDS COUGAR VILLAGE with a determined purpose. Relieved that summer school was over, his mind raced through the Friday afternoon agenda. Panting, he mumbled aloud, "Fall semester starts tomorrow and I have one more day of summer football practice—and then I need to find out what happened this morning."

He wiped his forehead and nose, now dripping with sweat. The early sunrise had created a sultry, late summer morning. The stifling, humid air hung like a thick blanket over campus, and Cullen wondered if cool fall weather would ever arrive.

The sixteen-acre athletic sports complex at Clear River College, known as Cougar Village, was a sprawling maze of fields, buildings, sidewalks, and paved alleys, all juxtaposed neatly between the West Virginia mountain landscape and the main campus. While the main campus at Clear River was arranged in a fragmented but student-friendly pattern of buildings and sidewalks, Cougar Village did not have the same carefully designed layout. Instead, the complex's buildings and sidewalks clumsily segued into one another. Someone could walk through Cougar Village and never exactly know where they were or what they were seeing.

Cullen stepped over a speed bump in the parking lot and ran towards the Cougars' football facilities building. He approached the three-story red brick building that resembled a perfect rectangle, complete with small, faded glass windows that stuck out in a random pattern. At the base of the first floor, under the only window on the southwest corner of the building, was a faded blue door. Cullen headed for it.

He'd learned all the shortcuts in the facilities building. As he darted through the blue door and rammed his shoulder into a gray door leading to the maintenance room, Cullen smiled, remembering how the freshman initiation by the upperclassman players involved four hours of isolation locked in this building. For the initiates, with only a flashlight and a bottle of water provided by teammates, the goal became finding a way out. Defying a record, Cullen made it out of the facilities building in ninety minutes, due in large part to his quick recall skills and ability to stay calm.

Cullen banged open the exit door at the end of the first floor corridor. Outside, from a distance, he saw a black Lamborghini that slowly stopped moving. The door swung open. Shading the sun from his eyes, Cullen smiled. "What are you driving now, Jordan Hancel?"

Jordan stood in front of Cullen. "You like it? My dad gave it to me as a senior gift."

Cullen approached the car and massaged it gently. "Wow."

Jordan slapped Cullen on the back. "Man, my only goals this year are playing football, getting drunk, getting laid and graduating."

Cullen scoffed. "It's funny that graduating falls last on your list of priorities."

Jordan poked himself in the chest with his thumbs, the same way a politician honors himself for accomplishing something in the name of the constituency. "You just worry about getting your senior slot receiver the football early—and often—and I will take care of everything else."

"You're the first guy I look to." Cullen had been throwing footballs to Jordan since they played together in middle school.

Jordan looked around the almost-empty parking lot. The four Weber Carburetors over the U2 engine in the Lamborghini purred softly. The car was a perfect mix of muscle and elegance.

"So what're you doing over here so early? Saving the day for Clear River College again?"

"I turned in my final essay for Petry's English class this morning." Cullen's smile disappeared. "Speaking of this morning, something happened about the time I left the library. Emergency vehicles were flying all over..."

"Dane Antonelli was found dead in one of the dorms."

Cullen's mouth dropped. Jordan Hancel seldom was up on what was going on. "How do you know? I mean, what are you talking about?"

Jordan's face scrunched up. "I heard it this morning on the radio." His white undershirt magnified the sunlight, forcing Cullen to squint. Jordan scratched his arm multiple times in a fit of nervous agitation. "Hell, I don't know. I wasn't even paying that close attention to it until I heard his name."

"No, not Dane! It can't be Dane! We were just with him a few days ago. He was at practice and…" Cullen closed his eyes tightly. "Shit."

Cullen edged backwards and his legs grazed the wheel well of the low-standing, front end Lamborghini. His eyes darted back and forth across the parking lot.

"I should have kept my mouth shut and waited for Coach to address the team," Jordan said.

"Was he alone when he died?"

Jordan dropped his gaze and stared at the pavement. "No, the radio said something about an Elizabeth, uh…Hastings, I think was her name, found him."

"Shit." Cullen locked a stern gaze with Jordan. "Coach Miles wanted us to work together as a team to hopefully have a special season."

Jordan shrugged. "I really don't know what else to say."

Cullen grabbed Jordan and pressed him against the car. "We were with him the other day at the stadium! Practicing pass routes! Remember?" The muscles in his neck tightened and the veins in his forehead sprouted above the skin. "If you weren't so busy trying to be the ultra-arrogant upperclassman and would have quit being jealous of him—"

"Man, quit jumping my case, Brewer. I liked him fine. He sure liked you."

"That's great, Jordan, just great." Cullen backed away from Jordan and rested a leg against the driver's side wheel. Jordan sidestepped around and faced Cullen, his posture rigid.

"Man, I don't know what I said or did, but I am just telling you what I heard."

Cullen shoved Jordan, swung around and strode across the parking lot.

"Where are you going?" Jordan called.

But Cullen was already walking away.

eleven

DR. BURCHAM STRODE ACROSS CAMPUS. Thick clouds hung in the sky over Clear River College as the scorching sun penetrated the high sky overhead, and the air remained humid.

Cars whisked behind and beside students, parents and faculty as the president left the administration building and crossed South Street, a sweeping, bending, single-lane road that connected the nature trail in the southeast portion of campus with academic buildings on the main campus. The road, seldom used for vehicular traffic, was quiet, although heat radiated from the asphalt.

Dr. Burcham stepped inside a service entrance corridor on the backside of the Fine Arts Center and walked onstage. Seated in the first two rows below the stage were newspaper, radio, and television reporters casually dressed, clutching cameras, recorders, and notepads. They were all awaiting the remarks from the president of Clear River College on Dane Antonelli's sudden death.

As Dr. Burcham stood in front of the podium, the dimly lit stage and auditorium created a dark backdrop. He could see only the first two rows of faces. The remainder of the Fine Arts Center was cloaked in darkness.

To his left, Jack Dillon stood offstage, hands crossed in a rather pious position.

Dr. Burcham adjusted the microphone and tapped it with his thumb. "I am Dr. Neal Burcham, president of Clear River College. I'm here today to make a brief statement about the tragedy that has affected our campus and our community. I cannot at this point take any questions after my statement, although my Chief of Staff Jack Dillon will be happy to provide other assistance." Dr. Burcham looked offstage. Jack nodded in agreement.

A slight tremor affected his throat, but he continued. "Today, our campus community suffered the loss of one of our students. Dane Antonelli, twenty, a sophomore from Clarksburg, West Virginia, was found dead at four-thirty a.m. by Upshur County EMS and the West Virginia State Police. Mr. Antonelli was found in a stairwell in Stokley Hall."

Dr. Burcham paused. Reporters frantically scribbled information on their notepads as cameramen tweaked levers, switches, and camera lenses. Several bright bursts of white light flashed from the audience.

"The cause of death is still under investigation and I will not speculate as to that cause. Dane was an outstanding student, a member of the Cougars football team, an active member of the Students Against Tobacco Coalition and a member of the Clear River College Campus Ministry Club. He maintained a three-point-seven grade point average during his freshman year. There are no disciplinary notations in his file."

The president swallowed hard and surveyed the room again before continuing. "I want parents, students, faculty, staff, and alumni to understand that this college is a community characterized by trust, confidence, and accountability. We take seriously our duty to provide a safe, secure campus for our students. Clear River College reaffirms its commitment to all our people, especially our students. Thank you."

Dr. Burcham marched across the Fine Arts stage amidst a clamoring of questions, each one asked slightly louder than the previous one.

"When can we expect to hear more from you?" one reporter asked.

"Has the Antonelli family been contacted?" another one asked.

Near the exit, a man in a dapper corduroy blazer with tapered trousers stepped out of the shadows. The man scowled. "Nice statement."

Dr. Burcham leaned toward Jack. "Mr. Hancel, have you met my new Chief of Staff, Jack Dillon?"

"We've met." Tom Hancel did not offer his hand.

Dr. Burcham forced a smile. "Jack, I believe you know Tom, the Chairman of the Board of Governors." His brow furrowed. "He's also a good friend of the college."

Jack nodded politely. "If you gentlemen will excuse me, I had better tend to the media."

As soon as Jack was out of sight, Tom glared at Dr. Burcham. "What the hell is going on here, Neal?" He maneuvered himself to occupy more space. "I can't believe we have had a student die on this campus."

The president placed his hand on Tom's shoulder. "I can understand your concern and frustration. Trust me, I am as shocked as you. We are going to find out what happened to that kid."

Tom wiped perspiration from his upper lip. "We are lucky..." He paused, turned his head, leaned closer towards Dr. Burcham, and whispered: "We are lucky the boy's family is not going to sue the college, or you, or the board. That would be a *very bad* situation for all of us." The more words Tom Hancel spoke, the more prominent and dragged out his slow, southern drawl became.

"I know, Tom, I know. Right now, we are staying ahead of the situation. Right now, I have to assure incoming and returning students, parents, faculty and staff that the campus is safe and that their safety is our number one priority."

Tom's nostrils flared. "You are implementing damage control, that's what you are doing." He leaned back and poked Dr. Burcham in the chest with an index finger. "You had better make sure this gets resolved and fast." He paused again, glanced towards the stage exit and leveled another determined look at Dr. Burcham. "The board, this school, and you do not need something like this hanging over the college. We have an ambitious year ahead."

Dr. Burcham blinked. The knot on his tie felt tighter. He envisioned Tom Hancel grabbing the tie and squeezing it around his neck until he expired.

Stepping backwards, Dr. Burcham stood on the balls of his feet, removed his glasses, and wiped the lenses with a cloth handkerchief. He turned abruptly. "I need to be going."

Tom grabbed the president's shoulder as he walked away, his short, pudgy fingers creating divots in the suit cloth. "During the first board meeting in September, we will discuss the college's transportation improvements. That damn road will be built, and you are going to support it."

The innate ability to be snooty and vulgar, a hallmark of Tom Hancel's personality, infuriated Dr. Burcham. Beyond Hancel, the sunlight created a blurred shadow on the doorframe. Where Dr. Burcham stood, the outdoors seemed miles away. "I have already given you my thoughts on the road proposal," the Clear River College president said, his voice controlled. "Unless the state comes up with money for building reconstruction and relocation, that road goes nowhere."

Dr. Burcham walked away, leaving Tom Hancel red-faced and muttering obscenities.

*   *   *   *   *

Serena ran towards the main entrance of the Fine Arts Center. She had managed two quick hours of sleep before leaving a snoring Crystal and returning to *The Record* newsroom. A note had been left in her mailbox about Dr. Burcham's press conference. Now, after sitting through what she felt was a charade, she wanted time alone with the president.

She turned beneath the small, decorative glass window cubes protruding from the main entrance canopy. As she neared the ramp by the stage exit door, she collided into something—or someone. "Excuse me!" she said, her voice more accusatory than apologetic. "Pay closer attention next time."

A tall, poised man wearing a royal blue shirt and tan shorts stared at her. A gusty breeze lifted his thick hair, allowing the sun to reflect off his brown curls. "Well, it's nice to meet you too," he said, his voice holding just a tinge of sarcasm. "I'm Cullen Brewer." His pastel-blue eyes drew Serena into them.

Slightly embarrassed by her brashness, she extended a hand. "I'm sorry. I'm Serena Johnson, assistant editor of *The Record*."

"The campus newspaper." Cullen nodded.

"That's right. And I'm sorry I snapped at you. Last night and today have been long and I'm looking for someone." Serena craned her neck to see past Cullen.

That's okay."

Serena smiled.

"Actually, I'm looking for someone too. Maybe we're looking for the same person?"

"Maybe we are or maybe we're not." Serena's journalistic suspicions froze the conversation. She didn't remember seeing Cullen in the audience at the press conference, but she knew he could have been backstage with the president. Did he have connections with Dane Antonelli's death? Or was his a fact-searching mission on behalf of someone else?

Three long, slender fingers waved in the stuffy air. "Are you okay? I think you wandered off the ranch for a moment." Cullen's grin revealed a small dimple in each corner of his mouth.

"I am investigating an unattended death."

Cullen's head bounced twice, feigning ignorance. "An unattended death? Here, on this campus?" He looked at the pavement.

"Yes. This isn't the first one ever at Clear River, and I am seeking answers—"

"To tough questions, right?"

Serena nodded.

"I bet you picked up that line by watching too many investigative journalism shows on television," Cullen said. "The fact that I finished the cliché proves it."

A strangled smile stretched across Serena's face. "Very funny." The smile faded. "Based on my first impressions of you, I bet whatever answers you are seeking, you will find. Why don't you tell me who it is you're looking for?"

Cullen grinned. "What if...what if you and I are looking for the same person, and I need his attention first, before your line of questioning flusters him and sidetracks my questions?"

Serena stomped her foot. "Why are you being so evasive?"

"Why are you so inquisitive?"

"Wait a minute, you said 'him.' That means you're looking for a man."

Cullen chuckled and placed his hands on his hips. "Looking for a man as opposed to what?"

Serena's gaze focused on the base of Cullen's right wrist. Through the mix of sun and shadow, she noticed the tattoo running around his wrist. In the middle of the tattoo, the initials QB spread across the front of the sketched football.

She tapped her pen against the legal pad, harder with each stroke, straining to think. "So that's it. Dane Antonelli was your teammate. So, you are here for that. And you are here as the representative of the student body." She tucked a moist strand of hair behind her ear. "You are here to see Dr. Burcham," shecontinued, forcing the words in Cullen's direction, enunciating each syllable perfectly.

"A student, Elizabeth Hastings or something like that, apparently found Dane, but it was too late for him." A lump formed in his throat.

Serena looked away, eyes darting back and forth as she processed the statement.

"Mystery solved," Cullen said. "Now, see, that wasn't so hard. You journalists always need a good source to get some resolution."

"I got it, didn't I?"

The screech of a metal stage door dragging against the stone ramp stopped the conversation. Dr. Burcham emerged from the stage entrance, his face flushed.

Serena and Cullen slanted their eyes towards him. Without either one declaring it, a race began.

twelve

CONLEY MASTERS, THE MEDICAL EXAMINER, lifted a fold of dense muscl near the ribcage and sewed through the muscle with heavy twine. With fingers soaked in blood, he adjusted the wide-brimmed, clear plastic helmet that now completely covered his face. Once the twine bored through the initial holes in the ribcage muscle, he would begin the process of sewing up the body.

Leaning closer, Conley began the weaving of string through muscle. Along with this body, three more bodies had been brought to the State Medical Examiner Office morgue. One, pierced with bullets, needed toxicology testing for a state police investigation. The second, a morbidly obese woman in her early forties, was suspected of having been poisoned by her boyfriend. The last body was a car crash victim killed on Route 35 near the Putnam and Kanawha County line outside of Charleston.

Conley had worked with so many bodies during his twenty-seven years as the state medical examiner that he could move from one autopsy to the next without needing the details. However, performing the procedure on younger victims always troubled him.

The metal operating table felt cold on Conley's elbows as he repositioned himself near the body. With a heavy tug on the twine, he made the final thrust with the needle and wove it directly around the nipple. A tie-off, and he was done.

Rising slowly, Conley let out an exasperated breath. The warm air trapped inside the mask created a haze over the mask surface. Turning away from the body, Conley lowered his hands under the sensor-activated sink nozzle. A generous stream of warm water oozed from the spigot, thinning the blood trickling across his fingers. Conley removed the latex gloves, washed his hands, and removed the mask.

He located a file folder near the sink ledge, adjacent to the operating table. He picked up the folder and scribbled notes on the parchment document.

Conley read over the victim information again. He stopped. Lowering the folder, Conley took one last glance at Dane Antonelli. Even though the autopsy had deformed the young man, Dane's angelic face set against his muscular body and wide shoulders appeared at peace.

Scribbling again, Conley signed his name at the bottom of the document, verifying the authenticity of the report. There was nothing unusual about this case, other than the person had suffered from slight tissue inflammation inside one heart valve, which was more than likely the cause of death. Conley placed the document report in the clasp folder, which brought some finality to the situation. Now he had to contact Davis Funeral Home in Clarksburg.

As Conley walked across the morgue and picked up the telephone, a burst of warm air rushed into the room, followed by the quick click of a door lock being turned. Conley turned around and saw nothing.

His face tightened. Reaching behind him, Conley surveyed the room as he removed the phone receiver and slowly dialed.

The soft, pleasant voice of a female representative from Davis Funeral Home answered. Conley identified himself, and began to say why he was calling.

Again, Conley heard a noise; this time, it sounded like the shuffling of feet. He quietly hung up the phone, opened a cabinet drawer below, and wrapped his fingers around a scalpel.

Then he held his breath. With the morgue building located in a seedy part of Charleston, Conley's work never proceeded uninterrupted. Sometimes, a homeless person would sneak in through the black metal door separating the lobby from the morgue room. Other times, paramedics bringing in bodies would leave the outside door ajar and a feral cat or some other animal came inside. For some reason, this intrusion felt different. Conley's palms sweated as he clutched the scalpel.

Conley swung around. He saw nobody. He scoured the room and noticed nothing amiss. As he sidestepped Dane's body en route to the lobby, he heard the rhythm of feet moving faster and felt another burst of warm air.

He raced to the back door. A faint streak of light dissolved into darkness as the door slammed shut.

thirteen

SERENA MANAGED TO LOCATE ELIZABETH HASTINGS through the campus directory. The directories were published on the last Monday in August, and today, Serena was thankful. After thumbing through several pages of students with the last name of Hastings, Serena stumbled upon Elizabeth. Initially, Elizabeth did not return the voice mail messages Serena left for her. After the third message, with Serena promising to list Elizabeth as an anonymous source, she reluctantly agreed to the interview.

Serena selected *The Record*'s newsroom for the interview. She assumed that Elizabeth would be more at ease around other students. The newsroom remained busy later in the day as reporters and copy editors met and decided story inclusion and placement. The incessant pecking of fingers on keyboards would provide a relaxing background hum.

Sitting at her desk, looking over her notes, Serena wrote down the names *Cullen Brewer* and *Dane Antonelli* and circled them. She had been intrigued by their meeting, mainly because she had heard Cullen's name mentioned multiple times, but without ever meeting him until now. Serena considered him a potential valuable source. Cullen could provide Serena a perspective on how the football team was dealing with the death of one of their own, but he would have to be kneaded and prodded for information, a challenge Serena felt she could handle.

"Serena?"

Her notepad clenched tightly, Serena turned toward the voice. "Elizabeth."

The unexceptional and unassuming girl teased her puffy hair as she slouched against the doorframe. Her pitted skin hid the radiance of smoky citrine eyes.

"Hi. Thanks for agreeing to meet with me," Serena said.

"I've never been interviewed by a newspaper before. I'm kinda nervous."

"Don't worry. I just have a few questions about what you saw in the stairwell at Stokley Hall."

She pulled out a chair for Elizabeth, and the girl cautiously sat down. Her eyes darted around the newsroom, alive with keystrokes and reporter-editor chatter.

Serena cleared her throat and tucked a tassel of hair behind her ear. "Did you know Dane Antonelli personally?"

Elizabeth shook her head. "No. I mean, he lived on the fourth floor and I lived on the eighth floor. We passed each other in the stairwells and in the lobby of the dorm sometimes, but we never spoke much. He always seemed like a nice person. He usually said 'hello' and smiled at me a lot, even though he didn't really know me."

Serena took notes in her own shorthand abbreviations. "Why were you in the stairwell?"

Elizabeth cast a glance at the ceiling, then dropped her gaze to the floor. Her lips twitched slightly.

"I had a chemistry final on Monday. It was my last assignment for that summer class. I had been making notecards of terms, things like ions, protons, neutrons..." Elizabeth looked at Serena. They locked into a stare, and Elizabeth smiled briefly before ducking her head.

"I'm listening," Serena assured her. "I may not write down every word, just the main points."

Elizabeth shook her head. "Like I said, I was making notecards and I decided to go downstairs to the lobby and get a Mountain Dew to help me stay awake. I took the stairs instead of the elevator, hoping the walk would keep me awake. As I went down the stairs, I heard moaning, the kind of moaning you hear when someone is sick."

Serena resumed scribbling. "Keep going."

"Whoever was making that sound, they sounded pretty bad. I stopped halfway down and listened for a few seconds, to make sure I wasn't hearing things. The moaning kept up. When I ran down the steps and... he was there...." Elizabeth cupped a hand over her mouth. "It was awful. Dane was there, sweating and vomiting and shaking really bad. And there was blood all over."

Elizabeth squinted, then shivered. "I don't ever want to see anything like that again."

Hearing how Dane looked in his final moments made Serena queasy. She let a long silence pass before asking, "Did you notice anything specific about Dane when you came upon him?"

"Not really. I just felt like I needed to reach out and grab him. Maybe I could have taken him to his room or into the lobby. I didn't want him left there on that cold, hard floor...alone. When I reached down for him, the life seemed to drain from his eyes. Then the eyes rolled back and stopped moving."

Elizabeth wrung her hands. "I'm sorry," she said, her voice growing softer. "You asked me what I remembered seeing. In addition to what I mentioned a second ago, I saw that Dane had bruises and swollen hands and some knuckles on his hands were really red."

"Like he had been in a fight?" Serena asked.

"Yes. I couldn't tell how badly messed up the hands were because he had one of them pulled close to his chest; the other hand was open and away from his body. There was also a torn piece of paper lying near him, but I didn't pay much attention to it."

"And you called 911 soon after?"

"Yes."

Serena stopped writing again. "Did you see anyone else in the stairwell? Or did anyone come upon either of you?"

"No." Elizabeth shook her head. "Wait. I did see the door leading to the lobby open slightly when I came down the steps. I thought I heard someone on the other side of the door walking away, but it could've been my own steps echoing in the stairwell. I really forgot about it when I saw Dane."

Turning a page, Serena caught Elizabeth taking a deep breath and turning uncomfortably in her seat.

"Have you told this story to anyone else?"

"Yes. A detective from the state police questioned me, and I spoke with Dr. Burcham about what I experienced."

The name fell on Serena like a lead weight. "You spoke with Dr. Burcham?"

"Yes."

"Why?"

Elizabeth scratched her chin. "He wanted to know what I saw, and I basically told him what I told you."

"And his reaction was...?"

"I could tell, you know, just by looking at his face, how upset he was about everything. He thanked me for doing what was necessary by calling 911 and telling my RA about what happened."

"That's it?"

A look of agitation crept across Elizabeth's face. "Yes, from what I remember, that's it."

"Did he ask you not to speak to anyone else?"

"Not really."

Serena let the words settle in her mind as she scanned the notes. "Thank you for coming and answering my questions."

Elizabeth sprang up from her seat and stepped to the door.

Serena reached out and snared her arm. "I will report what you have told me, but I will not name you as the source."

Elizabeth flashed a wry smile and left.

Serena went back to her desk and plopped into her seat. She turned the notepad back to page one. In the top right corner, she wrote the name NEAL BURCHAM in block letters and drew an arrow connecting his name to the *Cullen Brewer* and *Dane Antonelli* circles.

Satisfied, Serena reached for the campus directory, seeking the phone number for the president's office.

Serena walked across the newsroom to the phone and aggressively punched the numbers. She perched on a nearby chair as the attempted connection went through.

Someone picked up. "President's office."

At first, Serena didn't recognize the voice. "This is Serena Johnson from

The Record trying to reach Dr. Burcham."

"This is Jack Dillon. What can I do for you?"

"I really need to speak with Dr. Burcham," Serena said.

A bit of silence passed between them. Serena could hear Jack shifting the phone from one hand to the other.

"Dr. Burcham is not available. Is there something I can help you with, Serena?"

"I really need to speak with the president. I have some questions that only he can answer."

"What type of questions?" Jack asked, sounding annoyed.

"Really, I think it would be better if I spoke with the president..."

Jack silenced her. "He's unavailable. Maybe I can provide some answers to your questions or schedule you an appointment?"

Serena twisted the phone cord around a finger and sat more upright in the chair. "I understand Dr. Burcham spoke with Elizabeth Hastings concerning what she saw the night Dane Antonelli died..."

"I can tell you that the president did speak with Elizabeth, but he has no further comment on that at this time," Jack said.

Serena heard Jack take some deep breaths. "I am curious as to what they discussed and why Dr. Burcham wanted to speak with Elizabeth alone after the police had already taken her statement."

"That's something you will need to ask the president," Jack replied.

Serena tugged the phone cord tightly. "That's what I'm trying to do, sir."

"Well, I've already told you that he has no further comment on that discussion at this time."

As Serena prepared to ask another question, the line went dead.

fourteen

CULLEN STOOD INSIDE A SMALL POOL OF DIMMED LIGHT underneath a scorching September sun. Autumn might be two weeks away, but the streams of sweat gliding down his face were reminiscent of practice in early August, not mid-September.

The quarterback leaned in and looked through the chipped white plastic brackets of his facemask. Four players, each wearing a pale blue mesh jersey with the word "Cougars" stitched on it—along with silver leggings cut off at the knees—awaited his instructions.

"Now we're going to run a post-corner route," he said.

Two players nodded; two others grimaced.

"For the freshmen, this might be a bit difficult. Trust me, it gets better with repetition. We run an open offense. The more precise you become at running your routes, the better our offense will be."

Each player rose. Two of the receivers, Tay Anderson and Mike Ochoa, were veterans and first-team all WVIAC players from last season.

The other two receivers, Joey Gunnoe and Tyler Briggs, would likely play special teams during their freshman year, but they could see some work at wide receiver should a starter get injured or otherwise falter.

Whistles sounded, players grunted, and coaches screamed. The defensive unit for the Cougars worked through formations and tackling drills. The jarring sounds of bodies being slammed against the hard ground made Cullen tingle.

Focusing again on the receivers, Cullen continued, "If the cornerback plays off you when you're running the post, then the release will be easier.

You start by running a fly pattern. If he tries to jam you, make sure you get the inside position."

Cullen clapped. Each receiver broke away. Tay and Tyler lined up as receivers to the left. Joey lined up as a receiver to the right.

"Ready, on two... hut, hike!"

Cullen dropped back seven steps from a fictional line of scrimmage. Tay ran the streak route down the near sideline.

Tyler sprinted, made a sharp cut across the middle. Cullen pump-faked, pulled the ball closer to his collarbone and glanced right. Mike repeated Tyler's movements while Joey tripped and fell.

Cullen stopped retreating through the drop back. Shaking his head, he couldn't decide if he should be pleased or disappointed. Each receiver stopped running and focused on Joey, who clumsily picked himself up off the grass.

The receivers jogged towards Cullen, panting.

"Okay, not bad for our first time working as a unit." Cullen's eyes darted at Joey, whose face glowed crimson. "And don't worry about falling, Gunnoe. It happens."

Joey grimaced.

Cullen loosened his chinstrap and removed his helmet. "This time, I want you to run fifteen yards up the field and make your first cut. It will be to the inside, so you need to look straight ahead and make your cut. The second cut will be much sharper. When we do this for real, if you see a safety helping out over the top, make the cut. The defensive back may have his hands on you, so once you're headed for the sideline, turn and look around for the ball. There is a good chance the ball will already be in the air before you make your cut. If you can execute this play, it will pay off big in games."

The disjointed huddle fell silent.

"We'll run this pattern several times without interruption. After I make a read and throw the ball, whatever happens, come back and we'll run the play again."

Cullen was patient in allowing each receiver, especially the two freshmen, a chance to complete their routes. Each time he dropped back, planted his right foot, and delivered a perfect, tight spiral with plenty of zip. Tay caught nine passes, while Mike and Joey caught seven passes each and Tyler caught six passes.

Finally, Cullen removed his chinstrap. Practice was over for the day.

"Nice work, guys," Cullen called as his teammates jogged towards the sidelines. He settled the helmet under his arm and followed them. Once on the sideline, someone poked him in the back.

"Good throws out there."

Cullen turned.

Jordan's green eyes sparkled in the late afternoon sun. His face—smooth, manly, and symmetrically aesthetic—complemented his blond hair.

"Where have you been? We could have used you today. We were practicing post-corner routes, and I was showing Tyler and Joey how to run them."

Jordan tilted his head slightly. "Who?"

Cullen's eyes flickered. "Tyler and Joey, our freshman wide-outs." He shook his head. "Never mind."

"Dad and I went to some boring Board of Governors luncheon today. Coach said I could go."

Cullen headed towards the east stands. Clusters of cleats mashed into the grass field as players, coaches, and trainers whisked past him.

He turned. Jordan jogged toward him, wearing a salmon-colored polo shirt and brown corduroy pants. By comparison to everyone else, Jordan looked prepared to give a speech at a formal event instead of run routes and catch passes.

Cullen continued walking toward the locker room.

Jordan pulled a sheaf of papers from under his shirt. "You made *The Record* today."

"What are you talking about, Hancel? I haven't done any interviews since media day last week."

Jordan scowled. "Do you know Serena Johnson? She cited you in her story."

Cullen stopped walking. Just inches away from the east side stands and the lower level concourse exit ramp, he placed the football helmet on the ground and his hands on his hips. Facing Jordan once again, Cullen's lips tightened. "I know Serena Johnson. I mean, I don't really know her. I just met her two weeks ago."

"Well, I don't know her either, but that girl is smoking hot. We were in English Composition class together my sophomore year. I'd like to know her better, that's for sure." Jordan winked.

Cullen chewed his lower lip. "What did the article say and why did she mention me?"

"I'm not sure. Dad picked up a copy in the student center as we headed for the luncheon."

Jordan fumbled with the paper as more Clear River Cougars jogged past him. He unfolded two sheets of the newspaper before locating the story. He held the paper in front of Cullen. "See, your picture is here on the front page."

The small file photo had been taken by the college photographer during Cullen's freshman season. The page also featured a small photo of Dr. Burcham. The president seemed mature and regal next to Cullen.

Jordan turned the paper backwards. "It says, 'Clear River sophomore Dane Antonelli was found dead two weeks ago inside Stokley Hall. He was discovered in a front stairwell of the underclassman dormitory. Authorities do not suspect foul play, Clear River spokesman Jack Dillon said.'"

Cullen raised his arms. "I still don't see the connection between that and me."

Jordan read on. "'Police and university officials will continue investigating. Official autopsy reports from the West Virginia State Medical Examiner say no drugs were present in Antonelli's system at the time of his death.'"

Cullen opened his mouth to speak, but Jordan raised a finger, cutting him off. "'Antonelli was last seen leaving Darby's in Buckhannon at one-thirty a.m. on August 17 alone, according to a report filed by the West Virginia State Police and obtained by *The Record*. According to the Medical Examiner, Antonelli suffered a massive heart attack and internal bleeding resulting in death.'"

Jordan stopped reading. "Now it gets good."

Cullen folded his arms.

"This story is located next to the main one. 'Three days later, Dr. Neal Burcham was seen conferring with Student Body President Cullen Brewer after a press conference in which the Clear River College president provided little additional information about Antonelli's death or the investigation. Brewer also happens to be the senior starting quarterback for the Clear River College football team and an NCAA Division II All-American.'"

"At least she got my biographical information correct," Cullen said.

Jordan once again wadded the newspaper and jammed it inside his pocket. He looked at Cullen. "I want all the details. Tell me everything that wasn't in that story."

Cullen dropped his arms. "There isn't that much to add. Remember in August when you pulled up with your new car and we talked about Dane's death?"

"I do. Man, you took off like a bat out of hell." Jordan's face softened, although beads of sweat trickled down his nose.

"Well, I went looking for Dr. Burcham. When I reached the administrative building on campus, Dr. Burcham's secretary Barbara told me he was giving a press conference at the Fine Arts building. When I got there, I ran into Serena. She'd been at the press conference and she wanted to ask Burcham some follow-up questions."

Jordan rocked back and forth, absorbing the details. "Can we head under the stands? It's so damn hot out here. I don't like sweating unless I have to."

Cullen smirked. "Then you're playing the wrong sport at the wrong time of year." He patted Jordan on the back and they headed under the concourse ramp. The shade cooled their tingling skin.

"Dr. Burcham didn't say much when Serena and I approached him," Cullen reasoned. "He didn't seem real interested in talking with anyone else in the media about Dane. He said he'd meet with me later regarding my concerns."

Jordan stared straight ahead, remaining silent.

"I don't even know why I'm telling you this, Hancel. You don't even remember who Dane was. And you don't seem to care one way or the other about what happened to him."

"What concerns are you talking about?" Jordan spoke softly.

They reached the end of the concourse ramp. Ahead of them, a hallway split into two segments. The left hallway led towards the locker room and the right hallway connected to the facilities building.

Jordan's momentum moved him down the right hallway.

Cullen slipped ahead and faced Jordan again. "Dane was part of Cougar football and a fellow student. What happened to him was terrible, and as one of the team captains and the student body president, I'm going to make sure we honor his memory. We're going to wear stickers on our helmets with Dane's jersey number this year. During our Homecoming in October, we'll have a moment of silence before kickoff and retire his jersey. I'm going to invite his family to attend the ceremony."

Jordan raised his thick eyebrows. "Does Coach Miles know about all this?"

"Not yet. I'm going to discuss it with him, though."

"And Dr. Burcham?"

"I went over a few details before Serena Johnson started asking questions. That's when Dr. Burcham said he wanted more information at a later date and time."

"Damn, you really put some thought into this. I'm impressed." He grinned and shook his head. "Your damn compassion's gonna get you in trouble someday."

Cullen reared back. "What's that supposed to mean?"

"I learned from Dad a long time ago that you can't get too involved with people. People will let you down. You know, say one thing and then do something else. People should be treated as acquaintances. In other words, develop a relationship that benefits both parties, and then move on once it's over."

"In essence," Cullen said, "treat everyone like a business transaction."

Jordan flashed a wide smile. "You got it. It made my father a rich man with a lot of connections."

Cullen couldn't argue that point. Tom Hancel's intuition had made him a tycoon in concrete. Hancel Cement, Incorporated, started as a small company in Lewisburg, but had spread internationally with offices on three continents. Tom was also a proud Clear River College alumnus and a huge benefactor. Despite his reputation for being ruthless, Tom had always treated Cullen like a son.

Cullen playfully slapped Jordan again on the shoulder. "I've got game film to watch and chapters of *A Clockwork Orange* to read. I'll see you later."

The locker room smelled like dirty socks. Yet Cullen appreciated the tranquility of the lockers, each standing erect with helmets, pads, and cleats all hung in uniformity.

He sighed.

After a long shower, Cullen put on a white t-shirt, black underwear shorts, and jeans, and then returned to the outer hallway and headed for the facilities building.

He pushed open the blue double doors and walked through the main first floor hallway.

A man stood at the end of the hallway, examining the panoramic football team pictures on the wall.

Cullen approached, moving past the trophy and memorabilia cases lining the outer wall. Soon he was near enough to see tears creeping down the man's face.

The man was Dr. Petry.

fifteen

D R. JOHN PETRY NEARLY JUMPED. "Mr. Brewer. I'm sorry. I didn't hear you coming." He patted each pocket of his navy slacks until he discovered a tissue, which he dabbed on his moist cheeks.

Cullen reached a hand outward, and then drew it away. "I'm sorry, Dr. Petry. I didn't mean to startle you. I was passing through, heading back to my dorm..."

Still appearing flustered, Dr. Petry looked for a place to hide the wet tissue. Parts of the cloth dissolved in his hands, leaving speckles of cloth clinging to his fingers. "No explanation needed, young man. I have been teaching here for over twenty-eight years. So many students have passed through my classes. Sometimes, I reflect on events I've lived through."

Cullen sensed the tension in the professor's voice, so he said softly, "Think about the influence you've had on all of those students."

"That's an exaggeration. Most students sign up for my classes because English is required. They don't think of me as any different from any other faculty member in the department."

"I disagree," Cullen said. "Your classes have changed me."

The professor's eyes darted to Cullen, then returned to the picture on the wall. His face remained expressionless.

The panoramic photographs, in chronological order, jutted outward from the cinderblock walls. They were framed in blue and dated back to 1951, the first year Clear River College became an NCAA Division II football school.

The professor inched closer, gingerly touching the face of one player— a smallish boy with curly dark hair, a round face, peachy skin and almond-shaped eyes. The player wore jersey number 82.

Cullen watched, touched by the gesture. "Sir, I just wanted to say hello. But I meant what I said about your influence on me and my education."

Finally, a slight grin crept over Dr. Petry's face.

Behind Cullen, the entrance door flung open. Sneakers squeaked against the pewter tile floor, growing louder as the seconds elapsed. Dr. Petry continued stroking the picture, but Cullen turned around.

"Cullen Brewer, where the hell did you go after practice?" Coach Miles growled. "I let you work with those freshman receivers today and I expect a report on their progress. Please tell me they can catch the damn ball."

"Sorry, Coach," Cullen said, turning to face Coach Miles. "I just forgot to report. Everything went fine. Tay and Mike did great and Joey is coming along. Joey needs more confidence, but that will come with more reps and more work with the playbook."

Coach Miles moved close to Cullen's face. "For a senior quarterback who knows how I want things done, you sure act like a freshman. Our receivers, aside from Hancel, can't seem to run post-corner patterns." Coach Miles took a breath, tilted his head and looked around Cullen, focusing on Dr. Petry. "Is there something I can help you with, Doc? You're a little outside your element over here. You take care of academics on your side of campus. Trust me to have everything under control here."

Although he said nothing, Dr. Petry's rapid breathing echoed through the hall.

Coach Miles, of medium build with a thick neck, wide shoulders and a narrow waist, seemed larger than the hallway itself. "Oh, maybe you're here because we have an academic problem. Is Brewer skipping class?" The coach's tone grew more accusatory. "If that's the case, I can promise you I will run his ass until his guts ooze out of his mouth."

"No, Coach, I'm not skipping class," Cullen said, placing himself between Coach Miles and Dr. Petry.

Dr. Petry's breathing intensified. He shook his fist. "You ignorant fool," he snarled. "After all these years of coaching, you still won't listen to anyone. It doesn't matter if it's players, parents, other coaches, your own coaches—it makes no difference. You are a fool."

"No, I am in charge," Coach Miles barked back. "I will deal with my players and my team my way. Brewer did not do what I asked of him, and I have a right to know why in hell he didn't do it."

Dr. Petry leveled a determined gaze at Coach Miles. "Perhaps you should listen to the explanation before you make an accusation." He turned and faced Cullen, but pointed at Coach Miles. "This man, Mr. Brewer, is a tyrant and a barbarian. He has little regard for anyone except himself."

"You'd better watch it, Doc." Frown lines creased Coach Miles's brow. "I did not come here to argue with you. If you wanna talk and make accusations that are totally baseless, you go ahead and we can discuss this like men in private. Right now, I have a game prep I need to focus on."

"Discuss this like men, in private." The professor laughed. "I remember it well."

Dr. Petry leaned closer. The professor and the coach were now almost nose to nose.

"Brian rushed back here. He was scared you'd punish him if he defied your mandate." The professor leaned back. "But Brian never made it, did he?" Dr. Petry's eyes welled up.

Cullen took a step back. Everything now made sense. The professor had been admiring his son's photograph: his son who'd been killed. A knot grew in his stomach—the kind that makes vomiting the only remedy.

Coach Miles rubbed his nose. "I told you then I was sorry and I am still sorry about it. Not one day goes by that I do not think about that moment when your son was killed." Coach Miles pointed a finger at the professor. "But that was a long time ago. What happened to him was a tragic accident. I cannot do or say anything to bring your son back. And your son's accident has nothing to do with how I run my team or coach my players, and no one, especially not a professor, is going to tell me how to do it. If it were up to you and your goddamned academic ivory tower elitists, this college wouldn't have any sports teams, period."

"You cannot even call Brian by his own name!" The professor's eyes narrowed as he glared at Coach Miles. "You, sir, are a miserable misanthrope. Your teams might win games and conference championships and all the rest, but someday, your ruthless ways of handling people will cost you your career."

The coach moved his glare to Cullen. "Brewer, I need you to get some rest. Our first game is Saturday. I need you ready."

Dr. Petry turned sharply and strode past the coach. As he did, one shoulder collided with Coach Miles's shoulder, rocking his rigid stance.

Cullen ran after Dr. Petry. He didn't catch up with him until they reached the end of the hallway. "Dr. Petry, I'm really sorry about that back there. If I had known…." Cullen let the words trail away as the professor jogged down the stairs. "Coach Miles really *is* a good coach. He motivates us and challenges us. We are used to him, and quite honestly, the upperclassmen have learned never to take him personally. I mean, he played college ball for the Air Force Academy, he served in Vietnam… discipline is part of his package. I am so sorry about your son, though. If I had known…I mean, I am sure Coach feels awful about what happened…."

The words flowed from Cullen's mouth faster because Dr. Petry was walking faster. The professor stopped in front of the metal exit at the end of the hallway and seemed to stare into space as he said woodenly:

"Good day, Mr. Brewer."

sixteen

J ORDAN AND CULLEN leaned against the locker room wall. The rest of the team filed out ahead of them.

"Is your dad coming today?" Jordan asked. Cullen stared at the floor, then began running in place on a treadmill.

"This is going to be a tough one for us," Cullen said. "Coach Miles wants Southern Virginia State to serve as a measuring stick. This one will get us ready for conference play, no doubt."

Jordan rested a hand on Cullen, which Cullen ignored and instead ran faster.

"Is your dad coming or not?"

"Southern runs the ball well, throws the ball efficiently, and controls the tempo and game clock against opponents. We've got to be ready for that."

"Brewer..!"

Cullen stopped running. He leveled a solemn look at Jordan.

"I stopped asking my dad to come and watch me play after Mom died. Part of me wants him here, but I can't make him come. I'm not sure I could focus anyway, knowing that he's in the stands." His mouth quivered.

"He'd probably come drunk anyway and looking for a fight, which would probably involve me, which would lead to..." Cullen closed his eyes and shook his head in disgust. "Enough talking about him. We've got a game to get ready for."

Coach Miles had been preparing Cullen and the Cougars for the game all week. Before the game, he stood in front of the team in the locker room and said:

"As some of you know, the West Virginia Intercollegiate Athletic Conference rates as one of the oldest leagues at the smaller-college level. Every one of the schools in this league is competitive, and we'll face a new set of challenges each week. We got a win against Concord already under our belts, which is a good thing. But remember. men, there are no pushover programs."

Coach Miles, who loved teaching offense, started as an offensive assistant under former Glenville State head coach Rich Rodriguez, the 1993 NAIA National Coach of the Year; the next year, the WVIAC had joined the NCAA Division II ranks.

"Southern Virginia State, even though they are not a conference member, will be a good measuring stick for our program before we get back into conference play. Do not take them lightly. Last year, they beat three conference teams: Fairmont State, West Virginia State, and the University of Charleston. Let's come out focused, and ready to play."

As Cullen and Jordan left the locker room heading for the field, what Coach had said earlier in the week ricocheted in Cullen's mind: the Hawks brought an eight-game winning streak—dating back to last season—and a #20 NCAA Division II national ranking.

We got a big win over Concord last week, but we can't let down now.

"If we make a mistake, we'll pay for it," Coach Miles told the team, his face scrunched tight with anxiety. He barely noticed Cullen and Jordan arrive late to the huddle. "As long as we don't make mistakes, we'll be fine. But if we get behind, it's going to be hard getting anything going against that defense. Southern runs a base 4-3 defense, where two of their defensive tackles are going to stop Marcus from gaining yards running the football. Meanwhile, their defensive ends—who are quicker than our tackles—will rush Cullen."

As Coach Miles ended the meeting, the team captains headed onto the field and stood with the officiating crew at midfield for the coin toss. That done, Cullen gathered the offensive line, along with Marcus Turner, Mike Ochoa, Tyler Briggs and Jordan Hancel.

"Against their 4-3 defense, we're running traps." He pointed at Marcus. "We need you to run parallel to the line of scrimmage, wait for a block, and then hit the hole quickly. They will jam the line and bring pressure, so be ready. Once they penetrate, we'll use play action passes and take some shots down the field."

Jordan Hancel's wide eyes turned into slits. He smacked his fists against his chest. "We've got a chance here, guys, to beat a top twenty-five team at home. Let's do this! Let's beat these bastards."

Cullen glanced at Jordan, then looked over the offense, making sure they understood the plan. He lowered his helmet, adjusted his chinstrap, and screamed: "One, two, three...Cougars!"

Thick cumulus clouds hung over Cougars Stadium. On Saturday morning, a light rain had temporarily broken the humid, tropical atmosphere. However, the afternoon sun regenerated the humidity. The pungent smell of mud, now seeping to the surface of the field, mixed with the muggy air and created a stench as the Cougars and the Hawks took the field.

The opening kickoff from Hawks kicker Mike Maddox sailed through the end zone. Cougars, first down and ten, from the twenty yard line.

Cullen kept a close eye on Coach Miles so he could interpret his instructions. Cullen looked down at the sleeve on his right wrist, checking the coach's signals against the small chart printed on the sleeve. The first two offensive plays for the Cougars were trap runs, as Cullen predicted. Marcus Turner took the football from Cullen on the first snap from scrimmage. Guard Mike Bosello, the pulling guard, blindsided the quick, agile defensive end from the Hawks, creating a hole.

However, the center and right tackle failed to block out the two defenders momentarily uncovered: the defensive lineman left behind by Bosello and the Hawks linebacker creeping up on the line of scrimmage.

Simultaneously, the defensive lineman hit Turner high and the linebacker wrapped him up low. The Cougars netted one yard on the play.

Coach Miles signaled the next play from scrimmage—another trap-running play for Marcus Turner. However, this time the Cougars ran against the right side of the Hawks' line.

This time, Anderson was the pulling guard. Andre Gibson and Carmine DeRocha couldn't block the free defender. Despite Turner's best efforts—with his piston-like legs churning forward—he was tackled from behind for a loss of two yards.

As the offense sprinted back from the line of scrimmage into the huddle, Cullen took a deep breath. The blocking downfield by the wide receivers had been excellent, but the trap runs had failed at the point of attack. The offense gathered around him for the huddle. However, Jordan had Gibson and DeRocha in his own huddle. Jordan's face grew red and his arms animated as he obviously scolded the linemen. Carmine, trailing behind Jordan and Andre, bumped into Jordan, attempting to defuse the ensuing argument. Jordan reacted by grabbing Carmine's facemask and pushing the right tackle's helmet away.

Cullen jogged over. "You guys all right?"

Jordan scowled. "I'd be better if these damn idiots could block."

Cullen stepped in front of Jordan. "Okay. We'll get it. Let's go." He looked again at Coach Miles. This time, he signaled pass.

Cullen draped his arms over the backs of Jordan and Carmine. The symbolic gesture seemed to calm Jordan. Carmine ignored Jordan's presence in the huddle, staring instead at Cullen's mouth.

Cullen craned his neck upwards and caught a quick glance of the field. The mud became more defined between clumps of decaying grass as the Hawks defense, clad in soft green jerseys with white numerals, remained huddled on the opposite side of the line of scrimmage.

Cullen took quick note of the hashmarks outside of the line of scrimmage and the sidelines. With two flats on the field, one to the right and one to the left, Cullen knew this slow-moving play would require some quarterback movement in the pocket.

Moving into the shotgun formation behind center Andre Gibson, two wide receivers, Tay and Mike, lined up on the left side of the formation while Tyler and Jordan lined up on the right side of the formation. Cullen extended his hands forward. He barked the cadence, and the play began.

Jordan and Tay ran significantly more than five yards upfield. Mike, meanwhile, angled from the center of the field into the left flat and found a vacated portion of the field near the sideline, but no more than five yards downfield.

Cullen backpedaled farther, watching as Andre Gibson and Mike Bosello struggled to block the charging Hawks lineman. Cullen looked left, saw Mike Ochoa open in a one-on-one coverage with a Hawks cornerback, and threw a perfect pass that hit Mike in the chest.

Mike pivoted left, stutter-stepped to the right, and spun. The cornerback slipped and fell. Mike charged towards the sideline, past the first down marker, and gained fifteen yards.

The referee tossed out a yellow penalty flag. He turned to the Cougars sideline, and to Cougars fans indicated a holding infraction against Clear River. Mike Ochoa's catch and run for fifteen yards would be nullified by an offensive pass interference penalty.

On the next play, a bad shotgun snap forced Cullen to push the ball across the backline of the end zone for a safety. Southern Virginia State was ahead by the unusual score of 2-0.

The Cougars defense held the Hawks offense to eight yards on their next three offensive plays. When Clear River got the football back, the Cougars moved the ball into Hawks territory, but Marcus Turner lost a fumble at the Hawks' 42 yard line. Southern Virginia State took advantage, going 58 yards in eight plays and increasing their lead 9-0 on a nine-yard touchdown pass late in the second quarter.

Clear River's defense stopped Southern Virginia State on their first possession of the fourth quarter and the Cougars embarked on their best drive of the day—seven plays, 87 yards, capped off with a seven-yard touchdown pass from Cullen Brewer to Jordan Hancel. The score became 9-7 with 9:12 left in the fourth quarter.

On the Cougars' next offensive series, Marcus Turner lost a fumble at their own 31 yard line. A defender from Southern Virginia State scooped up the fumble and returned the football to the Clear River 18 yard line.

Coach Miles called a timeout.

Running to the defensive unit, which was getting ready to head onto the field, Miles barked some final instructions. "Blitz. You have got to put some pressure on White. Don't let him stand back there and go through his progressions."

The defense for the Cougars came onto the field first. White attempted a short pass to a fullback out of the backfield, but was sacked at the Clear River 24 yard line for a six yard loss.

On the next play, White took a deep drop behind the line of scrimmage. Once again, the Cougars blitzed. White avoided the defenders and carried the ball on a quarterback run for a nine yard gain.

On third down, Clear River blitzed from the outside of the line of scrimmage. White read the play, anticipated the blitz and threw a touchdown pass to Jamal Winston.

The Hawks beat Clear River at home by the final score of 16-7.

*   *   *   *   *

Serena peered over the tops of several workstations in *The Record* newsroom.

The newsroom featured little ventilation, creating a warm, stifling atmosphere that formed beads of sweat on her forehead.

Glancing at the computer screens, she saw flat, black, opaque squares staring back at her. Most of *The Record* staff had left the newsroom Friday evening and wouldn't return until Monday morning. Despite the absence of reporters pecking incessantly on keyboards, traipsing around the newsroom, and maintaining the usual jovial camaraderie, Serena enjoyed the stillness of the moment.

Her workstation was littered with loose-leaf sheets of notebook paper, pens with missing caps, pencils badly needing sharpening, and fluorescent yellow Post-it notes affixed to the computer screen. She grabbed a fistful of old, worn pages and discarded them in the trash can next to her desk.

She picked up the brown folder, removed *The Charleston Gazette* seal and tore open the folder. Inside, a hand-written note on unlined paper reminded Serena that the contents of the folder were sensitive and she had only two days to spend with it before it had to be returned.

Tracy came through for me again," she said aloud, her breath ruffling the yellow notes stuck on the computer screen.

City Editor Tracy Pritt had served as Serena's practicum adviser during her junior year at Clear River College. Serena earned placement at *The Charleston Gazette*, the largest newspaper in West Virginia, due in part to her tenacious coverage of campus issues for *The Record* and, of course, her excellent faculty recommendations. Working in Charleston provided Serena with invaluable real-world experience and an outlet for her relentless, albeit suspicious, attitude towards reporting to blossom.

When the details of the death of Dane Antonelli garnered attention from media throughout the state, especially the *Gazette*, Tracy frequently contacted Serena for additional information—information outside the traditional statements issued by President Burcham's office and statements released by the West Virginia State Police.

Serena had asked President Burcham for details contained in the autopsy report completed by the State Medical Examiner in Charleston, but her request was denied. With the approval of School of Journalism Dean Howard Shively, Serena filed a Freedom of Information Act request through the West Virginia Department of Health and Human Resources, proprietors of the state medical examiner's office. The DHHR stalled on the request and eventually denied it altogether. The reasoning: the autopsy report was not a public document.

From there, Serena once again contacted Tracy Pritt. Pritt had a source inside the DHHR that owed the editor a favor from several years earlier. When Tracy asked for a copy of the autopsy report, she went to the state capitol building, met with the source on the front lawn of the capitol, and collected the folder.

Since her follow-up story on Dane Antonelli's death appeared in *The Record* two weeks ago, the story had grown cold. Serena believed several aspects of the story didn't make sense.

First, how could Dane Antonelli, an otherwise healthy, muscular football player, die from myocarditis without someone within the football program being aware of his condition? Also, how did he end up in a dormitory stairwell in the middle of the night by himself? If Dane had suffered a heart attack—something Neal Burcham alluded to in several follow-up statements—then how did he manage the one-mile walk through campus without collapsing?

Serena mulled repeatedly over these questions. A dull ache arose from her temple, a sure sign of an oncoming headache.

She looked over her shoulder, carefully inspecting the doorway behind her. Silence. Holding the document away from her chest, she inspected the medical examiner's report.

Her eyes absorbed the information like dry ground absorbing water. The document stated the cause of death was myocarditis. No traces of alcohol or drugs were discovered in Dane Antonelli's bloodstream, although the victim suffered tissue inflammation around his heart. Several small, round scabs appeared below Antonelli's torso, near the naval and on the gluteus muscles. The coroner noted in the report that the spots resembled acne, a reminder that Dane was only twenty years old.

Overall, the report did not reveal any contradictory information, nor did it create additional questions for Serena. Yet she felt the story did not hold together on its own merits.

A vibration jolted Serena from her thoughts. Behind her, on the copy desk drawing table, her cell phone rocked and bobbled. The calendar icon on the phone expanded on the screen. Inside a text box, a reminder: the Clear River College Student Government Association was planting a maple tree outside the student center, and she needed to be there. Serena gathered her belongings and shoved the autopsy report in a large flap inside her purse.

Her next objective: a conversation with Cullen Brewer.

seventeen

SERENA MARCHED, arms and legs swinging rhythmically like pistons, from Branstone Hall to the student center.

The early September weather was heavy and close, the air tepid. The once-milky sky had now changed into a wickedly blue collection of fantastic shapes.

Serena approached the student center. The brick façade of the building, rising six stories from the ground, divided the outward surface into tiers of narrow columns. The low-slung roof had a canopy, attached by bolts and hinges to the rest of the structure. Under the canopy, several pockets of students gathered in small groups and spent the afternoon talking, eating, and smoking.

In front of the student center, on an expansive piece of grass that separated the main student center entryway from the sidewalk, several students dug with shovels. Dirt flung from the hole created a grimy sheen on the white sidewalks.

Serena jotted notes. First, she described the setting and the surroundings. Then, she counted the number of students—seven. A small, waifish maple tree rested on the sidewalk, its tiny branches bound together by rope.

Serena looked up.

Wearing a baby blue tee-shirt, tan shorts and sandals, Cullen limped along the sidewalk, his figure taut and coltish.

Serena tucked a lock of hair behind an ear and waved at Cullen. He waved back.

Cullen wiped perspiration from his forehead. "I imagine you want to talk to me. Sorry I'm late, but we had a tough game this afternoon against the Hawks."

Serena blinked. "Did you win?"

"Nope," Cullen replied. "We generated three hundred and fifteen yards of total offense, which is around a hundred yards fewer than our average. We had too many penalties, and we lost two fumbles that they converted into fourteen points. Practice next week is going to be no fun."

Serena watched the hole-digging continue. Her hair hung in perfect balance on her shoulders. A wispy strand of hair lay at an angle across her forehead and her smooth, porcelain skin gave her face and curvy body, resting inside a peach short-sleeve cardigan and tan shorts, an angelic appearance.

She shifted her gaze back to Cullen. "How did you do then, as the quarterback?"

"Fourteen for twenty, a hundred thirty-three yards passing, and one touchdown. And I'm sore," he replied matter-of-factly.

Serena swayed uneasily. The numbers meant little to her. "You'll win next week." She pushed her hair up. "I wanted to ask you some questions about this tree planting."

"I didn't get an opportunity to thank you for mentioning me in your exposé about Dane Antontelli's death. I didn't realize our conversation and the conversation we had with Dr. Burcham would be considered 'on the record'." Cullen carved imaginary quotation marks in the air.

Serena flinched. "Unless a journalist declares something off the record, you as the interviewee must know that your words can be considered part of the record."

Cullen shook his head. "I didn't classify myself as an 'interviewee' when we spoke. I thought it was just casual."

Serena's cheeks burned. "Then, for the record," she said, leaning towards Cullen, "I think having a tree dedicated in Dane's memory is a great idea."

Cullen blushed. "Thank you. Sometimes, as students arrive and graduate, we forget names and faces. Then something tragic happens and suddenly everyone knows a particular name. Dedicating and planting a tree makes Dane a part of this college community forever. I think we've got to find ways of making something positive out of something horrible."

"Good quote." Serena tapped the pen on her notepad and scribbled some notes. "What did Burcham think about the idea?"

"He was quite supportive," Cullen said. "He told me as long as we had money in the student government budget for the tree and members could volunteer their time, it was fine with him."

Serena rested the pen cap against her lip. "Did he tell you anything else about the investigation?"

"I didn't know there was one."

Serena stopped writing. "I believe there is something about Dane's death lurking below the surface. I also believe those details will not rise to the surface without more digging." She placed the tip of the pen on a new, clean line on the notepad. "You're sure Dr. Burcham didn't say anything else? The slightest detail could be important."

Cullen tilted his head. "No, not anything we didn't already know."

Serena stopped writing. "What is it we already know?"

Cullen felt uneasy. What sort of verbal joust was she starting? Beside him, the sounds of shifting earth intensified as well as the grunts of the men digging the hole. Soon, the hole would be finished.

"Look, Serena—"

"This can be off the record, if need be."

Cullen frowned. "I think you have this idea that I am hiding something from you and that there is a conspiracy at work here. I didn't know Dane very well as a person, but I feel like I knew him more than most other people, especially our teammates. Most of the time, upperclassmen mingling with underclassmen is considered a violation of an unwritten sports taboo." He paused, shook his head, and continued. "I don't see it that way. I believed if Dane was going to be a part of our team, then we had to make him feel welcome. As an offensive player, Dane was going to play in my unit. It's hard creating an atmosphere of trust between a quarterback and his unit without any rapport. Maybe that makes me different, but I felt it was right for me to reach out to Dane."

"What you did was noble," Serena said. "That whole upperclassman, underclassman dynamic is true in all areas of campus life. I'm involved in a sorority and we deal with many of the same issues."

Cullen's blue eyes glinted. "Serena Johnson is in a sorority?"

Serena set her jaw. "Before you start in on me, some of the stereotypes concerning sororities are justified, but we do a lot of community and charity work that goes unnoticed."

Cullen turned toward the sound of shovels scraping against concrete. "And you all have beautiful women in your organizations."

Serena crossed her arms. "What about Coach Miles? Has he said anything to you or the team about Dane?"

"No."

"Why is that?"

"That's just Coach and the way he is about things like that."

Serena turned a page on her tablet. "Seems that your coach hasn't said anything to anyone. What about your teammates? Have they said anything?"

"Nothing relevant."

Serena huffed, frowning at her notepad. "That's great, just great."

"Serena," Cullen said, expelling a long breath. "Everyone in our locker room has been affected in some way by Dane's death. But there are over fifty players on the team. It's impossible for me to say or speculate on their thoughts and feelings. I hope you understand."

She nodded. "I do."

A lanky, pimpled kid with glasses and greasy black hair shoved a stack of papers in front of Cullen. "We're almost done planting the tree." His voice had a nasal quality.

"Thanks, Ian," Cullen said. "Oh, Ian, this is Serena Johnson with *The Record*. She's doing a story on the tree dedication. I'm sure she'd like to get a quote from you." He flashed a sheepish grin at Serena.

"Nice to meet you." Ian tossed a dismissive glance at Serena, then turned back to Cullen. "These are the purchase order requests for the tee-shirts we're giving away for the Homecoming game. You gotta sign them so we can take them to Dr. Burcham and order the shirts."

Cullen patted his pockets, then looked at Serena's pen. "May I?"

"Sure." She handed her pen to him.

Cullen signed several forms and ruffled through the pages. "We're getting the shirts from the same distributor in Weston, just like before, right?"

"Yep," Ian responded. "T.J.'s Graphics."

With the last signature page signed, Cullen returned Serena's pen and then gave the papers back to Ian.

"Thanks, Ian. Tell everyone thanks for their work today."

Ian stood awkwardly and saluted. "Sure thing, boss."

As Ian disappeared into a group of workers, two moving shadows became more defined. Heading across the student center parking lot toward the administration building were Dr. Burcham and Tom Hancel. Tom was pointing at the ground and making agitated gestures while Dr. Burcham walked briskly, staring ahead and saying nothing.

The president stopped. He raised a rolled stack of papers to shield his eyes from the brilliant sunlight, gazed in the direction of the tree planting, and finally glanced toward Cullen and Serena.

"I wonder what those two are discussing," Serena mused out loud. Her voice carried a note of suspicion.

"That's Tom Hancel, the chairman of the Board of Governors, talking with Dr. Burcham."

"It looks like Mr. Hancel is doing all the talking," Serena said.

The men disappeared into the campus midsection.

Serena took in a deep breath, held it, then released it. She slowly turned her attention back to Cullen. "Thanks for talking with me. It's good seeing you again. I guess I'll talk to Ian and then finish this story."

Cullen touched her gently on the arm. "Thanks for letting me use your pen." He limped past her.

Serena finished her interviews, then went back to Branstone Hall and into the newsroom. Shutting the newsroom door behind her, she placed her notepad on her desk and retrieved the scrunched autopsy report from her purse. She walked over to the copy desk and turned on the halogen light underneath the table.

Unfolding the report, she reached into a file cabinet, removed a new clasp folder, and marked it with Tracy Pritt's address.

Serena glanced at the report one more time, and a striking image caught her eye. As the halogen light bathed the table surface, the images on the autopsy report became more defined.

She leaned down, inching closer. Serena studied the images at the top of the report, where the West Virginia state seal adorned all official government documents. Encased in gold, the mountaineer figure and the coal miner stood proudly, casting outward glances beyond the periphery of the circle. But something was missing—specifically, the trademark symbols usually associated with the two images.

As Serena pulled the document closer, she realized the coal miner inside the state seal was missing his pickaxe, while the mountaineer was missing his mallet.

Her mouth opened in amazement. Looking further down the document, the lines separating the columns of comments provided by the state medical examiner were uneven and blurred. The document was a forgery!

Serena repeated aloud something she'd said to Cullen earlier. *The slightest detail...*

eighteen

"I WILL NOT SUPPORT BUILDING A FOUR-LANE HIGHWAY through the middle of my campus." Every syllable of Dr. Burcham's words was accented with frustration directed at Tom Hancel.

Tom followed Dr. Burcham into the president's office. He folded his pudgy frame onto a sofa and ran stubby fingers through his silver hair.

"The fact that you mentioned my support of the idea in front of other board members at halftime today is preposterous and unacceptable." Dr. Burcham pointed a long, arthritic finger at Tom. "You had no right to speak on my behalf."

Tom huffed and settled into the sofa, glaring at the president.

Dr. Burcham turned away from the window, the amber sky now streaked fiery orange from the setting sun. He looked back at Tom.

Tom's square jaw, white teeth, and glazed-over blue eyes twitched anxiously. The president had seen this look before—Tom was preparing a response. Normally soft-spoken with a thoughtful drawl broken by frequent pauses, the chairman of the Clear River College Board of Governors took a good twenty seconds to weigh his position.

"I think you are missing the idea here, Neal," Tom said finally. "The Department of Highways can widen North Brent Street. Then Corridor 33 becomes a four-lane road leading into campus and then all the way to Burnsville and Interstate 79."

Dr. Burcham turned his back to Tom and looked out the window, resting a hand on the warm glass. "You are asking me to agree to something I don't believe this campus needs." He swung around and faced the chairman. "Explain to me how normal campus functions are to go on with a construction project this massive underway Building a four-lane road cannot be done in a summer, and I cannot just move the campus somewhere else."

"Agreed," Tom said. "But what you fail to see here is how this road can impact your recruiting. In case you've forgotten, this college is competing with several others for a small pool of in-state students. You, I, and the board know that an enhanced revenue stream coming from out-of-state student tuition is crucial. Students from other states will not come here if they can't find the damn place."

Dr. Burcham crossed his arms. "Are you forgetting that our primary mission is to serve the students of West Virginia? Our enrollment and revenues have been holding steady. What you need to do is convince your connections in the state legislature to appropriate more money, so we can be competitive with schools from other states."

Tom rearranged himself on the sofa and sighed. "If you'll just agree to the damn road, the state will cover its cost." He paused, stretching his arms and rotating his shoulders. "Also, you can sell this project as a jobs creator for the state. Think of how many construction jobs and support jobs can be added from the road widening project."

"What about the campus buildings that will be affected?" Dr. Burcham's eyes drilled into his nemesis. "Our maintenance staff did some exploratory digging between the student recreation center and the School of Education Building. They uncovered water and sewer lines that are crumbling and most likely will shatter during the construction process. I cannot risk half this campus not having electricity or running water so you can widen a road." Dr. Burcham scowled.

"Their relocation and reconstruction can be negotiated in the construction price with the state," Tom insisted.

Dr. Burcham walked away from the window and around his desk. The late afternoon sun cast deep shadows on the floor. He turned on a desk lamp, easing the effects of the oncoming darkness.

Tom rose. He looked at Dr. Burcham, and his entire countenance softened. "Neal, everyone wins here—the school, the state, your legacy— the legacy of this campus. You do not have to make a rash decision. All I am asking is that you consider the proposal and participate in an open, frank discussion with us at the next board meeting." Tom shifted his weight. "Plus, we all need something to distract ourselves from this Dane Antonelli mess. Right now, that's all anyone wants to talk about." Tom's voice grew softer as he spoke.

The president let out a long breath. "Why would you mention the Antonelli matter? These two issues are *not* mutually exclusive."

"All I'm saying," Tom continued, his voice reduced almost to a whisper, "is you can have another press conference, a bigger one, and announce something *positive*. The next thing you know, everyone will have forgotten about Antonelli and all the sniping will go away."

"Dr. Burcham?" A melodic voice echoed from the office doorway; the words slowly projected into the office. "I'm Serena Johnson from *The Record*. I don't mean to disturb you, but I saw you walking to your office. Mr. Dillon said it was okay to come in. I wanted to get your comments on the tree planting dedication organized by the SGA."

Dr. Burcham waved her in.

Serena stepped inside the office; the wooden floorboards creaked as she crossed.

"Serena Johnson." Tom smiled broadly. "You're the one who's been reporting on the Dane Antonelli case for the school paper."

"Yes." She turned to face Tom. "Yes, that's correct."

"A Pulitzer Prize-winning reporter in training." Sarcasm laced his words.

Dr. Burcham looked at Serena wearily.

Jack Dillon staggered into the office. "Dr. Burcham . . . "

"What is it, Jack?"

"I just got off the phone with the State Police. There's been a car wreck on Corridor 33."

No one spoke. All eyes were on Jack, waiting for more.

"One of our football players was involved."

"Oh, no," Dr. Burcham said. "Is it bad?"

"Yes. The injuries are pretty severe."

Dr. Burcham released his breath. "My God."

"There's more," Jack continued. "The second car in the crash belonged to Dane Antonelli.

nineteen

SERENA RESTED HER CHEEK AGAINST THE CAR WINDOW, her head throbbing. The meeting with Dr. Burcham had produced no new information. Serena felt defeated.

Crystal revved the engine of her Dodge Neon as she and Serena exited campus.

"Thank you for taking me," Serena mumbled into the glass, creating puffs of air that fogged over the window.

"Don't you mean, thanks for driving *us* to the crash scene," Crystal replied. "Besides, I've got nothing else to do. This could be exciting."

Through the side mirror, the Clear River campus disappeared. In a matter of seconds, the landscape changed from erect stone buildings into a forest divided by a paved road.

Starting in the Shenandoah Valley, Corridor 33 rises through the George Washington National Forest to the West Virginia state line, where the Potomac Highlands Region begins. For seventy miles, Corridor 33 winds up and down through valleys and mountains. Eventually, the road connects to the front entrance to Clear River College.

"I hate this road," Serena groaned. "The worst thing about leaving campus is traveling this road."

"Just be glad you're not a commuter," Crystal said.

Serena glanced at her watch. The time read 8:31, although it seemed much later. Her eyes ached with fatigue and her throat felt parched. Chasing raveling threads involving Dane Antonelli's death was exhausting. Serena wondered how reporters covering war zones and natural disasters kept up the stamina necessary to report the facts as they found them. Even her mentor, Tracy Pritt, managed some time away from work now and then. However, Serena became increasingly perturbed by that nagging reporter intuition that told her nobody was overly concerned with talking about Dane and what had happened to him.

Crystal accelerated, then braked lightly. Serena, now sitting upright in the seat, collected her curly hair in two handfuls and pushed it over her shoulders. "I cannot understand how Dane Antonelli's car can be involved in a crash," she said. "If he had a car here, why didn't his parents have it removed or towed back to Clarksburg?"

"Maybe they didn't know?" Crystal asked.

Serena scratched her chin. "It's possible. College students don't always tell their parents everything." She turned toward Crystal. "Apparently Dane's family is wealthy, so it's plausible they bought a car for him. But why would they not take it back after he died?"

Crystal looked left and right, then glanced in the rear view mirror. "You can't always tell how a family deals with grief and loss. Every family and every individual is different. Maybe getting the car back wasn't their first priority."

Serena settled into the seat. "If you're right, that means another Antonelli family member might be involved in the wreck or..." She faced Crystal again. "Or someone else took the car." She took her cell phone out of her pocket and placed it on the narrow shelf below the dashboard.

"Speaking of phones and messages..."

"I didn't know we were," Serena replied.

"Are you going to return the messages that have been left for you?"

Serena looked out the passenger window again. Rows of oak trees along with other deciduous trees marched high, wide and deep along both sides of the road. Their shadows wisped by the car. Sagging branches on the older trees hung near the road like tentacles. Between the trees, pockets of darkness spread into the forest.

"I will return those messages on my time and on my schedule," Serena finally said. "I can and will determine when they are returned."

"Well, I wish you would return them, because I'm running out of excuses to tell him."

Serena's eyes narrowed. "Matt Carmichael is a jerk. All I can remember is how he made me cry at least once a week for the last six months of our relationship."

"I remember some good moments when you were with him."

Serena forced her breathing to slow. "Things were great when we were together. At least, sometimes."

"So call him back. At least you can tell him you got the messages and get me off the hook."

Serena grudgingly nodded in agreement. The last time she had seen Matt Carmichael was at the Sigma Tau Epsilon Fraternity Formal in May. Matt's pale green tuxedo drew out the richness of his olive skin and green eyes. Matt swept her into a tight embrace the minute she arrived and kissed her passionately. Later that night, they made love. Serena, convinced it was the beginning of their future together, became enthralled with everything Matt. The next day, Matt ended the relationship and transferred to Bowling Green University at the conclusion of the spring semester.

Crystal sped over a bump in the road. The car bounced, then settled. "We're here," she announced.

A West Virginia state trooper, wearing a neon orange vest, extended an open palm at the oncoming vehicle. The thick blackness of night behind him revealed little, although it made him appear like a gigantic orange monster against the wooded backdrop.

"They're alternating traffic in each direction," Serena said softly. "This cannot be good." She dug in her pocket and pulled out a narrow laminated card. "Roll down your window and give him this." In the staff identification badge given to her as an intern at *The Charleston Gazette*, she looked refined and official. She flicked the card onto Crystal's lap.

Crystal slowed the car to a halt. She rolled down the window and showed the trooper the card. He read it, glanced at Crystal and Serena twice, and waved them through.

As the car crept ahead, they saw that fragments of two smashed cars littered the road. A metallic blue Mercury Sable had its right tire buckled inward, while the front bumper was strewn all around the road. A majority of the windshield glass was gone and lay on the pavement, resembling pieces of diamonds twinkling against the asphalt.

Serena leaned near the steering wheel and noticed a decrepit silver pickup truck with chipped paint resting at an angle in a small culvert. The hood of the truck was bent and the driver's door severed from the hinges of the frame. The rear left tire lay farther ahead in the culvert, resting alongside a large tree where thick roots bulged upward.

Emergency vehicles' rotating lights splashed everything with streams of red and blue. Several state police vehicles, including one truck with a spotlight mounted on the truck bed, painted the scene in a steady swath of white light.

Feeling a surge of adrenaline, Serena raised her head, her lips inches from Crystal's ear as she spoke hurriedly. "I'll probably be here for a while. Why don't you go back to campus. I'll call you when I'm through."

Crystal frowned, looking at the dashboard time display with concern. "It's getting late. Do you know how long you'll be?" Walking near the crash scene, Serena flashed her *Gazette* badge at several police and firemen. While most did not notice her, one state trooper gave the badge a courtesy glance before his large, hollow eyes returned to the crash scene.

Serena approached the broken Mercury Sable and began taking notes. She squatted down, resting her right knee on the pavement, which was still scarred by braking tires. Behind her, the damaged transmission in the truck still stuck in the culvert released a fading hiss.

The ambling footsteps against the asphalt crunched pebbles of shattered glass into the grooves of the road.

"Hey! I am actually glad to see you this time." Cullen kneeled beside Serena. He smoothed back some flops of stringy hair, his blue eyes searching her.

Serena opened her mouth and snapped it shut. "Oh my God, Cullen, are you all right? I didn't know you were involved. We need to get you to an ambulance."

"I wasn't involved in the crash. One of my teammates and friends, Tay Anderson, is hurt." Cullen stood. "Come over here with me." He led Serena by the elbow to the truck. The mix of shadows and light descended slightly as they approached the culvert. Jutting upward into the sky, the back of the truck looked like a half-uncovered artifact. Serena peered over. The hillside next to the truck slid away. The search light on the state police truck cast a pool of light next to the truck.

The swift current of Clear River raced below the hillside ravine. Swirling water gurgled frothy plumes of foam that crested gracefully as waves rose and fell while the water moved downstream. The rush of the water sounded relaxing, which tempered the somberness of the crash scene.

Cullen and Serena stood near the rear of the mangled truck. On the ground, Tay Anderson's toned frame lay still. Tay's head and neck were braced with a protector and his arms were strapped tightly against a wooden backboard. He was unconscious as paramedics prepared to load the gurney into the ambulance.

"Dr. Burcham and Mr. Hancel are also here," Cullen added, his voice a bit unstable.

Serena made a note on her pad. They must have left right after she'd gone looking for Crystal.

Cullen looked down at the thin, wiry paramedic tightening the straps around Tay's arms. "I've seen hard hits playing football, but nothing like this."

A wide-backed, husky state trooper walked towards Cullen. The trooper had small, square reading glasses pinching the bridge of his nose. Carrying a clipboard, he was making notes as he approached.

"Are you related to the injured victim?" The trooper glanced down at Tay before looking, somewhat disdainfully, at Serena and Cullen. He shook his head, appearing to silently strike the question from the record.

Car brakes squealed and a Lamborghini stopped. Its doors flung open. Jordan jumped from the backseat and ran to Cullen and Serena.

"Fuck, Cullen, I thought you had been hurt." Jordan tugged at his gray tee-shirt and settled his eyes on Serena. "Who's she?"

Cullen stepped back. "This is Serena Johnson, the reporter I was telling you about."

Jordan smirked. "Oh yeah, the hot chick from English Comp." He examined Serena with an arched eyebrow, tilting his head from her eyes to her feet.

Serena thought about extending her hand, but changed her mind. Jordan looked at Tay. "Shit, Tay, are you all right?"

The paramedic pushed Jordan aside and slid Tay onto a gurney, unlocking the wheels and dragging him away.

Serena took more notes.

The state trooper turned away from the group as Dr. Burcham and Tom approached. "Officer, I am Dr. Neal Burcham, President of Clear River College. This is Tom Hancel, chairman of the Board of Governors."

The trooper did not appear impressed. He shielded himself from Cullen, Serena and Jordan. They reacted by stepping closer to him.

Stepping away again, using his shoulder to separate the college students from the administrators, the trooper said to Dr. Burcham, "I'm Detective Jerry Parsons. Can we talk for a moment, alone?"

Dr. Burcham nodded. The trooper and the president walked away. Tom stepped past them and placed his arms around Cullen and Jordan.

"When we got the call..." He stopped talking and leveled a curious look at Serena.

She blinked rapidly at him but didn't move.

"When we got the call, I thought you two might have been involved. I know that sometimes you like to go out for drinks after home games."

"We were going to, but Cullen here is always late," Jordan said.

"I think there are more important issues here besides drinking," Cullen replied. "For instance, how did Tay get involved in this wreck, and why?"

"I agree completely," Serena added.

Jordan turned towards his father, whose face was peppered with beads of sweat that streaked down his neck. He pointed at Serena. "Why is she here?"

"She is apparently somebody's tag-along," Tom Hancel said gruffly.

Serena folded her arms and pressed her lips together tightly, glaring at the board chairman.

"I know Tay's getting help," Jordan said, "but that's what the emergency people are for. Can we go for those drinks now? Dad gave me my allowance."

Cullen slammed his palm into his forehead.

Serena, wondering if the phrase *spoiled brat* might be etched onto

Jordan's forehead, slipped away and stood behind Dr. Burcham and the state trooper, undetected.

The detective spoke with authority. "When we arrived, we found the Anderson kid awake and confused. He told us he was cruising at normal speed when the Sable appeared out of the blue. The best recollection he had was that the Sable was traveling at a high rate of speed down the middle of the road, right on top of the yellow lane dividing lines. The kid had no choice but to veer off the road and hit the ditch over there." The trooper pointed in a direction behind Dr. Burcham.

"What the kid said was right," Jerry continued. "The engine under the hood of the Sable was pretty warm. We don't know yet who was driving the Sable. We searched the car. We found empty, clear sandwich bags scattered on the backseat. There were no traces of anything in them that we could see, but we're going to send them to the state crime lab in Charleston."

Dr. Burcham studied the ground. "Who owned the car?"

"That's why we called you," the detective said. "We ran the plates. It's registered to Dane Antonelli. One of my men came up here to help on that investigation, and that's how we linked the two incidents." He pushed his glasses up the bridge of his nose.

"So did someone steal the car? If so, from where?" Dr. Burcham asked.

"That's another twist in this mess. I had one of my dispatchers in the Buckhannon office call the Antonelli family. They were unaware their son even had a car. To their knowledge, he caught rides with friends when he needed to go someplace. According to the kid's mother, if the family knew about the car, they would have come and picked it up weeks ago."

Serena dropped her pen. Dr. Burcham spun around. "Miss Johnson, this is a classified conversation between me and Officer Parsons. I ask that you go back to campus immediately." He nodded toward Tom, Jordan and Cullen.

"Take the other three with you," he added.

Serena rejoined the conversation. "With all due respect, Dr. Burcham, the information that is being discussed here is relevant to the Antonelli investigation. I think what Officer Parsons said needs another look."

"And that," the president said forcefully, "will be handled by the college and my office, not by you or anyone else on the staff of *The Record*. I will not have a witch hunt orchestrated by the campus newspaper on matters that do not concern them."

"Sir, this matter concerns the safety of the faculty, staff, and students at the school." Serena stood on tiptoes, attempting to match the president's posture.

Cullen slipped an arm around Serena's waist. The firm grip caused Serena to mumble a mewling sound as Cullen pulled her away.

Dr. Burcham smiled gratefully at Cullen.

"What are you doing?" Cullen asked, his voice a dull whisper. "You don't want to let Dr. Burcham know what you're doing."

Serena wiggled away from Cullen. "What was that?" she demanded. "I did not need a rescue! I was close to finding out the connection between this accident and Dane Antonelli."

"If there *is* a connection," Cullen said sarcastically.

"There is!" Serena shoved the notepad into Cullen's chest.

Cullen pulled it away from her. He walked under a cascading orange light spinning from the police cars and angled the notepad into a band of blue light. Squinting, Cullen scanned the information. When he finished, he studied Serena, although it appeared he was focusing on something different entirely.

"I'm sorry. I just know how the politics of this college work. If you upset Dr. Burcham and he finds you meddling, you'll be in big trouble."

Serena went limp. She tried speaking, but no words emerged. Caught between the investigative urge of a reporter and the temptation to lean forward and punch Cullen in the nose, she rocked back and forth.

Tom and Jordan Hancel walked near the Lexus as the trooper placed something into the palm of the president. Once again, Cullen led Serena away by the elbow.

"Remember last time we talked and you asked me if I knew anything at all that might be in some way related to this case?" Cullen said.

Serena gave an exaggerated nod.

"I need you to look into something for me."

Serena regained control of the notepad and arched her pen, positioning it for note-taking. "I'm listening," she said.

"Do you know Dr. John Petry in the English Department?"

Serena considered the question. "Not personally, but my roommate Crystal had him for freshman comp."

"Good," Cullen replied. "I ran into him after practice last week. He was in the facilities building looking at old team photographs. I talked to him, and then Coach Miles walked in."

Serena raised an eyebrow.

"They got into an argument. Apparently, Dr. Petry's son played for the Clear River Cougars a few years ago. Coach had called a practice right after Thanksgiving on a bad weather day. Dr. Petry's son died in a car wreck somewhere between Beckley and here."

Serena stopped writing. She remembered the autopsy report sent by Tracy Pritt. Believing the report might have been doctored, in this moment of honest confession, she contemplated telling Cullen what she knew. If Cullen confided in her, maybe he was beginning to understand her concerns. "I'll see what I can find out. In the meantime, can we get together sometime soon? I've come across some evidence and I need someone to see it. Can I trust you?"

Cullen hesitated. "If I become involved, you know what type of position you're putting me in?"

"Yes, I do, and I will be discreet."

Serena dropped the notepad again, this time from force. Her arms were pulled behind her back. Cullen, also forcefully grabbed, was spun away from Serena.

Cullen heard a slow click, followed by a snap. Serena flashed a look of confusion and fright.

Another trooper stood behind Serena. With her wrists handcuffed, the trooper marched Serena toward a patrol car.

twenty

"SO THE COPS ARRESTED HER?" Jordan pulled the white jersey over his shoulder pads and down his body.

Cullen tugged on the shoelaces of his cleats, tying them down with force. The morning had arrived quickly, but the images of the previous night were fresh in his mind.

"Not really," he said. "Dr. Burcham asked her politely to leave the scene. When she refused, he found another way to remove her. Once the officer brought Serena back to campus, he took off the handcuffs."

"So she's ready to fight another day. Damn, that chick never gives up." Jordan laced his cleats. "Dad thinks this girl is doing all of this for a job. You know, make a name for herself. Never underestimate the power of a determined woman. They own the world."

Cullen chuckled. The muffled conversations of teammates leaked between the grating sounds of metal lockers slamming shut. "What did you think about what happened a couple of weeks ago?"

"Not much really," Jordan answered, slipping on a black foam kneepad. "I think the sooner everyone realizes that Dane Antonelli is gone and we all move on, the better off everyone will be."

Cullen stopped. He had never felt the way that Jordan had. Now, with the car accident, his thoughts had shifted to sadness and confusion.

Tay Anderson had suffered three broken ribs in the crash and was told he would miss the next six or seven weeks of football. Cullen had spoken to Tay by phone, and his demeanor was unchanged. Tay was proud and boisterous, capable of swallowing a room whole with his personality.

The week of practice had been subdued without him. During the game, the challenges of moving the football on offense would intensify. Without Tay in the lineup, defenses would focus on and double-team Jordan. Mike Ochoa, Tyler Briggs, or the inexperienced Joey Gunnoe had to become a more legitimate threat at wide receiver.

As Cullen rose and moved towards the locker room exit, Jordan grabbed his back flap. "Let's go out there and beat the shit out of State and forget all of this. Besides, as far as all this Dane business goes, you can discover anything about anyone if you look hard enough. You know that, being a literature freak."

A slow smile rolled across Cullen's face as they jogged out to the field together.

*   *   *   *   *

Coach Gary Miles slouched over the defense, his hulking demeanor surly.

Cullen paced the sideline, tucking fingers into his waistband.

"Our philosophy on defense is what?" Coach Miles demanded.

When the linemen were slow to respond, the coach barked the question again. "Our philosophy on defense is what?"

This time, before anyone could respond, Coach Miles answered on their behalf. "Our philosophy on defense is run, hit, get excited and finish. We got too emotional in the Southern Virginia State game. We gave up big plays and got away from our fundamentals. Between missed tackles, bad blocking and poor tackling, you jackasses cost us the game. Not gonna happen today, not against West Virginia State."

West Virginia State's program had eight WVIAC All-Americans in its history, the most recent being Mike Mayer in 2002. Before the game, the Cougars sat on the bench as the school honored its former All-Americans, which included Mike Mayer along with Mike Gray, Mario Lewis, and Robert Ashley. Jim Abshire, the oldest West Virginia State All-American, who earned the honor in 1976, also stood at mid-field and waved at the crowd.

The defensive line bobbed and shuffled on the bench, staring at each other. The adrenaline coursed through their veins. Coach Miles's questioning of their integrity had fired them up.

The team captains moved out onto the field. The Clear River Cougars had won the coin toss and elected to receive. Last season, Clear River buried West Virginia State behind 197 rushing yards from Marcus Turner and four Cullen Brewer touchdown passes in a 31-7 defeat of the Yellow Jackets.

With Tay Anderson injured, freshman Joey Gunnoe was installed as the new kick returner. Gunnoe took the kick and returned it to the sixteen yard line. Cullen, standing on the sideline, remembered what Coach Miles said to the team captains in practice: "That boy can fly. If we can get his head on straight, he will be a pretty good football player."

Lakin Field, nestled on the banks of the Kanawha River in Institute and home of the West Virginia State University Yellow Jackets, had few fans in attendance. As Cullen led the offense onto the field, a chilly gust of late September air smacked his cheek. Overhead, the milky white sky, once sprinkled with low-hanging cumulus clouds, began to darken. Moving slowly down the Kanawha River, a large gray cloud crept closer. The grass at Lakin Field lay in clumps, covering large divots.

Coach Miles wanted the Cougars to move the football quickly down the field against a small but agile Yellow Jackets defense. The recipe for victory would be a repeat of the previou   year: have Cullen attack the defense with a variety of throws, then mix in draw plays and counter runs with Marcus Turner.

On the first play from scrimmage, Cullen held the center of the huddle circle together. "Slant route, on three. Ready, go Cougars!"

Cullen stepped under center Andre Gibson, who secured the football. Scanning the line of scrimmage, Cullen found West Virginia State revealing a man-to-man defensive front.

The strength of the Yellow Jackets' defense was stopping running plays. Cullen had decided to exploit the weakness of their pass defense.

Clear River broke the huddle in a single back set, with one receiver on each side of the field. Mike Ochoa occupied the left flat and Tyler Briggs stood poised in the right flat. Jordan Hancel stood close to Tyler Briggs in the right-side wide receiver slot.

Cullen looked left, then right. He changed the rhythm and called an audible. Jordan jogged down the line of scrimmage and stood on the outside of Tyler. Tyler nodded, understanding the play.

The center snapped the football. Cullen dropped back. His pass protectors—Luke Thompson, Mike Bosello, Andre Gibson, Arnest Anderson and Carmine DeRocha—held their blocks.

Jordan ran into a small space in the center of the field, behind the line of scrimmage and between the linebackers and safeties.

Cullen read the move and delivered a wobbly spiral that Jordan snatched from the air. However, a short, stocky Yellow Jackets defensive back, Daylon Bradley, saw Jordan running across the middle of the field. Daylon lowered his helmet into Jordan's chest. Jordan held on for a seventeen yard gain.

As Jordan stood up, Daylon lowered his helmet again, this time undercutting Jordan at the knees. Jordan fell backwards over Daylon, while the field judge tossed a canary-yellow penalty flag—unnecessary roughness. The fifteen-yard penalty gave the Cougars great field position and first down.

Jordan rose and delivered a forearm shove into the chest of Daylon. The defensive back responded by grabbing his facemask, jerking Jordan to the ground. The referees tossed several yellow penalty flags and, along with several players from both teams, interceded and broke up the scuffle. After separating the players, the referee indicated off-setting personal fouls, one against Daylon and one against Jordan. The down would be replayed.

Cullen bit his lip in frustration. On the sideline, Cullen saw Coach Miles slam a clipboard onto the ground and kick a clump of uprooted grass from the sideline onto the field of play. Coach Miles turned to a trailing official sauntering up the sideline. Arranging his hands in a cross formation, the coach requested a timeout. The official obliged.

Jordan jogged back near the line of scrimmage. Cullen slid in front of Jordan, blocking the pathway to the huddle.

"Pull yourself together!" Cullen demanded.

Jordan curled his lip. "They are playing dirty, like they do every year. After four years of this shit, I've had enough!"

Cullen interlocked three fingers inside the facemask of his senior receiver. "We cannot afford dumb penalties. You are on the road, and you are not going to get those calls in your favor." Cullen slapped the side of Jordan's helmet. "You're a senior and you're more talented than they are. Catch the football. Make plays. Beating those suckers will feel better than talking trash."

The rest of the offense approached the huddle as the head referee signaled the timeout was over.

Jordan nodded.

Cullen made eye contact again with Coach Miles. The next play call: a swing pattern.

Marcus Turner aligned himself to the left hip of Cullen. The three receivers in the formation—Jordan Hancel, Joey Gunnoe, and Mike Ochoa— stood patiently at the line of scrimmage.

Cullen backpedaled quickly into the shotgun formation. He stomped his foot and waited for the snap. Andre Gibson snapped a crisp, tight spiral.

A cold breeze tingled Cullen's fingers as he caught the snap.

Marcus leaked past the line of scrimmage, approaching the sideline. Coach Miles frantically waved his right arm, motioning for Marcus to run faster.

When Marcus reached the flat, after building momentum running up-field, Cullen drew back his throwing arm.

Yet something about the play didn't feel right. Cullen scanned the field behind him and saw Daylon Bradley coming on a corner blitz. Cullen released the football, but the pass was thrown wide and behind Marcus Turner. Daylon slammed into Cullen.

Marcus slipped two fingers around the football, but was pummeled from behind by a wide-bodied defensive tackle. The ball squirted free from Marcus's hands and rolled near the original line of scrimmage at the eighteen yard line.

Jordan juked a Yellow Jackets defender and sprinted after the ball. He gathered the football up, shifted his weight, spun and raced down the sideline until he reached the end zone. He kicked over an end zone pylon upon crossing the goal line. The eighty-two yard fumble recovery and touchdown run put the Cougars ahead 6-0.

The West Virginia State crowd fell silent. Cullen and the rest of the offense ran to the end zone, knocking Jordan to the ground and piling on top of him. They pulled Jordan up and jogged back to center-field. Jordan trailed slowly behind, again placing little pressure on the right ankle.

As the special teams unit ran onto the field to attempt the extra point, Jordan dug his left cleat spikes into the smeared image of a Yellow Jacket painted on the fifty yard line. He continued grinding his cleat into the soft earth, reconfiguring the yellow jacket.

Finally, Jordan stomped down on the Yellow Jacket image and spit a glob of saliva onto the insignia before trotting to the sidelines.

Fans jeered Jordan. Some of them even tossed food wrappers and empty soft drink cups onto the sidelines. Yellow flags flew. Without consultation, the head referee made the signal and said into his microphone, "Unsportsmanlike conduct. Fifteen yards will be assessed before kick-off." The referee stepped over to the sidelines and warned Coach Miles that the next infraction by any Cougars player might lead to an ejection.

The Cougar defensive unit responded to the challenge issued by Coach Miles at the beginning of the game. They allowed a touchdown on West Virginia State's first possession, but were stingy the rest of the game. Over the last seventeen plays of the first half, Clear River's defense allowed West Virginia State to generate only four yards of offense.

For the game, Clear River limited the Yellow Jackets to a miniscule seven yards rushing on thirty-one carries, and 200 total yards. Clear River totaled nine tackles for loss.

Cullen floated a sixteen-yard touchdown pass to Luke Briggs and another five-yard touchdown toss to Jordan Hancel in the third quarter, giving the quarterback over 200 yards passing and two touchdowns. But Cullen was hit nine times and sacked four.

At game's end, Clear River had raced past West Virginia State 21-7.

Cullen glanced up and down the sidelines looking for Jordan. For the season so far, the senior quarterback-receiver combination had connected for five touchdown passes in three games. But Cullen didn't see him.

He approached Coach Miles. "Coach, have you seen Jordan?"

"Try the locker room. The trainer's with him." Coach Miles sounded uninterested and kept glaring at the scoreboard.

"Is he hurt? I saw him hobbling."

"Hell, I don't know, Brewer. He's still in the locker room with the trainer. Go in there and find out."

Cullen slapped a few hands and dropped some congratulatory nods as he ran behind the Lakin Field stands into the locker room.

Inside, Jordan rested on a torn padded bench in the back of the locker room. The crease of his right arm covered his eyes, his elbow sticking in the air like a beacon. His right leg was arched with his heel resting against the edge of the bench.

This moment marked the first time Cullen had seen Jordan up close since the injury.

"I have a sprain," Jordan said dejectedly. "The trainer is coming back in a minute with some ace bandage wrap. Shit!"

Cullen rested his football helmet on the floor. "How did it happen?"

Jordan stared aimlessly at the cinderblock ceiling. His green eyes dissolved into glimmering pools, like two pieces of melted quartz. "I guess it happened when that prick from State clipped me from behind in the first quarter. I would rather have broken my damn ankle instead of spraining it. At least it would heal faster."

Muffled yells and cheers warned them that the rest of the team was approaching.

"Does Coach know about your injury?"

"He knows I'm hurt," Jordan said. "But I don't think he knows how bad."

"Any idea how long you might be out?"

Jordan sat up, resting his weight on his elbows, careful not to move his right leg. "Three weeks. Or it could be six weeks. It's hard to say. It just depends on if I can stay off of it and let it heal."

"Well, I guess you showed them how you felt about everything later in that quarter."

A slow smile rolled across Jordan's face and exploded under his nose. He winked at Cullen. "You liked that, didn't you?"

Cullen shook his head. "Coach is going to make you do sit-ups until you puke for that."

Jordan's face hardened. "Shit, I wanted to win the conference this year!"

Cullen's stomach twisted. The Clear River offense would be without its first and second receivers. With the main portion of the conference schedule left, the chances of a successful year looked grim.

He placed a hand on Jordan's shoulder. "We'll be fine. We'll get you and Tay back soon and we'll be fine."

Jordan, however, put his head down and did not look back at Cullen.

*   *   *   *   *

After the locker room emptied, Jordan said goodbye to the team trainers, swunghis legs forward and hopped off the table. He winced in pain and let out a groan.

Jordan navigated awkwardly between the benches until he reached the locker room door. He pushed it open.

The weather outside had deteriorated. Thunder rumbled in the distance as light rain spattered against the metal bleachers. The air had already grown colder. Chilly bursts of wind from the Kanawha River swirled through the concourse in a circular pattern.

He didn't see Cullen, and it was just as well. He just wanted to get back in his father's car and put his leg up and try to forget about the pain.

Giles McClure, the head trainer for Clear River College, had given Jordan a crutch, which he leaned on heavily. Jordan wiggled the crutch under his right arm and walked behind the concourse, heading for the parking lot.

As Jordan stuck the crutch into the chipped concourse concrete, he staggered from side to side, trying to find a walking rhythm. The rain managed to seep through the crevices between the stands, coating the ground and Jordan's shoulders with pools of water.

A small tan car was parked behind the field goal posts in the area normally reserved for an ambulance that might be called upon during the game.

Just beyond the final concrete entryway, a shadow appeared.

A man with a medium build wearing a gray, full-length coat buttoned in three places waited. The man wore a West Virginia State Yellow Jackets baseball cap pulled tightly around his ears, which jutted out sharply from his head. He wore black, fluffy ski gloves. The jacket covered his nose and mouth, with just enough of the nose exposed to see it had a wide bridge at the top.

"You need help?" the man asked; his voice light and even, a direct contrast to the clothes he was wearing.

Jordan felt another cold chill, this one from anxiety, run through him. "No, no, I think I've got it. Thanks, anyway."

"I would get moving if I were you," the man said. "Ankle sprains really hurt in cold weather."

Jordan studied the man and said nothing.

"Has your team cleared out of the visitors' locker room?"

Jordan nodded.

The man took a step closer. "Good."

Jordan watched the cloth flap around the man's mouth expand and contract as he spoke.

"It's the same injury I had last year, just the other ankle. Two years in a row we've played State and I've been hurt."

The man narrowed his eyes. "Yeah, but we never would've hooked up without them." He took a slight step back, removing the gloved hands from his pockets. "You might miss some time like you did last year."

"Cut the bullshit. Are you going to help me again or not?" Jordan mumbled.

The man pointed at Jordan's wrapped ankle. "How much pain you in? How much swelling?"

"Quite a bit of both, but I'm good until we get back to campus."

The man tucked one gloved hand into a pocket. "Did you get something for the pain?"

"No," Jordan replied. "Now hurry up, my fucking ankle is killing me."

The man flashed a sympathetic smile, which made the cold sensation coursing through Jordan subside even further.

"Here." He opened a clenched fist and revealed a folded sandwich bag containing one large blue pill and another smaller orange pill with parallel lines etched onto the tablet surface.

Jordan studied the pills and then looked at him.

"This shit ain't cheap, but it will work. The one pill will kill the pain; the other one will help with strength and healing," he added, the soothing voice becoming quieter and darker. "Trust me, until that ankle begins healing, the pain will be tough. Now I want paid."

"Look, man..." Jordan looked behind the figure at the Lexus, which had its headlights turned on, then resettled his attention on the man. "I'm good for it. I just can't right now."

The man emitted a hearty laugh. "I want my money and I want it soon." He grabbed Jordan's hand, pulled back his fingers and inserted a crumpled piece of paper inside the palm. Jordan instinctively clenched the hand again. "Send the money to that address. If you don't, that ankle won't be the only thing hurting on your body."

Jordan hedged. "Dude, I really need to go. My dad's waiting for me." Jordan grimaced again as he tried pivoting on the sore ankle. Piercing pain bolted up his entire leg. He wobbled, nearly falling over.

The man reached in and steadied him. Jordan cursed under his breath.

"I tell you what, Jordan. There's a water fountain at the end of the concourse. Why don't you take one of the pills before you leave, and I'll stand here and make sure you don't fall again."

Jordan steadied himself again. He swiped the bag and dumped the contents into the palm of his hand. Once again, he drove ahead with the crutch and dragged the ankle behind.

Jordan heard the man breathing heavily as the distance between them grew larger. It seemed like his eyes were boring holes through him. Jordan kept driving harder and faster, but the ankle and the rest of his body did not respond as quickly as he wanted.

He reached the rust-stained water fountain, took one of the pills and tossed it to the back of his tongue. He leaned in and downed a generous gulp of lukewarm water. The pill quickly slid down his throat.

As Jordan emerged from under the concourse, he saw his father step out of the car, walk around it, and open the passenger door. The rain fell harder, the skies darkened, and the wind howled.

Jordan looked back under the concourse.

"What is it, son?" Tom Hancel asked.

Jordan shook his head. "Nothing, Dad. Nothing at all."

twenty one

THE SECOND MONDAY OF SEPTEMBER had always been reserved for the first official student government meetings of the school year. Cullen was ready. He stood up, signaling the beginning of the meeting. As he walked to the podium, wearing a blue Clear River College polo shirt with tan slacks and dark brown dress shoes, he noticed Serena sitting in the back. She did not make eye contact with him. Instead, she kept feverishly turning pages in the same notepad she'd taken to the accident scene the previous week.

Dr. Burcham sat to the right of the podium. The president, calm and resolute, focused on each step Cullen made to the podium.

Cullen adjusted the microphone, cleared his throat and scanned the room. Student senators representing each of the five departments sat at three long, light brown tables. Placards indicated their names and the corresponding Clear River department they represented. The returning senators gazed off into the distance or chatted with one another. The new senators sat upright, eyes gleaming with anticipation.

Serena paused and made eye contact with Cullen. The track lighting overhead cast her in a shadow that elongated her taut figure and darkened her eyes.

"I call to order the first meeting of the Clear River Student Government Association." Cullen recited the words slowly and carefully. "To begin, our president, Dr. Neal Burcham, would like to address the body."

Cullen turned and extended an arm. Dr. Burcham rose, clad in a banal blue suit paired with a white shirt and purple tie.

The president's eyes met Cullen's, then he looked at the student governing body. Hushed conversations subsided as the president adjusted the podium microphone again.

Serena straightened her posture.

"Thank you, Cullen," Dr. Burcham began with a soft, confident smile. "Welcome, new and returning senators. The Student Government Association here at Clear River College is one of the most important organizations we have on campus. Led by your president, Cullen Brewer, the work you do affects each and every student, faculty, and staff member. You have a chance to represent your classmates and make this college a better place for learning and becoming adults."

Cullen interlocked his fingers and rested his elbows on the table as Dr. Burcham spoke. Serena sat with crossed arms. Cullen smiled as he recognized her skeptical pose.

Dr. Burcham paused and pressed his horn-rimmed glasses tightly against his nose. "As many of you know, we suffered a tragedy this summer when our fellow student and a member of the Clear River family, Dane Antonelli, passed away several weeks ago." Dr. Burcham's shoulders slumped slightly.

"I want to say how impressed I am with how this governing body, led by your president, planted a tree in honor of Dane outside the student recreation center Your kindness has ensured that we will never forget Dane, and that he will be forever in the hearts and minds of all who knew him at Clear River College."

The president dropped his clasped hands onto the podium, rattling the microphone and sending a slight piercing hiss into the audience. The noise startled a few of the senators.

Cullen looked over at Serena and saw her dig frantically into her pockets and pull out a small phone. Inserting a finger in one ear, she hunched forward, resting her elbows on her knees. She spoke in hushed tones. Creases in her forehead showed Cullen the conversation had Serena agitated.

She quietly stood up and rushed out the door into the small hallway outside the meeting room. Cullen watched her shadow rise up to the tops of the glass windows, then slowly slip away.

*   *   *   *   *

"Besides," Conley continued, "What proof do you have the report has been compromised? I maintain strict confidentiality with my paperwork and reports." He pulled the phone away momentarily and let out a dry, heavy cough.

"Nobody sees the reports but me, the family of the victim and the police, if necessary. Are you insinuating the police changed the document?" Conley exhaled a funny, disapproving laugh.

Serena was stuck. She remembered the note Tracy had written about reading and returning the report. She had done as instructed, although she'd told nobody about the photocopy of the report she still had. If Serena told Conley about viewing the autopsy report, she, along with the staff of *The Record*, could be in serious trouble with the college and with the state police. She swung her legs onto the booth seat and leaned back against the wall. Her jaw throbbed. She'd forgotten to unclench it.

Sometimes the best defense was a strong offense. Serena cleared her throat.

"What exactly did you discover when you examined Dane's body?"

"That information is confidential, so no comment."

Serena switched the cell phone to her left ear. "What did you determine as the cause of death?"

"I issued a statement regarding the cause of death. Dane Antonelli died from acute pulmonary distress."

As Serena prepared to ask another question, Conley cut her off. "Look, Miss..."

"Johnson," she said. "Serena Johnson."

"Yes, Miss Johnson." Conley cleared his throat. "Why don't you contact the Antonelli family for more information? If they want you to know more, they will tell you. But I'm very busy and I really must get back to work."

Serena slouched slightly against the wedge between the booth backing and the wall. "Sir, before you hang up..."

Conley exhaled a long breath. "Yes?"

"Nine years ago, you conducted an autopsy on a man named Brian Petry."

"It's possible that I did. I see so many bodies over the course of the years that sometimes names escape me."

"I understand," Serena said. Wetting her thumb, she rapidly turned pages in the notepad. Some of the older blue ink had begun fading and smearing on the pages. "According to your statement on that case, Brian also died from a car accident caused by pulmonary distress. Is this coming back to you?"

Conley shifted the phone around, sending bursts of static through the earpiece. "I, I would need some time to check my records." Uneasiness leaked through in his voice. "I must be going now."

Before Serena could formulate another question, Conley hung up.

*   *   *   *   *

Cullen counted the votes from student senators. By a unanimous vote of 11-0, the Clear River College Student Government Association approved $500 stipends for several campus organizations requesting funding.

As Cullen prepared to adjourn the meeting, he reminded the senators of the importance of the vote just cast.

"Since we started accepting bids from organizations four years ago, the number of pledges from student groups has risen. Make sure you encourage student involvement in these organizations and have groups continue to request funds as necessary."

Ian McDonnell stood up, upholding three fingers. Before he spoke, Cullen acknowledged his presence. "Oh, yes, see Ian about tee-shirts. We have extras left over from orientation and we would like you all to have the rest. We are adjourned."

Cullen stood on his toes, arching a casual glance at the back of the room where Serena had been seated. Her chair remained empty.

Moving back to the door, Cullen hoped Serena had not left the building. As Cullen walked through the door, he saw Dr. Burcham waiting, tugging on his lapels.

"Cullen, could we have a word?"

"Sure, Dr. Burcham." Cullen retreated to the opposite side of the stairwell and bent a leg, resting against the wall. "Sir, thank you for addressing the SGA. I always think it makes a positive impression on the senators, especially the new ones," Cullen said.

The president nodded. "My pleasure, Cullen. You have done some great work."

Cullen smiled. "Thank you, sir."

Dr. Burcham rubbed his chin. "Cullen, I don't want you to feel responsible for what happened to Dane or what's taking place with the rest of the investigation, including the car accident."

"I don't feel responsible." *Why would Dr. Burcham think he would?*

"Good," Dr. Burcham replied. His shoulders rose and his abdomen filled up with air, like someone had pumped oxygen into him with a machine. "Let the police and my office take care of the investigation. I want you to focus on football and your coursework. Graduation is coming up." He patted Cullen on the arm and proceeded down the stairs.

Cullen wondered why the president had chosen to mention the car accident. He waited a moment, and then headed for the cafeteria. Once there, he plopped four quarters into a vending machine and selected a Mountain Dew. He glanced around the mostly empty cafeteria.

Serena sat in the corner, slouched over a notepad, hands resting on the edge of the table with her nose mere inches away from the paper.

Cullen sneaked up behind her, startling her. He dropped into the bench seat across from her. "I'm sorry the meeting didn't keep your attention."

Serena drew her eyes slowly away from the notepad and gazed at Cullen; her shaded mahogany brown pupils were flat, heavy and dark. "I'm sorry. What did you say?"

"If I came by at a bad time, then I can come back," Cullen said.

"No, I need to talk to you." Serena tossed a curly clump of hair over her shoulder. "I had a phone conversation with Conley Masters, the state medical examiner, today. I wanted to see if there was any way Dane's autopsy report might have been altered."

Cullen unscrewed the bottle cap and swallowed a generous gulp of Mountain Dew. "What do you think is wrong with the autopsy report?"

Serena reached into her handbag and took out a piece of paper, which she carefully stretched across the table with her fingertips.

Cullen looked at the paper awkwardly and made a face.

"Read this," Serena commanded.

Cullen opened the pages and read over the document. As he moved through the information, his eyes widened. He lowered the paper. "Where did you get this?"

"It's from a friend of mine who works for *The Charleston Gazette*," Serena said. "You can't discuss this with anyone other than me. We could get in a lot of trouble if people knew I had it."

Cullen bobbed his head in agreement.

"Take a close look at the state seal and the lines on the document."

"The state seal is wrong," Cullen said flatly. "The coal miners near the rocks are missing their picks and the document lines are not even. An official state document wouldn't have those mistakes."

"Right," Serena said. "And there's more."

Cullen sighed. "I am not sure if I want to know any more."

"You will about this," she replied, sounding confident and proud.

"When I interviewed Elizabeth Hastings, the girl who came across Dane's body the night he died, she told me that Dane had scratches and cuts on his hands and that the knuckles on one of his hands were swollen, maybe even broken. The autopsy report makes no mention of those."

Cullen turned the page on the report. "You're right. There's nothing here about any of that."

"There's more. I did some research on Dr. Petry's son Brian and his accident. Conley Masters conducted the autopsy on Brian ten years ago. The cause of death was determined to be acute pulmonary distress. That autopsy report concluded that Brian had a heart attack on his way back to campus for football practice and lost control of the car. The impact of the crash killed him."

Cullen closed his eyes and exhaled.

"Dane also died from a heart attack, according to our report."

Cullen turned his head in disbelief, tracing the outer ridges of the bottle cap with his finger. "This report isn't our report. There *might* be a link between the two, but I still don't think that proves anything."

Serena raised a finger. "We do have some constants in this case." She counted on her smooth, slender fingers. "One, Coach Miles was the head coach in both deaths. Two, Dr. Burcham was the Clear River College president during both deaths, and three, both deaths resulted from heart distress, which I think is highly suspicious considering athletes, physically speaking, are more fit than most college students."

Cullen nodded. "But even with those constants, there still isn't a clear correlation between everything."

"What we need to find out is what police testing discovered inside the plastic bags in Dane's car."

Cullen leaned back and glanced at the door behind Serena. Discussing this with her made him uncomfortable. "You mean *you* need to find out. I told you, I'm really compromised here. I already know too much. Dr. Burcham is right. We need to let him and the police do the detective work."

Serena arched an eyebrow as she snatched the autopsy report back from him and put it in her purse. "Dr. Burcham told you this? When?"

"A few minutes ago, after the student government meeting. He told me to pass along the message to you as well." Cullen remembered showing up at the crash scene because of Jordan's frantic phone call. Cullen wondered if the simulated arrest by the state police was orchestrated by the president as a way of warning them to stay away.

Another voice interjected. "You'd be wise to listen to the president."

Cullen craned his neck, looking up at the two imposing figures standing next to the table. Detective Parsons stood next to them, along with another state trooper.

Cullen felt the muscles in his hands quiver with anger and adrenaline. Serena appeared unnerved.

"What a nice surprise, detective. Here to slap handcuffs on us again? It would be almost as humiliating to do it here in front of our peers as it was when you slapped them on us the other night."

The detective looked at Serena and Cullen, then inserted his hands into his pockets. He tipped his head at Serena.

"I just got a call from our Charleston detachment. It seems the medical examiner got a phone call from you this morning. Something about you think the autopsy report is a fake. Now, why would you think that?"

"I just told Serena that Dr. Burcham has told us to stay out of this and let you all handle it. Isn't that right, Serena?" Cullen prodded when she said nothing.

"Folks." The detective paused, clearing his throat and cutting a quick glance at the other trooper. "I want to remind you both that if you have any questions or suspicions about this case, contact my office or the president's office. Is that clear?"

Cullen nodded several times.

"Otherwise, you're interfering with an ongoing investigation, which could get you arrested."

"Understood," Serena grumbled.

"That goes for any physical evidence you come across or might be in possession of," Detective Parsons added.

Cullen wiggled in the seat and tried not to stare at or think about the autopsy report that sat inside Serena's purse. He unscrewed the cap on the Mountain Dew bottle and took a drink, smacking his lips after swallowing.

"Have a good day, folks," one trooper said. The two men left.

Serena curled her lip, revealing the edge of a canine tooth. "What a bully."

Detective Parsons froze and held up a finger. "Oh, and one more thing." He walked back to the table. "We are conducting a thorough investigation of all the autopsy reports within the office of the state medical examiner. We are going to ensure that there are no questions with the autopsy report." Then the two troopers strode briskly away.

Cullen watched Serena loosen the tight muscles in her face and her chest swell and stick out, like an athlete who had just made a great play in a game.

"Interesting," she said. She grabbed Cullen's hands. The football tattoo on his wrist wiggled with contact. "My friend, I hate to tell you this, but after today, you and I are in this together for the foreseeable future."

twenty two

SERENA NEEDED THE GUIDANCE OF HER EDITOR, Ben Caster, for the next step in the investigation. That word, *investigation*, etched in her mind, led to a dry lump in her throat.

As Serena watched students sauntering and sprinting, mostly in and out of classroom and administrative buildings on campus, a cooler breeze tossed her soft hair across her shoulders and the skies darkened overhead. The recesses in the clouds were mysterious; the slatted light streaking through them glinted off the stone facades of the campus buildings like embers. The tree-lined east quad of the Clear River campus became more devoid of students with each passing minute.

Serena strode confidently through the lobby of Branstone Hall. A cold burst of air twisted her hair again, although the cool gust felt good against her sweaty skin.

As she approached the narrow, crooked hallway leading past the School of Journalism Dean's Office and approached *The Record* newsroom, a surge of energy coursed through her. Showing Cullen the tampered autopsy report might have been a mistake, but witnessing his confirmation that the document was most likely not authentic gave Serena great solace. Something or someone did not want the truth about what happened to Dane seen by anyone else. The forgery proved it; now, could she get anyone else to believe her?

Serena waited for Ben to arrive for his Friday evening consultation hours. The processing computer mechanizations created a rhythmic hum that engulfed the newsroom. Serena learned that most of the senior reporters and editorial staff would be coming in soon, and the budget for the next edition would be debated and decided. Chairs were strewn throughout the newsroom in haphazard fashion. Serena shook her head and smirked. The collaboration and deliberation surrounding each daily edition and working with the other editors was what she loved most about the job.

A note in Ben's neat handwriting waited on Serena's desk. She tore open the folded piece of paper, taped diagonally across the computer monitor.

"We need to talk and soon about the Antonelli story." Serena read the note aloud, almost expecting a response. Instead, she wadded up the paper and shoved the note in her pocket.

She pulled out her chair from underneath the desk indention and collapsed, mentally tired. The prospects of completing neglected coursework in other classes created a small knot in her stomach.

Outside in the hallway, Serena heard an intermittent metallic sound, like metal scraping against metal. Curious, she stood up and looked into the hallway. At the end of the hall, a slender metal tube rolled around the floor in a semi-circular manner. Serena took a deep breath and walked slowly down the hall.

As Serena approached the tube, a rattling sound startled her. She turned and headed back for the newsroom.

Arching her head, Serena called softly: "Ben?" No answer. "Cullen?"

It must be Cullen, Serena assumed. Maybe he had more insight about the autopsy report.

An arm reached out and snatched her. She yelped. Struggling against the firm grip, Serena attempted a look at the individual. She backpedaled awkwardly as her shoes fought to gain traction. Before she could recover, a forceful push sent her body crashing into the hallway wall.

The collision forced exploding gulps of air from her lungs while the back of her head caromed against the plaster wall. Serena slid helplessly to the floor; her eyes blurred. The room and everything surrounding it grew dim. Then darkness took over.

*   *   *   *   *

Jordan stared disgustedly into the mirror.

He winced in pain, struggling to shift weight onto his injured ankle as he punched buttons on the cell phone.

"Hello?"

"Cullen, what's up?"

Cullen sighed. "Not much, just heading back to the village. I finished my first student government meeting, ran into Serena and talked with her, and I also talked to Dr. Burcham."

Jordan shifted his weight onto his good ankle. "Why in the hell are you still talking to that chick? Wasn't getting arrested with her embarrassing enough for your ass?"

Cullen grunted.

"I am surprised that she didn't write 'Clear River QB arrested in a stupid search for nothing'."

"Neither one of us was arrested," Cullen said, irritation peppering his words. "The police needed us to clear the scene, and they figured handcuffs were the best way for that to happen. How's the ankle?"

"Coach and the doctor think the swelling resembles a high ankle sprain instead of a normal sprain."

Cullen silently mulled over the information. "Those take longer to heal than normal ankle sprains."

"The doc said something about the large ligament above the ankle that joins the bones of the lower leg or some shit like that. I don't know. I want this better so I can play."

"We're not the same offense without you," Cullen added. "Without you drawing double-teams, I can't find open receivers downfield."

Jordan rested the phone against his jawbone. He flexed a bicep, noting with satisfaction the sharply protruding veins appearing through the muscle and outwards from his neck. "I think I'll be back soon."

"I hope you're right," Cullen replied. "Being positive helps; so does following the suggestions from the doctor and from Coach."

"Man, I'm starving."

Cullen chuckled. "I've never known you not to be hungry."

"Want to grab some food?"

Silence and static filled the line. "Sure. Let's go into Beaumont and get something. Or we can head south to Buckhannon or north to Fairmont. Doesn't matter to me."

"Sweet," Jordan said. "I've got Dad's credit card, so there will be plenty of booze for me tonight. I'll meet you by the stadium in a half-hour."

"That works." The earpiece clicked.

Jordan snapped the phone shut and pushed it into his pants pocket.

He glanced into the mirror, his eyes sunken into the recesses of the sockets. He bit his lower lip as he gradually placed more weight onto the sore ankle.

Hopping away from the mirror, he reached into a tissue, removed a large orange tablet and swallowed it.

Jordan tugged the small handle of the cabinet drawer below the sink. Without looking, he pushed aside various bottles of creams and gels and located the cologne. He grabbed it and then sprang back up.

As he settled in front of the mirror, the sudden movement made Jordan queasy. He felt his stomach churn and a cold sweat break out across his forehead. Jordan tried to calm the up-swell by rubbing his stomach, but that only made the sensations stronger. He leaned over the toilet and vomited.

After a few moments, a rush of bile filled his throat again, and Jordan repeated the vomiting.

A faint knock sounded at the front door. Jordan grabbed a dirty towel from the clothes hamper, wiping the drying vomit from his lips and the sweat from his brow.

When Jordan pulled open the door, Detective Parsons stood with arms folded, glaring at him.

Wearing a long, dark trench coat and gloves, the detective startled Jordan. He stepped back and let the towel lag beside him.

"Did I come at a bad time?" the detective asked.

"Uh, no. Come in." Jordan felt like he wanted to throw up again.

Detective Parsons entered the room and closed the door behind him. Jordan, a bit sheepish at the condition of the room, limped over to the bed and sat down. The physical stature of the detective filled the room. Parsons placed a pair of glasses on the brim of his nose.

"How's the ankle?"

Jordan tossed the towel in the narrow space between the bed and the wall. A slightly disingenuous grin from the detective made Jordan edgy. "It's getting better."

"Good. I wanted to ask you a few questions about your relationship with Dane Antonelli."

"Okay."

"A bartender at Darby's said you and your dad were there on August 17 and you saw Dane drinking with some men. Is that true?"

"Yes."

"And Dane and his group became somewhat belligerent, is that correct?"

"Well, not at first," Jordan replied. "I mean, Dad and I were there for an hour or so. Dane and those guys had been there a while before we got there. But the bartender, I think, asked them to leave not long after we arrived, so yes."

The detective jotted down notes on a small, narrow notebook.

"And did Dane say anything to you, or you to him?"

The line of questioning made Jordan nervous. He found himself rapidly tapping his foot against the floor.

"No, he didn't see me. But it was dark and smoky in there. Plus, he was wasted anyways."

"Any idea why the bartender asked his party to leave, other than being rowdy?"

"No."

Detective Parsons turned a page in the notebook. "Your father corroborates your story."

"You spoke to my dad?"

Detective Parsons nodded. "Yes, a couple of days ago." He looked around the room casually and then back at Jordan. "And how would you characterize your relationship with Dane?"

Jordan swallowed. "I liked the dude. He is, or was, a good player, I guess."

"We talked to Coach Miles. He said that you and Dane had a run-in at practice a few days before his death. Is that normal?"

Jordan rose from the bed and steadied his weight, favoring the ankle. "It is when you've got an underclassman acting like he's the shit and you've got a coach who tells you that he's going to be the current future, and the future future, and that you are expected to mentor him and help him and coddle him and make sure he gets a chance to show everyone how good he is. And your best friend mentors him and invites him everywhere, and you basically get overlooked by everyone as a senior just because some sophback comes around and wants to be the next you."

The detective leaned back, eyes widened. "Anything else?"

Jordan paused and collected himself. "Damnit, you wanted the truth and I just gave it to you. In fact, get out of my room. You need a warrant to be in here anyway."

"Not if you invite me in. And I don't need a warrant unless I'm searching your place." Detective Parsons sauntered around the room. "Do you know anyone that lives in Tennessee?"

Jordan scratched his head. "No. Why?"

"We found a torn piece of paper outside of Stokley Hall the night Dane was killed. It had a 615 area code, which is a Tennessee area code. We traced the number. It was a TracPhone that had been disconnected."

Parsons made his way to the bathroom, where he stuck his head inside the door and pulled back suddenly, his face scrunched.

"Whew. That smell. You sick or something?"

Jordan looked into the bathroom and hopped to the doorway. "Yeah, a little."

"That's an awful smell. You might want to go to the doctor."

"I'd feel better if you'd get the hell out of here!"

The detective looked back at Jordan again, up and down his frame, and stared at the ankle.

"Like I said, get that ankle better."

Detective Parsons escorted himself out.

Jordan went back into the bathroom. The acrid smell made his eyes water. He reached into a different drawer underneath the sink and found the syringe and needle.

*   *   *   *   *

As dusk descended onto campus, Cullen jammed both hands into pockets of his shorts. Exhausted, he couldn't wait to get back to Cougar Village and take a nap.

The week was nearly over. The Cougars faced a tough football opponent in West Liberty University near Wheeling on Saturday afternoon. Cullen hadn't prepared mentally for the upcoming game, aside from several hours of film study. Along with game preparations, a paper on the ethical business practices of Internet search engine company Yahoo needed completion. Despite these concerns, Serena Johnson had planted a thought in the recesses of Cullen's mind that became a primary distraction.

Cullen looked at the ground, staring intently into the cracks that split the sidewalk pavement into fragmented pieces, like a jigsaw puzzle that had not been put back together properly.

Cullen had met with Serena and seen the questionable autopsy report. The document appeared forged, yet a lingering question remained. Who altered the report? And why?

Cullen found himself nearly reciting his thoughts aloud. Shaking his head, he knew he needed to separate himself from Serena and the investigation. Cullen needed to refocus on football and school, just as Dr. Burcham had suggested—or rather, demanded.

Cullen raised his eyes. The image of Cougar Village became more defined, its main campus buildings dimming under the descending sun. As he strode between two large maple trees adorned with burnt orange and copper leaves, the steel poles of Cougar Stadium with the toothbrush lights mounted against them rose almost parallel with the mountainside behind it. Its steel and concrete edifice, however, seemed out of sync with its natural surroundings.

The calmness and near-reverence of an empty campus allowed Cullen a chance to get mentally lost in his own thoughts and clear a cluttered mind. A burst of air brushed against him as a heavy, cold object delivered a blunt pain on the back of his neck.

Cullen toppled forward, bracing a pending collision with the sidewalk by extending both hands outward. The weight and motion of the fall made the bones in his wrists creak. He blinked and rolled over, holding both arms upright in a defensive position.

A burly, immense man wearing black clothes and gloves, his nose and mouth hidden behind a scarf, leaned forward. Cullen, simultaneously enraged and frightened, watched as the man swiped the silver object. He struck Cullen with it on his right temple.

Cullen's eyes blazed. An explosion of crimson blood droplets splattered on his shorts.

He jumped up and lunged at the attacker. He managed to grab a fleshy roll of skin protruding from the neck, and dug his nails into the flabby flesh.

The man whimpered and mumbled, although Cullen couldn't decipher the words. Cullen lowered a left hand and punched the attacker in the abdomen.

A large rush of air burst from the man's nostrils as he folded at the waist. Cullen stared into his green eyes.

The attacker rose up and jammed the metal rod into Cullen's gut with both hands at tremendous force.

The impact nearly knocked Cullen unconscious.

Cullen thought his guts would explode. A swath of fresh blood poured onto his shirt.

The man took the end of the rod and slammed it against the side of Cullen's face. An incredible amount of pain distorted his vision, the skin on the side of his face tightening.

"Son of a bitch," the man sneered. The attacker reared back again, holding the rod with a tight grip. He struck Cullen across the face. The acrid taste of blood filled his mouth, and his tongue felt dry and large, like there was no longer enough room for it.

Cullen, woozy with pain, gasping for air, dropped into a three-point stance and pounced.

Catching his attacker by surprise, Cullen drove a left shoulder into the man's chest. He dropped the rod. Cullen kept both legs churning forward. The man toppled backwards and smashed into the sidewalk.

Cullen heard what sounded like shrieks and cries from other people in the background, but he ignored them.

Straddling the man with his knees pinning both arms against the sidewalk, Cullen pummeled his face.

The man yelped with pain at each blow.

The rod spun wildly on the ground. Cullen reached back, grabbed it and stuffed it under the man's chin, driving it into his throat.

The attacker's eyes widened and flickered.

"We'll see how well you fight when you can't breathe!" Cullen snarled.

"Stop!" The order was faint, from a distance. "Get off of him!" The voice, somewhat familiar, seemed far away. Cullen couldn't tell the direction of the sound, and he didn't care.

"The police are on the way. Stop it, both of you!" This time, the words sounded more urgent and authoritative. They came from behind Cullen.

Cullen flinched. That moment of pause allowed the man to jab an elbow into Cullen's crotch, knocking him sideways.

Cullen turned. The edge of the rod slammed into his eye socket. Immediately, the eye swelled and closed, leaving his vision darkened and his depth perception handicapped.

The attacker snatched the rod and stood over Cullen. He pounded Cullen's face and body with the rod, then with fists. Bones cracked. Skin tore. Muscles coagulated. Intense, paralyzing pain blazed through Cullen. Vomit climbed his esophagus.

Cullen kicked the man in the groin.

The attacker staggered and fell to one knee.

Cullen felt like every muscle in his body had torn and every bone had broken. His abdomen burned and tingled; blood streaked down his face onto his forearm.

Cullen dragged himself into an upright stance. Drawing all the energy he could muster, he kicked the man in the jaw with the heel of his shoe. Streaks of blood sprayed onto the sidewalk—along with two teeth. The man, now writhing in pain, spit out two more teeth.

Cullen grabbed the small steel pole.

The attacker siezed Cullen by the neck of his blood-stained shirt.

Sirens grew closer.

"Quit digging," the man dissed. "There ain't no story."

Sirens and screeching tires bounced off stone campus buildings. Exhaufed, wounded, and delirious with pain, Cullen leaned back and collapsed onto the concrete.

twenty three

DR. BURCHAM MOVED through the groups of people like a politician, striding without an ounce of pretension.

Walker Hall, buzzing with the hushed conversations of Clear River College dignitaries and alumni, faced the center of campus and featured over 20,000 square feet of space. Tom Hancel stood in front of an Italian marble fireplace with his chest sticking outward as if held up by a rope. He laughed gregariously and smacked the arm of another man.

Dr. Burcham approached, and Tom waved for the president to join the discussion. "Dr. Neal Burcham, this is Logan Hughes, West Virginia Department of Highways Commissioner," he said.

Dr. Burcham pushed his glasses up his nose and extended a hand.

Logan switched a half-consumed glass of wine to his left hand.

"It's a pleasure to meet you, Mr. Hughes. Thank you for coming to our Distinguished Contributors Dinner here at Clear River College."

Logan smirked at Tom, then leveled a friendly look at the president. "Just call me Logan, Dr. Burcham."

"Then I insist you call me Neal." Dr. Burcham straightened his posture as the smirk evaporated from the face of the commissioner. The odd silence of unfamiliarity fell on the group. Dr. Burcham looked past Logan and Tom.

Jack Dillon talked with a portly, hunchbacked woman wearing a sparkling silver necklace and several gleaming rings on her chubby fingers. Dr. Burcham watched Jack with admiration, because talking with dignitaries was something Jack excelled in doing.

"I was telling Commissioner Hughes here about the board's decision to build the four-lane road expansion on Route 33 through campus," Tom said.

Dr. Burcham giggled nervously, then patted Tom on the arm, squeezing the bicep tightly.

"Our board is committed to looking into the project, Logan," he said sternly. "I can assure you we are willing to conduct a thorough feasibility study on the matter and we will be in contact with your office."

Logan, his hair streaked white and his thin, freckled face radiating youth and vigor, swiveled the wine in a circular motion. "Let me be abundantly clear. In no way will this project require any college money. We are relying on federal and state highway appropriations to cover the full cost of the project."

Dr. Burcham looked again at Tom, who nodded.

"I am concerned about earlier reports coming from Charleston that the road might become a toll road in order to pay for bonds that would be needed for construction costs." The president swallowed. "I do not believe that we, as a college, can support a toll road, because it would be a financial detriment to our students and faculty."

Tom stamped his foot quietly in protest.

Logan flashed a puzzled expression. "You are aware of the possible impact this could have on your student recruiting efforts. Easier access to your campus will allow you to compete for in-state and out-of-state students. It might level the playing field for your college."

Dr. Burcham ran fingers across the creases of his mouth. "I am aware of that, Commissioner, but I am also concerned about the disruption to our way of life here. You cannot undertake a project of this scope without the logistics becoming a nightmare for our campus community."

Logan took a quick sip. "You have my assurances—and the assurances of the governor—that this road expansion project will be handled in an expedited manner with the concerns of the college at the forefront of all construction decisions."

"We have already done an earth and soil sample near the part of Route 33 that crosses through campus," Tom said, excitement garnishing his voice. "The state determined the soil pattern would make removal of the current road and green space easy and affordable for everyone involved."

"Speaking of the college," Logan added, "how is the investigation coming regarding the kid who was found dead—the football player? We hear bits and pieces about it in Charleston every now and then. Got it resolved?" He took another hearty drink of wine, the last trickle sliding down the glass and into his mouth.

Dr. Burcham reached down and collected Logan's arm, shaking the hand of the commissioner. "Thank you for coming this evening, Logan. It was a pleasure meeting you, and I can assure you I will relate your information to the board at our next meeting."

"As chairman of the Clear River College Board of Governors, I support this project," Tom said.

"If you'll excuse me." Dr. Burcham hurried toward the center of the room.

Jack had disappeared, and the room had fallen quiet as dark-suited waiters glided past tables, carrying trays laden with steelhead roe in coconut suspended from vanilla pods, granola-encrusted chicken with oatmeal foam, jelled apple cider floating in walnut milk, and vegetable ash, along with sweet potato and bourbon, pierced by a smoking cinnamon stick.

Meanwhile, the Jerusalem stone enclosing Walker Hall cast a mix of shadows through the bay windows.

Tom caught up to Dr. Burcham as he neared the head of the banquet table.

Dr. Burcham swung around. "You sandbagged me back there, Tom," Dr. Burcham said. "The next time you set me up like that, I will not hesitate to bring up your conduct to the board."

"My conduct? What about your conduct?" Tom asked.

Dr. Burcham's eyes narrowed.

Tom clicked his feet together. "I wanted you to hear from the commissioner that the state is supportive of building this road, and that it will not cost this college a dime."

Dr. Burcham dropped his chin.

"If we don't do this, the opportunity to build this road may never come again." Tom released a long-held breath. His voice softened. "Besides, Neal, we need something positive to deflect the focus off the Antonelli situation and onto something else."

Dr. Burcham looked up and stared steadily at Tom. "It has been my experience that when state government promises an ambitious project like this one and agrees to pay for it, there are always strings attached. The legislature will hold that road money over us like a sword of Damocles."

Tom leaned closer to Dr. Burcham's ear. "They might hold it over us if we *don't* agree to build it." The words, etched in his trademark southern slur, came out slowly, as if Tom recited them syllable by syllable.

"We will discuss this as a board."

"Neal—"

"Not another word, understood?"

Tom stepped back and nodded in defeat.

Dr. Burcham surveyed the room again and checked his watch. The conversations of the dignitaries and alumni circulated in the air around the banquet table. "Where is John Petry? He is the president of this group—and the keynote speaker."

twenty four

THE MEDICAL PERSONNEL and state police established the lobby of Pickens Hall as the triage and statement collection location. Cullen was placed on a large cushioned chair adjacent to the front desk of the residence hall. An overhead ceiling fan rocked and wheezed in a circular motion. The down-flow of air didn't provide Cullen any relief.

The paramedic, tall for a woman, stood up. Wearing a form-fitting blue responder uniform complete with finely pressed navy slacks and boots, she commanded respect. Her brown hair, tightly pulled against her scalp, revealed the clearness of her skin.

She held a small mirror for him. Cullen squinted, taking a long look into the slightly scratched and chipped mirror. The entire left side of his face, swollen and mangled, had pockets of dried blood crusted on the surface of the skin. A large gash over the left temple had been stitched. Swaths of skin ripped from his face exposed pulsing, bleeding, undulating jagged sores. The bones in his nose were crushed and swollen so badly that the orifice seemed like an otherworldly appendage.

Cullen tried breathing through his damaged nose, wheezing. He wore a rib protector that wrapped uncomfortably around his rib cage, but the defined muscles from his v-shaped torso expanded the foam. Gashes and cuts dotted his face and his left eye, which was almost swelled shut. A thin filament of blood disguised the blue hue of his pupil inside the right eye.

"I think you'll be fine, Cullen. Be sure and re-dress the bandages every four hours. We're going to take you to the ER at Fairmont General."

"There will not be a trip to the doctor," Cullen replied flatly.

The woman dropped down on her haunches. Placing a bony, slender finger under the dimple in his chin, the woman locked eyes with him. "You have been through quite an ordeal tonight. We are going to take you in just a few minutes."

Cullen grabbed her by the wrist. "I told you, I'm staying right here. If you want me to go to the ER, then arrest me!"

The paramedic stood, tugged her arm away from Cullen, collected the bloody gauze and bandages, and walked away.

Cullen told the responders he had been headed to Cougar Village prior to being attacked. The brick and tile interior of the hall made Cullen more uncomfortable each minute. A long, expansive counter bisected the main lobby, and tables, chairs, and a pool table scattered throughout the room in fits of disorganization made Cullen feel like a slightly disfigured wall ornament that had not been properly placed.

Around Cullen, men talked quietly to each other. Cullen found it ironic that Jerry Parsons, the lead investigator responsible for finding the person who stole the car belonging to Dane Antonelli, was also conducting this investigation. Cullen did not like meeting police under these circumstances.

Someone approached behind him. Dr. Petry walked around Cullen. The disheveled tuxedo shirt and crooked bow tie flapped slightly under the puffs of wind created by the ceiling fan, although Cullen did not look up. The stale stench of pipe tobacco wafted through the air.

"I'm certainly glad I stepped outside from the contributors' dinner to smoke my pipe when I did, or I wouldn't have seen anything. Who was that ghastly man and what did he want?"

Cullen rolled his shoulders. "I don't know and I don't know."

Serena approached Cullen. "Detective Parsons said you can go. He has completed his line of questioning with you. He feels like your description will aid in the search."

Cullen leaned forward, folded his arms, rested one elbow on each knee, and remained silent. Cullen let out a short breath and leaned closer to the window.

Feeling another presence close to him, Cullen shivered slightly. A different voice spoke, this one a halted tone. "Brewer, can I call someone for you?" Dr. Petry and Serena stepped aside as Jordan appeared.

Jordan hobbled around to face Cullen. He looked sideways at Dr. Petry and Serena, his mouth agape. "Jesus," Jordan said. "I came to meet you and get some food. Cullen, man, you're in bad shape. Who did this to you?"

"We were just getting to that," Dr. Petry said.

Jordan shot a sideways glance again at Dr. Petry and fixated on his floppy, white hair. The wrinkles around his eyes and mouth had deep grooves that carved into his skin, while his slouched posture seemed to suggest the professor may topple over at any minute.

"Cullen, please let us call someone for you," Serena pleaded.

Cullen sighed again and unfolded his arms. He had thought about calling his dad. He would want to know what happened tonight. Then, Cullen remembered the time of day and knew that nothing would interrupt his dad's drinking plans.

"My mom is dead and my dad is a drunk deadbeat. There's nobody to call."

Serena faced Jordan for confirmation.

Jordan lowered his chin.

"Oh, Cullen, I'm so sorry." Serena knelt next to him. She lowered her voice. "I think these two incidents are connected."

"I beg your pardon?" Dr. Petry asked.

"You have to ignore most of what Diane Sawyer Junior here says," Jordan said to the professor. "She sees a crime or some stupid story in everything that happens."

Serena looked up at Jordan, trying to balance himself with little weight put on his right ankle. "What happened to your leg?"

"Don't try and change the subject because I called you out for being a fraud."

"I'm not a fraud," Serena replied. "I read where your ankle is hurt. I'm curious, though, as to why your leg is covered in band-aids?"

Jordan rolled his eyes. "You try walking with one crutch and see how many times you trip and fall."

"I think we're forgetting about someone," Dr. Petry said, pointing at Cullen.

"Anyways," Serena said. "I was in *The Record* newsroom earlier. Someone grabbed me in the hallway and threw me against the wall."

"Oh my." Dr. Petry gasped. "Are you hurt? I can get another paramedic before they leave."

"You serious?" Jordan arched a thin eyebrow.

"Yes, I'm fine, and yes, Jordan, that's the truth."

Dr. Petry, smoothing out his wrinkled tuxedo shirt, studied Serena. "Did you call the authorities? Did the perpetrator take anything?"

Serena pursed her lips. "He took the file folder from my desk." She dropped her chin and bit her lower lip. "I was on my way across campus to cover the contributors' dinner for tomorrow's paper when I saw the lights and heard the sirens."

"Did you see who threw you?" Jordan asked, genuine concern in his voice.

"No," Serena replied. "It happened so fast, I didn't get a good look at him."

Dr. Petry rubbed his chin. "So, it's possible the person who attacked you attacked Cullen?"

"Man, he would have to be a fast runner to catch up with Brewer," Jordan said. "Brewer can fly for a quarterback."

"It's possible," Serena said. "Cullen could have been targeted." "You can stop talking about me like I'm not here!" Cullen demanded, startling the group. He arched his head. "Dr. Petry, thank you for calling the cops. The rest of you can leave."

The professor leaned close to Serena. "I really need to be going back to the dinner. I'm scheduled to introduce the distinguished guests."

The shuffling of emergency responders and equipment subsided behind the group. A shadow approached from across the lobby, gaining clarity with each step. Neal Burcham and Tom Hancel, taking long strides, came closer.

Jordan looked at them. "I, I think we had better go, gang."

Dr. Petry bent down and patted Cullen on the arm.

Serena crouched in front of Cullen. She reached for his hands, but he pulled them away. "Please, leave me alone."

"We will find out who did this, I promise," she said.

"You sure make a lot of promises," Cullen said. The tone of his voice and words, usually throaty and energetic, now were detached and clipped. "I'm sorry about what happened to you today. I'm glad you're okay."

Serena's face tightened and she moved closer to Cullen. "My autopsy report is missing," she whispered. "I think the person who attacked me grabbed that report and then got to you for good measure."

"I just don't want to think about any of it right now," Cullen said.

A short silence fell between them.

"I may not get to finish my senior year as quarterback of the Cougars, thanks to this mess," he added.

Serena paled.

"The team's whole year might be ruined, and it's all because of all of this."

"Why do you think your senior year is ruined?" Serena stammered.

"Take a look."

Cullen turned sideways in the seat, exposing more of his injuries.

Serena yelped and covered her mouth. Then she inched closer, her mouth agape.

Cullen barked, "Now leave. Please."

twenty five

"DOCTOR, WE NEED TO TALK." Detective Parsons grabbed Dr. Burcham by the elbow.

The barrel-chested West Virginia State Police detective Jerry Parsons clutched a clipboard under one arm with a small, rangy hand.

Dr. Burcham stopped. Dr. Petry and Jordan trailed closely behind him. In the distance, the president watched as the people slithering left and right inside the Walker Hall lobby grew in number. A hard blink did not change the movements.

Detective Parsons stepped forward. "My men think they caught the guy responsible for getting the Brewer kid in there," he said, the slow pace of his speech interrupted for heavy breaths of air. "A patrol car pulled over a man speeding in a red Ford Explorer on Corridor 33 near downtown Beaumont. The guy matched the description we received from the boy. After doing a walk-around casual search from outside the vehicle, my officers found the pipe used in the attack. We'll dust it for prints."

Dr. Burcham glared at the shiny badge pinned on Jerry Parsons's lapel. The evening sky, a magnificent, rich black sprinkled with stars, hung low over the discussion. "Who is he? Did he say anything about why he was here?"

"His name is Damon Jarousky."

Dr. Burcham shrugged.

The detective pushed up the wide-brimmed, green trooper hat with three fingers. "We ran his Ohio plates. Jarousky has no prior criminal record." He slid the clipboard back underneath an arm.

Dr. Burcham detached his slumping bow-tie and clenched it tightly. "So then, it's safe to assume this attack on Cullen Brewer was random and had no connection to your ongoing investigation into Dane Antonelli?"

"That's correct," Detective Parsons replied.

Two people walked up to Dr. Burcham. Turning, Dr. Burcham took a quick sideways glance at both Tom and Dr. Petry, and scowled. "Gentlemen..."

Tom revealed a slapstick grin that elicited a groan from Dr. Burcham.

Detective Parsons reached an arm around the shoulders of the president and led him away from Jordan and Tom.

"We also got the lab reports back on those bags found in the Antonelli car from a few weeks ago."

Relief floated over Dr. Burcham, but just as quickly, nausea growled in the recesses of his gut.

"The lab found Creatine residue in those sandwich bags," Detective Parsons added. "Creatine is normally used by body-builders and athletes to build muscle mass. We can't tell how long the bags were in the car, but it's possible that Dane Antonelli wanted to get bigger and stronger so he could be a better football player. We also contacted the Antonelli family regarding the car. We wanted to know if they wanted to pick it up or if we could impound it. The kid's parents had no idea their son had a car. They gave him a weekly allowance for his school and personal expenses, but they said it wasn't enough to buy a car unless he didn't spend any of it for a long period of time."

Dr. Burcham looked sideways at Detective Parsons and blinked hard.

The detective continued leading Dr. Burcham by the shoulder back toward Walker Hall. Clusters of men and women, dressed in various shades of black, emerged from the dinner ceremony in lockstep with their dates. In the middle of the clusters, Coach Miles engaged the couples with affectionate touches and handshakes.

"The lab also found residue inside the bags linked to a compound called *Bambuterol*." The detective stopped walking.

Dr. Burcham turned and faced him. He imagined that the striking, penetrating eyes of a police officer had tried on and shed various personae over the years, like outfits discarded in front of a mirror. Tonight, the personae hardened further into one of investigator.

Dr. Burcham removed his wire-rim glasses and cleaned them with a handkerchief. "What is Bambuterol?"

"It's a drug paramedics and doctors use to treat asthma," Detective Parsons answered. "I contacted Conley Masters, the state medical examiner in Charleston."

Dr. Burcham flashed a blank stare at the detective.

"The guy who did the autopsy on Antonelli."

Dr. Burcham raised a hand. "Yes, yes, the name escaped me for a moment."

Trooper Parsons exhaled heavily through his nose, widening both nostrils. "Conley did not see any signs of asthma present in the boy's lungs."

Dr. Burcham folded his arms. "So did Dane take it for something else?"

Detective Parsons scratched his chin. "Or he could have been combining the Bambuterol with the Creatine for another purpose. I just don't know. That's way above my pay grade."

Dr. Burcham nodded.

"One more point. Conley told me that he got a phone call a few days ago from a student on your campus." Trooper Parsons brought out the clipboard again, steadied it, moistened an index finger with the tip of his tongue, and turned a page. "Serena Johnson is her name. Conley said she accused him of false information in the autopsy report."

Dr. Burcham frowned. Every muscle in his body tightened. "How would Serena Johnson know anything about the autopsy report?"

"Good question," Detective Parsons answered.

twenty six

JORDAN FOLDED THE FLAPS of the small, rectangular cardboard box. On the bathroom sink, an orange pill had been pulverized into granular powder.

Jordan listened again as the voicemail from his father echoed from the bathroom into the bedroom. Tom spoke slowly, reminding Jordan to be careful over the next few days. He also issued profuse apologies regarding what happened to Cullen.

Jordan pressed a button, cut off the message and turned off the phone.

Hopping awkwardly across the bathroom floor, Jordan dragged his toes against the cool tile underneath. After being escorted back to Cougar Village by his father, Jordan had thrown his crutches into the garbage dumpster outside the residence halls. Jordan, tired and furious over what happened tonight to his best friend and teammate, needed to get healthy again.

He looked at a wrinkled white cloth, peppered with blood spots, next to the orange powder. Brushing the cloth aside, Jordan collected the powder into one hand. He allowed the gristly powder flakes to roll from the fingers into his mouth. The taste and texture of the powder nearly made him gag.

He swallowed and looked intently into the mirror.

*   *   *   *   *

Cullen looked up at the cracked mirror in the corner of the Cougars locker room. As he slid the clear, plastic mask over sore cheekbones, the rough edges of the mask chafed his skin, causing a nagging pain to shoot down his neck into his shoulders. Cullen wished that Dr. Richardson, the team physician, had not persuaded Coach Miles that wearing the facemask was essential to a complete recovery.

Frustrated, Cullen ripped off the mask and slammed it into the locker. He kicked the locker with his cleat, then lurched forward, clutching his ribs.

Cullen let out a scream of anger. The gesture felt good for a moment, then the searing pain of air coursing through his ribs made him regret the impulse. The empty locker room, a familiar place of respite for Cullen, now felt like a tempestuous kidnapper.

Staggering to a slouched position on the benches in the middle of the room, Cullen looked at the end of a long row of lockers. Stumbling down the row, Cullen steadied himself in front of the faded Prussian blue locker that once belonged to Dane Antonelli.

Cullen wished silently, desperately, that Dane could answer questions. So many unanswered questions fueled even more resentment for Cullen. Those thoughts placed Cullen on the same plane of thinking as Serena Johnson. And he wanted nothing to do with her or her line of thinking.

He thought about his mother and longed for her presence and love, especially now. This would be the moment where she would tell him, with soft eyes and a gentle embrace, that everything would be fine and that she was proud of him for everything he had done. Cullen closed his eyes and cleared the expression from his face. A bit of warmth passed through his body as he thought about her and his love for her.

Cullen swallowed a shallow breath to subside the stinging pain in his ribs. He reached up and touched his splotchy face, devoid of surface skin in many places, and softly touched his nose. The blinding pain nearly rendered him senseless. Cullen screamed—a frightening, horrific scream that channeled the pain and frustration into dulcimer tones that reverberated throughout the cavernous locker room.

Cullen listened as the sound grew faint. Grabbing two large tufts of hair, he closed his eyes. All of his ribs still maintained a dull ache; the perspiration forming under his brow ran down his cheeks, stinging his skin. The sensation made him feel sick.

Cullen cautiously picked up the protective facemask and pushed open the locker room door. Down the corridor from the locker room, Coach Miles talked to someone.

A faint stream of yellow light illuminated the otherwise dim corridor. The office, positioned at the end of the locker-room portion of the Cougars facilities building, did not disguise conversations well. Anyone roaming casually past the locker room and inching closer down the corridor to the office likely could discern any discussion taking place. Cullen headed for the coach's office, following the soft words that grew louder as he moved down the hallway.

Cullen reached the office door. He heard another voice. Cullen tapped on the door and edged it forward. Coach Miles, slouched at his desk, sat up, unmoved by the forced opening. More yellow light poked through a small window disguised by dusty blinds in the office. Behind Coach Miles, the highlights of the University of Charleston and West Virginia Tech game played silently on the television screen. Scattered in front of the coach were legal pads and sheets of paper in no particular order.

Coach Miles removed a clear pair of low-slung reading glasses, pinched the cartilage at the end of his wide nose, and plopped the glasses on the table. Reaching for the telephone at the end of the desk, he pressed a red button on the phone that turned gray.

He refused eye contact with Cullen. "You cannot play on Saturday, Brewer. You are going to sit out this game against West Virginia Tech. The off week is next week, and then you can come back and play against Wesleyan."

Cullen, dressed in a white undershirt and faded denim shorts, rested both hands on his hips. "I want you to answer something for me, Coach," he said. "No nonsense here, either."

Coach Miles quietly shuffled some papers on the desk. A faint whistle protruded from the television screen; an official stepped in to signal the play dead as the quarterback from the University of Charleston got knocked to the ground by two hulky defensive linemen from West Virginia Tech.

The coach sat up in the office chair and folded his arms—his burgeoning shoulders were far too large for the blue Cougars tee-shirt he wore.

"Make it fast, Brewer. We've got practice in thirty minutes and more game film to study."

Cullen wanted to speak, but no words emerged. His throat felt dry and scratchy. Meanwhile, the pulsating rib pain eased, but now the muscles in his face were burning.

A bemused look of curiosity washed over the face of the coach. "What do you want?"

Cullen moved a step closer to the coach.

"Dane helped lead East Fairmont High School to a state championship. He came here as a runner-up for the Kennedy Award. He was a two-sport athlete and was going to be a receiver this team needed. We needed a deep threat to go along with Jordan, and he was going to be the answer. Instead, he died. You never put him in a game outside of practice, and now he is dead. And all hell is breaking loose because of it."

The coach scowled. The veins in his neck bulged. "You watch it, son. I don't need anyone telling me who to play and when. You go on and on about Dane and his high school numbers. Well, that was then. What you did in high school doesn't mean squat when you come to college. When I recruit you, it's based on what can you do to help our team win championships." Coach Miles's eyes narrowed. "Dane couldn't learn to sense pressure coming from defensive backs and linebackers. He didn't understand that you still got to move and protect the football, even while you're focusing downfield. That's why we didn't play him last year until late in the season. I wanted him to start as a freshman, but you remember last year, at the end of the season in practice. You threw him pass after pass. He dropped most of them. And he had problems running routes correctly."

Coach Miles pressed his lips tightly together. "What does this have to do with you?"

Cullen shifted his weight between feet. He grabbed the back of a nearby chair.

Coach Miles raised both hands. "I'm sorry, Brewer. That was unfair."

Cullen stepped closer. "Who were you talking to just a minute ago? I heard you nearly shouting with someone."

Coach Miles tossed a hand into the air. "Dr. Burcham and I were talking on the phone, talking about what happened to you and the person who made you...like this."

"What did he say?"

"I want you to know, Brewer, that I came by Pickens Hall after Jack Dillon called me. Everything had cleared out by the time I got there. I, uh, I'm sorry for what happened."

Cullen's eyes stayed on the coach's. "What did Dr. Burcham say?"

Coach Miles kicked back the chair. The rusted chair wheels squealed in displeasure. Standing up, he approached Cullen, but stood to the side.

"We are going to have increased police presence when we practice and play games, at least for the rest of this season. There will be more police at the entrance to campus as well. I think it's a bit much, but that being said, keeping my team safe and making sure we're prepared for each game is a priority for me. In other words, our campus is going to be on a type of lockdown. The administration and the police don't know what happened to Dane or why you got attacked, and now we all suffer the consequences."

"But—"

"I suggest if you have any problems with it, you get ahold of Burcham and ask him yourself." Coach Miles retreated behind his desk.

Cullen processed the information and briefly looked up, staring at the ceiling. The stained ceiling tiles sagged in certain areas. He refocused his attention on the coach.

Coach Miles shuffled papers and placed them aside.

"I'm not sure you gave him enough time."

Coach Miles glared at Cullen. "We just need to move on."

Another tapping on the office door stopped the discussion. It thrust open and Jordan Hancel stood in the doorway.

"What's up, Coach? Cullen?" Wavy clusters of hair dangled over his brow as Jordan rocked back and forth with ebullience.

"Hancel, get in the film room and start watching tape." Coach Miles, once again, didn't make eye contact.

"Cullen, you're looking better, man," Jordan commented.

Cullen crossed his arms, feigned a small smile, and dropped his head.

"Where are your crutches?" Coach Miles asked.

"I don't need them. I'm ready to practice. I'm gonna play Saturday against Tech."

"I don't believe so," Coach Miles responded. "Not until Doc Powell clears you."

"He doesn't need to, Coach. I have rested, rehabbed the ankle, and I'm good as new."

Cullen turned to the coach. "Jordan was on crutches a couple of days ago. Either he was faking it then, he's faking it now, or he's had a miraculous healing."

Jordan shot Cullen a disgusted stare.

Cullen squinted. "What's that?" He pointed at a dark oval trickling from Jordan's nostril. "Your nose is bleeding."

Jordan touched the creeping blood droplet, which now began trickling in a more steady stream.

"Weather changing...gets me every year. Be right back."

Jordan disappeared as more people appeared in the doorway, this time rustling papers.

Center Andre Gibson burst into the office.

Andre, with his trademark fast-talking Northeastern lilt, spilled the words Cullen did not want to hear. "Hey, Cullen, you made the front page of the paper. Look!"

He shoved the paper into Cullen's chest, knocking the wind from his lungs and reviving the pain in his ribs.

Cullen glanced at the paper, then past it into the hallway, past the three stocky linemen.

"Serena Johnson." Cullen marched out of the office.

C ULLEN HELD THE FOOTBALL HELMET in one hand. An early fall chill descended on the field as the Cougars prepared to play their final game in September.

Coach Miles paced the sidelines, mumbling softly: "If we take care of ourselves, we'll be okay."

Hearing Coach Miles utter those words made Cullen uneasy. Although the coach recited the same statement in the locker room, the words might not erase the nine consecutive wins earned by the West Virginia Tech Golden Bears against the Clear River Cougars.

The West Virginia Tech Golden Bears started playing football in 1907. The Golden Bears split the conference championship with Concord in 1989. However, West Virginia Tech had defeated Clear River three of the last four years by a combined score of six points. Coach Miles refused to see his team lose again this year.

"Take care of everything out there, men. I mean all of it," Coach Miles barked to the offensive line. "We were up 21-0 a year ago against Tech and lost. We played well early, scored on the first three drives and then quit. I don't want to see any quit here today."

Cullen stepped closer and looked into the eyes of the tall, rail-thin sophomore backup quarterback. Chance Carpenter glanced up and flashed a quick, sheepish smile at Cullen.

"He has no idea what he's in for today," Cullen said aloud, nodding back at Chance.

Cullen took a deep breath. The temperate early fall sun warmed his skin. He looked up, watching small, fingerlike clouds speckle the blue sky. Small beams of pale gold light permeated the clouds and gave a slight sheen to the mashed grass at Cougar Stadium. A large gust of wind propelled a thicket of leaves onto the field from the stands, forcing spectators to pull and pick shards of dried leaves from their hair and clothes. The burst of wind made the still-swollen skin on Cullen's face tingle with pain.

Jordan bolted up from the bench, receiving a generous slap on the buttocks from Coach Miles. Jordan approached Cullen, flashing a broad smile. "I'm back, Brewer. I'm back, baby," he proclaimed. "I told you no ankle sprain would keep me from playing football."

"I can see that." Cullen watched the field. "I still don't know how you came back so quickly, but we need you today." He turned his eyes to study the face of his closest friend. "Stay close to the line of scrimmage. Chance is going to need a check-down receiver. Tech will blitz him all day long."

Jordan cocked his head sideways and removed a nylon glove from his right hand. "I really wish you'd quit talking to me like I'm a freshman. You and I have nearly rewritten the passing records at this school. I know how to catch the football."

His comment struck Cullen as odd. He'd known Jordan Hancel for most of his life, and Jordan had never accused Cullen of lecturing him. Before Cullen could fully process the thought, Jordan scratched at small, round bumps on his forearm. The scratching punctured the sores, which oozed a clear liquid.

"I am gonna catch four TDs today, Brewer. Just watch me." Jordan wiped away the liquid protruding from the bleeding holes and jogged onto the field for the opening kickoff.

West Virginia Tech took the game's opening kickoff and promptly went on a nine-play, sixty-two-yard scoring drive that ended with Mitch Isner's five-yard touchdown pass to Jamir Brown. A two-point conversion pass failed, but Tech led 6-0.

West Virginia Tech forced a three-and-out on Clear River's first possession. The Golden Bears offense then put together a ten-play, 69-yard drive ending with a one-yard touchdown run by quarterback Mitch Isner. The extra point kick made the score 13-0.

On the next offensive series for the Cougars, Chance Carpenter was sacked twice and threw an interception while trying to avoid a third sack.

Cullen paced the sidelines at a safe distance behind Coach Miles as the game continued deteriorating for the Cougars.

The coach grabbed players at random and verbally railed on them for lack of effort. When he found Chance, Coach Miles sunk fingers into his arm, screaming profanity-laced statements at the young quarterback. Cullen watched intently as Chance seemed to shrink under the verbal barrage.

In the second half, with West Virginia Tech leading 13-0, Chance Carpenter again was intercepted, this time on a screen pass thrown to running back Marcus Turner. Chance rushed the throw, and a Tech defensive lineman jumped the pass and returned it 46 yards for another touchdown.

Coach Miles slammed a clipboard on the ground. A loud chorus of boos rained down from the Cougar fans in the stands.

"Timeout! Timeout!" Coach Miles screamed, finally gaining the attention of a trailing official setting up the football for the next kickoff.

Coach Miles approached Cullen. With nostrils flared and pools of sweat splotching his face, Coach Miles sneered: "You wanted to play. You're gonna play. You're going in, Brewer."

Cullen slid the plastic protective mask over his face and squeezed the football helmet over the mask. Despite the fact that his ribs and muscles still ached from the attack, Cullen ran onto the field.

The fans erupted into a cascade of cheers and applause. Cullen looked around and grinned. He remembered why he loved playing football so much.

"Thank God you're back," Jordan proclaimed as the team gathered in the huddle after the ensuing kickoff. "That pipsqueak Carpenter had the arm strength of a wet noodle."

Cullen ignored Jordan and studied the resiliency of the rest of the offensive unit. Receivers Tay Anderson and Mike Ochoa bounced lightly on their heels, awaiting Cullen's instructions. Andre Gibson pulled all of the offensive linemen together in a tight circle. "Guys, Tech has had four sacks for twenty-seven yards and twelve tackles for a loss for forty-four yards. We need to change the tempo and score, but shit, we've gotta protect our quarterback better. He can't take no hits like that."

With a first down and ten from the twenty-seven yard line, Cullen called the play: the hook pattern. He told Jordan to run ten yards downfield and then cut in towards the center of the field. Meanwhile, Joey Gunnoe would block the defensive end, allowing Cullen a chance to step into the pass and make a strong throw. Tay Anderson would run deep down the far sideline as a decoy for Jordan.

As Cullen snapped the ball, Joey missed the block on the defensive end. Cullen felt the hot breath of the boorish defensive lineman charging after him. Downfield, Jordan made the cut at the thirty-six yard line and turned, arms extended back to the quarterback.

The Tech defensive lineman hit. Cullen threw the ball at the feet of Joey Gunnoe—incomplete. The pain from the hit struck. Nausea climbed his throat. As he rolled onto his back, the muscles in his ribs contracted and welled up with pain. Coughing and wheezing, he was helped up by Joey.

Jordan trotted into the backfield after several seconds, refusing eye contact with Cullen.

"Sorry, Jordan, I got rushed—"

"Save it, Brewer. I would've had a touchdown if you would've done your job."

Cullen glared at Jordan, forcing his brain to prepare for the next play. Since the hook play worked well on first down, Cullen called it again. This time, however, Joey would run the pattern and Jordan would block.

"They're going to expect me to look for Jordan on second down and long, so let's surprise them," Cullen said.

The rest of the offensive unit dropped their chins in agreement.

Cullen came to the line of scrimmage. West Virginia Tech stayed in a zone defense, so the linebackers would leave the middle of the field open. "Perfect," Cullen said, eliciting a soft laugh from center Andre Gibson.

Cullen retreated to the backfield to throw. From the corner of his eye, he watched Jordan run to the sidelines, right in front of Coach Miles. His arms were upright and flailing in the air as Jordan allowed the cornerback to run at full speed into Cullen.

The collision rocked Cullen. He fell back hard onto the ground, the back of his head slamming into the turf. The football, fortunately, sailed out of bounds. The full weight of the collision stole the air from Cullen's lungs and he gasped violently. His entire torso burned with blinding pain. Tears formed in his eyes. For a moment, he thought his ribs were broken.

As Jordan came back into the backfield again, he crossed over Cullen, driving the spikes of his cleats into the calf muscle of the Tech defender. The player yelped in pain.

"That's my quarterback, you prick. If you're gonna hit him, make a clean hit."

Incensed, Cullen wanted nothing more than to rip the toes from his friend's foot, but he remained in too much pain to move. The referee came over and signaled a timeout as Coach Miles ran onto the field.

Cullen managed to sit upright, looking for Jordan.

"Where is he? Where the hell is he?" Cullen demanded. "He let me get hit on purpose. I swear, I'll make sure he never does that again."

"Relax, relax," Coach Miles said, patting Cullen lightly on the shoulder.

While Coach Miles tended to Cullen, the fans began screaming.

Cullen leaned between the legs of his teammates, which resembled thick, round tree trunks, straining to see the sidelines. Jordan Hancel stood in front of the West Virginia Tech bench. Jordan spat toward the West Virginia Tech players standing on the sidelines, then slammed a navy blue Tech helmet into the ground.

Cullen closed his eyes, breathing shallowly from pain and nausea. There might still be time on the clock, but he knew this game was over.

twenty eight

SERENA SAW CULLEN TAKE A DEEP BREATH and wince, his hand on his ribs. She bit her lip.

"I heard about the game on Saturday."

Cullen couldn't help but smile faintly in return. He scoffed. "Yep, not one of the better days in the history of Clear River football."

"It sounds to me like Jordan might be the one who is history."

"It's Monday," he replied. "Do we have to start off the week discussing this?"

"I just thought..."

"We'll see," Cullen said, nearly cutting her off. "We're supposed to have a team meeting this afternoon. Apparently, Dr. Burcham had a meeting with Coach Miles on Sunday afternoon. This should be a great start to the week. I imagine we'll all be running laps until we collapse."

"I bet you read about the president's meeting with Coach Miles in the sports section of the newspaper," Serena said, leaning sideways and looking up at Cullen. She smirked with satisfaction.

Cullen couldn't help but smile faintly in return.

Serena and Cullen weaved in between and around several of the main buildings on campus, including the college Fine Arts Building. The late afternoon sun, with its dull orange hue, descended behind the middle of campus. The rays cast a slight shadow over Serena, sharpening the features of her hourglass figure.

Cullen shook his head to clear it. His mind was on the upcoming team meeting, the result of the Saturday game two days earlier against

West Virginia Tech, the possible suspension of Jordan Hancel, and what would become of the remainder of the season. Even the name *Dane Antonelli* crossed Cullen's mind for a fleeting moment.

"What do you know about Bambuterol?" Serena asked as Cullen trailed behind her. Without missing a beat, Serena pressed Cullen again. "I'm not sure what Bambuterol is or does, but I thought you might know."

She watched Cullen remove a crumpled piece of newspaper and unfold it quickly. Not breaking stride, he shoved the paper at Serena.

She nearly fumbled the exchange.

"I am not saying another word to you until you explain why you put the story of my attack on the front page of *The Record*."

"Your attack was not the main focus of the story," Serena said. "When I called the state police detachment in Buckhannon looking for the name of your attacker, the officer there told me that you decided against pressing charges."

Cullen raked fingers through his hair. "I wanted to put the whole attack behind me. I didn't know the guy or why he decided to attack me, but by pressing charges, I would have to go to Buckhannon and make a statement. There would likely be a hearing, and I need to be here." He tried to keep the annoyance out of his voice. "I just want to focus on football and graduating."

"But—"

"Also," Cullen continued, "I am the student body president. If I don't show resilience in the face of everything that has happened, our student body may lose hope in the school. I don't want to see that happen."

"That's admirable," Serena said, her voice firm to avoid further interruption. "But you realize the person you let walk away might have been the same person who accosted me in the newsroom hallway."

Cullen looked away. Both of them dodged a car crossing North Brent Street. The truck, packed tightly with several students, honked its displeasure.

"It's okay. There is no proof that the two incidents are related anyway. It's just something to remember."

Serena faced Cullen. "Who is Damon Jarousky?"

"I have no clue," Cullen said flatly. Then the name registered with him. He was the man accused of attacking him. Serena surely already knew that. "I told you, I am not going to press charges."

"The enrollment office has no record of him attending school here."

Cullen scratched his nose. For the first time since the attack, he could touch it without inciting pain. In fact, the swelling over his face had subsided. Unfortunately, the pain in his ribs and chest hadn't gone away.

"Weren't you asking me something about bamberol?"

"That's bam-bu-ter-ol," Serena said, pronouncing each syllable in the word carefully.

Cullen made a face. "What is so important about it?"

"My friend at *The Charleston Gazette* told me that her sources inside the state medical examiner's office told her that traces of Bambuterol, along with Creatine, were found in some plastic bags taken from Dane's abandoned car."

Cullen's face tightened. "Creatine is a nutritional supplement. The body naturally produces it, but you can take it as a supplement to supply more energy to your muscles. Some of the guys on the team take it to gain muscle mass."

Cullen paused. "I thought I told you I'm no longer interested in the Dane Antonelli investigation."

"I heard what you said clearly," Serena replied with slight agitation. "You are now a source for me, and I figured your knowledge of these topics could help me."

Cullen shot Serena a tense sideways glance. "Let's make a deal then."

Serena slowed her walk. "A deal?"

"Yes, a deal. I will be your source if you agree never to publish another story about me in *The Record*." He smiled. "Unless it deals with something good I did playing football."

They stopped walking. Cullen extended a hand and they shook.

Serena's phone rang. She reached into the pocket of her jeans and removed the cell phone.

Cullen raised his eyebrows and crossed his arms. "Maybe this is the answer to your question?"

Serena shook her head. "Hello?" After listening for a moment, her face turned hard. "I've been busy, Matt."

Cullen stood up a little taller and scrunched his face. Serena held the phone away. "Can you give me just a minute? I still want to find out what you know about Bambuterol."

Serena stepped away from Cullen and repositioned the phone to her ear. "Matt?"

"Who are you talking to?" Matt asked, this time raising his voice slightly.

"I am talking to Cullen. Not that it's any of your business."

"I know Cullen," Matt said. "He was recruited as a freshman to play quarterback behind me for the Cougars. Jordan Hancel came into the football program with him. We were supposed to be the three recruits that would restore the football program to glory at Clear River College." He paused. "All of that happened before you and I met, though."

Serena lowered the phone for a moment, her curiosity piqued.

Cullen stood back, kicking the air several times with his right foot, looking bored.

"What are you doing spending time with him?" Matt asked.

"Why do you care?" Serena asked. "Since we are no longer dating and you are going to school at Bowling Green, it's really inconsequential who I talk to and when."

"Had I practiced better as a freshman and sophomore, I would be the starting quarterback for the Clear River Cougars," Matt said. "Besides, Coach Miles always liked Cullen better for some reason."

"Aren't we bitter?" Serena asked with a slight bit of mockery in her voice.

"I moved on from that," Matt said.

Something about the way he said those words made Serena uneasy.

"The good part about being a two-sport athlete is that someone will recruit you to play at least one sport. Now I'm playing baseball at Bowling Green and I'm happy. What I miss is you."

Serena rolled her eyes. "Please, Matt. The whole time you were supposed to be with me, you were gallivanting around with that bimbo cheerleader from Charleston who cheered for Wesleyan. So let's just stop revising history to suit your purposes."

"I've been reading about what's going on at Clear River. Sounds like a real problem. That's tough to hear about that Dane kid."

"The problem will be resolved." Serena hoped what she'd just said would be proven true, and that she could be a part of the solution.

"I'm sure you're still playing investigative detective. Did you recruit Cullen to be your sidekick? How sweet. You've certainly come a long way since flunking out of Journalism 101 and then being assigned to write about the cafeteria menus and dorm checkout procedures during your first semester as a student reporter." Matt chuckled.

Serena imagined his defined Adam's apple bobbing up and down with each laugh. She seethed with anger. "This conversation is over!"

"When can I see you again?"

"Oh, never sounds good."

"Don't hang up on me!" Matt commanded.

"Goodbye, Matt."

As Serena pulled the phone away, she noticed Cullen walking to the library with both hands stuffed in his pockets.

Matt hollered her name.

Serena drew the receiver slowly back to her ear. "What?"

"Bambuterol," he said. "You wanted to know about Bambuterol. It's a steroid. Athletes are not allowed to use it—it's on the NCAA list of banned performance- enhancing drugs."

twenty nine

SERENA PULLED CULLEN BY THE ARM, leading him to Smith Library. "You walk fast."

"Call it the quarterback scramble." Cullen flashed a pearly-white smile. "Everything go okay with your phone call?"

Serena panted, trying to catch her breath and speak at the same time. "Yes, just dealing with a mistake from the past."

"I didn't think Serena Johnson made mistakes," Cullen said playfully.

"Very funny." Her eyes brightened. "Matt the Mistake. That has a good sound to it."

"Matt who?"

"Carmichael," she muttered, slightly embarrassed.

"He's an arrogant jerk," Cullen said. "Did you date him?"

"Unfortunately, yes."

Cullen frowned. "I never saw much of him after the beginning of my sophomore year. He and I battled for the starting quarterback position."

Serena wiped sweat from her forehead. "Matt told me that he plays baseball at Bowling Green now."

"Good for him."

"We need to research Bambuterol and find out what this drug is and what it does."

Cullen shortened his stride behind Serena, careful not to step on her as they moved through campus.

"Are you and Matt Carmichael together?"

"That's not important right now," she replied, sharply.

"Fine. Just asking."

Cullen watched her downcast eyes lock onto the ground and a furtive glance dance across her face. "It's a long story. Maybe sometime I'll tell you."

He nodded. "I'd love to hear it."

Serena arched her head back. "Bambuterol is a steroid."

Cullen blinked, dropped his jaw and settled an uneasy stare on Serena. "Is that why you answered the phone?"

"No," she said, pushing a clump of hair behind her shoulder. "Matt told me about it."

"How would he know?" Cullen asked.

"I don't know. I didn't talk to the creep long enough to find out."

Serena burst through the exterior door into the computer area of the library. "Get on a computer and start looking for information about Bambuterol. I'll be right back."

"Yes, ma'am," Cullen replied mockingly, giving her a half-hearted military salute. He chuckled dryly at the gesture.

Serena pulled away.

"Where you going anyway?"

She turned back to him. "The fifth floor, medical research section."

Cullen found an open computer, sandwiched between a student slumping over the keyboard at one terminal while another student snored quietly at the other. Cullen decided the best place to start looking would be the NCAA website. Perhaps the organization governing college athletics would have information about Bambuterol on their site, especially if student athletes were forbidden from using it.

Typing in the information, Cullen located the NCAA homepage and dragged the mouse over the section headings "Rules Compliance" and the menu screen "Safety." Once he clicked on the drop-down menu, he found a section of by-laws on performance- enhancing substances.

Not surprisingly, Bambuterol was listed, along with street drugs, stimulants, anabolic agents, and diuretics and other masking agents. Cullen scrolled down the page, looking closely at the classifications for specific stimulants. He discovered Bambuterol listed as a "Beta-2 Agonist."

A heavy book dropped on the desk from above. "Got it! Bambuterol."

Serena had found a medical encyclopedia with a section on performance- enhancing substances that anyone could use for enhanced weight training, weight gain, or the building of muscle mass. Cullen l ooked back at Serena, who bobbed her head forward twice, enticing Cullen to read the entry.

"I found this information on the NCAA website. Matt was right—Bambuterol is a banned substance for student athletes."

Cullen began interpreting the complex medical jargon inside the encyclopedia pages.

Bambuterol is a long acting beta-adrenoceptor agonist (LABA) used in the treatment of asthma; it also is a prodrug of terbutaline. Commercially, the AstraZeneca pharmaceutical company produces and markets Bambuterol as Bambec and Oxeol. The adverse effect profile of Bambuterol is similar to that of salbutamol, and may include fatigue, nausea, palpitations, headache, dizziness, tremors and mood changes. Administration of Bambuterol with other drugs, including pain-controlling stimulants, increases the risk of hypokalemia (decreased levels of potassium in the blood). Bambuterol acts as a cholinesterase inhibitor, and can prolong the duration of action of other drugs whose breakdown in the body depends on cholinesterase function. Bodily activity returns to normal approximately two weeks after Bambuterol is stopped. It can also enhance the healing of non-debilitating neuromuscular and tendon and ligament injuries.

Cullen leaned back and massaged his temples. "I have no idea what all of that means, but it does not sound good."

Serena reviewed the material, leaning over his shoulder. "Basically, this drug allows you to get more oxygen to your lungs and doesn't mix well with other drugs. But it can be used to help heal muscles."

He looked back at Serena, who vigorously chewed on the inside of her lip.

"I think we are getting one step closer to figuring out what is going on," Serena said.

thirty

CULLEN LEFT THE LIBRARY, walking with long strides toward Cougar Village while Serena tried to keep up.

The horseshoe-shaped road that cut away from the north end of campus had a large, lush field dotted with three dormitory buildings and a cafeteria. The buildings, spaced apart evenly, allowed the fullness of the grass to be the dominant feature. Behind the field, the toothbrush-like light towers of the football and baseball fields emerged like talons on the feet of a giant eagle.

As they approached the entrance to Cougar Village, the sudden slamming of van doors and slow grind of cable wires across the grass and pavement caught their attention. Behind the dormitories and cafeteria, several small and large box-shaped and rounded vans littered the remaining green space.

Serena took notice of the names emblazoned on the sides of the vans and trucks. Colorful letters gave prominence to news organizations such as WSAZ, WOAY, WCHS, and *The Charleston Gazette*. The area, now a flurry of activity, featured people sidestepping each other while dragging camera cables, microphones and monitors across the field and stationing the equipment away from each other. News reporters checked their watches and chatted on cell phones.

Cullen stopped walking and rested both hands on his hips. "This can't be good."

Serena squinted through the descending late-afternoon skyline. "It looks like everyone is headed for the facilities building near the football field."

Cullen sighed. "Now what?"

Serena thought for a moment that Cullen was implying she leaked the information.

As Cullen took another step closer, a frail, thin reporter dressed in a tweed suit approached him and asked for directions to the football coach's office. Cullen complied with the request while Serena stood apart, answering another telephone call.

When the man slinked away, Serena walked in front of Cullen.

The reporters and cameramen piled through the two main doors leading into the facilities building. Cullen's face looked pale and sickly. "If Bambuterol is a steroid and traces of it were found in those bags in Dane's car, then Dane could've been a user." His eyes darted back and forth as his brain worked at piecing together the information.

"That's exactly what I'm beginning to think," Serena said. "And whoever stole Dane's car knew that if the car was examined, traces of that stuff in the bags would be found. Maybe you and I were attacked by whoever is responsible because they felt we were getting too close to the truth."

Cullen looked at Serena again, his eyes ablaze with worry. "What about Dane? Do you think Bambuterol could have been involved in his death?"

"I don't know." Serena looked away for a moment. "You saw the autopsy report. We both agreed that it had been altered. Unfortunately, I lost the report."

"What?" Cullen's mouth hung open.

"Whoever grabbed me in Branstone Hall took it."

Cullen gazed up at the cirrus clouds swimming slowly overhead. "Great. That's just great."

Serena glanced down at her phone. "Look, I need to leave. I've got a meeting to go to. I'll talk to you later."

Cullen nodded and Serena skipped away behind him. He crossed the field and headed for the facilities building.

Once inside, echoing voices cascaded throughout the hallway leading to the locker room and coaches' offices. Television cameras and equipment were juxtaposed awkwardly in the narrow corridor, making Cullen feel claustrophobic as he worked his way forward.

As Cullen neared the doorway to the locker room, reporters stuck microphones and small recording devices into his face and asked questions. Cullen found the gesture off-putting and charged ahead through the blue door.

Inside, Cullen heard the hushed tones of a conversation near the back of the locker room, near the showers. Approaching slowly, he turned the corner and saw Coach Miles and Jordan standing close together, their backs to him.

Cullen spoke softly, careful not to startle them. "Coach, there's a ton of reporters in the hallway. Are they here because of our meeting today?"

Coach Miles and Jordan froze. Jordan stepped back, revealing a syringe in his hand.

thirty one

DR. BURCHAM PINCHED THE BRIDGE OF HIS NOSE with two fingers. Jack Dillon, always handsome and composed under duress, stood in the president's office with his chest extended outward. "I have notified all parties of your request for a meeting. Everyone should be here within the hour."

"Thank you, Jack," Dr. Burcham said.

Jack scribbled notes on a legal pad. He stepped away from the door for a moment, then reappeared. The president glanced up. "Sir, Tom Hancel would like a moment with you."

Dr. Burcham exhaled, slouching forward slightly. "Send him in. Please tell him to keep his comments brief. I'm in no mood for lengthy chit-chat today."

"Understood." Jack retreated into the hallway, and in a moment Tom Hancel emerged.

Unbalanced and disheveled, Tom waddled into the office with rolls of thick paper tucked under his arms. He reached the desk and dropped the papers. The weight of them rattled some of the ornate markings protruding from the polished wood frame.

Dr. Burcham opened his lips, but Tom snatched the words away. "Department of Highways blueprints for the new road."

The president leaned back into the chair, folding his arms. "This has not been run by me or the board, Tom. Until that happens, you can gather these plans and march right out the door you came through."

Tom cocked his head sideways. "Dr. Burcham, these blueprints mean the DOH is on board and has done all the preliminary work. The permits have been processed. All we need now is your approval, and then I can go to the board and we can get started."

Disgusted, Dr. Burcham pushed back the centerfold of one roll of blueprints. In the upper left corner, a suppliers list was affixed to the blueprints. Dr. Burcham held up his hand. "Hancel Cement is named as a major supplier on this project." He looked at Tom over his glasses. "You personally stand to benefit financially from this project. No wonder you're determined to see the highway widened through the campus."

Tom stared at Dr. Burcham.

"Don't you see this as a conflict of interest, Tom? You are on the Clear River College Board of Governors, and your cement company is going to profit handsomely from this road project."

Tom leaned closer to the president. "According to the state, there is no conflict of interest. Hancel Cement supplies most of the cement needed for highway construction projects in the northern part of the state. My company has a contract with them. The state has a need and we have the supplies for the job. I see nothing wrong with that."

"I'm sorry," Dr. Burcham said. "I cannot take the risk. The appearance of impropriety is too great." He pushed the blueprints away and stood up. "I need to inform the board of your involvement in the project. I don't think they will appreciate you running to Charleston behind their backs. This issue is tabled."

A faint grin slid across Tom's face. "I don't think you'll do that, Neal," he responded in a hushed voice.

Dr. Burcham glared at him. "I beg your pardon?"

Tom crossed his arms. "There is a full-blown crisis going on here at the college. There is one student dead, the student body president has been attacked, there is state medical examiner evidence that may have been tampered with, and you and this office are no closer in solving the case or cases now than when this whole mess started."

Dr. Burcham tore off his glasses and threw them on the desk. "And your son embarrassed the school at the football game Saturday night. I will not be lectured by you about conduct."

Tom's eyes remained steadily on the president.

"Your son is facing suspension for the remainder of the season. That decision is in the hands of Gary Miles, but if I were you, I would focus on that situation and not this road expansion project." Dr. Burcham jabbed the air, his words falling out so quickly they nearly garbled.

"Don't you try and change the subject," Tom said, the tension in his words reverberating his puffy cheeks. "I have been privy to everything and I am sure the board would like to know about your little conversation with Detective Parsons of the state police." He winked.

"Let me be clear: you were privy to the conversation because Cullen Brewer and your son are friends and teammates, and you are on the board," Dr. Burcham said. "Do not overinflate your importance to this college because of your place on the board."

"Let *me* be clear," Tom replied, clearing his throat. "If you do not go along with this road expansion project, then I will tell the board the information you are concealing about the Dane Antonelli case." His gray eyes narrowed. "And I will recommend they begin proceedings to remove you as president."

Dr. Burcham reared back. Nervously, the president tapped fingers against the edge of the desk. For all his bombastic blustering, could Tom execute what he threatened? Could he?

Tom shifted his weight between his feet, his resolute expression remaining hard.

"I will not be threatened or blackmailed." Dr. Burcham's hands tightened into fists. "I am the president of this college and I will always do what's in the best interest of this school and its students."

Tom laughed nervously. "Remember, you work at the discretion of the board, not the other way around. So, do we have an agreement?"

A knock at the door interrupted the conversation.

Jack wrapped his head around the inside of the door. "Serena Johnson is here, sir."

Dr. Burcham leaned around Tom. "Send her in, please."

Tom pursed his lips. "I am glad we could reach an agreement."

Serena gingerly entered the room as Tom retreated and forged past her.

The president ran both hands along his trousers and smoothed his hair. "Thank you for coming, Miss Johnson. Please have a seat."

*   *   *   *   *

Serena bypassed the visitor's chair near the desk and sat on the couch.

Dr. Burcham moved to the overstuffed armchair adjacent to the couch. Serena's knees trembled. She now sat in the office of the most powerful person on campus and she remained unsure of the nature of this meeting.

"Miss Johnson," Dr. Burcham began, spinning a coaster across the small table at the foot of the couch, "let me begin by saying that I appreciate the good work you do as a student journalist for *The Record*. I think you represent our Journalism School and Clear River College quite well. Dean Shively speaks highly of your work, as does your editor, Ben Caster." He settled into the chair and crossed both legs.

Serena wanted to respond strongly and confidently, but she couldn't muster the words.

"However, there are some college matters that need to be handled administratively. While I respect the right of our student media to pursue and investigate the news, there comes a point at which a responsible journalist must step back so an investigation can proceed."

"Are you talking about the Dane Antonelli investigation?" Serena felt the office absorb the weight of her words.

The president rose from the chair and retrieved an over-stuffed file folder from the desk. "I am," he responded, his tone more grim. "Let me be frank with you, Miss Johnson—"

"Please call me Serena...sir."

Dr. Burcham lifted his head, this time looking at her through the bottom of his glasses. "Fine then, Serena. I understand that you contacted Conley Masters about suspicions regarding the autopsy report he completed on

Dane. Why would you do that?"

Serena hated being blindsided and forced to defend herself. "I had reason to believe the report had been altered and some of the information falsified." She stared at the floor. From the corner of one eye, she saw the president studying her.

"And how did you come across a copy of the report?"

Serena twiddled her fingers nervously.

"Did you take it?

Serena sniffed. "No. I did not take it."

"Then how did you get it?"

Serena felt her mind lock like a steel trap. Dr. Burcham wanted her to reveal her source. She remembered Tracy talking about the importance of sources and how a good reporter needs sources to get information, especially secret information that a reporter could not access independently.

"Serena, I know that Tracy Pritt from *The Charleston Gazette* sent you the information."

Serena was stunned. She found it difficult to breathe.

"I have spoken to Don Pettigrew, the managing editor of the paper. Tracy Pritt had been covering this investigation in Charleston. Miss Pritt admitted to sending you the autopsy report. Mr. Pettigrew has placed Miss Pritt on administrative leave."

Serena didn't know whether to rise up and punch the president or cry. Tracy had been her mentor, encouraging her to pursue her passion of becoming an excellent investigative reporter. Now Tracy was suffering the consequences.

Tears of frustration welled up inside the corners of her eyes. She couldn't make the situation any better.

The president sat closer to her, a satisfied smirk on his face. "I also spoke with Dean Shively this morning."

The mention of his name made every muscle in her body tense.

"He and I agree that you will be suspended from your reporter duties for the remainder of the fall semester. The dean will meet with you at the beginning of the spring term to determine whether or not you may return to *The Record* as a reporter. This decision does not inhibit your progress towards graduation."

A long moment passed in which the only sound was the rhythmic ticking of the wall clock behind Serena.

"Serena," Dr. Burcham said in a tone tinged with disappointment and sympathy, "if there is anything else that you need to say about this situation, I suggest you speak up now. If you have an accomplice working with you, I need to know the name because if I find out more information later, your problems might worsen."

"I have nothing more to say," Serena replied, the words falling out of her mouth as if she had heaved them with great strain.

"Good. Please see yourself out."

Serena stood, nearly catching the seam of her jeans between the folds in the couch. She lowered her head and left, although she felt the president glaring through her as she disappeared.

Dr. Burcham tucked the file folder under one arm, moved around the desk to the telephone, picked up the receiver, and checked the time.

An energized voice answered on the other end of the phone. "President Burcham's office."

"Jack."

"Yes, sir?"

Dr. Burcham looked out the window at the students traversing the campus below.

"Find Cullen Brewer and Jordan Hancel and send them to me. Also, notify the board that we need to meet soon. The matter is urgent." He stepped back. Another television news van cut through campus heading for Cougar Village.

"And find out what's going on over at Cougar Village."

thirty two

JORDAN SQUEEZED THE SYRINGE TIGHTLY. Coach Miles looked away. The small plastic tube nearly disappeared inside his collapsed hand.

"Brewer, Hancel and I are talking. The team meeting has not started yet, and yes, I am aware of the reporters in the hallway!"

Jordan, his jawline clenched, was covered in sweat as he took a step back in retreat. Cullen trained his eyes to slowly look back and forth at both men. Jordan looked terrible—eyes gaunt and skin sagging, pasty and white. Both legs, openly exposed under loose-fitting boxer briefs, featured bloated calf muscles that appeared ready to burst.

Jordan dropped his head and rested both hands on his hips.

Cullen felt his mouth drop. The inside bend of Jordan's arm was littered with small red welts, and the veins climbing and scattering across his arms were a brutish, dull purple.

"Get out of here, Cullen. This matter does not concern you!"

The carotid arteries bulging from Coach Miles' neck increased the wave of uneasiness spreading over Cullen.

Jordan peered at him from the wall, a look of unhealthy aggravation painted on his face.

"Coach, what's going on with that syringe? And Jordan, what are the red marks on your arms?"

Jordan took a step closer. "The only thing that is keeping me from further ripping your face to shreds is the fact that Coach is here. My season is over, and it's all because you couldn't complete two passes. So don't you act concerned, you high and mighty—"

"That's enough," Coach Miles growled, stepping between Cullen and Jordan. He tapped Jordan on the breastbone with two fingers. "The reason you are being suspended has everything to do with you and this needle, and less to do with Cullen. You spitting on the West Virginia Tech bench has nearly ruined the season for us. Now you need to leave. I don't allow players no longer associated with the team to be in the locker room."

"Season's over anyway, Coach," Jordan said. "We will never win the conference title now. My senior season is over, and it's because of that prick over there!" He pointed at Cullen.

"Get dressed and get ready for the meeting, Hancel. Make no mistake, our talk is far from over."

Jordan walked around Coach Miles. He planted a shoulder into Cullen, attempting to nudge him aside with the force of the impact. Instead, Cullen grabbed Jordan by the arm, swung him around, and fired a fist that crushed the base of his nose.

Jordan shouted an inaudible expletive as he fell to one knee.

"You seem to get plenty of nosebleeds these days, so there's another one."

Coach Miles ran between them.

Cullen shrugged away from Coach Miles's intervention. He reached down, pulled Jordan up by the shoulders and slammed him against the wall.

Blood oozed from the stricken nose, which changed colors from peach to magenta, like a chameleon being chased by a predator. Jordan attempted to wipe away the blood with his arm, but Cullen pinned the arm against his chest.

"Enough! That's enough!" Coach Miles shouted.

The locker room began filling up with players. Some of them rushed to the rear of the room to catch a glimpse of the unfolding fight.

Coach Miles wedged two hands between Cullen and Jordan.

Cullen pressed Jordan against the wall with more force.

Jordan began coughing—a wet, racking hack that made his body go slightly limp.

"What's the needle for, Jordan, huh?" Cullen demanded. The blood emanating from the busted nose trickled between the gaps in Cullen's fingers.

"It must be something. What's in it? Bambuterol? Is that what has you acting like a fool?" Cullen temporarily released his hold on Jordan. He considered what Serena had told him about Bambuterol. Although the name seemed like a vocabulary word from a foreign language, it resonated. If the drug was a performance-enhancing steroid, then it could be the reason Jordan healed from the high ankle sprain so quickly. Cullen dismissed the thought. Jordan would never take a steroid. Right?

Coach Miles used the moment to pull Cullen off Jordan. By now, a chorus of excitement ran through the locker room as teammates, some encouraging more fighting while others shouted for it to stop, huddled around the men.

Once separated, Coach Miles pushed Cullen back. "What did you say about Bambuterol? Do you know what that is? What that can do to a player?"

Cullen crinkled his nose.

Coach Miles dropped his head slowly. "You think Hancel is taking steroids, and that I know about it? Or at least caught him using?" He moved closer to Cullen.

The locker room grew silent. Jordan disappeared into the crowd of players.

"I do not, nor will I, support players using drugs of any kind on this team. You understand me, son?"

Cullen kept breathing deeply, watching the coach. Coach Miles liked to gauge reactions. Cullen did not flinch.

"I'd expect this type of nonsense from a freshman, but not from my senior starting quarterback. Pathetic, Brewer, absolutely pathetic. Now get away from me before I puke in your face."

Cullen gave one long, intense stare at the coach and stepped aside.

Coach Miles wiped away sweat and headed past the players. "I want everyone to sit down and not say a word until I get back. I especially do not want to hear a word from Brewer or Hancel about what happened here."

*   *   *   *   *

Coach Miles flung open the locker room door and stepped into the hallway. Microphones of various shapes and sizes appeared in front of him, blocking the corridor walkway.

Pockets of bright, phosphorescent white light blinded him; Coach Miles attempted to shield the light with one hand.

"Coach Miles, can you tell us about the future of Jordan Hancel and if your team will be able to compete for a WVIAC championship without him?" A tall, baby-faced reporter waited for a response.

When Coach Miles said nothing, another reporter shouted from the back of the room: "Coach, is there any connection between the attack on Cullen Brewer and the death of Dane Antonelli?"

Coach Miles scowled as the questions continued. Reporters talked over each other, and understanding the meaning of each question became nearly impossible.

The coach exhaled and took a step forward. Behind him, the locker room grew quiet.

"Folks, I have coached football for a long time. Once in a while, you coach a team that's special. When you coach that team, you find they possess an intangible that many other teams don't have, and that's a champion's heart. A team that possesses a champion's heart will rise above the negative and prove themselves at play. That's what we have with this group of Clear River Cougars. This season has been trying for everyone, and yet we still have a chance to have a winning year. That desire, those intangibles, cannot be taught. Thank you."

Coach Miles gave a faint wave and went back into the locker room. The room seemed smaller when he returned. The team, now seated, remained silent. Cullen stood up. Jordan, with wads of toilet paper inserted in each nostril, shifted uncomfortably. Coach Miles relaxed and settled in front of the room. Dr. Burcham stepped out of the shadows in the back and faced the team.

thirty three

"DON'T TALK TO ME." Cullen waved a hand dismissively at Jordan. "It's not my fault that it's the middle of October, the season is half-over and you're suspended for the remainder of the season."

Jordan tapped a bloodied gauze bandage against his nose as they left the facilities building.

Cullen glanced back at Jordan. "My father ruined his life and my mother's life because of drugs. I can't believe you! How many times did we talk about this growing up? My God, Jordan, you were at my house when he would come home, so drunk and out of it on pills that all he wanted to do was fight with me and her!"

Jordan appeared much more maligned and melancholy than earlier. He trailed behind Cullen, walking listlessly. From a distance, news reporters shouted questions at him, but he ignored them.

Dressed in a blue tee-shirt and white nylon shorts, Cullen felt the weight of the day grinding against his body. Fortunately, his ribs were no longer sore and the facial swelling had lessened.

"What do I tell my dad, Cullen? He's going to be so pissed. He loves me being a football player—a member of the Cougars. If I can't play football, what do I do?"

"You'll figure it out." Cullen didn't break stride. "Go to class, focus on school. That is, if Dr. Burcham doesn't suspend you or throw you out of school. I think his coming into the locker room was a warning. It meant he stood behind Coach."

Jordan ran forward and grabbed Cullen.

Cullen whipped around, his right fist clenched. "Did you not get enough earlier?" Jordan held up two open palms. "No, I don't want to fight you. Do you seriously think Burcham will give me the boot?" Jordan looked away, his deep-set eyes heavy and fatigued. "He can't do that, can he?"

Cullen felt a moment of sympathy for Jordan, but then the feeling subsided. He unclenched his fist. "You'll figure it out." He moved closer to Jordan. "Are you using or not?"

The question hovered around them both for a moment. Jordan looked down, then over Cullen. He slouched slightly. His blue shorts, slightly torn at the thigh, hung low on his narrow waist.

Cullen wondered if this might be the other side of Bambuterol or any type of steroids—the the side that comes after the drug sends people into a fit of rage.

"I am not using steroids or any drugs like that."

Cullen grimaced and shook hid head. "I don't believe you. How did your ankle heal so quickly?"

Jordan seemed puzzled by the question. "I healed the ankle by rehabbing it day and night. I told you I wanted to get healthy quickly so that I could play again and we could win a conference title."

"How much Bambuterol have you taken?"

Jordan folded his arms. "What in God's name is Bambuterol?"

"I think you know," Cullen replied.

A chunky, well-dressed female reporter carrying a microphone walked past them. Cullen paused as she passed, then continued. "It's a steroid," he hissed. "Bambuterol is banned for student-athlete use by the NCAA. They consider it a performance-enhancing drug."

Jordan guffawed. "It sounds like you and your girlfriend Serena have been spending too much time in a science lab, coming up with crazy theories and trying to pin them on somebody. Well, that somebody is not me!"

"I don't believe you. You have always been brash, but spitting on the Tech coaches and players? That's not you. Not to mention, you failed to block that blitzing Tech defender and I got crushed. I could have had my ribs broken, and all you did was blame me for the incomplete pass."

Jordan ran his tongue across dry lips. "For the last time, I am not taking drugs. I am not taking steroids or Bambuterol or anything else."

"Not taking drugs?" Cullen stomped his foot. "I saw you taking a syringe full of liquid and jamming it into your body. I'd call that using drugs."

Jordan stepped closer to Cullen, resting a hand lightly on his chest.

"It's not drugs. It's something for pain and something to help the ligaments and tendons in my ankle heal faster."

The rush of frustration and adrenaline had Cullen ready to pounce, but he resisted. "Tell me what you're taking."

"I don't know the name exactly."

"That's great, Jordan. Just great! You know what the drug does, or you think you know what it does, but you can't even name it. You're unbelievable." Cullen clamped his jaw tightly shut and pointed a finger directly at Jordan. "There's always a price to pay for drug use. Just ask me, or my dad. Or my mother, if she was still here!"

He turned away from Jordan and let the silence pool around them. He hesitated, and looked at Jordan again. "The police found traces of Bambuterol in the bags from Dane's car. The drug might have been the reason he died in that dorm stairwell at the beginning of the year."

The statement softened Jordan and his defiant expression. "Who told you that?"

"Serena did. She got the information from a reporter in Charleston."

Jordan, mouth slightly agape, let a wisp of air pass through his teeth. "God. Cullen, we knew him. You knew him better than anyone. For a while, I was jealous because you invited him to go bowling with us and those were activities we always did together. Then I realized that he was a pretty good guy and you were trying to mentor him."

After a moment of tense silence, Jordan rubbed the stubble on his chin. "Brewer, I am more angry at you now than I was before."

The statement rattled Cullen slightly. "Why?"

"Just because Dane might have been using and because he might have died from that drug doesn't mean that I have been using or am using right now."

"That's a lie! I saw you! What do you expect me to think? The Jordan Hancel I know would never have intentionally let me get hit during a game or spit at an opponent. I'm not even sure I know who you are anymore."

Cullen studied Jordan for a reaction. Instead, Jordan walked past Cullen and headed for the main part of campus.

"So that's it? You're going to just walk away and not talk about this?"

Jordan stopped and tugged his sagging shorts over his hips. He pivoted enough that Cullen could hear his voice. "What I am tired of is your self-righteous attitude that condemns anybody who thinks, acts, or does anything you don't like. What *you* have become is really pathetic."

Bulging veins protruded from Jordan's neck, face, and arms. The corners of his mouth foamed with spit as he became more enraged. "You are my best friend, Brewer. I always stood by you. On the field, I stood by you. I stood by you when your drunken daddy beat you silly with anything he could get his hands on; I have stood by you through everything here at school. Now, you're turning your back on me by accusing me of being a drug user. Some friend you are!" Jordan threw his hands down dismissively at Cullen, turned, and walked away.

After several steps, Jordan collapsed on the sidewalk.

thirty four

"WOULD YOU LET GO OF ME! I slipped, that's all. It happens," Jordan said. "That wasn't a slip," Cullen said. "You collapsed. The entire weight of your body hit the ground."

"I am not talking about this with you!" Jordan shoved Cullen's hands off him.

Cullen gripped Jordan tightly around the waist as Jordan placed a low-slung, flimsy arm over Cullen's shoulder.

Small clusters of students approached them. Jordan stared tiredly into their faces while Cullen marched through the groups.

"We are fine, everybody. Jordan here slipped and fell but he's going to be okay."

With each word recited, Cullen squeezed harder.

Jordan began to take longer, more absorbed steps, putting more weight into his movements, as the two made their way through campus.

Cullen wanted to take Jordan to the student center, where cold drinks and comfortable chairs might defuse the tense situation. Students continued asking questions and talking among themselves while others used their phones to take pictures of Cullen dragging Jordan across campus.

The view of campus became sharper. The late afternoon autumn sun again bathed the buildings and sidewalks in a faint tangerine glow that softened the hues of everyone walking under it. From a distance, Cullen saw the tree that the Clear River Student Government Association had planted for Dane Antonelli. The tiny tree, branches leafless and bearing the burden of the ropes and weights holding it into the ground, stood alone in the middle of a field of green grass.

"What is she doing here?" Jordan asked.

Serena, hair pulled back in a pony-tail, moved through the clumps of students. Her eyes radiated a quiet intensity that caught Cullen by surprise.

Jordan raised and extended a rigid finger, which slightly grazed Cullen's ear.

"She got you started on this garbage about Bambuterol and drug use, didn't she?"

A lump formed in Cullen's throat.

Serena stopped and flashed Cullen a disapproving glance. She had asked Cullen to stay quiet for now about Bambuterol, and he hadn't kept his promise.

"Well, you can stop gawking at me," Jordan said, "because I am not using drugs. Not Bambuterol or anything else you two can dream up."

Serena looked behind Cullen and Jordan. "I'm not here to see either one of you, believe it or not. Crystal called me on her way back from Biology. She said there were news reporters back here, and that Coach Miles had a meeting with the football team." She appeared anxious, tapping a small notepad against her wrist and looking side to side. "Crystal also said that there were surveyors looking at the empty recreation field. Did you see anyone over there?"

Cullen looked around. "No." He loosened his grip on Jordan.

Jordan retracted his arm and stood up straight. Both arms and knees were littered with wide gashes, as fresh streams of blood had clotted at the surface since the fall. He leveled a gaze on Serena. "Are you here to spy on the maintenance men too?"

Serena looked at Cullen instead. "Last year, a backhoe dug a hole near the recreation field, but the hole was relatively small and contained. Then the students were discouraged from using the field. I thought I could find out more information by coming over here and talking with the construction crew."

She paused and cocked her head. "May I have your permission to continue my investigation, Jordan?"

Jordan shook his head and rolled his eyes. "Whatever."

Cullen let the words form in his mouth. "I know student organizations have asked the student government office to use the field for fall and spring recruitment purposes, but we get stonewalled by the president's office when we ask for permission. I'm glad you are looking for answers."

"It doesn't really matter, though," Serena said, tucking a loose strand of hair over her ear. "I'm no longer on the newspaper reporting team, so I'm operating only as a concerned student."

Cullen flinched. "What are you talking about?"

"Dr. Burcham suspended me." Serena's eyes became misty. "Someone told him about me getting a copy of the Antonelli autopsy report."

She looked at Cullen as deep lines etched across his face and the dimples near his mouth sank into the skin. "Go on."

"He called me into his office this morning. I had to tell the truth. I had a feeling I would be in more trouble if I lied. I still don't understand it. He even knew that Tracy Pritt at *The Gazette* sent me the report. I feel like I let her down. The paper suspended her as well."

Cullen waved awkwardly at the air, stopping Serena. "The state police detective. Serena, he must have told Burcham." He leaned closer. "Remember, he responded to the scene on Route 33 when Dane's car was found abandoned? He also investigated my attack. He has to be the one that said something. I'm sure in piecing together the entire investigation, he went back to the beginning and checked with the medical examiner in Charleston."

Serena allowed herself a faint smile. "Now *you* sound like the investigative reporter."

Cullen glared at Serena. "You're not going to stop investigating what happened to Dane, are you? Remember, you and I were both attacked over this. "

Serena squinted. A look of disbelief washed over her face. "Wait a minute, Cullen. Wasn't it you who told me to leave the matter alone and that you didn't want to be involved? Now, you want me to continue. This is quite a change."

"We might have another story to investigate." The thought of Jordan using steroids and Coach Miles's knowledge of it made Cullen seethe. The muscles in his neck and face grew tense.

Cullen swallowed, and cut a sharp look at Jordan. He wanted to tell Serena about the syringe, but he held back.

Serena studied him. Her mouth twitched, almost as an instinctive sign that she knew Cullen might be keeping something from her.

"I'm starting to believe that everything that has happened so far this semester is connected," she said. Cullen cut another quick glance at Jordan, who folded his arms and looked bored.

"Definitely connected," Cullen added.

Serena stepped closer to Cullen. Her eyes raked over his body, making Cullen feel slightly uncomfortable. And slightly something else. Interested? He couldn't help but suck in his gut and stand a little straighter.

Serena refocused. "I'm going to find those workers before they leave. If I find out anything..." she paused, lowered a disparaging look at Jordan, and then refocused on Cullen. "If I find out anything, I'll let you know."

Cullen appeared relieved. "Thank you. In the meantime, I need to get Jordan out of here and get ready for our game next week against Glenville."

*   *   *   *   *

Serena had already trotted away as Cullen spoke; the words hung in the air. The soft, golden autumn light cascading across campus blurred the silhouettes of Cullen and Jordan as Serena looked behind her.

The construction workers dragged large black crates from a truck parked near the field. One man, thin with sharp shoulders and a narrow face, pointed at the other two men. Both of them nodded and continued dragging the crates.

Serena approached them cautiously. The group leader dismounted a small, burnt-orange camera from a sagging tripod.

"I am so sorry," Serena said. "I didn't realize this part of campus was closed for construction."

"It's not closed." The man's voice was gruff, as if he had to force the words out of his mouth. "We're just taking some pictures."

"Pictures of what?"

The man appeared annoyed by the question. "Survey work. For the four-lane highway that's going to run through this part of campus."

thirty five

CULLEN FLOPPED ONTO THE DESK CHAIR in his dormitory room. The walk back to Cougar Village had been silent for him and Jordan. Cullen fully expected him to make disparaging remarks about Serena or claim that she and Cullen were exaggerating a situation that wasn't real. However, Jordan didn't even look at Cullen before he took the back entrance into the hall.

Cullen leaned back in the chair and dropped his arms, searching for his backpack. Normally, the Prussian blue cinderblock room remained cool and quiet, but tonight the room seemed warm and exceedingly small. The foldout bed jutting outward from the wall remained littered with papers, folders, and bed sheets that hadn't been tucked or straightened in weeks.

Hanging on the corner of the desk was the golden locket, the one that held the picture of his mother. Cullen grabbed the locket, squeezed it tightly in his palm, and held it near his heart for a few seconds. His eyes became glassy with tears.

His mother had been so lively and vibrant before she was diagnosed with cancer. Cullen stared for a moment at her picture, looking down at the name *Juanita Brewer* etched into the face of the locket. She looked so elegant, with high-planed cheeks and wide eyes and light curly brown hair. Juanita always taught Cullen to look for the positive aspects of any bad situation, and she served as a buffer between Cullen and his dad. For some reason, his mother had loved his father, despite his incessant drinking and fits of rage. Juanita reminded Cullen that Wendell provided the necessities for their family and that he really loved them both, he just had an odd way of showing it. The thought of Wendell's *love* now made Cullen want to vomit.

Setting the locket aside, Cullen reached into his backpack and removed an American Literature anthology, a plastic sandwich bag, two pens, and several multi-colored file folders. Then he removed three cheese sticks—large, rectangular tangerine-colored sticks that made his mouth water.

He jammed one into his mouth and opened each folder. One folder contained a set of offensive plays for the next football game against Glenville State. The other folder contained the assignment sheet for an American Literature essay on the role of Pearl in Nathaniel Hawthorne's *The Scarlet Letter*, and the final three folders contained student government forms that required his signature.

Cullen decided to proceed with the essay first. Opening up the textbook, he scribbled some notes about Pearl, the bastard daughter of Hester Prynne, and tried to analyze her character. He jotted notes as his mind worked. *Pearl: infantile and petulant. Jordan: narcissistic and callous.* Cullen leaned back and drew a line through Jordan's name. He hadn't intended to focus on Jordan, although Jordan seemed as real in his subconscious as Pearl did within the pages of the book. Cullen moved closer to the page. He knew Pearl well.

As the daughter of Hester Prynne and Arthur Dimmesdale, she was jaded. Her hate manifested in a refusal to connect with others. She created a self-fulfilling isolation from everyone except the one person who affected her life through a similarly drastic lack of empathy—Hester.

As ideas crossed his mind, Cullen kept scribbling, nearly tearing small holes in the paper as he wrote.

Cullen grinned. "I have my thesis statement," he said, expecting someone to congratulate him.

A door lock clicked from a room down the hallway, followed by the shuffling of feet past his room.

Cullen continued writing. Trying to manage time effectively, he wrote feverishly, focusing on printing words on paper regardless of their relevance to the thesis. The more he wrote, the more exhausted he became.

A loud rattle at the door jolted Cullen awake. He rose from the desk, his arms and hand heavy. He checked the alarm clock near the bed. The time read 2:18 a.m. Cullen had been asleep for nearly six hours.

The rattle evolved into several pounding vibrations, spaced seconds apart. Cullen stood up; he crinkled his nose at the stale stench that wafted from his shirt. Scanning the disheveled dorm room, he couldn't find a clean shirt, so he removed the old one and strode to the door.

"Just a second," Cullen announced as the pounding got louder.

Wiping the corners of his eyes with two fingers, Cullen pulled back the door.

Jordan fell onto the floor, sprawling at Cullen's feet and shivering violently.

thirty six

"JORDAN. WHAT IS WRONG WITH YOU?" Jordan didn't respond. Instead, he rolled to one side and drew his knees against his chest. A puddle of perspiration formed on the carpet as Jordan shifted back and forth.

Cullen stepped over him and looked into the hallway. The late-night silence on the floor was broken only by the slight moaning emanating from Jordan.

Cullen stepped back inside the room and dropped to one knee. He grabbed Jordan by both arms and dragged him into the room. Jordan groaned louder—a slow, throaty rumble that made Cullen shiver. As Jordan rocked side to side on the floor, still clutching both legs, Cullen shut the door behind him. He leaned an ear to the door to make sure the incident hadn't drawn the suspicions of anyone else.

Jordan scratched his legs and arms, digging into the skin with such force that small, pea-sized welts on the skin surface punctured and began bleeding. One trickle of blood ran down the right leg onto the carpet. Cullen stepped behind Jordan again, looking for a towel to staunch the bleeding.

"Stop it!" Jordan commanded. "I'm fine. Quit fussing over me like I'm some helpless woman. I'm just not feeling good."

"That's nonsense. You know it and I know it." Cullen tossed the comment behind him as he searched for a clean towel.

"I just wanted to talk to you about the game on Saturday," Jordan mumbled.

Cullen ignored the comment.

"I'm so cold," Jordan said, his teeth now rattling together violently. "Having the flu sucks."

Cullen covered the bleeding leg with the towel and sat back from Jordan. He gave a long, cautious glance.

The skin on Jordan's face and limbs was oily with stretch marks throughout the inner joints. On the inside skin of both arms, pockets of small red or purplish acne appeared. His bloated face and jaundiced skin made Jordan appear disfigured. The skin eruptions throughout Jordan's body were infected; abscesses and cysts littered his arms and legs. Jordan looked like a creature that had been genetically altered in a lab. Cullen barely recognized him.

Resting on his knees, Cullen slid both arms around Jordan and drew him close, trying to provide enough warmth to calm the shivering. Jordan had always been in peak physical condition, but now Cullen struggled to lock his fingers around the waist of his friend. Jordan responded by gesticulating violently and scratching at Cullen's arms with both hands.

Cullen loosened his grip slightly as Jordan's fingernails dug into his skin. Jordan began coughing, a wet, racking hack. Bursts of vomit pulsed from the corner of his mouth, and Jordan began choking on them.

"This," Jordan mewled, "is the worst part about being sick. Puke." He paused. "Would you get off of me, Brewer! I'm okay. I can handle this."

Ovals of blood blotted the towel and Jordan continued shaking. Cullen managed to wrestle Jordan onto his back.

Jordan stared at the ceiling. His hard, round pupils dilated. The skin around both eyes, now deeply wrinkled, contracted and rescinded with each movement.

After what seemed like hours, Jordan stopped moving, stopped vomiting, stopped groaning. His body went limp. He snored slightly and breathed slowly.

Cullen bolted toward his desk. He pushed the rough draft of his essay to one side and began pulling open desk drawers. His first thought was Coach Miles. He needed to know what had just happened. Coach Miles surely had some idea what Jordan had been taking. In a way, Cullen wished he hadn't seen them in the locker room together.

As he sifted through wadded-up pieces of notebook paper and sticky notes, Cullen thought about Serena. *Do I have her number? Can I find a number for* The Record *newsroom?* No, she no longer worked there. A knot formed in his gut.

Behind him, Jordan stirred. He smacked his lips together and clicked his tongue against his cheek.

Cullen stiffened. The name John Petry lurched across his mind. Dr. Petry would know what to do. Cullen dug frantically into the desk drawer. He managed to pull out the course syllabus from the summer class. Even though Dr. Petry's office hours would be different this semester, Cullen had a phone number and a way to reach him.

Cullen put the syllabus on the desk.

Jordan clung to the ends of the bed, using them to pull himself up. He steadied himself, then spun around and shoved Cullen in the chest.

The gesture knocked Cullen off-balance and into the corner of the desk.

Jordan jammed a finger into his breastbone. "Do not tell anybody what happened here, you understand?" Jordan barked. "Pretend tonight did not happen."

Cullen feigned an impish smile and raised his arms, palms open, at Jordan. "Jordan," he said, "you're sick. Call your dad and have him take you to the doctor."

Jordan blinked, looked down at the dried streaks of blood and vomit on his legs and arms, and shook his head. "I told you, I don't want anybody to know about tonight. Do not *ever* mention this again!" Jordan leveled a hypnotic, psychotic glare at Cullen. The veins in his neck, arms, and face bulged outward from the yellow surface of the skin.

Jordan backpedaled slowly. He bent down, collected the blood-stained towel, opened the door and slammed it behind him.

Cullen exhaled and let his body relax. Instantly, the adrenaline that had been pumping through his body stopped, leaving him drained.

As Cullen looked for another clean towel to wipe up the dried vomit from the carpet, he noticed two small pills—one a pastel blue and the other a soft orange—on the carpet. Cullen picked up the pills and held them up to the phosphorescent light shining from the ceiling.

The light had the ability to make everything and everyone under it appear sickly. Cullen couldn't identify any marks on the pills. He closed his fingers around them and gritted his teeth.

thirty seven

SERENA MINIMIZED ONE WINDOW on the computer monitor and moved to another computer terminal.

Littered in front of the second screen were sheets of paper, adorned with words and phrases that were highlighted and underlined. Each computer screen had archived newspaper stories from *The Charleston Gazette*. Serena had access to the databases, given to her during her summer internship, which expired on October 10. She had reached the end of her access. She moved in a balletic weave between the terminals. Behind her, Crystal cleared her throat.

"This is necessary," Serena hissed. "I have to do this—just in case I missed something."

Crystal tossed a tuft of hair over her shoulder and checked her watch. "You've been at this for over two hours, and all I have seen you do is bounce back and forth between two computers and write down bits of information here and there. I'm not sure that what you're doing is working."

Serena stopped. She cocked her head sideways. "Crystal, good journalism is about gathering disjointed pieces of information and looking for a connection—and that's what I'm doing right now." She glanced down at her notes. The newspaper had done very little reporting on the expansion of Corridor 33. She managed to find a small paragraph inside a larger story written during the West Virginia legislative session in 1992, when then-Governor Gaston Caperton discussed the need for West Virginia to maintain and expand its infrastructure, especially its highway system.

He had used Corridor 33 as an example of a highway that needed state and federal highway construction dollars to expand and bring more economic development to the northern part of the state. Apart from that, Serena couldn't find any information on the highway expansion project.

She mulled over the possibility that the plan could be a secret deal between the college and the legislature, so the road could be expanded without other colleges in the state griping that the legislature had given Clear River College preferential treatment.

"What did Matt have to say the last time you talked to him?"

The question stopped Serena again. "I'm way too busy to think about that right now."

Crystal lowered her head. "Okay, sorry for asking. I just thought getting your mind off what you're doing for a bit might help you refocus."

"I should have returned his phone calls when you told me," Serena added. "I knew Matt well enough to know that he'd just keep calling until I did answer."

Crystal drew a long smile that ignited some playfulness in her voice. "Weren't you with Cullen when Matt called?"

"Yes, I was," Serena replied brusquely. "I had to tell Cullen about what happened to me when I met with Dr. Burcham—and I needed him to know my suspicions about Dane and Bambuterol."

"What did Matt say when you told him Cullen was there?"

"He wasn't too pleased," Serena said. "Although the two of them played football for the Cougars for some time before Matt transferred. Actually, it was Matt who told me that Bambuterol was a steroid. Cullen knew nothing about it."

"Interesting," Crystal commented, accentuating the first syllable for effect.

Serena dropped into a chair in front of the computer terminal and scratched her forehead. "I cannot find anything about Corridor 33 being expanded in any archived stories."

Crystal pulled up a chair and sat beside Serena. She placed her elbow on the ledge of the terminal and rested her round face in her hand.

"Are you sure you didn't misunderstand what the construction crew told you?"

"I'm sure of it," Serena replied. "They were quite shocked when I approached them and started asking questions. Something is going on. I just knew that recreation field had been sitting idle for too long. The school must know about the highway expansion plans."

"That would explain why the school won't let students use that field anymore."

"Exactly," Serena said.

The slender glass panels in the library filled with soft yellow light that cast streaks of sunlight into the room. The natural light was comforting, making Serena stir in her seat along with other drowsy students. Through the window, the cloak of dark shadows rescinded from campus buildings like a curtain being pulled up from a stage.

"I need to get ready for class at nine," Crystal said. "By the way, are you coming to the Phi Mu Sorority Fall Dance next week? Some of the money collected at the dance will be donated to the Upshur County Homeless Shelter."

Serena steepled her hands together and stared intently at the computer screen. "I hadn't thought about it. Probably."

Crystal rose. "Why don't you ask Cullen to be your date?"

"I'm sure he has other plans." A lump formed in Serena's throat. She would love nothing more than to go on an actual date with Cullen—a date that didn't involve anything about construction or steroids or Dane Antonelli.

"It might be a good public relations move for him, as the student body president, to be in attendance," Crystal added. "Plus, more money from attendees means more money for the sorority and for the homeless shelter."

"We'll see," Serena replied, a bit annoyed. "Right now I have to find out about Corridor 33."

Crystal rolled her eyes and walked away.

*   *   *   *   *

Cullen trekked through campus, watching the faces of students flash past him.

Today, the passing students were pinned under a faint blue sky, making the Clear River College campus seem more grandiose, with a cluster of mammoth academic buildings that seemed to shrink everything and everyone around them.

Cullen removed the folded syllabus from the pocket of his jeans. He'd tried calling Dr. Petry earlier that morning, but all he had reached was the professor's voicemail. Cullen left a message, but decided seeking out the professor, armed with the two small pills he confiscated from Jordan, was a better idea. The thought of having those pills wrapped in toilet paper and resting in his pocket made Cullen sick and furious. He'd considered going to see Coach Mile this morning as well about the pills, but he didn't want to provoke a confrontation before practice.

As he stopped near the curb of Jefferson Street, with the large arms of two maple trees cradling him from the sun, Cullen watched small clusters of students scurrying down the stairs of Branstone Hall and through the exits of the library, making their way to the student center in the middle of campus.

Although the students seemed unalarmed, Cullen felt a tingle at the tips of his fingers. He decided to trail behind the students.

The students pointed and whispered to each other as the wave grew larger. Now, most of Jefferson Street was filled with students as they gathered in smaller groups outside the student center.

Serena parted the crowd and found Cullen. The pearl-white skin on her face was ashen and the tips of the curls in her hair were tainted with oil. "They broke into the student government office," she said.

The words drew the attention of students nearby. They formed a pocket around Cullen, pushing into him.

The collision made Cullen step into Serena. The two touched and Cullen caught a whiff of her perfume. He blinked—hard.

"Who broke into the student government office, Serena?"

"The police. The campus police are inside. I came from the library to the student center to get some breakfast. I saw two police officers go upstairs. I followed them down the hall to the student government office. I thought they might be looking for you. I...I tried to stop them but they told me if I didn't step aside they would arrest me."

The more Serena spoke, the more strained her voice became. Cullen inserted a hand between himself and a portly girl wearing flannel pants who insisted on charging into Cullen, thereby squeezing them closer together.

"Why would they do that?"

"Something about the forms you signed last month. The ones you signed when we planted the tree for Dane Antonelli. That little wormy guy, Ike or something, brought them to you when we were talking."

"Ian, you mean? Why did the police tell you that?"

Serena grimaced and dropped her head. "I told them I was a member of student government."

Cullen craned his neck upwards in exasperation. "Serena, you are in enough trouble. I can't have you claiming to be a member of student government when you're not."

"I thought you might be in trouble."

"Not yet," Cullen pressed.

Serena nodded.

"Are the police still there?" Cullen asked.

"I...I think so."

Cullen grabbed serena by the shoulder and spun her around, moving them between three students huddled near the entrance to the student center.

"Come on. Let's go."

The two raced around the lower level of the student center and tore up the two-tiered staircase to the second-floor student government office.

Cullen sprinted down the narrow hallway, Serena bouncing awkwardly behind him. The brown door at the end of the hallway had been dead-bolted, but now the mutilated central piece of the lock lay in the corner against the wall. The secondary door lock had been pulverized by a heavy, blunt object. The door to the office was ajar, but a thin, narrow band of yellow police tape spanned the door frame. A paper sign read *Office Closed by Order of Clear River Campus Police.*

Cullen slammed both hands into his hips in frustration. "Damn. They have the area taped off."

Serena came around Cullen. "Let me go in first. You cover me."

Before Cullen could react, Serena stuck her thumb in front of Cullen. Serena transformed into a childlike character playing a game of tag with friends. He flashed a sarcastic smirk towards her. Indeed, Serena seemed to shrink in front of Cullen as she bent down and crept into the room.

She slipped under the police tape and pushed the door open gingerly. Finding a light switch, Serena flipped it. Once the overhead lights flickered and lit up the room, Cullen breathed in quickly.

In the middle of the room, both sets of faded pewter file cabinets had been overturned and the individual filing drawers had been removed. File folders and their contents were strewn across the room. Faint impressions of heel prints appeared on some of the loose pages. The horseshoe-shaped table in the center of the room had been moved, and the chairs once surrounding the table had been turned over.

Serena squatted lower to the ground and scooped up the loose pages. She cut a sideways glance at Cullen.

"We are taking a huge risk here by messing with this room," she said.

The color evaporated from his face as he paced in semi-circles around the room.

"Don't bother, Serena. It doesn't really matter at this point."

She continued collecting papers, positioning them awkwardly in her hands. She looked around, seeking a place to rest the papers.

Cullen heard the faint, hollow echoes of slight movements outside the office door. He scratched his face and walked to the entryway. As he reached for the doorknob, a hand grabbed his wrist and yanked him to the ground.

The figure pointed a Colt .45 at Serena.

"Campus Police! Don't move, either of you. You are both under arrest for trespassing."

thirty eight

CULLEN FELT THE GIRTH OF THE OFFICER grind his chest and ribs into the cold floor. He gasped as the large hand with thick fingers jerked his head sideways. Both hands were pinned behind his back.

Cullen could not see Serena, but her palpable fear surrounded the room. He heard a click. Handcuffs ensnared his wrists and dug into his skin.

"Serena!" Cullen shouted. His words were muffled against the floor. As the side of his face remained wedged into the floor, a stream of saliva trickled from his lips.

"Perpetrator secured," the officer on top of Cullen called behind him.

"I need to see some I.D.," the smoky voice of a female officer demanded of Serena. She slipped her hands into the air as the female officer strode to her. "No I.D.? Lock your hands behind your head and turn around." A moment of silence passed between them. "Do it. Now!"

Serena did as instructed. From the corner of her eye, she watched the other officer yank Cullen from the floor, turn him around, and rest him against the wall inside the doorway. The officer ran both hands down his legs, making Cullen squirm. The officer moved back up the right pant leg and noticed a bulge protruding from the right pocket. The man grimaced and stuffed his hand inside the pocket, pulling out a clump of paper towels wadded up and crushed.

"What's this?" the officer asked. Cullen stared straight ahead, grinding his teeth together, feeling the dimples on his face swell and twitch with each passing second. He hoped the cop would not unfold the paper towels, but it was too late.

The officer let two small pills, orange and pastel blue, fall into his hands. "Joan, I got some drugs off this one."

Serena was spun around and placed against a small glass window next to the entryway into the student government president's office. She puffed, sending a strip of auburn hair into the air and causing the officer's nose to twitch.

The female officer turned to Cullen. "Let me see those." She grabbed the wrist of her partner and pried the pills from his hand. Cullen cut a quick glance at Serena. Her face remained expressionless except for her eyes, which widened at the sight of the pills.

"This is a crime scene," the woman announced to the group. "We put the yellow tape on the door to keep people like you out. It looks like we're going to kill two birds with one stone here. You a user, son?"

Cullen looked away, although his armpits began to sweat.

"Nah, I bet you are a dealer. Using drugs is probably too messy for you. In any case, you both are coming with us."

Serena gulped. The woman nodded to her partner. With the pronouncement made, the male officer grabbed Cullen and shoved him out the door as Serena was led behind them.

Cullen shrugged off the officer trying to maintain a firm grip on his shoulder as the group went back down the hallway to the top of the student center second-floor steps. Dozens of students had filtered inside the student center. They whispered and pointed at Cullen and Serena as they were led down the steps.

From the crowd, John Petry emerged. Clutching a faded leather briefcase on his hip along with a Styrofoam cup, the professor stared in the direction of Cullen and Serena.

Serena wriggled uncomfortably. "Not so hard," she grumbled at the woman officer. Dr. Petry stepped in front of the group. "Excuse me, what is the meaning of this?"

A rush of hope overwhelmed Cullen. He wanted to run straight for Dr. Petry, but he held firm.

The professor purposely stiffened his posture, uprooting his normally slumped shoulders. The teal shirt rippled and folded in a slovenly manner against Dr. Petry while the faded brown corduroy pants hung low on his wide waist and narrow hips. His hand gripped the briefcase.

"Sir, we need you to move," the woman officer said. "We have two suspects we need to question."

"Question about what?" Dr. Petry asked. "These are two fine young people. They do not deserve to be paraded through the student center like cattle at a meat market."

"Sir, I need you to move!"

Dr. Petry did not budge.

The wiry officer slid a hand around his belt, feeling for a night stick. The female officer raised a hand and her partner stopped searching.

"I demand you release these students," Dr. Petry said.

The woman tilted her head. "Under whose authority?"

"I am a faculty member at this college and these are two of my former students." Dr. Petry looked at Serena, whose face filled with blood. "I do not know why these students have been handcuffed like this, but I am sure you have apprehended the wrong people."

The officer released her grip on Serena. "These students were trespassing on a secured police scene. Plus, we've caught the boy carrying drugs."

Dr. Petry flashed a look at Cullen.

Cullen allowed a twisted smile to cross his face.

"Have you even bothered to ask them who they are or why they might have been there?"

"Sir, if you would step aside, we will have a chance to ask them that and much more." The woman extended her arm and an open hand to the right, gesturing for the professor to move. Instead, he stared down her arm to the fingertips and his eyes retraced the stare.

"May I say something?" Cullen asked.

"No," the woman responded.

Cullen dropped his head, but he saw the gray eyes of the professor harden and the wrinkles in his face deepen and become more resolute.

"This is Cullen Brewer, student body president at Clear River College, and Serena Johnson, reporter for *The Record*, our campus newspaper. I can assure you these students had a right to be wherever you arrested them, but not for the reasons you think."

Dr. Petry spoke in such a booming, declamatory manner that the student center lobby rang. The male officer cowered as the words passed through the space.

"Cullen and Serena. It doesn't matter to us if your names are Mary and Joseph. Both of you were trespassing in an area that had been clearly marked, and one of you has drugs in your possession."

The woman took a step back. She looked at Cullen, then at Serena, and cleared her throat in affirmation. "Explain the drugs, son. Why are you carrying drugs inside your pocket?"

"We can explain," Serena began.

Cullen interrupted. "I have a friend..."

Serena tensed her posture and pleadingly looked at Cullen, who felt his heart pounding inside his chest.

"There is someone I live with who I think might be using drugs—steroids, as a matter of fact. I found these pills in the bathroom of my dorm. I gathered them up to turn them in."

The woman folded her arms. "Gathered them up for what purpose?"

"I don't really know," Cullen said, his voice falling quiet. "I am not really sure if I'm right. I'd like to hang onto this until I can tell my coach or ask someone what to do."

"So, this supposed roommate of yours is a friend? Do you know him well?

"Sort of, ma'am."

The woman looked up and down, sizing up Cullen. "Is all of this true?" she asked.

"Every bit of it," Cullen replied.

The officer looked away for a moment before settling back on Cullen and Serena. "Let's get them out of here so we can question them further."

Cullen heard Serena inhale deeply while every muscle in his body tightened.

The woman snarled, "I'm taking the pills with me. Let's go, folks."

Cullen stepped forward. "Wait...."

The warm, flimsy hand of Dr. Petry touched his shoulder. Cullen fell silent.

Dr. Petry stepped around Cullen and in front of the woman. "What exactly is going on here, ma'am?"

"I want to know that too," Cullen added. "I followed the crowd of students over here." He turned and nodded at Serena. "She did the same thing. She's probably over here to cover the story for the school paper. When we found out something happened to the student government office upstairs, we wanted to check it out. Is there something we can do to help, Officer . . . .?"

"Cutler. Sergeant Cutler."

Cullen jumped back in the discussion, feigning concern and trying to deflect focus away from the drugs held tightly in Sergeant Cutler's hand. "Is there something we can do to help you?"

Finally, Sergeant Cutler softened. Her square jaw and emerald green eyes darted around the group.

Cullen got a chance to look at her for the first time. She had a thick torso, broad shoulders, and round breasts that rested perfectly inside the trademark blue campus police uniform with the college logo emblazoned on the side. The jagged badge and other uniform trademarks sutured against the green cloth defined her figure. Cullen guessed the woman was in her late forties.

"We were called here by the college president. Apparently, some state purchase orders were processed without the necessary funds and some documents had been removed entirely. We were asked to come here with representatives from the accounting office, as well as a representative from the bank; remove all the files and paperwork from the office; and escort anyone with access to the accounts from the premises. I have already taken a statement from Ian McWorter."

Cullen stopped massaging his wrists. "Ian is the parliamentarian for student government. That is just odd. I don't understand. I signed those purchase orders at the beginning of the term. I ordered shirts, cups, and hats with the college logo on them to use for orientation and other campus recruiting programs, as well as for student organizations to use them for recruitment purposes."

Sergeant Cutler didn't seem impressed.

"We do it every year," Cullen added.

"Look, son, all I know is that the money for those purchase orders was not there and the president asked us to gather some information. We tried to do it as quickly and quietly as we could, and then you two showed up."

"I don't think emptying an office counts as 'quietly'," Serena said, drawing a quick, disgusted look from Sergeant Cutler.

"So the bank and the accounting officer asked that the office be searched?" Dr. Petry asked.

"That's correct," Sergeant Culter replied.

Dr. Petry looked away from her and locked eyes with Cullen and Serena. "That doesn't make sense. I have been teaching here for over thirty years. Money for college memorabilia for student clubs and for recruiting purposes has always been a part of our mission as a college. In fact, students are charged activities fees each semester to cover those materials."

Cullen's eyebrow crinkled. "Dr. Petry, I swear we had money in our accounts to pay for those purchase orders. I wouldn't have signed off on those orders if I'd known the money wasn't there."

Dr. Petry made a sympathetic but puzzled face.

Cullen turned back and looked at the state troopers. "There has to be some type of mistake here."

Sergeant Cutler shrugged her shoulders. "You'll have to take it up with accounting. That's all I can say." She checked her watch. "We're going to go and re-secure the room upstairs, take these pills back to our office, and then we'll leave. And we'll get those students to back off so you have some space."

As the officers trotted away, Dr. Petry set down his briefcase and rested both hands on his hips. "Do you to know how lucky you are? If I hadn't been here, those police probably would have arrested the both of you! Mr. Brewer, I cannot believe you would carry drugs on your person."

"Dr. Petry." Cullen led the professor a few feet around the stairwell while Serena followed. "We really need to talk."

Cullen looked back at Serena. Still shaking slightly from the experience, she nodded at Dr. Petry in agreement.

"After what happened today, I'm not sure there is anyone left we can trust."

"Am I going to be pulled into something I might regret later?" Dr. Petry asked.

"It's possible," Serena answered.

Dr. Petry reached into his shirt pocket, pulled out a faded, matted leather notepad and flipped through the pages.

"Come to my office at Franklin Hall on Monday morning at nine," he said, making a note in his pad. "And be prepared to tell me everything."

thirty nine

"THE AREA HAS BEEN SECURED, SIR."

"Excellent, Jack, thank you." Dr. Burcham ran the extra spool of phone receiver cord through his long, slender fingers as static filled the line.

On the other end of the line, Jack took several deep, loud breaths over muffled conversations.

"One more point, sir, before I let you go."

"Yes? What is it?"

"I spoke with Sergeant Joan Cutler and her partner from the campus police department. They responded to the call to remove the student government files from the office and then secured the area. It appears two students re-entered the sealed area."

Dr. Burcham sat up straighter in his chair. He spun the chair around and, while remaining seated, propelled the chair closer to the window behind his desk.

"Did they get the name of the students?"

"Cullen Brewer and Serena Johnson."

"Oh, my," Dr. Burcham groaned. "I didn't have time to tell Cullen about the student funding requests being denied, and now he clearly is looking for answers. Miss Johnson is trying to play detective, no doubt."

"That's what I concluded as well, sir," Jack replied. After a moment of silence, he added, "There's something else, sir."

The president pulled his glasses from his face, withdrew a cloth handkerchief from the pocket of his starched dress shirt, and wiped the bridge of his nose. "Yes?"

"Sergeant Cutler placed in her report that John Petry from the English department was at the bottom of the stairs as they escorted Cullen and Miss Johnson to the lobby."

Dr. Burcham twisted his mouth. "What does Petry have to do with this?"

"Apparently, they found drugs in Cullen Brewer's pocket."

The president swiveled his chair back around to the desk. "I beg your pardon?"

"That's correct, sir."

Dr. Burcham scattered papers and folders across his desk. Resting the phone receiver against his ear, Dr. Burcham sifted unsuccessfully through stacks of paper.

"Everything all right, sir?"

"Yes, yes," Dr. Burcham replied, slightly agitated. "I'm just looking for a phone number." He managed to reach the bottom-right corner of his desk by shoving aside the blueprints for the widening of Corridor 33 through campus. They hit the floor and rolled near the couch in the middle of the office.

"What type of drugs?"

"I don't know, sir. They were destroyed."

"I can't believe that Cullen Brewer would be using drugs." He sighed. "Sometimes the students you least expect to get into trouble are the ones that disappoint you the most. I expect to see Cullen in my office soon to discuss the student government funding being denied."

"Indeed, sir."

"Jack, thank you for the call and for checking with the police."

"You're welcome, sir."

Dr. Burcham hung up the receiver and searched for John Petry's office number, but instead came across the football office number for Coach Miles. He made a mental note to contact him as well.

The president felt a burst of air settle across the room. Tom Hancel slouched into the office.

"I'm sorry for barging in, Neal, but I didn't see Jack in the front atrium. What's going on over at the student center? I drove in this morning and became concerned about the crowd of students over there. It looked like they were staging a protest."

"Not quite," Dr. Burcham said. "We have had some improprieties concerning student government's appropriation of money for various organizations and merchandise for recruiting. I asked the accounting department and the bank representatives to go to the office and search the records."

Tom leaned back and looked around the office. "Neal, this office—along with accounting—normally sets the student activity fee rates for all students at the school. If you think there's some misappropriation of money, we need to be advised about the situation."

"I planned on doing that at our meeting this afternoon," Dr. Burcham replied. "As the president of this college, I thought immediate action needed to be taken."

Tom leaned closer to the president, glaring at him.

Silence lay heavily in the room. Dr. Burcham broke the frozen stare first and began resifting the papers on the desk.

Tom stepped away from the desk and walked across the floor; the heavy steps caused the polished wood floorboards to sag slightly under each footfall. He flopped onto a couch as the faint musky fragrance of cologne and vanilla wafted behind him. He peered across the room and noticed the road expansion blueprints slightly open on the floor.

Dr. Burcham leaned forward, resting his elbows on both knees, and peered at the documents.

"I assume you're going to stay here until the meeting starts?" Dr. Burcham asked.

"That's my plan." Tom pulled a phone out from the inside pocket of his sport coat and checked the time. "Ah," he said quietly.

Dr. Burcham didn't look up from the desk. "Everything all right, Tom?"

"Yeah, I guess. It's just I haven't heard from Jordan in a couple of days. That's not like him. He always calls me at the end of each week."

Dr. Burcham reorganized the papers into three neat stacks on his desk. "Your son might be busy with classes and getting ready for midterm exams."

"Maybe." Tom turned away and stared ahead. "I expect you to report to the board as soon as the meeting begins about what happened earlier."

"I will," Dr. Burcham replied. "Jack will get the files and bring them to the meeting as well, if you'd like me to make a presentation on the problems with the requisition forms that were signed."

Tom snickered. "Speaking of reports, the board is going to expect you to make a decision soon on the road expansion project."

Dr. Burcham stood up and scrunched his forehead. "There is not a decision that needs to be made just yet."

Tom interlocked both hands and cracked his knuckles. "You're wrong there. The legislature transportation subcommittee is holding their interim meetings next month in Charleston. The state has money appropriated from the feds to spend on highway construction. They will expect a report on our plans."

"*Your* plans, Tom. *Your plans.*"

Tom relaxed for a moment as Dr. Burcham walked around the chair adjacent to the couch and folded himself into the seat cushions.

"Everyone benefits here, Neal. The college will benefit, and so will I, your legacy, and the particular board at Clear River College. We have a chance to be a part of something special."

"In case you've forgotten, this college has more pressing needs at the moment. This campus doesn't need to be disrupted by a road project that goes nowhere."

Tom laughed a soft, disapproving laugh and pulled himself against the back of the couch. "Let's just see what the board decides."

Forty

THE STARTING OFFENSIVE UNIT MARCHED behind Cullen, who tucked the silver Cougars football helmet tightly under one arm, looking down at the ground and watching each foot walk in lockstep with the team's cadence.

He hadn't seen Jordan in the locker room. Coach Miles had told Jordan to stay away from the team before games. As Cullen and the team emerged onto Russek Field, the West Liberty University Hilltoppers were already huddling around their head coach on the far sideline.

The lines of teammates behind Cullen dispersed in different directions. Cullen walked to the sidelines. The playing surface, surrounded by a cushioned jogging track, had a state-of-the-art MondoTurf that looked and felt like real grass. When Cullen pressed a cleat into the turf, the cleat spike bounced up in sprightly fashion.

Looking around the stadium, Cullen saw that nearly four thousand people lined the stands under the press box. West Liberty was celebrating an alumni day for their football program, which featured twelve WVIAC All-Americans since 2007. Cullen looked on as former quarterback Zach Amedro and wide receivers Kashif Walls and Almonzo Banks received plaques from the West Liberty Alumni Association.

The far sidelines behind the recipients rested against robust trees with full limbs of leaves splotched in a variety of colors and patterns. The trees were dotted with red-orange leaves and set under a low-hanging sun and milky sky. Cullen suddenly felt a refreshing surge of optimism.

"Athletics is mercilessly fair," Coach Miles shouted to the team from behind Cullen. The coach cut quite a striking image with his strong nose, close-cropped sandy hair, bushy eyebrows and hawkish gaze exploiting, intimidating, and influencing the team huddled around him.

"There are no shortcuts, no easy solutions, no miracle ways out. We are undermanned here today, men. However, if we take care of the football, play good defense, and make some plays, we can win."

Some of Cullen's offensive line bobbed and weaved as the coach spoke. Their eyes glinted with competitive spirit as Cullen made his way to the bench.

"We can do this today, fellas," Cullen barked. "They are young, undersized, and inexperienced. Coach wants us to throw on first down, throw on second down, and throw a touchdown on third down, and that is what we're going to do." He stepped back from the bench as the kickoff team and starting defense strapped on their helmets and adjusted their shoulder pads. Cullen locked eyes with Coach Miles.

Neither said a word. Cullen had avoided Coach Miles for most of the week since Jordan was suspended. Cullen had said nothing about Jordan visiting his room or the pills he'd found. Likewise, Coach Miles had said nothing directly about Cullen and Serena being interrogated by the police, although Cullen was sure the coach knew all about that incident.

The unspoken silence held for several seconds. Coach Miles's eyes were inflamed with adrenaline, yet the pools of quartz-green color inside each eye quivered slightly. Coach licked his lips, expecting to say something. Cullen instead puckered his mouth and drew his hands together in the shape of a fist. Coach Miles did not release the stare, but stepped aside and walked past Cullen.

It took West Liberty only two minutes and six offensive plays to take the lead. Hilltoppers quarterback Austin McAmis scored on a three-yard run following a sixty-eight yard drive.

The first offensive series of the game for the Cougars ended in a three-and out, in which Cullen was sacked twice and threw an incompletion.

Following a Clear River punt, the Hilltoppers drove eighty-eight yards on thirteen plays for another touchdown.

Cullen stood on the sidelines as the crowd erupted into a cavalcade of cheers, creating a distracting ringing in his ears.

Coach Miles approached Cullen, pumping his fist and letting a clipboard slap against his knee. "If you would like to wake up and play some football, son, we could sure use your help."

Cullen looked away and shuffled his feet. "I got sacked on the last couple of plays because I held onto the ball too long. I'll get rid of it next time."

"We're almost at halftime, Brewer. The way our defense is playing, you may not get too many more opportunities."

"I'll make the adjustments," Cullen said coolly.

"The line is trying to zone-block for you," Coach Miles added. "Have them do some more linear blocking. Tell them to dig their heels in and stop the pass rush from the defensive line. That should give you more time."

Cullen attempted a response, but Coach Miles cut him off. "And spread the ball around. Throw to some different receivers. Try to hit Tay Anderson on a slant. The way West Liberty is blitzing, if you can find Tay, you'll get some yards on the slant."

Beads of sweat formed on Cullen's forehead. "Hitting that slant is easier with Jordan in the lineup," he said. He stepped back, expecting Coach Miles to pitch a blustery fit.

Coach Miles exhaled a deep breath and gripped the clipboard tightly with two hands. He lowered his chin and stared at Cullen so intensely Cullen thought the look would bore a hole through his chest.

"If you've got something to say, Brewer, then just say it. But don't sit here and play verbal footsy with me."

"I said all I needed to say last week, Coach," Cullen replied.

The carotid arteries in Coach Miles' neck sprouted through his skin while the veins around his temples swelled with indignation. "You have no idea what you saw or what you're talking about, and I'd suggest you watch your mouth, Brewer. I can put you on the bench if that's where you want to be."

Cullen took another long look at Coach Miles. The coach, at that moment, seemed defenseless and pathetic. Cullen shook off the glance and the comment. "I'm ready to go in, Coach."

Coach Miles looked to the field of play as the two referees motioned for the offensive unit.

Cullen took the field, with teammate and running back Marcus Turner behind him in the backfield and three receivers, Tay Anderson, Mike Ochoa, and Joey Gunnoe, standing on each side of the line of scrimmage. Cullen reminded the offensive line to linear-block and not zone-block, as Coach Miles had suggested, but the true test would come on the first play.

A fifteen-yard completion on the slant route to Tay Anderson moved the football from the Clear River nineteen yard line to the Clear River thirty-four. On the next snap, Marcus took a deep handoff from Cullen and danced through a gaping hole into the West Liberty secondary. A pair of Hilltoppers tacklers tried to wrestle Marcus to the ground near midfield, but Marcus broke stride, shrugged them off, and pulled away from the pursuit. He didn't stop until he crossed the goal line.

As the second half began, Cullen watched from the sideline as the defense stepped up. An interception of West Liberty quarterback Austin McAmis ended a promising Hilltoppers drive deep into Clear River territory. The interception, returned by Cougars cornerback Jamir Bonner, set up a touchdown that tied the game 14-14.

After another defensive stand by the Cougars, Cullen took the field with the offensive unit, reminded them about the linear blocking scheme, and completed a pass to Tay Anderson on a 25-yard slant. He rifled two more passes—one to Tay Anderson, the other to Joey Gunnoe—and sent Marcus Turner on runs that set up a one-yard quarterback sneak for a touchdown. Game, Cougars.

Cullen walked off the field for the final time when the game ended. Sloping his shoulders, he felt the normal tightness in his throwing arm while both hamstrings protested with pain. He listened as four thousand disgruntled Hilltopper fans sauntered underneath the bleachers, grousing as they went.

From under the tunnel two reporters emerged carrying small recorders. One radio reporter, a short, gaunt man with a cherubic face, ran up to Cullen and stuck a recorder out.

"Cullen Brewer, you completed thirty-four of forty-eight passes for two hundred fifty-six yards and two touchdowns with no interceptions. That extends your career passing yardage record to 13,783, while moving you up to number two on the Division II career total offensive yardage list. Your thirty-four completions give you 1,180 for your career. How do you feel about those accomplishments?"

The reporter spoke at such a frenzied pace that Cullen couldn't process all the statistics being quoted. "I'm just glad we won today. Considering we were without our senior wide receiver, Jordan Hancel, I think we did all right." He allowed his mind to wander. This would have been a chance for Dane Antonelli to play and showcase his skills. Dane could run a slant route better than Tay Anderson, that much Cullen remembered from working with Dane in summer practice. Cullen felt his heart beat faster.

"Can you discuss Jordan Hancel's suspension and what that has done to your team?"

Cullen hedged, wondering if the reporter somehow knew about the Bambuterol and about Jordan taking pills. As the silence hung in the air, the other reporter tapped his foot, encouraging Cullen to respond.

"Jordan has been an important part of our team and he will continue to be. We miss him on the field."

"Cullen is pretty good at massaging the truth, that's for sure."

The words penetrated Cullen's ears like a tattoo needle under the skin. He looked around and saw Jordan standing behind him. The reporters pivoted quickly to pummel Jordan Hancel with questions.

Cullen wasn't interested in any more questions. He looked back at Jordan, who was brushing off the reporters. Cullen pressed his lips into a tight, thin line and walked to the locker room.

forty one

BY MID-OCTOBER, leaves began dropping from the trees around campus. Cullen pulled a few crumpled leaf bits from the bottom of his shoe's sole as he spoke to Dr. Petry.

"Have you told me everything, Mr. Brewer? Miss Johnson, is there anything you would like to add?"

Serena shook her head.

"Dr. Petry, we've told you everything," Cullen said.

"And you're certain those pills Mr. Hancel discarded in your dormitory room are some type of performance-enhancing drug or steroid?"

"I'm not exactly sure, but there is that strong chance," Cullen replied.

The professor laced his hands behind his head and leaned back in his chair. The office remained in the same condition as before, with multi-colored file folders scattered on the desk, piles of typed essays tucked inside several literary anthologies, and drawers of file cabinets slightly ajar, revealing a rich blackness inside the openings.

"Sir, we don't want to get you involved, but we don't think there's anybody else we can trust."

Dr. Petry arched his stare higher, fixating on the creases between the faded white ceiling tiles. He tugged at his oatmeal-colored sweater as a clump of snow-white hair hung over his brow, partially covering his left eye.

"There seem to be constants that link various parts of your stories," Dr. Petry said. "We need to determine what these constants mean and how they affect the persons involved."

Serena looked at Cullen, puzzled. Glancing back at her, he found, to his surprise, that she had never looked more beautiful. Her face was radiant, her skin a soft peach, and her curves were accentuated by a pale gray Clear River Cougars sweatshirt and dark jeans that hugged her hips.

Cullen refocused on the professor. "We're doing what you've taught us to do with literature. Look for the common threads and motifs of the story, and see how the characters fit and don't fit with those stylistic devices."

"Precisely," Dr. Petry responded.

"I think I need to take more English classes," Serena mumbled. She stood up straighter. "If we go with this idea," she continued, "then our constants would be Dane's death, the abandoned car, the autopsy report that we felt was falsified, Bambuterol, Jordan taking drugs, and now the student government requisitions being denied."

Cullen could almost hear Serena thinking these thoughts inside her head as she spoke.

"No, no, those constants are much too trite, much too disjointed," Dr. Petry replied.

"Then how do we connect them better?" Cullen asked.

The professor pushed back his chair and walked around the desk. The small office didn't provide much room for group discussions, but Dr. Petry leaned against the edge of the desk and crossed his arms.

Serena took a step aside near the door, while Cullen stood against one of the file cabinets, locking shut a previously opened drawer.

"We have to think about the items Miss Johnson mentioned in more general terms," Dr. Petry said. He pointed an index finger outward while he spoke. "Indeed, we have those separate incidents, but we need to think about how they come together to form a larger, identifiable whole."

"Wait, we do that in journalism," Serena said, her eyes becoming more focused. "With reporting, we look for disparate facts and see how they fit as parts of a puzzle—a unified chunk of information."

Cullen slapped a closed fist into an open hand. "So let's try this again. If we take what Serena has said, and we connect it to a larger whole, then what we are left with is basically individuals influenced by circumstances."

Dr. Petry tipped his head at Cullen. "Yes, Mr. Brewer. Keep going."

"Dane's death, the attacks, the evidence that keeps disappearing for some reason or another..." Cullen stared at the floor.

Dr. Petry crossed his legs.

"I think I have it," Cullen said. "Every time we get closer to finding out what really happened to Dane, something happens. Something—"

"Or someone," Serena interrupted.

"Or someone," Cullen said, nodding, "stops us from moving ahead." He sucked in a deep breath. "It's almost like someone is trying to stop anybody from finding out what happened."

The deep-set wrinkles carved into the face of the professor became more prominent. "Now you must ask yourself, *who* has the power to squelch any investigation? *Who* stands to benefit most from seeing the truth hidden?"

"The answer to that question brings us back to some other constants," Serena said. "This time, the constants are people with authority and influence."

"Dr. Burcham has influence," Cullen said. "So does Jordan's dad, Tom. He's chairman of the college's board of governors."

"And don't forget your coach," Serena interjected. "He has some influence on people."

Dr. Petry remained motionless as Cullen and Serena began listing names, then he asked, "Now that you two have created a list of names, what is the common connection they all share?"

Cullen began to reply, but Serena cut him off. "The connection is, all of these people have become involved in this Dane mystery, and everyone has a connection to Dane—either a large connection or a small one."

"Nicely done, Miss Johnson," Dr. Petry replied. He nodded approvingly.

"Dr. Petry, we can't forget about you. Your name is also involved in this whole mess."

The professor rolled his shoulders uncomfortably. "Well, Mr. Brewer, I never imagined you getting involved in something like this, or associating yourself with these types of people. I feel like I should not be involved any further in this situation. This is a matter between the both of you and your associates and the police."

Serena pursed her lips together. "Your son. Your son Brian is the connection you share in this situation."

Cullen cut her a sharp look. "Serena..."

Serena's cheeks reddened. "I'm sorry, Dr. Petry. That was totally out of line."

"No, it was not out of line, Miss Johnson. My son, like the Dane boy, will forever have a connection with this school."

Dr. Petry stared away longingly.

"Dr. Petry, I didn't tell Serena about your son. She did some research and found out about what happened."

"No additional explanations are needed, Mr. Brewer. As Miss Johnson knows, that type of information is a matter of public record. Anyone can have access to that information at any time for any purpose."

Cullen took an uncomfortable step backwards.

Dr. Petry relocated to his seat behind the desk and dislodged a stack of essays from one of the literary anthologies. He pulled the essay close to his nose and scoured the words.

Serena turned to face Cullen, expecting him to do or say something. When Cullen shrugged his shoulders, Serena rolled her eyes.

"Is there anything else I can do for you?" the professor asked, avoiding eye contact.

"Dr. Petry..."

"I have done all I can do. In fact, I have probably done more than I should. I do have a code of ethics to maintain as a faculty member of this college. I fear I am overstepping my boundaries."

Serena stiffened. Cullen watched her eyes narrow. He had seen this look before—the Serena-readying-for-battle look.

"Sir, knowing more about the death of your son might help us answer all our questions. I know your son played football for the Cougars and died from a sudden massive heart attack. Heart attacks are quite rare for someone in good physical shape like Brian. The state medical examiner even mentioned it."

The air in the room grew warmer.

"Miss Johnson, the death of my son is not a trivial matter, nor is it something that I want to revisit at this time." Dr. Petry's voice grew deeper and raspier as he spoke. "My son's car accident cannot help you. Anyway, the accident was ten years ago. I must move on."

Serena took a step forward, hovering over Dr. Petry. "If you have moved on, then why do you go and look at your son in the Cougars football team picture?"

Dr. Petry leveled a gaze on Serena as he dropped the essay. Cullen lowered his head and shielded his eyes with his hand. He wanted to shrink and scurry away.

"Cullen did tell me about that incident," Serena admitted.

Dr. Petry extended a hand and waved it back and forth at them. "The two of you need to be careful as you proceed in this conversation. You are preparing to cross a line with me that would sever our commonalities."

Cullen reached out and slipped his fingers around Serena's elbow. "We need to go, Serena. Dr. Petry helped us make the connections we need, and I think our stories are safe with him."

The professor remained locked in a steely stare with Serena. "I admire your tenacity, Miss Johnson."

Serena bit the inside flesh of her cheek.

"Did you know that my son was a biochemistry major here at Clear River? He loved science and math as a kid, and between that and football, he had few other passions." Dr. Petry rubbed his eyes, now moistened with tears. "Over the course of his career here, Brian's behavior changed dramatically. He had always been so polite, so articulate, so gracious to me and his mother."

"He got those traits from you, no doubt," Cullen interjected, trying to lighten the mood, but Dr. Petry looked at Cullen with disdain.

"Brian would usually call me and his mother at least three times a week, but as he became a sophomore and a junior student-athlete, he became more insular, more focused on football and getting bigger, getting stronger, getting more time to play during each game. He kept telling us that Coach Miles was counting on him to help the team win a conference championship, that he had to do whatever was necessary to help the team reach that goal. Mildred and I could not buy him clothes because he kept outgrowing everything." Dr. Petry paused.

"Meanwhile, his behavior became more erratic. He would get overly aggressive and irritable over silly things...disagreements over trivial matters. On Thanksgiving Day during Brian's senior year, he became enraged because Mildred didn't make oyster dressing to go with the turkey."

The professor shrugged. "Mildred tried to explain, but Brian would hear none of it. Instead, he shouted at her and smashed dishes. I had never seen Brian so angry."

"Then what happened?" Serena asked.

"When I intervened, he nearly struck me with a fist. He swung at me with such force that when I moved out of the way, his fist smashed into the kitchen counter, causing a small dent."

Serena and Cullen exchanged glances. Serena opened her mouth, but Cullen cut her off.

"Brian's increased strength... had you noticed him getting stronger?"

"I noticed his tight-fitting clothes."

Cullen nodded to Serena, who made a face.

After a pause, Dr. Petry stiffened. "How do you know about my son's increased strength?

"We don't—or didn't—exactly," Serena answered. "We think there might be a connection between Dane Antonelli's death and the attacks on Cullen and me and everything else that has been going on lately. It involves a drug called Bambuterol."

Dr. Petry stiffened further. "Miss Johnson, Mr. Brewer, can you prove this?"

"Not yet," Cullen replied. "But we have looked into the drug and its effects. There are some parallels with what happened to Brian and everything that's going on now."

"Dr. Petry, what happened after Brian took a swing at you?" Cullen paused and took a deep breath, mustering up the courage and tact to ask the next question. "How did your son die?"

"He gathered his belongings and said that Coach Miles expected them to be ready for practice first thing on Friday morning. I suspected Brian was lying, but before I could confront him, he took off and headed back to campus. He didn't even stay for dinner. It was so cold, so snowy that night. Mildred begged me to go after him, but I didn't...." The professor's voice quivered and trailed away.

"I never saw my son again. After the funeral, Coach Miles gave Mildred and me the same condolences and platitudes we heard from other friends and family. However, he never once said that he regretted making those boys come back to campus for practice. He didn't seem genuinely concerned that one of his players, one of the young men he swore would become a better football player and a better man by being involved in the football program, had died."

Cullen now stood next to Serena, watching her creamy skin turn pale as Dr. Petry recounted the events. His heart broke for the professor, but rage surged through his body. Coach Miles, another constant, had shown that same dismissive attitude when Cullen caught him and Jordan with the syringe in the locker room.

Dr. Petry reached into a desk drawer and pulled out a tissue, with which he dabbed his moist eyes.

"Dr. Petry, I am sorry for what happened to Brian," Cullen said.

"I think I understand what's going on here," Serena said, calmly and diplomatically. "It is starting to make sense. The symptoms Brian showed nine years ago are the same symptoms Cullen sees in Jordan now."

Cullen looked at her, puzzled. "So?"

"So, I think..." She carefully weighed her words before she spoke. "I think we have some of our questions answered."

"I never expected my Brian would do that," Dr. Petry replied curtly. "But as time has passed, the thought has crossed my mind frequently."

Serena rested her hands on the edge of the desk. "Brian majored in biochemistry, so he would have known what steroids could do for him physically and how they could help him gain a competitive advantage."

Cullen ran his tongue over dry lips and smacked them together. "And there's a good chance Coach Miles knew Brian took steroids and did nothing about it, just like he ignored me when I saw him and Jordan huddled around that syringe."

Serena grabbed Cullen by the arm and forcefully pulled him to the door. "We need to go."

"Go where?"

"Back to the beginning," Serena said, leaning in to Cullen and whispering.

"Knowing what happened to Brian might be the missing link we needed. You and I need to sit down and start from the beginning, and look at everything we know and everything that has happened. I have a feeling we're closer to finding out what really happened to Dane and how everyone is involved."

Cullen looked back at Dr. Petry. "Thank you, Dr. Petry. For everything."

Serena pulled Cullen again, this time leading him through the office suite and down the Franklin Hall hallway.

"Shoot," she exclaimed and stopped. "I forgot something."

"What?" Cullen braced for the answer.

"I forgot to tell Dr. Petry that I saw some State Department of Highways employees taking pictures and soil samples of the vacant recreational field. When I questioned them about what they were doing, they shied away at first. Apparently, the state is going to expand Corridor 33 into a four-lane highway. Part of it will run right through campus."

Cullen's eyes moved left and right rapidly, trying to process the information. "Tom Hancel."

"Come again?" Serena said.

"Tom Hancel, Jordan's father. He owns a concrete company in Bridgeport. They have supplied concrete for state highway projects in this part of the state for years."

Serena made a face. "How do you know this?"

"Because he brags about it all the time. He makes a killing off those state contracts."

Serena touched her cheek with an index finger. "Isn't Tom Hancel the chairman of the Board of Governors?"

"He is."

"Is he involved somehow with all of this?" Serena questioned.

"I don't know, but he has plenty of money and plenty of influence at this school."

Serena rocked forward and past Cullen. "We have work to do."

forty two

DR. BURCHAM REACHED for a crumpled set of pink message tickets stuffed into the hanging basket.

As he looked inside the doorway to his office, the dark interior was quiet except for the droning of the sleeping computer. The sound would be hypnotic if anyone had been inside to hear it. The blinking message light on the phone, resting on the corner of the desk, remained dim.

He reached up and turned on the lights. Once the overhead lights illuminated the room, the silhouette of Tom Hancel came into full form.

Surprised and slightly annoyed, Dr. Burcham glared at Tom. "What are you doing in here? I ran to the student center cafeteria to get some lunch. If you need to see me, Jack can make an appointment for you. My Fridays are normally free for meetings. In fact, I have some students coming to see me in a few minutes."

He looked over his appointment calendar. "You're like everyone else, Tom; if you need to see me, make an appointment."

"If I need to see you, I will see you. I do not need to make an appointment like some homesick student."

Dr. Burcham removed his black sports coat. His mauve tie hung low and slightly unknotted around his neck. He'd already unbuttoned the sleeves of his white shirt and rolled them up to his elbows.

"I figured you needed to explain the way you stormed out of that board meeting last month." Tom pushed himself up from Dr. Burcham's chair and trudged across the office.

"Did you get ahold of your son?" Dr. Burcham asked, skimming through the pink message receipts.

"Yes." Tom's face relaxed a bit. "Yes, I did. Jordan said he hasn't been feeling well. He sounded tired when I talked to him. But yes, I was glad to hear from him."

"Good." Dr. Burcham wadded up several of the messages and dropped them into the trash can. He locked eyes with Tom. "Anything else?"

"We need to talk about your future." Tom drummed fingers against his bulging torso.

Dr. Burcham suppressed a chuckle. "My future? Why would I want to discuss my future with you?"

Tom sucked air slightly through his teeth. "Remember when I reminded you a few weeks ago that the board is ultimately responsible for what goes on at Clear River?"

"I understand the organizational structure of this college quite well. This college operates under policy governance. The board sets short-term and long-term goals for the college, and I am responsible for achieving those goals. Do we really need to go over all of this, Tom?"

"We do," he replied sharply. "There are some members of the board who are not happy with your performance of late. I have been consulting with other members, both in and out of executive session meetings—"

"Cut the nonsense!" Dr. Burcham walked around Tom behind the desk. "Just say what's on your mind."

Dr. Burcham fell into the chair, steepled his hands, and waited for a response. He looked down at the floor, at the small granules of dust clustered around the wooden prongs on the desk.

"The board has sent me to ask for your resignation."

"That's ridiculous. On what grounds?"

"Several." Tom coughed softly in an attempt to clear his throat. "The Dane Antonelli investigation is a large part of it."

"That matter is closed," Dr. Burcham replied defiantly. "I have been working with Detective Parsons of the state police exclusively. The autopsy has been completed and traces of drugs were found in the young man's car. All indications are that he died of an apparent heart attack."

"The board feels the incident wasn't handled properly and that a lack of institutional control from the president's office has influenced other parts of the college."

Dr. Burcham's nostrils flared. "Give me an example."

"Well, two students were attacked. There was a nasty incident with the football team, leading to suspensions. And now the Student Government Association office has been cleared out and sealed over requisitions? I'll admit, that's a pretty gutsy decision and I knew nothing about it."

Dr. Burcham leaned forward. "The suspect in those attacks was arrested. If Cullen Brewer decided not to press charges, that is not my problem. And we cannot have student government authorizing the spending of student activity fee money without going through the proper procedures. As for the football team, *your* son is the one who spit on those players and coaches from West Virginia Tech, and not anybody else. He's been suspended and the rest of the team has been warned." He glared at Tom. "So then—explain to me, Mr. Chairman, how those reactions by this office show a lack of institutional control!"

Tom opened his mouth, but no words came forth.

Dr. Burcham surged up from the chair, cutting him off. He stood steadfast before Tom. "What is really going on here is that I told the board I would not support the road expansion project, and you responded by interrupting me and attempting to censure my comments. That's why I left the meeting. I am the president of this college and I am going to be treated with respect. The board should know that your company stands to profit handsomely from this arrangement, and that you went to Charleston and spoke on behalf of me and the board without our consent. Under college bylaws, *that* is grounds for your resignation."

Tom tilted his head up. "The board knew about my visit to Charleston. They agreed it was the right course of action."

"So you decided to exempt me from discussions on this matter because I have been against the project from the beginning?"

Tom shrugged. "You were preoccupied with several other crises that needed your attention. The board is not happy with the way everything has been managed and they think a change is necessary."

The words hit Dr. Burcham in the chest like a missile. "I have been a chief academic officer and college president for the majority of my tenure in academia, and I have never been told by a board member, or a board collectively, that my performance was not good enough. The fact that we are at an impasse over this Route 33 expansion project does not mean that we cannot work this out."

Tom rocked back and forth on the balls of his feet. "The board is tired of talk, Dr. Burcham. They want action and results, not excuses." He poked the air with a finger in the direction of Dr. Burcham. "The decision has been made and is final. The board of governors at Clear River College expects your resignation within thirty days."

Tom turned and took long strides to the front door. He looked back for an instant. Dr. Burcham fell back into the desk chair and sat, mouth agape, slouching forward and resting one elbow on the desk.

"This is the best decision for you and for the college," Tom called back.

Dr. Burcham spun the chair around and stared out the window.

forty three

CULLEN AND SERENA FOUND A SMALL CORNER TABLE on the second floor of the library, isolated from anyone else. Serena unfolded several sheets of paper from a notebook. Cullen sat back in his chair, a bit astonished at the amount of preparatory work Serena had completed before the meeting. A small peach-colored paper fell to the floor.

"I outlined everything that has happened from the beginning, starting from when they found Dane dead in the stairwell in Stokley Hall."

Cullen looked away briefly. A lump formed in his throat. In some ways, Cullen felt in his soul that Dane had been gone for just a few short days. In other ways, it felt like Dane had been dead for years.

"So much has happened to so many people since Dane died, I feel like he's been hovering over us since that night."

"Well . . . " Serena smoothed over the rough edges of the paper. "What happened to him that night has affected all of us in some way. What's troubling is that nobody is any closer to figuring out what is going on and how all of this is connected."

Cullen rubbed his chin. "I just don't see what we're going to discover by doing this ourselves. We've been in the middle of everything."

"Willingly and sometimes unwillingly," Serena stated, looking at Cullen with soft eyes.

Cullen rested both hands on the edge of the table as he looked closely at the outlines. Serena had created meticulous notes, details and facts highlighted and color-coded with a key at the bottom of one of the pages explaining what the color combinations meant.

She pointed to the left of the page. "Here, I have everyone involved, including Dane, you, me, Dr. Burcham, Dr. Petry, the police, Jordan, the attacker, Tracy Pritt, the medical examiner, Ian, Tom Hancel...Is there anyone I'm forgetting?"

Cullen hesitated. "Matt Carmichael."

"Oh, Lord." Serena pushed back into her seat and slipped her arms through the hand rests. "Thanks for mentioning him."

"He did give us a key clue about Bambuterol," Cullen said. "Neither one of us knew anything about it."

"And we still don't know why it ended up in those bags in Dane's car, either."

"I think we can assume," Cullen said, touching the name *Dane Antonelli* written in large, blocked letters on the page, "that he was taking steroids."

Serena nibbled on the cap of a blue pen and looked thoughtful. When she didn't speak, Cullen filled in the silence. "I think we can also assume that Jordan Hancel is taking them too and that Brian Petry took them in the past."

Cullen removed the blue pen from Serena's hand and drew an arrow connecting the two names.

"It does make sense," Serena said, staring at the arrow and retracing it with her finger. "We need to know where the steroids are coming from and who is distributing them."

Cullen squirmed. He grabbed the papers from the table and held them up to the light. Serena craned her neck upwards.

"Be careful. We don't want anyone to see that information," she hissed.

Cullen rotated the sheets around as a stream of hollow orange light, beaming through a small portico window in the library, illuminated the writing on the page perfectly.

"We have a doctored autopsy report, an attack on you and me, an infiltration of steroids on campus. Can all of this be done by one person? Or could one person be leading a group of people to carry out everything?"

"Possibly," Serena said. "It would have to be well-planned and well-executed, but I think one person or a group of people could do all of this."

Cullen smirked, flicking his eyebrows up and down playfully. "That's the key to it, then. We need to find the one person or the group of people that might be connected to everyone."

Serena took back the paper. "What about the guy that attacked you, Damon Jarousky? Could he have done it?"

"I don't think so." Cullen shook his head. "When the police asked me to press charges and I told them I didn't want to, they informed me Damon didn't have a record. Plus, he doesn't attend Clear River College."

"Maybe he was sent here by someone else to send you a message," Serena suggested. "I remember you thinking we were attacked for getting too close."

"That's true. I still feel that way."

"I wish we could find out who he was involved with or why he was sent here."

Cullen sucked on his lips. "He didn't tell the police why he came to the Clear River campus. I think he told them my attack was a case of mistaken identity, or some lame excuse like that."

Serena scoffed. "That *is* a lame excuse." She added additional notes to the copious ones on the pages. When situations required analytical determination, she seemed physically larger and stronger. Now, though, Serena appeared small and vulnerable.

"If someone is behind all of this," Cullen continued, "then chances are it's not over."

Serena pursed her lips. "It's over as long as we don't keep investigating what happened. In a way, now that I'm kicked off *The Record* as a staff member, we can keep searching without letting anyone know what we're doing."

Cullen leaned back into the chair and rested one hand on each knee. Serena rotated the paper so the names of involved participants now faced inward.

"Remind me. Who suspended you from the newspaper?" Cullen asked.

"Dr. Burcham. I guess my reporting got a little too close for comfort." She sighed. "At the beginning of the year, my goal was to become the first Clear River student to win West Virginia Associated Press Student Reporter of the Year. I guess that goal is over."

Cullen stared at the floor, the palm of his hand covering his lips.

"Cullen, are you there?" Serena teased.

Cullen leaned over and picked up the piece of paper from the floor. "I'm listening. And I'm sorry about the suspension, but I was just thinking about Dr. Burcham. The president's office would be the only entity on campus that could have denied the money for those requisition requests for student government. If Dr. Burcham had no problems in suspending you for investigating Dane's death, then he could have said no to those requisition requests."

Serena went back to sorting the pages. "Why would he do that?"

"I'm not sure," Cullen said, his voice trailing off. "I've been involved with student government before, and he's always been supportive of our efforts."

"It could be a way to punish you for helping me."

Cullen unfolded the piece of paper. Serena reached a hand toward Cullen, signaling him to stop.

Instead, Cullen read the note wide-eyed and displayed a broad smile. "I forgot you're in a sorority."

Serena's face glowed pink.

Cullen let out a chuckle. "Based on what I know about you, sororities do not seem like your scene. I assumed someone like you would find them phony and unnecessary."

"I joined Phi Mu as a freshman," Serena replied. "I'm not as involved as I should be because of classes and working at the newspaper."

Cullen waved the piece of paper in the air. "So, are you going to their fall formal tonight?"

Serena scowled. "Maybe. I don't know. Crystal, my roommate, is bugging me to go. She has a date, though, and I'd be the third wheel."

Cullen watched Serena wringing her hands and tapping her foot nervously. He leaned closer, trying to see if his presence would force her to look up.

"Yes," Cullen said.

Serena jerked back and scrunched her face. "Yes, what?"

Cullen grinned. "Yes, I will be your date to the fall formal."

Serena inhaled a large gulp of air, which sent her mind scrambling for thoughts and words. "Oh, Cullen, I didn't, I mean, I don't want you to feel obligated—"

"I don't."

"I...I do not want you to feel committed to go with me out of pity."

"I am going with you because I want to go with you, not because you assigned it to me or because I feel a need to go out of some duty or obligation."

She exhaled. "Thank you."

"No problem." Cullen winked.

"Back to our discussion earlier...do we agree, then, that we need more information about everything and some stronger threads between the facts before moving on?"

"Yes. And I wish I had more time to connect the threads, but I need to go see Dr. Burcham before tonight."

"Okay," she replied. "But dress warmly tonight, because it's expected we'll get the first big snowstorm of the season."

"I love fall." Cullen stood up, flashed a weak smile and collected his belongings. "I'll see you at the Phi Mu house later."

forty four

A S HE PREPARED TO MEET DR. BURCHAM, Cullen weighed several options. He could confront the president, stating his dissatisfaction and possibly creating a stir. Or he could go in controlled and slightly shy, but prepared to nuance the conversation about the denied requisition requests. That might ultimately lead to their reinstatement.

Cullen traversed campus while the late afternoon sun slanted down. The billowing cloud cover wove together like a gray-colored cloth, holding a damp chill that made Cullen's muscles ache. Cullen climbed the narrow, steep stairs of the administration building with vigor. He felt ready now to storm into the president's office with purpose.

As he pushed open the frosted glass door leading to the office, voices emerged from inside the next room. The desk in front of the second doorway, normally reserved for Jack Dillon to serve as the president's gatekeeper, sat empty. The two voices from inside the office seemed muffled, but they came through clearly enough that Cullen could make out the words.

"I am a senior faculty member at this college," one voice said. "I do not appreciate my classroom being interrupted by a student assistant summoning me to a meeting with you. What is the meaning of all of this?"

Cullen backed himself flatly against the wall near the door, sliding himself close to the door frame. He tossed several quick glances at the front office door, preparing himself for a possible intrusion.

"That's just like you to get involved in something that does not concern you. The police didn't need you tervening in their investigation," said theother voice.

Cullen tilted his ear closer to the opening between the door and the hitched frame. A streak of dull white light coming from the office burst through the opening. Cullen surmised that one voice belonged to Dr. Burcham. The other person sounded like Dr. Petry.

"I cannot believe this office would condone such a public spectacle towards two students. Having them handcuffed and interrogated for some sort of a charade being played out in front of other students. That is absolute nonsense and displays conduct not becoming of the mission of this college. Miss Johnson and Mr. Brewer are two good students, two bright students, two students who are leaders and who make a difference within our college community. Instead of respecting their contributions, you set out to badger them and shame them. What you did was disgraceful."

"I suggest you watch your tone," Dr. Burcham replied. "I am responsible for granting you professor emeritus status at the end of the school year. If that matters to you, you will drop this issue."

"Emeritus status is something that is earned by diligence and scholarship related to the current issues of my discipline," Dr. Petry replied. "I do not need a pronouncement from this office granting me that status. I will not be bullied into it, nor will I be threatened to have a public acknowledgment taken away from me."

"Cullen Brewer and Serena Johnson are intruding on an investigation that has been handled and resolved," Dr. Burcham said. "I can't allow them to play police and look for something that isn't there."

Cullen scraped his back against the wall, trying to inch closer. Neither man inside the room noticed the noise. Cullen wanted to let Dr. Petry know he was outside, supporting his argument, just as the professor had supported him and Serena.

"Have you spoken with either student about their suspicions and fears?" Dr. Petry asked. "These two students have been a part of this situation since the beginning. I think if you would take the time to listen to their concerns, you would make more reasoned decisions in their regard."

Dr. Burcham raised his voice. "I do not have time to listen to discredited theories."

"It would behoove you to speak with them," Dr. Petry said coolly. "I think they are justified in their suspicions."

Another slight pause. "What is *that* supposed to mean? Do not come in here and speak in innuendos.."

Dr. Petry cleared his throat. "I have been around students a long time, actually in the classroom working with them every day. Unlike you, who have been in the ivory tower of administration for the better part of your career, I can tell when a student brings forth genuine concern and when the concern is misguided, misplaced, or being used to hide something else. In talking with Miss Johnson and Mr. Brewer, I find their concerns are worthwhile, and it's the responsibility of this office to listen to them."

Cullen held his breath. The muscles in his legs and feet tightened. He no longer felt like he could hide from the conversation. He sorted through the thoughts pulsating in his mind. Dr. Petry might be forced to reveal the content of their conversations. If so, he and Serena could get into further trouble and not be able to find the person responsible. Dr. Petry did not deserve a rebuke for helping and listening. It was time to intervene.

Dr. Burcham spoke again, his voice louder and more inquisitive. "Oh, so you have talked with Serena and Cullen about everything?"

The question pierced Cullen's mind like a bullet. He slid across the wall, ready to race around the door and burst into the room.

But as he prepared to reveal himself, the main office door opened.

forty five

CULLEN GASPED, held his breath, and pulled the smaller door close to him. He pressed the door so tightly against his body that he turned his face sideways to keep the frame from smashing his nose.

Someone walked over to the desk and picked up the telephone, jostled pens and papers, then stopped moving altogether. Cullen heard himself letting air out of his nose slowly, creating a slight wheezing noise in the room. The movements in the office started again. Footsteps approached the door. Cullen flinched, expecting to be discovered.

Instead, the person slipped into the office where the two men continued talking, although Cullen had lost the gist of the conversation.

"Excuse me, sir, it's nearing three. Your next appointment should be here shortly."

The arguing stopped. "Thank you, Jack."

Cullen pushed the door an inch or so back from his face, trying to catch some air. The pattering of footsteps halted next to the door. Cullen remained motionless.

Jack Dillon took another large step, dropping something onto the desk, and then opened the door. The latch clicked behind him.

Cullen let out another long breath. Pockets of sweat dotted his face. After clearing his mind for a moment, he refocused on breaking up the conversation in the next room.

Cullen slid from behind the door. As he turned the corner, Dr. Petry said, "I did what a responsible faculty member should do. I listened to their concerns."

Cullen barged into the office. "That's not entirely true."

Dr. Burcham gave Cullen a feral look. The antagonistic mood of the room crested and then broke.

Dr. Petry didn't look at Cullen.

"Dr. Petry has listened to everything Serena and I have said."

The president folded his arms. "I beg your pardon?"

"I heard everything," Cullen continued. Dr. Petry turned sideways and raised his eyebrows at Cullen.

"There is no sense in denying it. I came here to talk with you about the student government requisitions that were canceled. When I came in, I heard the two of you arguing."

Dr. Burcham uncrossed his arms.

"The truth is, we've talked to Dr. Petry about our suspicions with Dane's death and everything that's happened since then." Cullen stopped speaking, attempting to gauge a reaction from the president. Dr. Burcham's beady eyes narrowed. They studied Cullen closely, darted over to Dr. Petry, then back to Cullen.

"Sir, there are some serious problems going on."

"Since that young boy died," Dr. Petry interrupted, "nobody in this room has been the same. Listen to what Mr. Brewer has to say."

Dr. Burcham checked his watch. "I have a three o'clock appointment. I'll give you two minutes."

Cullen nodded and steadied himself.

Dr. Petry flashed him a slight wink.

"I will make this brief," Cullen said, feeling the muscles in his throat constrict. "When Dane died, Serena got a copy of the autopsy report from Charleston. She brought it to me to look at. We determined that the report had been forged. The official seals and the lines in the document looked odd—like someone had re-created the form using a computer. Then, when the police searched Dane's car, they found traces of Bambuterol in the plastic bags in the back of his trunk. Serena began investigating that angle. Then Serena and I were attacked, and we're not sure if the same person did both attacks."

Dr. Burcham sighed. "Move it along, Cullen. I already know all of this."

Cullen's mouth became dry. "Bambuterol is a steroid. It's a performance-enhancing drug banned by the NCAA. Those bags found in his car were laced with Bambuterol. I too thought Serena might be thinking up silly theories, but then came the incident involving Jordan," Cullen said.

"Jordan Hancel?" Dr. Burcham asked. "How is he involved?"

Cullen took a deep breath and looked at Dr. Petry. He gave a stern, reassuring glance that encouraged Cullen to continue. "Jordan suffered a high ankle sprain earlier in the season. Those injuries are usually painful and take several weeks to heal. Jordan came back so quickly. Then I started noticing his nose bleeding. What's more, I would see him with sores on his skin. After that, he started acting weird, which led to the spitting incident that got him suspended."

Cullen allowed a question to cross his mind: was now the time to implicate Coach Miles? If he mentioned Coach Miles as part of the explanation, there would be problems. Coach Miles would become the constant factor that Dr. Petry had talked about earlier.

Cullen cracked his knuckles. "I think that Jordan may be using steroids," he concluded. "We haven't spoken in a couple of weeks, mainly because he came to my dorm room under some type of steroids-induced rage and then left. Later, I found a couple of pills on the floor and I put them in my pocket."

Dr. Burcham leaned forward. "Have you confronted Jordan about this?"

"Yes, several times. Each time I do, he gets angry and changes the subject." Cullen paused again and mumbled softly, "Coach Miles has suspicions about Jordan too." Cullen stared at the president and noticed the energy in his face lessen. Dr. Burcham's mouth twitched and lips moved, but he stopped before any words escaped.

"Do you have any proof regarding the steroids? Do you still have the pills?"

"No. I had the pills until you had the police handcuff and search me and Serena. They took them. They thought those pills belonged to me."

Dr. Burcham raised an eyebrow. "How do I know you're not using steroids yourself, and trying to deflect the blame to Jordan or Dane or someone else?"

"If I may," Dr. Petry said. "I saw the police bringing Serena and Cullen down the student center stairs. When I asked questions of the police, they explained everything. I did nothing more than inform the officers that Mr. Brewer and Miss Johnson are students that exemplify high standards and high character at this institution, and I asked them to reconsider arresting them."

Dr. Burcham rested the edges of his fingers against the side of his face as a gesture of frustration.

"I want to make sure I understand. The both of you think we have a steroids scandal at Clear River College that killed one football player and is spreading to others. You think someone is out there arranging all of this, like some sort of orchestra conductor, and that the entire problem is not resolved. Is that what you are telling me?"

"Yes," Dr. Petry replied stoically.

"And sir, I know you had Serena removed from the school newspaper as a reporter because she kept meddling with the investigation. I wonder if those student government requisitions got denied as retaliation for my part in helping her." Cullen held his breath.

Jabbing the air with a finger, Dr. Burcham's eyes widened, coupled with flared nostrils. "You are accusing me of using the power of this office to punish you and the student government organization? You are insinuating that this office has not conducted a thorough and complete investigation into this situation I have cooperated with the state police at every moment and I have done my very best."

Dr. Petry leaned back. "There are two types of investigations. One type tries to resolve problems, establish solutions and set benchmarks for the future. The other type simply attempts to minimize damaging impact."

"Or sweep the problem under the rug," Cullen added.

"Enough. Both of you!" Dr. Burcham barked. "I do not have to explain my reasoning to either of you." He shot a look at Cullen. "I denied those requisitions to send you a message to keep better track of student government finances. Furthermore, you were taken into temporary custody because you and Serena trespassed on a crime scene. Both of you made that decision and you are lucky you didn't get taken to jail."

Cullen clamped his jaw. "I think you denied those requisitions as a way to distract me from everything else."

"That's ridiculous," Dr. Burcham protested.

Dr. Petry looked at Cullen. "If you feel strongly about that position, you can appeal this matter to the board of governors."

"And the board will side with me," Dr. Burcham proclaimed. His horn-rimmed glasses slipped to the tip of his nose as he spoke. He shifted his weight uncomfortably. "I'm sorry, Cullen. I find your story preposterous. And Dr. Petry, I find your involvement and conduct unbecoming of a faculty member. As a result, I will consider a further consequence for you in the near future."

Cullen advanced toward Dr. Burcham, arms pumping. "I am telling the truth!" he shouted.

Dr. Burcham folded both arms in a defensive posture that made Cullen step back.

"Cullen, stop it! Do not do this," Dr. Petry commanded, ensnaring Cullen by the arm.

"I am telling the truth! I am telling you the truth!" Cullen yelled as Dr. Burcham stepped aside.

Cullen exhaled, igniting a headache that started pounding inside his head. Standing in the room, hurt and disappointment washed over him. He was alone. The college president didn't believe him, and now Dr. Petry would be punished for his involvement.

Cullen flung his arms, breaking the slight embrace held by the professor.

Dr. Burcham dug the heels of both shoes into the carpet, scraping himself against the floor as he attempted to lean back into the desk. Sweat ran down both cheeks, fogging his glasses.

"I am telling you the truth, and before long, if you don't listen to what I am saying, something else bad is going to happen. Whoever is responsible for causing all this havoc has not been caught yet!"

Cullen looked around, kicked the toppled chair, and stormed out of the room, slamming the door behind him. The entire office suite shook.

forty six

THE LONG WALK TO COUGAR VILLAGE helped Cullen displace his anger.

He called Jordan's phone a few times, but got no answer. Frustration overtook his rage, but it returned once he realized that he'd never made transportation arrangements to take Serena to the Fall Formal.

As evening approached, Cullen dressed in his best—and only—suit. His stomach gurgled.

He called a taxi to take him off campus, down Corridor 33 near Buckhannon. The cab smelled musty and old. The driver sang along with a country tune blaring over the radio. Cullen managed to slump against the window and watch the trees, adorned with burnt red, orange, and gold leaves, as they whisked past. As the cab puttered past the spot where Dane's car had been discovered earlier in the semester, he felt a pang in his gut.

When the cab reached the outskirts of Buckhannon, his stomach gurgled again and he found his palms sweating.

Cullen got out of the cab and stood in front of the Phi Mu sorority house. The Spanish-style hacienda sat on a narrow corner lot near the end of a dead-end street that cut close to the turning lane of Corridor 33. Thin clouds slipped around the eaves and overhangs of the house, covering them like a blanket. The temperature grew cooler and a swirling wind sent leaves careening down the sidewalk and into the streets.

Elegantly dressed women stood smoking and gossiping on the small front porch, arm-in-arm with their handsomely-dressed dates. Cullen recognized a few of the couples as former classmates, but their names escaped him. The gurgling in his stomach stopped, replaced by nervous quivering. If he could just scream, he might feel better.

Cullen entered the house and searched for Serena. The main floor featured dark wood floors and brightly painted walls. Each of the three main rooms had large tables decorated with flowers and framed pictures of sorority activities. In the main living area, where couples danced, talked, and gathered snacks and drinks, a loveseat and chair faced a fireplace. Wood crackled and splintered under bright orange flames.

Serena appeared, wearing a one-shoulder cream-colored chiffon gown. As her shoulder grazed Cullen's arm, her exposed skin felt like silk. A bow centered on the bodice of the gown held the asymmetrical dress strap tightly against her shoulder.

Cullen blinked hard. "Wow. You look amazing."

Serena's right eyebrow rose. She smiled, her eyes smoldering. "Thank you. You look great yourself."

Cullen felt both cheeks warm. "Thanks."

Serena laughed.

Cullen grinned. He looked around the formal room. All the furnishings appeared to be antiques, and all were in excellent shape. He almost felt like he was in a museum.

"Are you okay? What's wrong?" she asked.

"Nothing. This just isn't how I pictured a sorority house."

Serena laughed. "What did you expect, a bunch of cackling hens?"

Cullen laughed nervously. "No, not at all. It's just, well, the frat houses I've been in have been... some of the messiest places."

"We clean up well," Serena said. "Especially tonight, since we've let some roosters into the henhouse."

She punched Cullen lightly on the arm and led him into the living room with the fireplace. "Let me introduce you to some of my sorority sisters."

Serena led Cullen over to a cloth-covered table in front of a large bay window. A rather stocky girl, slightly bent forward at the waist, stood up, nearly bumping into them.

"Cullen, this is my roommate and best friend, Crystal."

Crystal turned, her face caked with makeup and cherry-colored lipstick. In her left hand she held a plate of food.

"*The* Cullen Brewer? Serena has told me everything about you. It's so nice to finally meet you."

Cullen shook her hand. "Nice to meet you too."

Crystal looked at Serena. "So far, everyone on the guest list has shown up. We should have fun tonight." She flexed her eyebrows twice, displayed an impish grin, and nodded at Serena and Cullen. A fast-paced dance song echoed into the living room from the adjacent room near the front door.

"Well," Cullen said, "would you like to dance?"

Serena's eyes lit. "You can dance?"

"I have to dance away from blitzing defenders every Saturday."

A cell phone resting on the arm of the fireplace chair throbbed. Serena glanced behind her. "Excuse me for just a moment."

As Serena walked over to the chair, Cullen looked at Crystal. "This food looks delicious."

Crystal handed him a small plate and explained each dish.

Cullen glanced back at Serena. As she talked, she stomped her foot and shook her head, her hand pointing at the ground. The more she pointed, the louder the fire crackled.

Cullen picked up two sausage meatballs, chips, and pretzels with a mustard dip, and began to nibble.

"Where's your date?" Cullen asked Crystal as he crunched down on a pretzel.

Crystal grimaced. "Well, I'm in charge of the Fall Ball every year, and by the time I get everything organized, I don't have time to ask anyone for a date."

Cullen sucked in his breath. His question had been tactless. It was none of his business and he feared he'd embarrassed Crystal. He looked at her and forced a smile. "Well, since Serena is on the phone, what do you say we dance?"

Crystal nearly dropped her plate. "Sure!"

Crystal led Cullen into the room, littered with guys and girls dancing with full glasses and bottles of beer held high above the clusters of dancers. Liquid swiveled in the glasses and bottles as the dancers moved.

The dance music evolved into a slow, melodic love tune. Crystal grabbed Cullen by the wrists and threw his arms over her flabby, round shoulders.

She interlocked her fingers around Cullen's waist and pulled him against her, nearly knocking the wind from him.

They swayed back and forth for a few minutes before Serena approached. "May I cut in?" she asked, a bit wounded.

Crystal smiled and released her grip. As Serena stepped into his embrace, Cullen glanced around. Couples danced closely and intimately, some even kissing softly.

Serena appeared frazzled. Her hair, once soft and flowing seamlessly past her shoulders, now seemed tousled.

"Look, I had no idea Crystal would dance with me like that," Cullen said defensively. "I felt bad that she didn't have a date, so I asked her to dance while you were on the phone."

"I don't care about that," Serena replied, in the same wounded tone she'd used a moment ago.

Cullen looked down at her, his eyes wrinkled in concern.

"I'm sorry," she said. "It's nothing. I got a phone call from Matt, and it just makes me upset when he calls."

"Why?"

Serena rested her head against his shoulder.

Cullen continued moving them with the music, which had passed the crescendo point and faded.

Serena pulled away again. "One of the reasons we broke up is because Matt views women as possessions. I wasn't someone he wanted to be with. He just wanted to treat me like an object, taking me off the shelf and spending time with me when it suited him. He expected me to sit there and be pretty when he was busy with his other girl toys. Then, he cheated on me. He got tired of me and went for the next easy hit that caught his eye."

Cullen listened. He couldn't quite relate to her complaints, but knowing she was upset was all that mattered. He pulled her tightly against him and hugged her. He nuzzled her neck slightly with his cheek and whispered, "I'm sorry. You don't deserve to be treated that way."

Serena returned the embrace, then stepped back. "I'm sorry, too. Let's not talk about Matt. How did your meeting with Dr. Burcham go this afternoon? Did he confess to anything?"

Cullen grimaced. "Speaking of things I don't want to talk about…"

"Oh, okay."

He pulled her closer. "I will say this: I called his bluff on the requisitions. He denied canceling them to punish me."

Serena nodded, somewhat relieved. "Good."

"Dr. Petry was in Dr. Burcham's office, though."

Serena's eyes widened. "Why?"

"Apparently, Burcham gave Petry a tongue-lashing for helping us with the police in the student center."

"I hope Dr. Burcham knows that Dr. Petry helped us because he wanted to, not because he had to," Serena said.

Cullen gave her a steady look. "I think I made that point pretty clearly."

Serena stared at Cullen as the music stopped. Other couples rushed past them into the next room.

Something jabbed his arm. As he turned, Crystal stood with a silver serving plate full of drinks. "Drinks, anyone? I thought you all might be thirsty."

"Absolutely." Cullen scooped up the frothy amber liquid in a plastic cup and tossed it back.

"What is it?" Serena asked cautiously.

"My special blend of Long Island Iced Tea," Crystal said proudly. "I can't cook or fix many things, but I can fix this drink quite well."

Cullen wiped a trickling stream of liquid with a shirt sleeve. "Man, that's really good, Crystal." He grabbed another drink and swallowed it again in one gulp. "I was thirsty." He grabbed two more drinks and steadied one in each hand.

Crystal gave Serena an inviting nod and pushed the tray closer towards her. Serena took a glass and sipped.

Minutes passed. Cullen blinked hard. The room spun. They stood near the fireplace now, which made him uncomfortably warm. He tried focusing on Serena, but blurry eyes made it impossible.

Serena moved her lips, but he couldn't discern the words. He felt himself falling away from her as she lunged to grab him.

Then the room went dark.

forty seven

CULLEN AWOKE to something prodding him.

"Wake up! Don't make me have to call 911."

The voice sounded gruff, but distant. Cullen tried to open his eyes, but they felt too heavy, as if some force kept them closed. He tried to lift himself up, but his arms and legs wouldn't cooperate.

"I can't...I can't move," Cullen whispered. His mouth and throat felt parched.

"You're slightly hungover, that's why," the voice said again, this time more smoothly than before.

Something grabbed Cullen by the wrists and flung his body up from a stationary position. Cullen nearly vomited from the jerking motion, but he didn't. He had been seated on something soft, something with a backrest attached.

"Come on, Brewer, wake up."

Cullen opened his eyes. His head throbbed and the light stung his eyes. "I don't feel so good," he grunted. He slouched back into the seat.

As Cullen turned his head from side to side and tried focusing on something, he identified Jordan standing in front of him.

"Jordan! What are you doing here? Where's Serena?"

"How should I know?" Jordan answered. "I just got here."

"What time is it?" Asking the question sent a sharp pain down the back of Cullen's neck, which made his stomach queasy.

"It's late. Or early, depending on your point of reference." Jordan dropped to one knee in front of Cullen. "Man, you are trashed."

Cullen squinted, stroking the top of his shirt. It had become unbuttoned. He fumbled with the shirt, trying to fix it. After a few seconds, he gave up.

"Are we late for practice?"

"Yep. You are seriously trashed," Jordan snickered.

Cullen heard another male voice laughing alongside Jordan, but he didn't recognize it.

The haze over Cullen's eyes faded. He blinked and Jordan came into focus. With pale skin and that shock of blond hair, Jordan appeared alert but disheveled. Wearing a dingy, dark-colored sports coat with a dirty white shirt and faded jeans, he looked like a homeless bum. His beat-up tennis shoes and stained white socks that collapsed around his ankles completed the look. Cullen drew back. The smell hit his senses. He wondered when Jordan had last bathed.

Cullen pulled himself up. The nausea intensified and he held his stomach. He wanted to puke. In fact, puking might make everything better.

The chattering and shuffling of feet on the first floor of the house had gone away. The burgundy-shaded drapes inside the sorority house's downstairs windows hung over the panes and shielded the moonlight from the room. Cullen realized he was shivering.

Jordan appeared amused by Cullen trying to make sense of everything. "Coach Miles is looking for you."

"Wha, what? Why?"

"I don't know. I was over in the weight room this afternoon when he barged in. He asked me if I'd seen you. I said no, but I thought you were going to the Phi Mu Fall Formal tonight. He said something about you and Dr. Burcham and something that happened in Burcham's office."

The haziness in Cullen's mind made linear thinking difficult, but he did remember calling Jordan earlier. He couldn't remember if he had told Jordan about the party. And he definitely wanted to forget about the meeting with Dr. Burcham.

"Who was with you earlier? I thought I heard someone else laughing at me," Cullen said.

"Nobody important. I came down here to party. Looks like you beat me to it," Jordan replied.

Cullen stumbled to the left and collided with a silver-ensconced light hanging over the food table. In an attempt to balance himself, he stuck a hand into a dish filled with dip. He jerked his hand, which now smelled like ranch dressing, away. Cullen veered to the right and then stopped moving.

"I need the bathroom, Jordan."

"It's upstairs." He pointed to the ceiling.

Cullen brushed Jordan aside and stumbled through the living room to the front entryway. On the first floor, small groups of students were talking and drinking, although most of the original crowd had left. Cullen peered into the living room, nearly falling over as he looked for Serena. He didn't see her.

Cullen grabbed the rickety wooden handrail and pulled himself up the stairs. The slatted wooden steps bowed and squealed under the pressure of each footstep. He tripped on the top step and hit the floor hard, landing on both wrists. He managed to crawl into the bathroom and kicked the door shut behind him.

The bathroom held the outside chill within the ceramic tile floors, which Cullen found refreshing. He located the toilet, rose up, and vomited copious amounts of bile.

The dizziness and spinning stopped. Cullen's mind refocused. He looked around the narrow bathroom and began thinking of Serena. The last time he'd seen her, they were both drinking. He needed to find her.

He cleaned himself up, then quietly opened the bathroom door. The hallway led to several bedrooms: three on the left and three on the right. Some of the bedroom doors were closed, others stood open.

In the far right bedroom, bare feet dangled from the edge of a bed. Cullen approached the room and looked inside.

Crystal lay sprawled across the bed, her gown hanging low around her breasts. She was snoring loudly.

Cullen stepped backwards and proceeded left down the hallway. He noticed one door slightly ajar at the end of the hall. Hushed voices came from inside.

"I've wanted you for so long."

"Don't. Please, I've had too much to drink. I don't want our time together to be like this. Please." The female voice sounded sweet but distressed.

The male voice became sharp. "You've played hard to get for a long time. I'm gonna give it to you and you're going to like it."

Cullen held his breath, tightening the muscles in his still-unsettled stomach.

"I don't want to. Please, get off of me."

What sounded like a zipper unzipping filled the momentary silence. "You know you want some of this."

"I said no!" A slap resounded.

Cullen stepped closer and looked into the room. The descending moonlight cast a faint glow. Then he recognized a mashed bow bulging from the side of a dress. Serena! She lay on the bed, pinned there by a man who seemed rather tall.

Cullen charged into the room. "The girl told you no!"

Serena gasped. Cullen grabbed the man by his suit jacket and spun him around. Matt Carmichael stood in front of him. Cullen's eyes returned back and forth between Serena and Matt. Cullen punched the man squarely in the jaw, sending him falling back onto the bed. Serena scurried out of the way, but not fast enough. Matt landed on the edge of her dress. Serena toppled to the floor.

Matt bounced back up. He hit Cullen with a punch to the stomach, then an uppercut under the chin. Cullen's teeth rattled as a stinging pain in his stomach made him want to puke again. Matt reared back and swung at Cullen again with a closed fist. This time, Cullen blocked the punch with his forearm and countered with a right to Matt's stomach.

Cullen drove a knee into his solar plexus. Matt moaned, but attempted to lunge at Cullen. Cullen slammed the side of his head with another fist, and he flopped onto the floor.

Serena bolted from the back of the bedroom, breathing heavily and trying to speak. "Cullen, stop!"

Cullen looked at her, eyes wide and expressive. "That bastard was going to rape you."

"God, get him away from me, please, Cullen. I didn't want to have sex with him, I promise."

"I know. I stood in the hallway and heard you say no. If I hadn't been standing there, he would've raped you."

Matt rolled over and grabbed Serena by the ankle. He jerked it forward. The gesture caught Serena by surprise and she cascaded backwards, her head slamming against the bedpost. Serena rolled to her side, motionless.

Cullen froze. "Serena!"

Matt then landed a punch into Cullen's crotch.

The excruciating pain ravaged Cullen's entire body. He fell to his knees, gasping for air.

Matt balanced himself on one knee and swung an elbow. Cullen pulled back, but the elbow crushed the bridge of his nose. Streams of blood poured from both nostrils.

Cullen grabbed his nose, adjusting it in an attempt to reset the bone and cartilage.

Matt slithered away to the doorway.

Cullen stood up, wobbling and woozy but trying to balance himself. Matt turned back around and Cullen exploited the movement. He punched Matt below the ribs and Matt yelped in pain—and collapsed.

Cullen slowly walked over and knelt in front of Serena. He scooped her up carefully in one arm and balanced her. He lightly patted her cheeks and whispered her name. Serena stirred and mumbled. "Cull...en. Call the po...lice. I want Matt in jail."

Serena became heavy as Cullen steadied her. With pain shooting through his groin, legs, and face, he sniffed, which agitated the pain further. Carefully, Cullen laid Serena down so her head rested easily against the floor.

He found a napkin on the nightstand and held it against his bloody nose. "I'm here, Serena. Are you okay?"

"My head hurts," she replied.

Matt kicked, digging his feet against the floor and pushing his body backwards into the hallway.

"I'll be right back," Cullen whispered and gently stroked her cheek.

In the hallway, Matt grabbed the stair handrail and pulled himself to his feet. Cullen stormed after him.

Matt's sports coat had been torn and his pants hung low around both hips. Hearing Cullen approach, Matt turned and swung. He missed.

Cullen grabbed him by his forearms.

"Man, somebody is getting some upstairs," Jordan hollered from downstairs, his voice echoing into the stairwell.

Jordan appeared at the bottom of the steps. At the same time, one of the adjacent bedroom doors opened behind Cullen, momentarily startling him.

Matt dropped to the floor, pulling Cullen to him with all his might.

Cullen resisted, then jumped and landed both feet on Matt's thigh, which was scissored under another leg and against the floor. A ripping sound signaled muscle being pulled from the bone. Matt screamed in pain and released his grip on Cullen.

Matt fell backwards, momentum carrying him down the stairs. Cullen stared as Matt tumbled sideways, limbs flailing in different directions. Jordan hopped out of the way. Matt hit the front door, shaking the entire house.

As Matt turned over, something burst from his torn pants pocket. Scattered across the floor were pea-sized pellets which Cullen could see from the top of the stairs.

A beefy guy with small, calloused hands and a wiry blonde girl with beady eyes and a narrow nose approached from one of the bedrooms, wrapped in a bed sheet. Before they could speak, Crystal emerged from her room, rubbing her eyes.

"What is that noise?" Crystal asked sleepily as the couple glanced around.

Bending at the waist, Cullen struggled to catch his breath. "Go help Serena. She's in the other room. Matt attacked her. She hit her head."

"Matt Carmichael?" Crystal asked.

"Yes, Matt Carmichael. Now help her!"

Instantly, Crystal and the couple darted into the room.

As Cullen made his way down the stairs, Jordan knelt beside Matt, whispering into his ear and collecting the small pellets from the floor. Two pellets slipped past Jordan, and Cullen nearly stepped on them as he came off the last step and reached the foyer.

Some of the remaining guests hovered around the entryway, glassy-eyed and barely standing, while others talked quietly, pointing at Jordan and

Cullen, who now stood over Matt.

"Get that piece of shit off the floor, right now," Cullen commanded Jordan with such anger that Jordan's eyes grew large.

Matt rolled over, facing Cullen with an arm hiding his lips. He moaned again, making his olive-toned skin and fiery hazel eyes dart to the left and right.

Jordan shook his head. "Fuck, Brewer, you didn't have to throw the guy down the stairs for hitting on your date."

Matt forced words through gasps of air. "Jordan, get the pills and get rid of them. We don't want anyone seeing them."

Cullen clenched both fists, ready to pounce on Matt. "Shut up!"

Jordan took a step back, his hands up. "Sorry, Matt. I just buy, I don't clean up your messes . . ."

Cullen looked sideways at Jordan. Jordan curled his lips tightly against his face, a look of guilt forming in the ridges around his eyes. Cullen bent down and picked up two of the small pills. Jordan's face grew white while Cullen inspected them. The size and texture of the ones closely resembled the pills Jordan had left in his dorm room earlier.

A rush of air wheezed through Cullen's teeth. He glared at Jordan. "These are the same pills you left in my room. What are they? Don't you fucking lie to me."

Jordan looked at Cullen with the same tired, expressionless face that Cullen had seen from him for the last month.

"I got it now." Cullen threw the pills at Jordan. They ricocheted off his chin and hit the floor. "That's how you recovered so fast from that high ankle sprain, isn't it? You took drugs so you could play sooner, instead of letting your ankle heal on its own time. All that crap you said, accusing me of being righteous and trying to draw unnecessary conclusions."

The dark circles under Jordan's eyes twitched and the ridges of skin under his sockets creased.

Cullen shoved him lightly. The motion made his groin muscles ping with pain.

"You're a joke. A cocky, self-indulgent joke. All I heard from you this summer was you wanting to help the Cougars win a conference title and to have a great senior year. You didn't mean any of it! It was nothing but bullshit!"

Cullen shoved Jordan yet again, this time more forcefully. Jordan took a step back, and Cullen stepped closer. "You cheated yourself and this team. Do you know how much worse off we are as a team without you? Do you?" He grabbed Jordan's shirt and shook him. "Answer me!"

Jordan glared at Cullen but said nothing.

"You're done, Jordan. I'm going to tell your father and I'm going to tell Coach Miles." He shook him again. "Then again, Coach probably already knows." Cullen flailed his hands in disgust. "I nearly went to jail because of your drug problem."

Jordan's head bobbed while his eyes twitched and darted around the room.

"It's over; your football life, your school life, everything. I'm also going to Dr. Burcham first thing Monday morning and I'm telling him all of it. Then, I'm calling Detective Parsons."

Jordan's chin dropped. He appeared infantile and helpless. "Please, Cullen," he whispered so only Cullen could hear. "Don't do this. Don't tell anybody."

"Tell me, how long have you been taking drugs? And when did you start hanging out with losers like Matt Carmichael?"

Jordan stiffened. "C'mon, Brewer." He shrugged, and nearly instantly his personality reverted to the cocky, arrogant Jordan. "We've known Matt for a long time. Remember? We were all teammates at one time. He was your mentor, right?"

"Bullshit. We were competitors. Then he transferred to another school, which makes him no longer a part of anything here."

Cullen pushed Jordan again, this time with both hands.

Jordan retreated again, his back against the wall.

"Keep talking or this is going to get even uglier."

"No, Jordan." Matt whimpered. "Don't tell him anything."

Cullen spun around. Matt propped himself up on his hands and knees, like a wounded creature. Cullen kicked him in the ribs.

Matt wailed, then collapsed onto his stomach and rolled around on the floor trying to breathe.

"Shut up," Cullen barked. He glared at a frail-looking blonde attempting to aid Matt. She backed away.

"This is not the way to handle this," Jordan pleaded. "Matt has nothing to do with it."

Cullen flexed the muscles in his legs.

"Matt had nothing to do with it? Come on, Jordan. Serena was nearly raped tonight. She's upstairs right now, nearly unconscious because of this prick. And you're going to stand there and tell me he had nothing to do with it? You just admitted that you bought the shit from him."

Jordan made a face.

"Are you honestly listening to yourself and what you're defending?" Cullen scanned the foyer. Raising his voice made the broken nose throb unbearably.

A pill rested against the door frame. He picked it up and held it close to Jordan. "This right here has changed everything for you. Is this all you care about? Hanging on until you can get more pills for your next fix? Damn it!"

"Cullen?" A faint voice called. Cullen glanced up the stairs. Serena hovered near the top step with Crystal, who was holding her steady. "What's going on with you and Jordan and Matt?"

Cullen blinked.

Matt struck Cullen on the back of the neck, dropping him to the floor. He then punched Jordan in the jaw, knocking him sideways. The force of the punch landed Jordan on his back, dazed.

Matt pulled open the front door and ran. Aided by the edge of the front step, Cullen managed to collect himself. Blurred shadows of people rushed near him and around him, offering to help.

Serena slowly came down the steps on Crystal's arm.

Cullen stood and ran after Matt.

The cold, biting air slapped Cullen in the face and jolted his nose, the sting nearly causing him to cry. A fresh stream of blood trickled from a nostril. Cullen blinked hard, trying to clear his blurry vision and follow Matt's movements.

He stumbled to the end of the sidewalk, where he ran into another towering figure.

Jordan steadied him with an open hand. "What in the hell are you doing?"

forty eight

"GET AWAY FROM ME. You're a liar!" Cullen shouted.

Jordan ensnared Cullen in a modified headlock. "What are you talking about? I think you've had a little too much to drink, and it looks like Matt isn't doing so well either."

Cullen tried shaking free, but Jordan tightened the hold.

Matt hobbled to the end of the street, where he disappeared.

"Let me go!" Cullen demanded. "You have to let me go!"

"No, I don't think so. Look at you, your nose is all bloody."

Cullen growled, trying to break free.

After several seconds of pulling and tugging, Jordan released his grip on Cullen.

"I can explain," Jordan said breathlessly.

Once Cullen would've been amused, waiting to hear the excuse Jordan would concoct on the spot. But that day had come and gone.

"Steroids," Cullen growled, looking at him sternly. "That's what's going on here. You've been taking pills—and for quite some time." Jordan made a face, then looked away.

"That's right, Jordan. Steroids. Drugs. You know, performance-enhancing drugs, the type that are banned by the NCAA."

"Watch it, Brewer. You're making accusations about something that could get you in a lot of trouble. Who in the hell do you think you are to accuse your best friend of taking drugs? I can tell you this, if I am a drug user, don't you think I'd be the first person to admit it?"

I caught you and Coach in the locker room with that syringe, Cullen thought, but he held the comment.

"Cullen, when you're sick and you take cold medicine, that's a drug to help you feel better," Jordan said. "A performance-enhancing drug, per se. When you have a headache and take an aspirin, that's a performance-enhancing drug. I had a bad ankle sprain and I took the medicine I needed to get better."

Cullen's skin burned from the cold night air, but the heat from his anger warmed him. "Yeah. And cold medicine and aspirin are legal. Go take a look inside the house; the pills are everywhere." He massaged the back of his sore neck.

From behind, a car engine roared. Cullen grabbed Jordan by the arm, leading him in a direct sprint in the direction of noise.

"Whoa," Jordan exclaimed as the momentum of the pull forced him to follow. Large, fluffy flakes of light snow began falling around them.

"We're taking your car," Cullen wheezed as he inhaled cold gulps of air.

Jordan stumbled alongside Cullen. "Why?"

"Because we're going to follow Matt and call the police," Cullen said, his strides getting longer.

Jordan stammered something Cullen couldn't make out. "Don't argue with me! Just do it!"

Jordan broke to the left, heading for the black Lamborghini parked on the opposite side of the street. Cullen hadn't even noticed the car, cloaked as it was in the still darkness of the night.

Jordan and Cullen got in. The cold leather interior made Cullen shiver. Jordan coughed heavily, a dry hack that shook the car.

"Turn around and follow Matt," Cullen ordered. "We can't let him get away."

The U2 engine erupted and heaved as Jordan pumped the pedal, turning the car around in the middle of the street. As the car spun left, Coach Miles walked into the street behind it. Everything on the street faded into the darkness as the car sped away.

Jordan tapped the pedal lightly. With his right hand, he fiddled with the heater settings.

"Mash that pedal harder, Jordan. I know Matt's your new buddy, but I swear, you'd better not let him get away."

Cullen looked ahead and barely made out the pulsating red taillights on the car. Even though Matt had a generous lead on them, Jordan was closing the distance quickly.

Jordan veered left and cut a sharp right turn, paying close attention to the blind corners on the highway. The light snow became steadier and covered the road in a light glaze that shimmered in the headlights beam.

"Corridor 33 is a bad road to drive when it's raining, not to mention snowing," Cullen said.

Jordan gripped the steering wheel with both hands.

The rear tires on the car slid to the left slightly. Jordan compensated by turning the wheel to the right, stabilizing the car. A faded green road sign whisked by. Cullen didn't notice the sign completely, but he did see the marking that Beaumont was ten miles ahead.

"Why is Matt going into town?" Cullen asked tersely.

Jordan chewed on his lower lip.

"If you don't want to tell me, that's fine. I thought you might know, that's all."

Jordan sat up a bit straighter. "He'll go through Buckhannon, head for Interstate 79, and go north. Then he'll jump on Corridor 33 west of I-79 to get back to Columbus."

Cullen rested against the headrest. The Lamborghini spun more sharply this time, then wove around the steep slopes between the mountains of Corridor 33. Cullen looked out the window and saw that rocks and dirt littered the highway. He yawned to release the pressure in his clogged ears. As they climbed into higher elevations, the snow grew thicker; it was already piled along the shoulder.

The car climbed and fell sharply with the curvature of the road. Heavy bands of snow fell. The roads were now covered in white, rapidly filling the fine outline of Matt's tires.

"We're getting closer," Jordan said softly.

Cullen squinted as the Ohio license plate on Matt's car come into focus.

"Jordan, go easy here."

"I've got it, Brewer." The back end of the car swung first to the left, then to the right.

In front of them, the maroon car veered sharply to the right. Jordan tapped the brakes, slowing the forward momentum of the Lamborghini, yet the car shook and bounced as the rear brakes tried locking into place.

"Jordan, watch out!" Cullen shrieked.

Jordan swung the wheel sharply left, sending the car into a sideways skid. Cullen felt the seatbelt strap dig into his chest as his head hit the passenger side window. Jordan whipped the wheel counterclockwise, stomping the brake pedal with both feet.

The tires screeched. Finally, the car stopped. Cullen bounced back into the seat as Jordan loosened his hold on the steering wheel.

Cullen, regaining focus, said sharply, "What happened to Carmichael's car?"

Jordan finally looked at Cullen. "That's what you are worried about after what just happened?"

Cullen opened the car door. The snow reduced visibility, but he could hear a dull hiss coming from a few yards ahead. The mistiness of exhaust and brake dust hovered above the road and the putrid smell of scalding rubber tires filled the air.

Cullen began shivering while Jordan got out of the car and stopped next to him.

"Walk slowly and keep your eyes and ears peeled," Cullen said.

Out of the misty snowfall, the back end of a car appeared.

Cullen and Jordan stopped walking. It was maroon with Ohio plates.

The right front bumper of Matt's car had clipped the edge of the guardrail, bending the front bumper. The guardrail had bowed in the middle and separated from the steel joints that secured it to the highway. The right side of the car rested at the edge of the road, where the shoulder and the hillside slipped below the surface into darkness. The right rear-view mirror had been dislodged from the car and lay on the road. The front hood was bent like a teepee. Smoke from under the hood escaped into the air. The rushing water from the Clear River whooshed along below the embankment.

Finally, Jordan spoke. "Brewer, there's someone else inside the car."

Tate police! Drop the gun, son."

forty nine

AS CULLEN SHIELDED HIMSELF from the snow with one hand, the shadows of two men moved restlessly inside the car. Cullen clenched both fists as the car doors opened.

Matt Carmichael bolted from the driver-side car door, then slipped and skidded on the road surface. As he fell, a Colt 38 Special spilled onto the road. Its bright nickel finish and medium-toned walnut grip blended into the snowy landscape.

Cullen stepped toward the gun; the husky passenger in the car flung open the passenger-side door and lumbered awkwardly, trying to slither inside the narrow space between the open door and the damaged guardrail.

Cullen cut a sharp look at Jordan. "I'll take Carmichael," he said, nodding towards them. "You keep an eye on that guy."

Cullen stepped around the left rear bumper and approached Matt, who kept slipping on the slick road. Cullen slammed the open car door shut. It groaned and clanked against the door frame, rattling the entire vehicle. Cullen grabbed Matt by the shirt and slung him against the door.

"Looks like someone forgot all the twists and turns on Route 33."

Curling his lip, Matt bristled. Every muscle in his face wrinkled with disgust. "Cullen Brewer, the big hero," Matt mocked. "So what? You want a medal for catching me with drugs and discovering your friend is a user?"

Cullen lifted Matt and pressed him harder against the car door. "Don't let that other guy move one inch, Jordan," Cullen hollered over the car, although he could still hear the man grunting and pulling, trying to slip through the narrow opening near the guardrail.

"What I want to know is how you're involved in all of this besides trying to rape your ex-girlfriend."

Cullen tried to calm the chills shooting up and down his body by focusing on Matt.

"Serena and I are not through," Matt laughed. "She means more to me than a cheap trick. Serena got too involved in everything and she got you involved. Everything was fine until she had to play investigative reporter... and dig into the case."

Cullen leaned closer. "Case, what case?"

Matt shivered and his teeth began chattering. He kept twisting, trying to free himself from Cullen's grip. Cullen watched Matt's eyes bulge and slant sideways, looking in the direction of the gun. Cullen slowly planted one foot on the pavement, reached back with another foot, and kicked the gun away. It scraped against the road until it landed in a tuft of snow alongside the highway.

Cullen drove a knee into Matt. The force of the move, landing right above the solar plexus, slumped Matt forward. The inside car light, flickering but still illuminating the cabin, highlighted several pages of paper and file folders strewn throughout the interior.

"What are those papers, Carmichael? Tell me or you'll get another knee to the gut."

Matt mumbled something.

"Louder!" Cullen demanded. Matt said nothing.

Frustrated, Cullen threw Matt to the pavement. Matt hit asphalt hard, collapsed into semi-consciousness and lay still.

Cullen tugged firmly on the door handle. The door wouldn't budge, but he kept pulling. Finally, it moved a small distance from the frame. Cullen slid hisnear-frozen fingers into the crevice and pulled again. The creaking door opened.

Frantically, Cullen collected the papers strewn around inside. He scanned the pages randomly. He found a legal pad with names, phone numbers, and ounces and grams written in the right margin. The words *Bambuterol, Oxycodone* and other drugs that he didn't recognize or couldn't pronounce were written at the top of the page.

A cold gust of air wisped into the car. Cullen paused and took a deep breath, but the cold air made his lungs sting and ache. He wiped dried blood from around his lips and refocused. One name made his heart palpitate: *Dane Antonelli.*

Cullen kept looking. From behind him, he heard Matt stirring. Cullen looked and found that Jordan's name also appeared on the purchase order list; next to it, he saw the names *Bambuterol* and *Oxycodone* highlighted.

Cullen felt a sudden and overwhelming sadness. The fact that both Dane and Jordan were involved with Matt and drugs didn't seem real.

In the floorboard of the backseat, Cullen found another file folder. The West Virginia state seal, emblazoned on the front of the folder in large blue print, stood out like a lighthouse beacon against nightfall.

The cabin light grew dim. Cullen snagged the folder and pulled it open. Inside, the autopsy report for Dane Antonelli was stapled to the folder. Cullen couldn't recognize any distortions on the document, but something echoed in the recesses of his mind.

Bruises on the hands and fingers... On the last page, near the sketc hed drawing of a sample body, Cullen saw the word "cuts" with an arrow drawn to the hands.

"Cullen, what's going on?" It was Jordan's voice.

A gunshot exploded into the night. Then silence.

Matt slapped the side of the gun against Jordan's face, knocking him to the ground. Before Cullen could react, he felt a hard tug on his waist. He leaned back to find the barrel of a gun pressed between his shoulders.

"Slide out of the car, slowly, and drop the papers."

Cullen retreated as instructed. The barrel of the gun did not move. The raspy voice of Matt Carmichael punctured the silence.

"Arms up! Palms out! And turn around slowly." Matt drove the gun barrel further into Cullen's back, the cold steel making him shiver.

Matt spun Cullen around so the two were face to face.

"Dane was one of your users," Cullen said.

Matt nodded. A psychotic grin crossed his lips. "He is. Or *was.*" He shrugged. "We knew each other better than you know."

"And you stole the autopsy report from the medical examiner and replaced it. The fake one is the one you wanted everyone to see."

Matt gripped the gun handle tighter and jabbed it again into Cullen. "Did you ever wonder why an otherwise ripped athlete would die from a massive heart attack after showing few signs of illness?"

Cullen's eyes twitched, but his body remained motionless.

"But you transferred before he arrived on campus. You were no longer a member of the football program."

"I met Dane at the summer football camp Coach Miles put on three years ago," Matt continued. "Dane wanted to play college football... badly. He impressed Miles with his performance at camp. Dane told Miles he would walk on if that's what it took to play."

Cullen quivered. The temperature had dropped and the winds now howled through the ravine. Pressing his lower back into the car, he slowly spread both legs apart, widening his stance.

"Miles told Dane to hit the weight room during his senior year of high school and get stronger."

Cullen took another small breath. "Miles tells everyone that."

"That's right. I told Dane after camp that I knew of a way he could get stronger faster. He called me later that summer."

"Then why did you transfer to Bowling Green, if you and Dane had an arrangement?"

"Mainly because of you," Matt replied through gritted teeth. "I knew that Miles would go and watch you and Jordan play at James Monroe from time to time. He told the other coaches that you could bring a level of offense to this program that would scare the shit out of every other defense in the league. If I didn't have a great sophomore year, I knew Miles would consider playing you as a true freshman."

Cullen again heard slight groans from the other side of the car. Matt prodded Cullen with the gun. "Don't move," he warned.

Cullen hoped that Jordan was unhurt, thinking the moaning could be from the other passenger.

"So, why target Dane after the fact?" Cullen asked.

Matt looked perplexed. "Everything was going well until Dane decided to chase the pills with alcohol. Not smart. I told him not to, but he didn't listen. Sophomores...!" Matt clucked his tongue.

"I bet you were pleased with yourself, because Dane did get stronger."

"He did, and then he started needing more and more pills," Matt said. "I came to town before the season started. He called and wanted a huge amount of them, enough to last through to the offseason. Jarousky made the delivery. The only place open on a Friday night where you could have a drink and make the deal was at that shithole Darby's downtown. Jarousky went there to make the deal with Dane, but he brought some of his buddies, so Jarousky got him and his buddies loaded and then made the deal. I came to campus looking for a second chance with Serena. She would be graduating this year, I would be graduating this year...I really wanted a future with her. I thought maybe we could even discuss marriage."

Cullen couldn't contain an impish grin, even under the circumstances. "I'm pretty sure Serena wants nothing to do with you."

Matt curled his lip in anger, revealing the root of a canine tooth. "You know nothing about us. Just because you overheard one of our conversations doesn't mean you know shit."

"I know that she hates you for what you did to her. Cheating on her and then leaving. I guess that's really what you are, Matt—a cheater *and* a quitter."

Matt drove the barrel of the gun deeper into Cullen. Cullen felt the pressure of a forearm around his throat as the gun pinched his skin.

"One more word and you're done."

Cullen felt true panic course through him. He needed to keep Matt talking, if for no other reason than to think about an escape.

"I bet you attacked Serena too in the J-school hallway." Cullen managed to gurgle the words as Matt had his forearm pressed against his throat. But the accusation made the pressure relent for just a moment. "Yeah, Serena told me about that too!" Cullen coughed loudly as spittle dribbled down his chin.

Matt leaned into Cullen harder, the pressure of his body smashing Cullen into the car, siphoning off even more air from the lungs and throat.

Cullen laughed softly, further enraging Matt. "So, what do you think is going to happen now? You think you are going to walk away from this and everyone will forget about it? There is no escaping this for you."

"Shut up!" Matt demanded.

"The only thing that is going to happen to you, Matt, is prison. Look what you've done. Attempted rape, assault with a deadly weapon, and an accessory to murder...You really think this will end well for you?"

"I said *shut up!*" Matt barked.

"And Serena. You think she wants to be with someone like you after what you've done to her and everybody else?"

"She will want to be with me," Matt replied. "She has never stopped thinking about me."

Cullen coughed slightly. "It'll be easy for her to forget you when you're inside a cell at Mount Olive."

Matt thrust his forearm back into Cullen's throat, siphoning off more oxygen and pinning him tighter against the car frame.

"You think you know about us and what we had? I went to her dorm room and that beast-looking roommate of hers told me she didn't know where Serena might be. I assumed she was lying to me, so I walked all over campus and couldn't find her. I called her phone, left messages, and she ignored me. I decided to give up and go have some drinks with the group, then Jarousky called me and said we had trouble. Dane had been spotted *and* he didn't have enough cash to pay for the blow."

The cold, fatigue, and lack of air began to slowly take over Cullen and his ability to reason. He processed the information, but struggled for questions. The snow peppered their shoulders and cascaded around them.

"Unfortunately, your rich buddy Jordan and his daddy were at the bar and saw the deal taking place. If those two identified Dane buying drugs, then everything was over. Jarousky followed Dane back to the dorm. When I got there, both of them were pushing and shoving, and the next thing you know, Dane doubled over."

Matt paused.

"Cullen Brewer!"

Cullen saw a burly man, presumably the passenger in the car, clutching a knife.

The man balanced himself on the frozen road, ungainly and graceless—resembling a bully. Dressed differently than Matt, the gray hooded sweatshirt hugged his body tightly and a furry dark beard jutted outward from his face in multiple directions. Cullen looked at the man's small knife with its large blade.

The stance of the man and the way he held the knife seemed familiar. The man flinched and gripped the knife tighter in his left hand.

The thunderous groan of engines fractured the still silence of the snowy night. The engines sounded far off, yet they grew louder, their vibrations echoing into the curves and tree-lined woods of Corridor 33.

Cullen kept his eyes on the knife. The man held it in the same manner as the man who had attacked him on campus, when he'd been holding the steel rod.

Cullen took another step. "Damon Jarousky."

Damon narrowed his eyes. "I told you to stay out of this!" The words were enunciated with a heavy, thick accent. Cullen knew that burly voice.

"You told me once to stop digging," Cullen said, causing Damon a look of bewilderment. "Tonight, I'm done digging."

Cullen widened his stance. Looking down, Cullen noticed Matt moving his feet within close proximity to his own. Feeling his heart thumping, Cullen raised a foot and crushed the heel of his shoe into Matt's toe.

Damon moved towards them. Cullen could see Damon wobbling from the corner of his eye. As Damon tried to regain balance, Jordan grabbed his leg. Damon fell forward, with Jordan growling through gritted teeth, refusing to let him go.

Matt stepped back. Cullen smashed his foot again. As Matt dropped his arms, Cullen lunged at the gun. Matt tightened his grip on it and Cullen thrust an elbow into his chest. Matt didn't let go of the gun and both he and Cullen stumbled back and fell on the road.

The gun discharged. Cullen felt a small metallic ball pierce through his abdomen, tearing through muscle and flesh. Cullen punched Matt again in the chin before his arms went limp from weakness.

Cullen heard Serena calling his name, followed by the pattering of feet growing louder and closer.

Matt pushed Cullen away. As Matt tried getting up, he was shoved to the ground by Detective Parsons.

"State police! Drop the gun, son."

fifty

SOMETHING THICK and flat pressed against Cullen's eyes. A bright light agitated him for a moment, awakening him from a deep sleep.

"Definite head trauma, but fortunately, we have brain activity."

Cullen tried to speak, but his mouth was covered by a thick mouthpiece taped from corner to corner. When he swallowed, his tonsils collapsed around a thin plastic tube that made him gag.

"Rest easy, Cullen. You have a long recovery ahead of you."

The voice sounded calm and reassuring, yet unfamiliar. Cullen opened his eyes to see the shadow of a man dressed in a white coat, followed by two sprightly women, slip away to the left.

A few moments passed, and then a more familiar face appeared.

Serena sat in front of him, her eyes stained with tears. She looked radiant and teary at the same time.

Cullen wondered if she was coming to him in a dream. But a warm hand slipped over his. "How are you feeling?"

Cullen wanted to tell her that he felt fine, other than being a little tired and sore, but he couldn't formulate the words.

"The doctor said you needed to get lots of rest, but I had to see you."

Serena was fine. Cullen's heart skipped. She was fine. His memory was sketchy, but he held a vision of her injured and unconscious.

"You took quite a fall last night." She smiled, bringing more warmth to the room. "I'm glad that we found you when we did."

Cullen closed his eyes. He was too exhausted to hold them open.

Serena continued speaking and Cullen strained to listen, but her voice grew distant.

*   *   *   *   *

Cullen awoke, this time finding himself raised at a slight angle and able to discern his surroundings.

The long, narrow room featured light gray furniture and fixtures, and smelled like disinfectant. A television jutted from the wall above him. To the left, a monotonous blip repeated. He tried wiggling, but his right arm and leg didn't move.

From across the room, he could hear Jordan and Serena talking. Dr. Petry sat with them.

"This is all my fault, all of it," Jordan said. "Now Brewer is lying there..."

Serena folded her arms, looked away, the turned to face Jordan. "I can't believe that you and Matt were involved in this whole drugs thing. Cullen could have been killed!"

The volume of her voice was loud enough that Cullen stirred a bit in bed, straining to listen more closely.

"I know," Jordan said flatly. "I told Detective Parsons everything from the beginning. It's the least I could do to try and make this right."

"It may never be right," Serena said, speaking in a hushed voice.

Cullen cut his eyes to the left as more people entered the room. A man dressed in a forest green uniform with a gun belt spoke to Serena, Jordan, and Dr. Petry. Serena was dressed differently than the last time she stood before him.

The thought of a gun being so close to him unnerved Cullen. He deduced that if he closed both eyes again, the dream might change. So he did. He waited, and then reopened them. Nothing changed.

The officer approached Cullen, his expression stern but kind. Cullen relaxed. He'd seen him before, but couldn't remember his name.

"Son, I wanted to let you know that we took care of everything. Matt Carmichael has been arrested and charged with attempted murder, drug possession, and attempted sexual assault."

Cullen stared up into the ceiling, noticing the dust particles clinging to the light fixture. He blinked.

"Matt also admitted that he and Damon Jarousky and their associates distributed steroids to Jordan and Dane. This feller had a pretty extensive pill network going. Carmichael claims Jarousky got him into the business as a way to make some big money, and then they started pill-pushing. Pretty involved, if you ask me. Now, our office has not spoken with the Upshur County prosecutor yet, but chances are Carmichael is facing some significant prison time."

Hearing those words brought Cullen peace. The muscles in his body relaxed.

Dr. Petry approached, grinning widely and patting Cullen on the leg. "Mr. Brewer, your stubbornness and persistence aided you and Miss Johnson greatly. The Clear River College community owes you a great deal of gratitude."

Questions littered Cullen's mind. He knew something else needed to be explained or said, that other details needed clarifying, but he couldn't ask anything. Instead, he bit down harder on the plastic mouthpiece still wedged tightly inside his mouth.

Jerry Parsons stood alongside the professor while Serena hovered between them.

"We still have more work to do, but I wanted you to know we got the guy responsible for what happened to your friend and teammate."

"Thank you, Detective Parsons," Serena said. Dr. Petry extended a hand and Detective Parsons gripped it tightly.

Detective Parsons led Dr. Petry and Serena away from Cullen. "The doctors asked me not to mention any of this right now for fear of upsetting him." The detective shielded them from Cullen by turning away and standing in front of the bed.

Serena and Dr. Petry nodded.

Another wave of tiredness overcame him. He closed his eyes for a brief moment.

The voice of an unfamiliar woman startled him awake. Cullen could now only look up at the ceiling instead of around the room, but a woman spoke with a frank, robotic voice.

"Coming up next on Eyewitness News, chaos at Clear River College leads to several resignations . . . and more questions. But first...."

Cullen tried pulling himself up to see the screen, but his muscles wouldn't contract. The droning, beeping noise on the machine beside him quickened as he moved.

The door to the room opened. Cullen couldn't see anyone, but seductively sweet perfume wafted through the room. *Serena.*

"Let's go ahead and turn this off." She stood on her tiptoes and strained to switch off the television.

Cullen craned his neck just enough to see her low-cut gray sweatshirt and jeans accentuate her milky skin tone beautifully.

"We need to make sure you get some rest."

Unable to speak, Cullen groaned several times.

Serena looked at him. "Oh, okay. Sorry. I'll leave it on."

She walked across the room and sat next to him as the newscaster spoke again. "Clear River College is in disarray after a scandal rocks the school. Following the suspicious death of student Dane Antonelli in August, Clear River College has seen a rash of attacks and activities that have caught the attention of law enforcement. On Friday night, Clear River student, Cullen Brewer, the starting quarterback for the Cougars football team, and Damon Jarousky were found in a ravine near Corridor 33 outside of Beaumont in Upshur County near the college. Brewer is at Mercy Hospital in serious but stable condition. Jarousky was pronounced dead at the scene."

Tears rolled down his cheeks. Jarousky had died. Maybe it was even his fault.

Serena sprung up from her chair and touched his hand. "I can turn that off."

"Noooo," Cullen managed to mumble, sliding the mouthpiece over to one side of his mouth.

"This incident is the culmination of many unanswered questions resulting in several resignations from top officials at the college. Eyewitness News has learned that President Neal Burcham will resign at the end of the month, along with Head Football Coach Gary Miles, who has been at Clear River College for eleven seasons and has led the football team to three WVIAC conference titles. The chairman of the Board of Governors, Tom Hancel, was asked to resign by the West Virginia Higher Education Chancellor. A separate investigation into possible irregularities between

Hancel's construction company and state contracts will also begin soon. Chancellor Turner says the Clear River Board of Governors will choose a new chairperson, interim president and football coach immediately while the search begins for their new, permanent successors."

Cullen smirked. He wished he could rise up and race over to campus to see Dr. Petry, but the moment of bliss faded into despair. What did "serious but stable" mean? His injuries must be severe.

Serena leaned close to him and kissed him softly on the head. "I knew you would be glad this is over. We were going to tell you yesterday, but you fell asleep."

Cullen tried to speak.

"Don't try speaking yet, just relax."

A commercial for a Charleston law firm concluded and the news returned.

"I hope that pig Matt gets what he deserves." Serena turned to the television in anger. She softened and then looked back at Cullen. "I never did thank you for coming into the bedroom that night and getting Matt off of me. If you hadn't been there...."

Cullen mumbled again, blinking twice.

The hospital room door opened; this time two nurses charged in and began disconnecting and reconnecting tubes and wires around the bed.

"All right, Mr. Brewer, we're going to take you down the hall for some tests. The doctor wants to see how your arm is healing and run some other tests on your head."

The older nurse, a middle-aged woman with swept-back silvery hair, looked at Serena. "Excuse us."

"Yes, yes indeed," Serena replied. "I'll be right outside, Cullen."

"Mr. Cullen," the older nurse said, "your father arrived, and he'll be in to see you after we're done with the tests."

Cullen gripped the sheets tightly as the other nurse unlocked the bed wheels and pulled the bed forward.

The ceiling overhead began rotating and spinning wildly, which made Cullen slightly dizzy as they pulled the bed into the hallway.

Other nurses moved aside as Cullen was pulled down the narrow hallway. At the end of the hall, Jordan leaned against a wall, arms folded, talking to Serena.

The nurses stopped the bed in front of two large swinging doors. Jordan looked rested and calm, with a shock of blond hair falling over his face.

"Hey, Brewer! I wanted to come by and see how you are doing."

Cullen was glad to see his friend.

Jordan leaned closer. "I'm glad you are doing well," he whispered. "I wanted to tell you I'm sorry. For everything."

Cullen blinked again.

"Also, I enrolled myself in a treatment and recovery program here at the hospital that's going to help me recover from coming off the steroids. I thought you should know."

The two nurses appeared again. "Okay, Mr. Cullen, it's time to go."

Jordan patted Cullen's arm as Serena touched him lovingly.

Epilogue

Jordan steadied Cullen, while Serena held his backpack.

"Don't move too fast," Serena reminded Jordan, who froze momentarily after extending a lean leg forward.

Cullen stopped. He turned his head and looked back at the Brewer farm set against the Monroe County mountains. The acreage looked like a fist: five gnarled little hills split by freshly plowed snow paths that were veined with winding lanes, leading into the face of the mountains.

Serena patted Jordan on the arm. "Watch him while I go and open the door."

"You all don't have to treat me like I'm a cripple," Cullen called to Serena, who was preoccupied with trying to get the key inserted into the rusted door lock.

"We are just glad you are getting better," Jordan said, his voice a near-whisper. Jordan pressed his arm firmly into Cullen. Cullen let out a short breath. "Easy, Jordan, I don't want my ribs broken."

"Got it!" Serena exclaimed, slowly pushing the front door of the trailer back. She turned to face Cullen, who balanced himself on the rotted front porch step.

"I never thought it would feel so good to see this place," Cullen said. "This farm hasn't felt like home for a long time, but I'm glad to be here."

"Let me get your cane," Serena stated as she disappeared behind the front door. Cullen raised an arm and pressed it against the door frame. He tilted his head towards Jordan. "I sure won't miss the trips to St. Joseph's Hospital each week for physical therapy, but at least the semester is over and I don't have to worry about classes."

Serena held out the cane in front of Cullen. Jordan sighed and took it from her. "You okay?" Jordan asked, dropping his gaze and peering up at Cullen.

"Yes, guys, I'm fine," Cullen said sharply, snatching the cane from Jordan. Cullen drove the rubber cane tip into the floor and nodded at Jordan. Jordan slowly loosened his hold on Cullen and casually removed his arm.

Cullen wobbled for a moment, looking down to ensure the cane was supporting him.

"Damn, it's warm in here," Cullen said, tugging on the neck of his Cougars sweatshirt. He looked around the living room, which was slightly cleaner than it was in August, although the stale smell of old cigarette smoke tangled with a musty smell coming from the kitchen still made his nose burn.

Serena stood in front of Cullen; she pressed her arms at her sides as if she was awaiting instructions. Cullen looked past her down the hallway and nodded. "My room is down that way."

Jordan stepped away and Cullen limped ahead, leaning on the cane for support. Serena ran in between him and Jordan and collected the backpack. Without looking, Jordan took it from Serena and slowly followed Cullen down the hallway.

Cullen turned on the overhead light. Even then, his bedroom was dark and cluttered. A black futon, shoved against a small window on the far wall, was littered with cups and ashtrays.

"It looks like Dad took over my room," Cullen surmised, before approaching a small chair sitting next to a table.

Jordan came into the room as Cullen let out a groan while gingerly lowering himself onto the chair. Cullen took off his sweatshirt and tossed it aside.

"How is your dad doing?" Jordan asked, the words trailing off.

Cullen turned to face him. "Good. He has been going to AA meetings in Union for the last several weeks. Part of the treatment requires him to call me after each meeting." Cullen swallowed. "I'm not used to it, but it's nice. I guess my injuries made him rethink some things."

"That's good," Jordan replied. He said down on the floor and leaned forward, his hands clasped in front of him.

"And your dad," Cullen inquired, "how's he doing?" Cullen watched Jordan's downcast eyes as he pressed his hands together tightly.

"Okay, I guess," Jordan replied. "It's been tough for him to be completely cut out of everything at Clear River. He's been through a lot. The board refused to let him vote on Burcham's replacement and, apparently, the State Department of Highways terminated their contract with our cement company. Dad had to let five people go because of a lack of business."

A long silence passed between them. Cullen scratched his chin. "Wow. I didn't know. I'm really sorry."

"It's fine, really," Jordan replied rapidly. "I was going to tell you a few weeks ago, but the doctors at St. Joe's said that you needed to focus on regaining your strength. Brewer, look...I realize how much I messed up." Jordan continued staring at the floor. "I got mixed up with those steroids... I...I just wanted us to have a great senior year and then I got hurt and all of this shit started going down. If I had known what would happen to you and my dad, and to Coach, and to Burcham..."

"...and Dane," Cullen added. The color drained from Jordan's face.

"Yes, and Dane."

"You and Coach had that in common," Cullen said softly. "Win no matter what. It cost you both a lot. But, forget about it. What's done is done. We have always been friends and we will always be friends."

Jordan smiled. "Our lawyer told me what you wrote about me in that letter. Thanks for doing that for me. We sent it to the prosecutor in Buckhannon. I think it will help me with the charges."

Cullen remained silent.

"We'll find out in the spring." Jordan looked sideways, and then raised his gaze back to Cullen. "At least you only have one semester of school left. It might take me a little longer to finish, if I can get reinstated by the new president."

Down the hallway, they heard a loud crash, followed by a faint apology coming from Serena, directed at nobody.

Cullen widened his eyes, while Jordan furrowed his brow. "Would you mind?" Cullen asked, throwing a thumb behind his shoulder.

"Yeah," Jordan said. As he went into the living room, Cullen heard Jordan and Serena talking, Serena in hushed tones while Jordan had a stronger edge in his voice.

Reaching for his backpack, Cullen awkwardly hooked a shoulder strap with the tip of the cane as Serena appeared in the doorway. He studied Serena and curled an eyebrow at her.

"Everything all right in there?" he asked.

She licked her lips quickly and bobbed her head just as fast. "Yeah, everything's fine." Cullen dragged the bag towards him and he could feel Serena staring at him from the corner of his eye.

"Let me help," she interrupted, untangling the strap from the cane and unzipping the bag, dumping its contents onto the floor. "What are you looking for, a pen, or something to write with?" She paused. "Oh, I bet you are looking for your pain medicine."

Serena kept shaking the bag as the contents scattered on the floor. A few loose papers hung loosely in the air for a moment before landing. As Cullen reached for them, Serena pushed his arm aside. "I'll get it for you."

"Serena, stop."

She gathered the various sheets of paper, stared at them, and held them away from her. A vexed look crossed her face. "Graduate school applications to Marshall and WVU."

Cullen blushed. "Yeah, I am looking at going to graduate school next year."

Serena rocked back on her heels. "I think that's great. Why didn't you tell me?"

"Well, I still have to get apply and get accepted. I thought about going into education, you know, so I could teach and maybe be a football coach someday."

Serena inserted the loose pages inside the folders and laid them on the floor. "I think you would be excellent, Coach Brewer."

She smiled sheepishly at Cullen and knelt in front of him, taking his hand and stroking her thumb over the knuckles.

Jordan came back into the room, holding a small radio. "The championship game is on."

Cullen sat up straighter in the chair. "Awesome. I can't wait." The cheers and applause from the crowd echoed through the radio. "Good afternoon, and welcome to the WVIAC football championship game between the West Virginia Wesleyan Bobcats and the Fairmont State University Fighting Falcons, from University of Charleston Stadium in Charleston. I'm Larry McKay, along with John Dickensheets and Jason Lee ready to bring you all of the action..."

"This is going to be a good game," Cullen mumbled.

"I've never listened to a football game on the radio before," Serena added.

Jordan rolled his eyes and threw his head back, looking at the ceiling. "And who invited you?"

Serena slapped Jordan on the chest, making him cough.

"We lost to Fairmont State at the end of the year, didn't we?" Cullen asked, already knowing the answer.

"Yeah," Jordan replied. "Chance threw three picks and the defense gave up 178 rushing yards. We went from potential conference champions to finishing four-and-seven. Shit."

As the play-by-play emanated from the radio, Cullen leaned back and closed his eyes.

Author's Notes

Founded in 1924, the West Virginia Intercollegiate Athletic Conference (WVIAC) rates as one of the oldest leagues at the small-college level.

The league's 15 member schools include: Alderson- Broaddus College, Bluefield State College, University of Charleston, Concord University, Davis & Elkins College, Fairmont State University, Glenville State College, Ohio Valley University, Shepherd University, West Liberty University, West Virginia State University, West Virginia Wesleyan College and Wheeling Jesuit University. The University of Pittsburgh at Johnstown and Seton Hill University joined the WVIAC for the 2006-07 season. Pitt Johnstown and Seton Hill are the WVIAC's first out-of-state members since 1932.

The WVIAC moved into the NCAA Division II ranks in 1994 after a long affiliation with the NAIA. The conference was the only one in Division II to place a team in the national quarterfinals in men's basketball, football and baseball during the 1998-99 academic year. In 2002 the WVIAC, along with two other conferences, became the first league to earn four bids to the NCAA Division II Men's Basketball Championship.

Commissioner Barry Blizzard, who has held the post since 1987, led the move into the NCAA. Blizzard, a native of Bramwell, West Virginia, previously served as the athletics director at Bluefield State. The long-time conference chief has served in a variety of national leadership positions, including a stint as president of the Division II Conference Commissioners' Association. He is currently the chairman of the NCAA Division II Nominating Committee.

Alumni of conference members include

West Virginia State's Earl Lloyd (the first Aftican-American to play in the National Basketball Association), Pitt Johnstown's John Murtha (former US representative), and Wheeling Jesuit's John beilein (current Michigan men's basketball coach).

The conference's basketball tournament is one of the longest-running events in collegiate hoops; the 74th annual event eas held earlier this year at the Chareston Civic Center. Attendance ar the WVIAC tournament ranks among the highest in Division II. The conference also boasts a 10-station radio network for the tournament.

Women's sports were incorporated into the WVIAC during the 1981-82 academic year as the West Virginia Intercollegiate Athletic Association was absorbed. Currently, women's championships are offered in softball, golf, tennis, track, basketball, volleyball, cross county and soccer.

Men's championships are conducted in football, cross county, soccer, basketball, baseball, golf, tennis and track.

The league was recognized by the State Journal as one of "55 Great Things About West Virginia" in the magazine's April 2007 edition. The WVIAC is headquartered in Princeton, W.Va.

WVIAC Chronology:

1924-West Virginia Department of Education helps organize the WVIAC in a meeting at the Waldo Hotel in Clarksburg. Charter members include Alderson, Bethany, Broaddus, Concord, Davis & Elkins, Fairmont State, Glenville State, Marshall, Morris Harvey (Charleston), New River State (WVU Tech), Potomac State, Salem, Shepherd, West Liberty State, West Virginia University, and West Virginia Wesleyan.
1927-West Virginia University exits the league.
1929-Morehead State (KY) joins the WVIAC.
1932-Alderson and Broaddus Colleges combine to form Alderson-Broaddus.
1933-Morehead State (KY) leaves the conference.
1946-Beckley College joins the league.
1949-Marshall exits the WVIAC.

1955-Bluefield State and West Virginia State join the WVIAC after being members of the Central Intercollegiate Athletic Association.

1957-Wheeling College becomes member of the WVIAC.

1962-Bethany leaves the conference.

1963-Potomac State leaves the WVIAC.

1977-Beckley College leaves the conference.

1986-West Virginia Wesleyan leaves the WVIAC for two years.

1988-West Virginia Wesleyan rejoins the conference.

1994-The league became a member of the NCAA's Division II.

1999-Ohio Valley becomes a WVIAC member.

2006-WVU Tech leaves the conference.

2006-The University of Pittsburgh at Johnstown and Seton Hill University become the first WVIAC members from Pennsylvania as membership grows to 16 schools.

2010-Salem International University leaves the conference.

2011-First national championship in any sport (individual or team) was won by Shawnee Carnett in the 800m.

Current WVIAC Schools:

Alderson-Broaddus College
101 College Hill Drive
Philippi, West Virginia 26416
Nickname: Battlers
Students: 800
School fact: Alderson-Broaddus is a four-year, liberal arts college affiliated with the American Baptist Churches USA and the West Virginia Baptist Convention.

Bluefield State College
219 Rock Street
Bluefield, West Virginia 24701
Nickname: Big Blues
Students: 2,063
School fact: Fully integrated after 1954, Bluefield State has a primary academic emphasis in professional and technical programs.

University of Charleston
2300 MacCorkle Avenue, S.E.
Charleston, West Virginia 25304
Nickname: Golden Eagles
Students: 1,315
School fact: In 2003, the school resumed playing football after abolishing
the sport in 1955.

Concord University
Vermillion Street
P.O. Box 1000
Athens, WV 24712-1000
Nickname: Mountain Lions
Students: 3,100
School fact: The college was founded in 1872, soon after West Virginia split
away from Virginia during the Civil War.

Davis and Elkins College
100 Campus Drive
Elkins, West Virginia 26241
Nickname: Senators
Students: 751
School fact: Related to the Presbyterian Church, the college is located in
Elkins, two hours east of Charleston, three hours south of Pittsburgh, and
four hours west of Washington, D.C. It's some of the most scenic country
in the eastern United States—accented with a vibrant arts scene and great
tourism destinations.

Fairmont State University
1201 Locust Avenue
Fairmont, WV 26554
Nickname: Fighting Falcons
Students: 7.450
School fact: The Robert C. Byrd National Aerospace Education Center
located in nearby Bridgeport, West Virginia, offers multiple programs
in aviation.

Glenville State College
200 High Street
Glenville, West Virginia 26351
Nickname: Pioneers
Students: 1,505
School fact: The college, often referred to as the Lighthouse on the Hill, is West Virginia's only centrally located public college.

Ohio Valley University
1 Campus View Drive
Vienna, West Virginia 26105-8000
Nickname: Fighting Scotts
Students: 527
School fact: Ohio Valley University is a faith-proclaiming, residential, iberal arts university located between Parkersburg and Vienna, West Virginia.

University of Pittsburgh Johnstown
450 Schoolhouse Road
Johnstown, Pennsylvania 15904
Nickname: Mountain Cats
Students: 3,032
School fact: Founded in 1927, the University of Pittsburgh at Johnstown is the first and largest regional campus of the University of Pittsburgh.

Seton Hill University
1 Seton Hill Drive
Greensburg, Pennsylvania 15601
Nickname: Griffins
Students: 2,014
School fact: In 2002, Seton Hill was officially granted university status by the Pennsylvania Department of Education.

Shepherd University
P.O. Box 5000
Shepherdstown, West Virginia 25543-5000
Nickname: Rams
Students: 4,400
School fact: For the northern Shenandoah Valley region as a whole, the University is a center for noncredit continuing education, public service, and convenient citizen access to extensive programs in art, music, theater, athletics, and other areas of public interest.

West Liberty University
101 Faculty Drive
West Liberty, West Virginia 26074-0295
Nickname: Hilltoppers
Students: 2,600
School fact: Established as West Liberty Academy in 1837 (26 years before the state was admitted to the Union), it was created to respond to the need for higher educational opportunities west of the Appalachian ridge.

West Virginia State University
P.O. Box 1000
Institute, West Virginia 25112-1000
Nickname: Yellow Jackets
Students: 5,000
School fact: It is one of the original 1890 Land-Grant colleges and the smallest land-grant institution in the country.

West Virginia Wesleyan College
59 College Avenue
Buckhannon, West Virginia 26201
Nickname: Bobcats
Students: 1,360
School fact: Wesleyan's student life program features 19 NCAA Division II athletic teams, regionally-renowned performing arts programs, community

engagement, including scholarships and service and leadership programs, over 70 campus organizations, outdoor recreation and intramurals programs, nine fraternities and sororities, and religious life.

Wheeling Jesuit University
316 Washington Avenue
Wheeling, West Virginia 26003
Nickname: Cardinals
Students: 1,200
School fact: Wheeling Jesuit University, one of 28 colleges and universities in the Jesuit tradition of academic excellence and service to others, educates the whole person-- caring for the mind, body and spirit of each student.

CPSIA information can be obtained
at www.ICGtesting.com
Printed in the USA
LVOW08s1618050717
540359LV00007B/1302/P